APR 1 4 2011

Also by David Bezmozgis

Natasha and Other Stories

THE FREE WORLD

THE
FREE
WORLD

DAVID BEZMOZGIS

FARRAR, STRAUS AND GIROUX

NEW YORK

Farrar, Straus and Giroux
18 West 18th Street, New York 10011

The passages in italics on pages 76 and 169 are from Soviet and Kosher: Jewish
Popular Culture in the Soviet Union, 1923–1939 *by Anna Shternshis, courtesy of
Indiana University Press.*

Library of Congress Cataloging-in-Publication Data
Bezmozgis, David, 1973–
    The free world / David Bezmozgis.— 1st ed.
        p.   cm.
    ISBN 978-0-374-28140-3 (alk. paper)
    1. Jews, Russian—Italy—Fiction.   2. Immigrants—Italy—Fiction.   3. Jewish
families—Fiction.   I. Title.

PR9199.4.B495F74 2011
813´.6—dc22

                                                                    2010033122

Designed by Abby Kagan

www.fsgbooks.com

1   3   5   7   9   10   8   6   4   2

to Hannah

and in memory of
Mendel Bezmozgis (1935–2006)
Jakov Milner (1915–2006)

Now the Lord said unto Abram: "Get thee out
of thy country, and from thy kindred,
and from thy father's house, unto the land that
I will show thee." —Genesis 12:1

JULY

1

Alec Krasnansky stood on the platform of Vienna's Western Terminal while, all around him, the representatives of Soviet Jewry—from Tallinn to Tashkent—roiled, snarled, and elbowed to deposit their belongings onto the waiting train. His own family roiled among them: his parents, his wife, his nephews, his sister-in-law, and particularly his brother, Karl, worked furiously with the suitcases and duffel bags. He should have been helping them but his attention was drawn farther down the platform by two pretty tourists. One was a brunette, Mediterranean and voluptuous; the other petite and blond—in combination they attested, as though by design, to the scope of the world's beauty and plenitude. Both girls were barefoot, their leather sandals arranged in tidy pairs beside them. Alec traced a line of smooth, tanned skin from heel to calf to thigh, interrupted ultimately by the frayed edge of cutoff blue jeans. Above the cutoff jeans the girls wore thin sleeveless shirts. They sat on their backpacks and leaned casually against each other. Their faces were lovely and vacant. They seemed beyond train schedules and obligations. People sped past them, the Russian circus performed its ludicrous act several meters away, but they paid no attention. Alec assumed they were Americans. He guessed they were in their early twenties. He was twenty-six, but he could pass for younger. In school and university he had run track and had retained a trim runner's build. He also had his father's dark, wavy hair. From the time Alec was a boy he had been aware of his effect on women. In his presence, they often became exaggerated versions of themselves. The maternal ones became more maternal, the crude ones became cruder, the shy ones shyer. They wanted only that he not make them feel foolish and were grateful when he did not. In his experience, much of what was good in life could be traced to a woman's gratitude.

Looking at the two girls, Alec had to resist the urge to approach them. It could be the simplest thing in the world. He had studied English. He needed only to walk over and say, Hello, are you Americans? And they needed only to respond, Yes.

—Where in America do you live?

—Chicago. And where are you from?

—Riga, Latvia. The Soviet Union.

—How interesting. We have never met anyone from the Soviet Union before. Where are you traveling to?

—Chicago.

—No. Is this true?

—Yes, it is true. I am traveling to Chicago.

—Will this be your first time in Chicago?

—Yes, it will be my first time in Chicago. Can you tell me about Chicago?

—Yes, we can tell you about it. Please sit down with us. We will tell you everything about Chicago.

—Thank you.

—You are welcome.

Alec felt Karl's hand on his shoulder.

—What's the matter with you?

—Nothing.

—We have seven minutes to finish loading everything onto the train.

He followed Karl back to where their parents were arranging the suitcases so that Karl and Alec could continue forcing them through the window of the compartment. Near them, an elderly couple sat dejectedly on their bags. Others worked around them, avoiding not only helping them but also looking them in the face. Old people sitting piteously on luggage had become a familiar spectacle.

—I see them, Karl said. Move your ass and if there's time we'll help them.

Alec bent into the remaining pile of suitcases and duffel bags on the platform. Each seemed heavier than the last. For six adults they had twenty articles of luggage crammed with goods destined for the bazaars of Rome: linens, toys, samovars, ballet shoes, nesting dolls, leather Latvian handicrafts, nylon stockings, lacquer boxes, pocketknives, camera equipment, picture books, and opera glasses. One particularly heavy suitcase held Alec's big commercial investment, dozens of symphonic records.

First hefting the bags onto his shoulder and then sliding them along the outside of the train, Alec managed to pass them up to the compartment and into the arms of Polina and Rosa, his and Karl's wives.

Karl turned to the old couple.

—All right, citizens, can we offer you a hand?

The old man rose from his suitcase, stood erect, and answered with the formality of a Party official or university lecturer.

—We would be very obliged to you. If you will allow, my wife has with her a box of chocolates.

—It's not necessary.

—Not even a little something for the children?

Karl's two boys had poked their heads out the compartment window.

—Do as you like. But they're like animals at the zoo. I suggest you mind your fingers.

Alec and Karl shouldered the old people's suitcases and passed them into their compartment. Alec noticed the way the old man looked at Polina.

—This is your wife?

—Yes.

—A true Russian beauty.

—I appreciate the compliment. Though she might disagree. Emigration is not exactly cosmetic.

—Absolutely false. The Russian woman blossoms under toil. The Russian man can drink and fight, but our former country was built on the back of the Russian woman.

—What country wasn't?

—That may be so, but I don't know about other countries. I was a Soviet citizen. To my generation this meant something. We sacrificed our youth, our most productive years, our faith. And in the end they robbed us of everything. This is why it does my heart proud to see your wife. Every Jew should have taken with him a Russian bride. If only to deny them to the alcoholics. I'm an old man, but if the law had allowed, I would have taken ten wives myself. Real Russian women. Because that country couldn't survive five minutes without them.

The old man's wife, the incontrovertible product of shtetl breeding, listened to her husband's speech with spousal indifference. There was nothing, her expression declared, that she hadn't heard him say a hundred times.

—To women, Alec said. When we get to Rome we should drink to it.

Alec helped the old couple onto the car and scrambled up as it began to edge forward. He squeezed past people in the narrow passageway and found his family crammed in with their belongings. Perched on a pile of duffel bags, his father frowned in Alec's direction.

—What were you talking about with that old rooster?

—The greatness of the Russian woman.

—Your favorite subject. You almost missed the train.

Samuil Krasnansky turned his head and considered their circumstances.

—The compartments are half the size.

This was true, Alec thought. Say what you want about the Soviet Union, but the sleeping compartments were bigger.

—You want to go back because of the bigger compartments? Karl asked.

—What do you care about what I want? Samuil said.

Samuil Krasnansky said nothing else between Vienna and Rome. He sat in silence beside his wife and eventually fell asleep.

2

Somewhere south of Florence, Polina lifted Alec's head from her shoulder and eased it into a cleft between two lumps in the duffel bag that functioned as their bed. As she lowered his head, Alec opened his eyes and, after the briefest moment's disorientation, regarded Polina with an inquisitive smile. This was Alec's defining expression and it had been the first thing she had noticed about him. Before he had become her husband, before the start of their affair, before she knew anything about him, Polina had seen him in one or another of the VEF factory buildings, always looking vaguely, childishly amused.

—If Papatchka offered me life on a silver platter maybe I'd also go around grinning like a defective, Marina Kirilovna had said to Polina when Alec made his first appearance in the technology department.

Marina Kirilovna occupied the desk beside Polina's at the radio factory. In her mid-forties and a widow twice over, Marina Kirilovna treated men with only varying degrees of contempt. They were sluggards, buffoons, dimwits, liars, brutes, and—without exception—drunks. The tragedy was that women were saddled with them and, for the most part, accepted this state of affairs. It was as though women had ingested the Russian saying "If he doesn't beat you, he doesn't love you" with their mothers' milk. As for her own departed husbands, Marina Kirilovna liked to say that the only joy she'd had in living with them had been outliving them.

Later, when Marina Kirilovna began to suspect Polina's involvement with Alec, she had admonished her.

—Not that it's my business, but even if your husband is no prize at least he's a man.

—It isn't your business, Polina had said.

—Just know that it will all be on your head. No good can come of it. Believe me, I'm not blind. I see him skipping around like a boy with a butterfly net. And if you think this business might lead to a promotion, then half the women at the factory are eligible for it.

At the word "promotion," Polina had almost laughed. The suggestion of some ulterior motive, particularly ambition, was risible in a way the widow could not have imagined. First, the mere idea of ambition in the factory was ludicrous. Thousands of people worked there and—with the exception of the Party members—nobody's salary was worth envying. But, beyond that, if anything had led her to consider Alec's overtures, it was her husband's ambition—insistent, petty, and bureaucratic. In the evenings she was oppressed by his plots and machinations for advancement, and on the weekends she was bored and embarrassed by his behavior at dinners with those whom he described as "men of influence." By comparison, Alec was the least ambitious man she had ever met.

One afternoon, as she was preparing to leave work, Alec had approached. He was accompanied by Karl.

—My brother and I are going out to seek adventure. We require the company of a responsible person to make sure that we do not go to excesses.

—What does that have to do with me?

—You have a kind and responsible face.

—So does Lenin.

—True. But Lenin is unavailable. And, at the risk of sounding unpatriotic, I am sure we would prefer your company.

Even now, with her forehead pressed against the cool window, it was hard to believe that this invitation had led to this humid passageway on a train bound for Rome. Straining to see beyond her own reflection, Polina marveled that the predawn countryside she saw was Italian countryside, the black two-dimensional cows Italian cows, and the geometry of houses Italian houses, inhabited by Italians—and when the train sped past the rare house with a lighted window, it seemed barely comprehensible that, awake at this hour, there were real Italians engaged in the ordinary and mysterious things Italians did in their homes in the earliest hours of the morning. She regretted that she didn't have a quiet place to sit at that very instant to compose her thoughts and set them down for her sister.

In Vienna she had already written to her twice.

My dear Brigitte,
On our way to an appointment with our caseworker this morning
we saw a little girl and her brother vomit in the pensione
courtyard. These same two also vomited in the courtyard
yesterday morning. Both times, their mother, a woman from
Tbilisi who seems incapable of opening her mouth without
shouting, raced out into the courtyard, swinging her slipper. This
woman comes in from the market every evening with a bunch of
spotted bananas roughly the size of a large cat. But you can't
blame her. It takes everyone a few days just to get accustomed to
the bananas. They are not expensive, but if you want to economize
you can buy ones that are overripe. They are even cheaper than
apples. You'd think they grew them in Austria. I can't begin to
describe the pineapples, or the chicken and veal in the butcher's
shops. All the émigrés, including me, walk around overwhelmed
by the shop windows. It doesn't seem quite real, but rather like
something in a movie. And considering how little money we have,
it might as well be a movie. The second evening we were here,
Igor and I explored a street lined with clothing stores. There were
stores for men and for women. Austrians were rushing in and out

carrying bags and boxes, all of them dressed like the mannequins in the store windows. Compared to them we looked like beggars. I was wearing the pale yellow dress Papa brought from Stockholm. The dress is almost four years old. You remember how excited I was when I got it? I'm embarrassed to think of it now. Wearing it in front of all of those people, I wished I were invisible. That way I could admire everything but avoid people seeing me and the horrible dress. Any single article of clothing worn by the Viennese would be the envy of all Riga. And it isn't only a question of the latest styles. It is the materials, the quality of the work. Naturally, I expected this. What I hadn't expected were the colors. There were dresses and blouses in colors I had never seen. How strange it is to think that I had lived my entire life without seeing certain colors. In one display there was a silk blouse of a deep lavender I associated with exotic flowers. I was so taken by it that I lingered too long by the window. Igor encouraged me to go inside and take a closer look, which I didn't want to do. He teased me and pushed me playfully to the door. This attracted the attention of a saleswoman. She was in her forties, dressed very smartly. I suppose she was amused by us. She spoke to us in German, some of which Igor understands. She wanted to know what it was that had appealed to me. Igor pointed to the blouse and the saleswoman invited us into the store so that I could try it on. She was very kind and wanted to help us but I literally had to wrest myself out of Igor's grip to avoid going into the store. I wanted to apologize to the woman for my rudeness, but I don't know how to say even that much in German. She must have thought I was crazy. But all I could picture was trying on the blouse and somehow damaging it. If that had happened, I don't know what we would have done.

Because she wasn't accustomed to using the aliases, Polina had had to rewrite parts of the letter two or three times. To refer to Alec or to her sister by a different name still felt ludicrous. It seemed like a children's game, playing at spies and secret agents. Her sister, however, embraced the game. When she met Polina in Kirovsky Park to say goodbye, she came armed with a list of preferred alternate names.

—I never liked my name anyway. It's so average. Nadja. It's the name of a cafeteria clerk.

They had met on a bright Sunday afternoon. Polina had arrived first and claimed a bench under a linden tree, not far from where the men played dominoes. This had been a week before they left. All week, all month, she and Alec had been getting papers notarized, valuables appraised, haggling with the seamstresses who sewed their custom duffel bags, supervising the carpenters who constructed the shipping boxes, and arranging clandestine farewells. All this time she had slept poorly. In the mornings she would open her eyes overwhelmed by the tasks ahead of her. Polina realized, as she sat on her bench, that it had been weeks if not months since she had last had such a moment to herself. The day was warm and cloudless, a rare treat in Riga even in late June. Along the paths, young mothers pushed buggies, and grandmothers shuffled after their grandchildren, trying to entice them with a flavored wafer or a peeled cucumber. All around her were the fellow inhabitants of the city of her birth, each one possessing the individuality and anonymity of a city person. Polina derived pleasure from the sensation that, at least at that moment, she was indistinguishable from them. No one could identify her as a traitor to the motherland, a stateless, directionless person. She smoothed her skirt and looked up through the branches of the tree. Feeling the warmth on her face, Polina considered herself as if from the sun's perspective. Observed from such a height, she imagined that she could pass for a green leaf among green leaves or a silver fish among silver fish floating in the common stream.

From a distance, she recognized Nadja's buoyant, fidgety walk. In low heels and a skirt, and swinging a small handbag, Nadja, at twenty, looked like a girl experimenting with her mother's wardrobe. Because of their age difference and because of her sister's nature, Polina harbored feelings for her that were more maternal than sisterly. To friends, their mother often remarked that, unlike other children in similar circumstances, Polina had never rebelled against the idea or the fact of a little sister. Although she was eight years older than Nadja, Polina's own memory did not extend to a time before her sister's existence and so she couldn't say who had exerted the greater influence in forming the character of the other. Had she become maternal because of Nadja, or had Nadja remained childlike because of her? In this sense Nadja shared something with Alec, the difference being that Alec's childishness seemed to protect him from the world whereas Nadja's seemed to expose her.

—I've always liked the name Anastasia, Nadja had said. That or maybe Brigitte or Sophia.

She had dropped down beside Polina and set her small handbag on the grass at the base of the park bench where she was liable to forget it. The same people in the park who would not have been able to identify Polina as a traitor to the motherland also would not have been likely to identify the two of them as sisters. Polina had inherited their father's coloring: pale skin, blond hair, gray eyes, and angular face. Nadja resembled, if anyone, their mother: dark hair, wide mouth, hazel eyes, and a starburst of freckles on her nose and cheeks—though her chief distinguishing feature was the slight gap between her two front teeth, which she displayed whenever she smiled or laughed.

—I suppose you can choose any name you want, Polina had said.

—What are you choosing for yourself?

—I don't know. Something simple.

—And Alec?

—Igor.

—I never saw him as an Igor.

—When he was small he had a friend named Igor whose father could bend nails with his teeth.

—What was his friend's father's name?

—I didn't ask. But he didn't want to be the father. He wanted to be Igor. He wanted to have a father who bent nails with his teeth.

—I wouldn't be surprised if Alec's father could bend nails with his teeth.

—Probably. If he had to.

—And what will we call Mama and Papa?

—Mama and Papa.

—That won't create problems?

—I don't think so.

—We could just call them Him and Her.

—I'd rather not. Things are bad enough as they are.

Even if her relations with her parents had not soured, Polina supposed that their father, a Party member and a sea captain, would have objected to having her letters addressed to their apartment. She planned to post her letters to Arik Farberman, a friend of Alec's and a refusenik who had been trapped in Riga for the last five years. Arik served this function for other émigrés who left behind family members—Party officials, esteemed professionals, or just the habitually cautious—who did not want letters from the West arriving at their homes. The false names were in case the mail was seized.

When she and Nadja had embraced to say goodbye, Polina felt her sister's hair against her face and the sharpness of Nadja's silver seashell earring against her cheek. When they drew apart, the earring had left an imprint that Nadja pointed out so as to avoid the subject of their separation. Polina also did not want a dramatic scene. She saw them meeting in another lifetime, two old women at an airport, straining to recognize each other.

As they rose from the bench and started off down the path, Polina noticed that Nadja had forgotten her purse. Nadja doubled back to retrieve it.

—There's nothing in it anyway except the paper with the fake names.

—Who will remind you now not to lose your purse? Polina had said.

—Every time I lose my purse I'll think of you, Nadja had said and smiled.

3

This is Rome? Samuil Krasnansky heard a man his age inquire in the hall.

Slight variations on the same question rippled through the car.

—Can this be Rome?

—Such a small station for such a big city?

—Do you see a sign that says Rome?

—You can read their language?

The train came to a halt and radiated its heat into the heat of the early morning.

—It's not Rome, Karl said when he returned to the compartment. Rome is another hour. But someone from HIAS is here. We're to get off the train.

Samuil Krasnansky looked out his window and saw Italian militia with their submachine guns lined up the length of the platform. He did not like being under foreign guard, but he preferred the Italian militia in their blue uniforms to the Austrians in their green. The Austrians offended his sensibilities. When last he had seen Austrians like these they had been marching in long, dejected columns under Soviet command. He had been a young officer then, a revolver on his hip and the soles of his boots worn down by the rubble of Eastern and Central Europe. Men still chose their words carefully when addressing him. Fussy women with clipboards had not felt entitled to pry into his thoughts and personal affairs.

Once again the baggage had to be deposited onto the platform. The same method they had used to get the baggage into the train was now reversed. His daughters-in-law descended and stood waiting beneath the windows. His sons wrenched the bags and suitcases from the floor and the sleeping berths and lowered them to their wives. Samuil and his wife, Emma, were assigned the task of looking after the grandchildren. Emma held each boy by the hand. At first, still half-asleep, they were obedient. But that lasted only a short while, until a suitcase slipped out of Rosa's grasp and crashed loudly and heavily to the cement. From the train, Karl cursed and Rosa responded that he had handed her the suitcase improperly. She could not be expected to manage all that weight if he practically dropped it on her. She wasn't going to risk her head for souvenirs and tchotchkes. She had the boys to think about. Did Karl want the children to grow up motherless orphans? If that's what he wanted then he had nearly succeeded.

At the sound of the word "orphans" the boys started to revolt. They didn't want to be orphans. They didn't want their father to cripple their mother with the suitcases. They thrashed in Emma's grip and tried to free themselves to assist their mother.

—Stay, don't move, Samuil instructed them, but they didn't heed him.

—Boys, you can help your mother by behaving, Emma said.

Just then another bag fell from the window and somehow wedged itself between the train and the platform. This time it had been Alec who had released the bag. It was one of the duffel bags, extremely heavy and unwieldy, and Polina tried in vain to dislodge it.

—Why even have them down there if they can't catch the bags? Samuil said.

—They're doing their best, Emma said.

—I could do less damage with a hammer.

—With your heart don't get any ideas.

—I can't stand here and watch their bumbling.

When Emma spoke again in protest, Samuil glowered at her and said, Not another word. He stalked to the train. Awkwardly, grasping for decent handholds, he and Polina ultimately managed to free the bag.

—Now let's have the rest, Samuil said, his face crimson with the exertion.

Karl gazed down from the window, wordlessly.

—What's the matter with you? Samuil demanded. You forget what you're doing up there?

—For God's sake, be careful, Emma implored.

—Don't speak to me as if I'm an invalid, Samuil snapped.

With three of them receiving the bags, the job progressed faster. Soon they found themselves before another woman with a clipboard at the doors to the bus. Meanwhile, Italian porters appeared and heaved their belongings into its belly. A Russian interpreter accompanied the woman and called out the names of the émigrés. One after another they passed before him to be counted and checked off the list.

—You think terrorists couldn't attack the buses? a gaunt, intellectual-looking woman said to Samuil.

—Rumors. Fearmongering, Samuil said.

—They'd hire all these soldiers because of rumors? the woman asked.

—Attacks have already happened, a man behind Samuil offered. That's a fact. Palestinian terrorists.

—Italian Fascists, corrected another man. Shot up a train compartment. A woman from Odessa, mother of three, lost an eye. A tragedy.

—They always change the routes, Rosa said. I heard it from HIAS in Vienna. Sealed orders. Even the train engineers don't know where HIAS will meet them until they get to the station.

The interpreter called out "Krasnansky" and Karl cleared a path to the front of the line. The others fell in behind him.

—You're one family? the interpreter inquired.

—Three families. Same last name, Karl said.

—But related?

Karl withheld his answer.

—No point playing games. It's all in the files.

—Who's playing games? Karl said.

—Don't worry, there's no penalty. You have three family heads. Go find your seats.

Samuil and Emma settled for a pair of seats near the back. Once they were on the road it became evident that the bus lacked proper ventilation. For relief Samuil slid his window open but encountered resistance from the woman behind him.

—I have a young child, sir, do you want her to catch pneumonia?

—We're elderly people, you'd prefer we suffocate?

—Citizens, let's be civilized, another voice chimed in.

—We could exchange seats, Emma suggested.

—And wake my child? the woman said.

—If your screeching hasn't woken her, moving won't either, Samuil said.

Samuil thought, as he had time and again, that the Soviets had wisely managed to rid themselves of the least desirable elements. In his long life he had never had the misfortune of being cast among such a lot of rude and unpleasant people.

Gradually, the bus approached the suburbs. Up front, the Russian interpreter assumed the role of tour guide. The road they were on was called Via Flaminia, built by the ancient Romans. Those familiar with the famous saying "All roads lead to Rome" might be interested to know that they were now on such a road. It was interesting to consider, the interpreter continued, the traffic that the road had conveyed over the centuries. Roman legions used it when returning from their campaigns against the Gauls. Merchants from across Europe traveled its length from antiquity through the Middle Ages. Barefoot pilgrims walked it for hundreds of kilometers on their way to the Via Conciliazione, at which point they crawled on their knees to St. Peter's Square. The carriages of kings and aristocrats had passed here, as had convoys transporting Italian troops to the Alps during the First World War. And during the Great Patriotic War, German Panzers had descended this way from the north to occupy Rome after the Italian king sued for peace with the Allies. It would not be an exaggeration, the interpreter said, to propose that the history of Western civilization could be plotted along this road.

—Their history: imperialist aggression, dogmatic theocracy, totalitarian monarchy, and fascism, Samuil muttered to Emma.

When they penetrated the ring road that circumscribed the city, the interpreter announced that they had officially entered Rome.

—Rome: the word tolls like a bell, the interpreter said.

Their route took them through a neighborhood called Parioli, the interpreter explained, home to many of Rome's wealthiest and most powerful people.

Morning found these people emerging from their apartments. The boulevard was bordered at either side by a wall of pastel-colored stucco buildings. Trees in full leaf dotted the boulevard and nearly every window was ornamented by a flower box. Here and there, Samuil noticed young men in tailored suits holding open the doors of black sedans for older men in tailored suits. The superior quality of the suits and the cars was the only exceptional thing about this scenario. Not eight months earlier he had himself been a man with a sedan and a personal driver. For twelve years, he had stepped from his building promptly at seven in the morning to find the black Volga at the curb. Rain or shine, Arturs preceded him to the rear door of the sedan. The man always executed his duty with proper decorum—neither too formal nor too familiar. He also provided for Samuil that day's editions of *Pravda* and *Izvestia*, folded neatly on the backseat. Before Arturs, Samuil had had a Russian driver who was far less reliable. Felix had been the man's name. His mustache always looked greasy and he had a pronounced stutter that intensified when he was nervous. Nothing had tried Samuil's patience so much as enduring Felix's excuses for his tardiness. Most frequently, he blamed a neighbor in his communal apartment.

—H-h-h-h-he oc-oc-oc-occupies the tah-tah-tah-toilet with nah-nah-nah-no re-re-re-regard for others.

—You've informed him that his behavior is compromising your job?

—H-h-h-h-he resp-resp-resp-responded in a ru-ru-ru-rude manner.

—Well, either straighten him out or wake earlier.

When Felix had shown no improvement Samuil had dismissed him.

He had experienced none of these problems with Arturs. Samuil had observed that, broadly speaking, compared to Russians, Latvians possessed a superior regard for discipline. Samuil attributed this to the years of German influence. One could criticize the Germans for many things, but it was difficult to fault their discipline. Arturs had been a good man; Samuil did not even blame him for his denunciation, which, in any case, had been rather pro forma.

Samuil preferred not to think about that day. He had had no defense. In fact, he had, in principle, agreed with his accusers. He had attended similar meetings in VEF's main theater and had also furiously denounced traitors to the state. Given his position, he neither expected nor received mercy. He prepared himself for the worst. He even allowed Emma to press upon him his blood pressure pills. He had carried the pills in his trouser pocket and had not felt the need for them until Felix with the greasy mustache rose in the front row, pointed his finger, and cried: Hyp-hyp-hypocrite!

On the street, the stucco apartment blocks gave way to large, gated villas. Palm and poplar trees jutted above the gates. Samuil saw garden terraces on the rooftops; on a balcony, gathering the wash from a line, he saw a maid in uniform; on the walls of another villa Samuil saw what was unmistakably a swastika graffito.

—Imagine, another passenger said, they do not even remove such filth from the walls.

—In Leningrad such outrage would never be tolerated.

Rome was a city divided, the interpreter went on. Parioli, being home to wealthy and powerful people, was traditionally a Fascist neighborhood. Other neighborhoods were Communist in nature. Typically, one could identify them by their graffiti. Fascists or Communists, all Italians liked to write on walls. This should come as no surprise given the Italian origin of the word "graffito." That said, it was illegal to deface public property and any émigré found doing so would risk criminal charges. But this was getting off topic. A complete list of things that were forbidden to them would be provided at the first Joint meeting. Meanwhile, if they looked out their window to the right they would be able to see a section of the Villa Borghese park. It was a good place to go for a walk or for a picnic. It also contained a museum with an impressive art collection. Not to be missed was *The Rape of Persephone*, a masterpiece by the sculptor Bernini.

4

I n Vienna, Alec and Polina had had a tiny, but private, room. In Rome they had no such luck. Karl, Rosa, and the boys were given a room of their own but Alec and Polina were directed to share a room with Samuil and Emma on the fourth floor of the hotel. The elevator was either broken or off-limits, it wasn't exactly clear which. On the ground floor, a sign composed in both Russian and Italian had been posted on the elevator doors. In one script was written, *Elevator is not functioning*, though in another script someone had scribbled the words *"For Russians"* before the word *"Elevator."* To ensure that nobody misunderstood the prohibition, the hotel's manager planted himself in front of the elevator doors. He was a grim little man, his face a mask of blunt suspicion. To Alec he seemed like a bad comic actor. The effect was reinforced by the man's red hair, which he styled in a pompadour roughly the size and hue of a cheap fox fur hat. Who could get angry at an Italian gnome with a red pompadour? Alec mentioned this to a man who lurched past him, crippled by the bulk of two suitcases. The man hissed curses at the manager as he mounted the stairs.

—Swine. Son of a whore.

—What's the point? He's a clown.

—How many floors do you have to climb?

—Four.

—So who's the clown?

Theirs was one of the rooms not equipped with a toilet. A shared bathroom was down the hall. It served three other rooms, each occupied by four people. Karl, who helped Alec bring up their bags, recommended the use of their bathroom. It would demand climbing another flight of stairs, but at least they would not be hostage to the bowel and hygiene peculiarities of a dozen strangers.

When Karl returned to his room, Polina stated to Alec that she'd rather take her chances with strangers than ask Rosa's permission every time she had to pee. From his parents' half of the room there was silence. Alec didn't need to look to confirm the magnitude of his father's disapproval; he was an expert in the many tones of his father's silences. He could have written a dissertation about them.

—We had it much worse during the evacuation, Emma said. People would have paid anything to have such a room for even one night.

Samuil remained silent. He refused to respond to Emma's pacifying overture, even though the war was one of his favorite subjects.

—You know, I've thought about it, Emma said, and what is this except another evacuation? Emigration, evacuation; I don't see such a difference. At least this time everyone is together.

—Think before you speak, Samuil said. In the war you ran from the enemy. Now who are you running from?

To Alec's relief, this interlude of family harmony was interrupted by a knock on the door. Alec hopped over a suitcase, opened the door, and was greeted by the momentarily startled face of Iza Judo. Alec, whose own expression must have mirrored Iza's, could not at that instant imagine a less likely visitor. He said the only thing that came to his mind.

—Iza, how did you know we were here?

Iza shrugged ambiguously.

—I heard, I guess.

Alec had never been so happy to see Iza Judo—hadn't supposed that the sight of Iza Judo could bring him happiness. They had never been close friends. Sometimes they socialized in the same company. In the summers, they played soccer together on the beach in Jurmala. He'd never particularly liked Iza, preferring Iza's brother, Syomka. The two were identical twins, although nobody would ever mistake one for the other. Iza had shaved his head when he enrolled in the Institute of Sport, where he specialized in judo. Syomka grew his hair long and studied engineering and languages to become a translator of technical literature.

Alec tried to think back to when he would have seen Iza Judo last. He remembered a small party at the dacha of a friend. There had been half a dozen men and four women. Alec and his friend had met two girls at a café and invited them back to the dacha. Iza had arrived later with other friends and two girls. One of the girls had been very drunk and she had wedged herself at the kitchen table with a guy named Robik. Robik presumably held something in a closed fist and the girl kept whining, incessantly and mind-numbingly, for him to show her what it was. *Robik, show me. Come on, Robik, show me. Robik, show me.* At the same time Iza had been trying to make headway with the other girl. The girl was slight and dark. She wasn't particularly pretty, but she had an idea of herself. Part of this idea included the belief that she was too good for Iza Judo. She was also sober. When she was no longer willing to tolerate Iza she tried to leave. Iza blocked her way and then, somehow, managed to catch her head in the door. That nearly ruined the evening. The girl threatened to call the police, but eventually she calmed down, accepted a drink, and spent the night with Alec's friend. Alec spent the night with the girl he met at the café. He no longer remembered her name. Mainly what he remembered was that as a child she had owned eleven pet bunnies. Even then, when he spoke of her, he referred to her as Eleven Bunnies.

Alec invited Iza in and cleared a place for him on the bed. Iza seemed to deliberate over the invitation. Hanging from his shoulder by a vinyl strap was a medium-size valise. Iza eyed this valise before he finally accepted the invitation and picked his way through the bags to take his seat.

—I wish we had something to offer you, Emma said. But as you can see . . .

—Don't trouble yourself, Iza said.

—I'm surprised you're still here, Alec said.

—Australia. Even the embassy is run by kangaroos. We've waited seven months.

—Before you left, Syomka mentioned an uncle in New Jersey.

—He lives in a home for geriatrics. We've never even seen a picture of him. If we'd gone to visit him and a nurse wheeled out the wrong old Yid we wouldn't have known the difference.

—So why Australia?

—First, Syomka heard good things. Second, for America, they fly you out of Rome in about a month. But Syomka thought, We're in Italy, what's the hurry? So I thought, All right. New Jersey or Sydney: once we get there it will be all the same shit. Pardon my language, Emma Borisovna. And what about you?

—Chicago.

—You have relatives?

—My mother's cousin from Vilnius, Alec said. They settled two years ago.

—Chicago's a big city. I don't know much about it. But people go there.

The conversation then hit an uncomfortable lull. Iza sat on the bed, at something of a loss. Alec kept expecting him to give some indication as to why he had come to see them, but Iza offered nothing and looked instead as if he was hoping that someone would explain the same thing to him. Eventually, Emma eased the awkwardness and asked Iza about his parents.

—Still there. My brother-in-law doesn't want to leave. He's the transport coordinator at the fruit and vegetable terminal. They live well. Everywhere he goes he carries a watermelon. My sister has the two kids. Our parents don't want to leave without them. Me and Syomka, they're happy to be rid of. They figure we'll settle somewhere first and then it will be safer for the others to follow. We're like the minesweepers.

—I'm sure that's not what they think, Emma said.

—Maybe; maybe not. In any case, they didn't want to be separated from the grandchildren. I don't blame them.

—Of course not. A family should stay together, said Emma, intoning what had effectively become her anthem.

—And how do your parents feel about Australia? Samuil asked.

—They are getting used to the idea.

—You didn't consult with them before you decided?

—We are here, they are there, you understand. If the day comes when they are able to join us—and I hope it will—then they will have to come to Australia. Or, if they don't like it, they can always go to Israel. This may not sound very nice, but it's the truth. Now, of course, you are traveling as one family and so, naturally, it is better.

—Naturally nothing. It remains to be seen what is better, Samuil said.

With that, Iza rose and excused himself. He had enjoyed his visit but had to attend to some affairs. For practical advice, he recommended settling in Ladispoli instead of Ostia. Ostia was overrun by Odessans. Ladispoli was populated more by people from Moscow, Leningrad, Latvia, Lithuania. In short, it was more civilized. But both towns were on the seashore. Both were close to Rome by train. If they liked, he would make himself available to help them find an apartment. Having lived there for seven months, he knew the system. He could protect them from the *meklers*, the unscrupulous apartment brokers. And, if they required, with his experience, he could also help in other ways. For instance, if they had optical equipment—cameras, lenses, telescopes—to sell, he could secure them a much better price than they would get on the open market.

—That's very generous, Emma said, as Alec accompanied Iza out of the room.

In the hallway, when Alec said goodbye to Iza, he noticed a handful of men roaming from room to room, knocking on doors each with his own shoulder bag.

—Well? Samuil said, when Alec returned.

—Well, Alec replied.

—Glad to see your friend?

—What do you think?

—I just hope you didn't agree to sell him anything.

—Of course not.

—Or tell him what we have. All the time he sat there, his eyes were on our bags.

—I said, Thank you and goodbye.

—With a character like that, what he can't buy he'll steal.

—I wouldn't worry about Iza, Alec said. I know him. If he poses a danger to anyone it's to himself.

They had no other visitors. After they put the room into some semblance of order, Samuil reluctantly followed Emma up the steps to see Karl and the grandchildren. In their former life, Alec had never seen his father do anything reluctantly. He did what he wanted or he did nothing at all. Almost in spite of himself, Alec couldn't help pitying his father——even knowing that the only reason Samuil consented to climb the flight of stairs was that he preferred to sit in a room with Karl, Rosa, and the boys than to sit in a room with Alec and Polina.

—Quick, Alec said, before they come back.

—I haven't slept. I haven't washed, Polina said.

—Sleeping, washing. You're the most beautiful woman in Rome.

Polina gazed at the squalid, overheated little room.

—This is Rome?

—We could open a window.

In the afternoon, everyone was called down to the cafeteria for lunch. Since the Joint Distribution Committee had yet to provide them with Italian currency, the meal was furnished by the hotel. Two Italian waitresses shuffled through the cafeteria, dispensing bread rolls and apricot preserves. For families with *bambini* they also brought milk. After the rolls were exhausted the waitresses disappeared into the kitchen. It soon became evident that the rolls constituted the entire meal.

—This must be a mistake, Rosa said.

Later, when they were served a dinner of lettuce followed by macaroni, a former dissident circulated a petition among the émigrés. He promised to file a formal grievance with both HIAS and the Joint. A number of people signed, though Alec declined and Karl forbade Rosa from adding her name.

—These people control our fate and you want to antagonize them because of a salad? Karl said.

When his turn came, Samuil sneered at both the petition and the petitioner.

—I didn't sign your petitions before and I don't intend to start now.

—What do you mean by "your" petitions, *comrade*? retorted the dissident.

—You know very well what I mean. It's lucky for you we are no longer back home, because, over there, I assure you, no Zionist agitator would be so quick to call me comrade.

—My luck then, *comrade*, the dissident said, and moved on.

Alec, Samuil, Polina, and Emma retreated to their room. In one suitcase, Emma had stashed several dozen packets of dehydrated chicken noodle soup. In the same suitcase, she also found a box of crackers. Polina had several cloves of garlic, four potatoes, and a Spanish onion which she had bought in Vienna. There was also half the salami that she'd packed for the train. Alec withdrew a pot from one of the duffel bags and lined up with his neighbors by the bathroom to fill it with water. Everyone in line held either a pot or a kettle. Back in the room Emma set the pot to boil on a glowing hot plate. On another hot plate, Polina had placed a frying pan into which she deposited sliced onions and potatoes. The water had just started to boil when the lights in their room dimmed, flickered, and then cut out entirely. Immediately, shouts and curses rang through the hotel. Alec waited a few moments for his eyes to adjust to the dark, and then, by the vestigial glow of the hot plate, sought out the bag that contained their flashlights. The flashlights were jumbled in with windup, skittering toy chicks; tin Red Army soldiers; pocket knives; abacuses; miniature wooden chess sets. As a mark of Soviet ingenuity, the flashlights did not require batteries. They were mechanical, powered by a long metal trigger. One repeatedly pumped the trigger, thereby generating light and a faint buzzing sound.

Pumping his flashlight at the rate of a quick pulse, Alec stepped out into the hallway. Other people emerged from their rooms also pumping their little flashlights. The effect was reminiscent of the countryside at dusk. It was as if, one after another, nocturnal insects were awaking to pursue their nightly business. Before long, Alec could no longer distinguish individual sources. The buzzing lost all cadence and dominated the hotel. Alec heard it from the floors above and below and, all around, he saw the flitting yellow halos cast by the low-wattage bulbs. Not far from him, crouched against the wall, a boy spooned soup from a metal bowl which his mother illuminated by flashlight. Alec looked the length of the hallway and saw doors open to every room, the occupants peering out or congregating in groups. At the end of the hall, a man strummed a guitar and sang the first line of a melancholic war ballad: *Dark night, only bullets whistle on the steppe.* Interspersed throughout the hallway, other voices joined in and obliged him to continue. Alec passed an elderly woman who leaned against the railing, like a bygone movie heroine, singing, immersed in sentiment. For the first time, a sense of community pervaded. People suspended their quarrels and commiserated about the shitty hotel: no elevator, no food, no power.

As Alec turned back toward his room he heard the familiar piercing voices of his nephews. There was a bounding on the stairwell and two darting beams of light. The boys raced down the steps and then along the hallway, shining their lights into people's faces. The boys were seven and five; the two-year age difference half that of his and Karl's. Yury, the elder, and the more reserved of the two, looked like Karl, square and sturdy, and tried to emulate Karl's laconic manner. Zhenya, on the other hand, though only five, showed the ill effects of his mother's and grandmother's coddling. He was overfed and impudent—qualities that Alec hoped he would outgrow. Emma was fond of pointing out that he himself had been a hundred times worse than Zhenya at that age.

After irritating half of the people in the hallway, Yury pointed his flashlight into Alec's face.

—Looking for someone? Alec asked.

—The captain, Yury said.

—What captain?

—The *submarine* captain, Zhenya chimed. Can't you see we're going down?

—I knew we were in trouble.

—The captain is wounded, Yury said.

Before the boys could run away, Karl descended the steps and called to them. Grudgingly, they scuffed over to him. Karl led them to Emma, who had arranged four bowls on the floor near the entrance to their room.

—Sit, Karl said.

The boys slid their backs along the wall and dropped down.

—Eat, my darlings, Emma said. Grandmother made a tasty soup.

—How are we supposed to eat it? Zhenya demanded. There are no spoons.

—I'm sorry, darling, Emma said. Grandmother couldn't find the spoons.

—Lift the bowl, drink, and don't complain, Karl instructed.

Alec stood beside his brother and directed his flashlight at the wall immediately above Karl's left shoulder. The wall, a grimy off-white, diffused just enough light to illuminate the side of Karl's face. Karl's expression suggested that he was not at all seduced by the anarchic, carnival atmosphere in the hotel. His mind operated on another plane. Alec would see a circus and want to join; Karl, meanwhile, would estimate the cost of feeding the elephants and conjecture that the acrobats suffered from venereal disease.

It was going to be like this every night, Karl said. The sooner they could get out of the hotel the better.

—You know that the Joint covers the hotel for eight days, Alec said.

—You want seven more days of this?

—I'm ready to go now.

—The hotel manager has a deal with the Joint. So long as the trains keep coming, his hotel stays full. That's why he serves us slop. And so long as he serves slop, people plug in their hot plates. There's a bus driver on our floor from Tula. He's been here four days. Every fucking night a fuse blows.

—Why is he still here?

—He takes the train to Ladispoli every day. Brokers demand extortionate prices for hovels. Our bad luck. It's summer. High season. Romans want to get away from the city, lie on the beach, swim in the sea. The bus driver comes home after a day of pleading and weeps in the bathroom so his wife and children won't know.

—So what does that mean for us?

—The bus driver has a sad and trusting face. One look at his face and you want to plunge a knife in his back.

—And our faces?

—My face is whatever it needs to be. As for yours: there may be a sexually frustrated woman with an apartment available. In any event, I don't intend to come back here and weep in the bathroom.

5

There was no limit, it seemed, to Polina's sense of dislocation. The border crossing at Chop had been nightmarish, but at least the nightmare had conformed to some perverted Soviet logic. What was cruel and nonsensical about it was cruel and nonsensical in a typical way. Then on the brief stopover in Bratislava, where they had to change trains for Vienna, she had already begun to feel a heightened sense of foreignness—even though they were still only in Czechoslovakia, where it was not too difficult to find people who spoke Russian. Vienna was overwhelming, every step felt like an embarrassing misstep, but at least Alec had understood the language. And yet, compared to Rome, all that had preceded seemed mild and rational. When, on their first morning in the city, she and Alec stepped onto the sidewalk outside their hotel, Polina had the distinct impression that every car and pedestrian was rushing deliberately at her. She had never before seen quite so much human traffic. Cars, mopeds, and people surged in response to some inscrutable choreography. She watched an old man cross the street and somehow avoid being killed by several cars and one moped carrying two barechested teenage boys. On the sidewalk, a mother passed holding the hand of a little girl. The girl was no older than four or five and chattered away in singsong Italian. This little girl, Polina thought, stands a much better chance of fending for herself in this city than I do. She can put one foot in front of the other. She can cross a street. In Vienna, they had heard rumors about Rome. The city was dirty. Crime was rampant. To walk near Termini, the central train station, was effectively to surrender your valuables. As a city, they were informed, Rome's claim to being part of Europe was purely geo-graphical. Vienna was Europe; Leningrad was Europe; Riga; Mos-cow. With its withering summer heat, filth, and disorder, Rome was Africa.

HIAS had distributed maps to all of the family heads and ex-pected them to fend for themselves. Polina's sense of direction was good, but when they set out on the first day Alec and Karl took charge of the maps. They quickly got lost. They boarded the correct streetcar but took it going the wrong way. By the time Karl and Alec realized their mistake, they'd already been riding for ten minutes. They clambered off and reversed their steps in the mid-afternoon heat. Every few blocks they stopped so that Emma could take a drink from a thermos of water. Because they had already spent their money on a streetcar going the wrong way, they didn't have money for a streetcar going the right way. At one point, Emma saw a park and insisted that Samuil needed a rest, and they all huddled under the shade of a palm tree. Rosa, who had left her boys with the bus driver's wife, complained about a woman who at breakfast had fina-gled an extra serving of milk by claiming that her son was only twelve years old.

—Twelve years old. Stalin didn't have such a mustache.

They recognized their destination, when they reached it, by the large group of émigrés milling about in front. They pressed their way through the crowd and presented themselves to a security guard. The guard, an émigré like themselves, made them recite their names and their city of origin before he let them pass. Though it was unnec-essary in such heat, he stressed that the use of the stairs was expressly forbidden. They rode the elevator four floors and followed a hallway into a large waiting room filled with people. There were not enough chairs for everyone; some people sat on the floor while others leaned against the wall. The stout, matronly Georgian and Azeri women had fallen silent. Some tried to cool themselves with the black silk fans that they'd brought to unload at the markets. Their men gazed into their shoes or at the ceiling. The only exceptions to the general torpor were three old men bent over a small chessboard, and a young, pretty, dark-haired woman who was teaching her son to read using the signs tacked along the walls. The boy formed words by sounding out each letter. In a clear, earnest voice that, unexpectedly, stirred Polina's heart, the boy enunciated:

AVOID LIVING IN THESE HIGH CRIME AREAS.

ENGLISH CLASSES OFFERED.

ROOM AVAILABLE IN CLEAN APARTMENT. ROME. CALL LUIGI.

DRIVING OR OWNING MOTOR VEHICLES IS FORBIDDEN.

DESTINED FOR CANADA OR AUSTRALIA? GOOD COMMAND OF ENGLISH? JOINT AND HIAS HIRING INTERPRETERS.

—What's your name, little boy? Polina asked.

—Vadik, the boy answered.

—You read very well.

—He can also recite poetry, said his mother. At two he was already singing "The Regimental Commander." If he's in the right mood he can also do Marshak.

—Would you like to recite a poem? Polina asked.

—About Lenin? the boy asked.

—If you like.

The boy snapped to attention, pressed his fingertips to his bare thighs, below the hem of his shorts, and raised his chin for better projection.

—They taught him that stance in kindergarten, his mother said.

With feeling and conviction, the boy chimed:

—When Lenin was little / With a head of boyish curls / He also gamboled happily / Upon the snowy hills / Stone upon stone / Brick upon brick / Gone is our Lenin, Vladimir Illich / Deep in the Kremlin / A kind heart resides / Sad are the workers / Sad too am I.

By the conclusion of the poem, others had turned to listen and when the boy was finished there was a smattering of applause.

—Now do one about Brezhnev, a man called.

—Don't be coarse, a woman responded.

—Pay him no mind, a third added.

—Very nice, Polina said to the boy as he relaxed his pose.

—If you can believe it, he knows more of them than I do, the boy's mother said.

—You must be very proud.

—Thank you. I wish I could take the credit. But it was the kindergarten. Where are you from?

—Riga.

—Do you know Leningrad?

—Hardly at all.

—Do you have children?

—No, Polina said.

—Well, there is a wonderful kindergarten. The best in the city. My husband pulled every string, called in every favor. We had money saved for a car, but once we learned there was a chance, we parted with nearly all of it. It's probably the same in Riga.

—Probably.

—It was a wonderful kindergarten. Excellent teachers. Progressive pedagogical methods.

—All right, she understands, the husband interrupted, the kindergarten was good.

—At recess the children played in an apple orchard, the wife continued.

—This is her big regret, the husband said. The kindergarten.

—He says that now, but you should have seen him when we picked up Vadik from the kindergarten for the last time.

—Well, the fact of the matter is, I've heard mixed things about the educational standards in America, the husband said. Students in the fourth grade who don't know the capital of France, can't do simple arithmetic or sign their names.

Inside the classroom, Polina eased into one of the little school desks. Alec appeared and slid into the place directly behind her, even though there was an empty desk beside her.

—I like this better, Alec said. It's like a fantasy.

—Which fantasy is this?

—The two of us in school together. Young love.

—This is a new one?

—Hard to keep track.

—So how does it go? You pull my braids, dip them in the inkpot?

—I sit all day and admire you. Stare at the back of your neck. Dream about you. Get yelled at by the teacher.

During the orientation, as the woman from the Joint was speaking, Polina twice had to reach back and slap at Alec's hand when he tugged her hair.

—Are you even listening to what she's saying? Polina whispered.

—After class, meet me in the hall. I'm having difficulties with algebra, Alec said.

When the orientation was over, Alec leaned forward and said he thought they should rent an apartment in Rome.

—So you were paying attention for that, Polina said.

As part of her talk, which escalated sometimes into a harangue, the woman from the Joint had dissuaded people from trying to rent apartments in Rome. The best and most expedient housing solution for everyone was to be found in Ostia and Ladispoli, where the Joint and HIAS had established satellite offices. Ladispoli and Ostia also now boasted Jewish community centers, created for the émigrés, where there were regular lectures, cultural events, and even programs for children. That past March, in Ladispoli, a professional director, formerly of the Moscow Theater, had helped stage a spectacular Purim pageant. And in April, in Ladispoli as well as Ostia, with the help of the Italian Jewish community, they had managed to organize Passover seders for more than one thousand people. Needless to say, these were very moving celebrations.

—If the Romans are heading to the shore to escape the heat, it might be easier to find a place in the city, Alec said.

—I don't think it's a good idea, Polina said.

—You're not serious.

—Your family will be in Ladispoli and we'll be in Rome?

—That's part of the appeal.

—They'll say it was my idea, Polina said.

—No they won't.

—They'll think it.

—I'll make it clear, Alec said.

—I'd be happier if you left things alone, Polina said.

—Happier sharing an apartment in the suburbs with Rosa? You'd be miserable.

—A happier miserable, Polina said.

6

I n Ladispoli, the hub of Russian activity was Piazza Marescotti, a short distance from the beach. It served as bazaar, employment agency, and social club. When they arrived, Alec saw an old man holding a sign that advertised tutoring in math and physics. Another man offered English lessons. There were women offering to mind children. A few people, men and women both, had also spread blankets on the ground and laid out a selection of small items. Many others were there just to trade gossip and kill time.

Karl was the first to spot a familiar face. It belonged to Boris Tsiferblatt, known at the Riga Dynamo gym as Boris the Bodybuilder. He was at the piazza advertising his services as a mover.

—I see you're putting your training to good use, Karl said after an enthusiastic greeting.

—I've got my hand in a few things, Boris said. But people come and go every day. It's a good way to make a little extra money.

They had left Rosa behind with the children, and traveled together to look for a place to live and also to make a phone call to Emma's cousin in Chicago. It was a Tuesday, one of two days when Emma's cousin had written that she could be found at home. On other days she had her job at the bakery, her driving lessons, her English classes.

On account of his sideline, Boris said that he sometimes got leads on apartments. The day before, he'd seen a family off to Philadelphia. They'd had a good three-room apartment. In the coming days, he knew of other people going to Baltimore and San Francisco. San Francisco: in the Soviet Union the name had possessed magic. California. America. Australia. Canada. Now when people spoke of these places, they spoke mainly about the relative strengths of their economies or the nature of their industries. Boston was in decline. Hadn't New York City filed for bankruptcy? Calgary, mind you, was booming. They compared climates. San Francisco was wonderful if you didn't mind rain every day. Atlanta was forty degrees in the shade and you were lucky to find a white cop. San Francisco had the ocean and a famous bridge; New York City had culture and phenomenal buildings. To live in these places you could marvel at them every day, but who did? In the same way you took a beautiful girl and made her into a wife. The wife remained enchanting, full of mystery, to everyone else. Strange men saw her on the trolleybus, concocted brute or intricate fantasies of seduction, while you waited for her to come home with the groceries and wash your socks.

—We are six adults and two children, Emma said.

—It's not impossible, Boris replied. Maybe not an apartment, but a small cottage. There are cottages.

From Piazza Marescotti they went south along Via Ancona to the post office, which housed the international call center. It had a small seating area where people waited for their calls to be connected. One operator accepted the phone orders from behind a long wooden counter. Beyond the seating area, three numbered phone booths were visible. From one of them, Alec heard a man's hoarse voice shouting in Russian. *I can't hear you well. Can you hear me? The furs? The furs? Hello? Mentka, you hear me? Yosik wrote you what? Your furs? He was with us at the border. He's a liar. He saw with his own eyes that the furs were confiscated.*

Holding a piece of paper with her cousin's name, address, and phone number, Emma approached one of the operators at the counter. Karl, Alec, and Samuil drew up to the counter with her while Polina found a chair beside the window. The operator was a woman in her middle thirties, plump though not unattractive, with a hairstyle too fashionable for her job and her face. Because of her hairstyle, Alec expected her to be curt or impatient, but she listened attentively as Emma repeated the words "Chicago, Illinois, America" and her cousin's name, and pointed to the digits of the phone number as they were written on the slip of Soviet graph paper. Emma looked meaningfully at the operator, as if, in the absence of a shared language, concentration and desire could effect understanding. The operator peered back at Emma. Then she pointed to Emma and spoke one word. When Emma didn't respond, she continued to point and said several more words, hoping, perhaps, that given a broader choice of words, Emma might encounter one she recognized.

—What did she say? Emma asked Alec.

—I don't know.

The operator pointed to herself and drawled: "Gisa."

—What does she want? Emma directed her question nonspecifically at Alec, Karl, and Samuil.

—Your name, Samuil grumbled. Tell her your name.

They had spent immoderately on the train to Ladispoli. But Samuil hadn't wanted decisions made about an apartment without him; Alec had insisted that Polina come and see the place for herself. To compensate for the expense, Emma had planned ahead and instructed everyone to conserve their dinner rolls from the previous evening. Rosa had sent them off with lingonberry jam from her private stash, and so, as they waited for their call to be connected, Emma unpacked the bread and jam and prepared their lunch. Sharing the waiting area with them were an elderly Italian, an Arab laborer in stained jeans and work boots, and the wife of the Russian man who denied stealing his friend's furs.

The Russian completed his telephone call and left with his wife. ("So?" his wife asked as they walked out the door. "You'd think I hadn't done enough for him," the man spat.) The operator connected the Italian, and Alec watched as he limped to his designated booth. Every few minutes Emma checked her watch.

—What do we do? Emma asked.

—We've already waited an hour. You want to cancel the call? Samuil asked.

—Rosa is waiting with the children. What will she think?

—She'll think. She'll think we've been delayed, Karl said.

—If we knew how to call the hotel, Emma said, they could inform Rosa and maybe put our food aside.

—Do we know how to call the hotel? Samuil asked.

—No, Emma said.

—So why blabber about it?

—I only thought, Emma said dejectedly.

Just then, the operator's phone rang.

—Emma. *Numero due*, the operator said, and motioned to the appropriate booth.

Emma sprang up and rushed to the booth, beckoning for the others to follow.

—Hurry, so everyone can have a chance to speak, she said.

Everyone rose, except for Polina, who shook her head and said, The woman doesn't know me. Go on. You talk.

The woman didn't know Alec all that well either. He had seen her perhaps three times in his life. She was his mother's first cousin. As children they had been close. They had, in fact, shared the family house. During the war, they had evacuated together and spent the war years in the Kara-Kalpak region of Uzbekistan. Shura, the cousin, had met her husband there and, after the war, settled in Vilnius, his town. Emma had meanwhile returned to their house in Latvia, and soon was married to Samuil. Over the intervening years they had corresponded. On occasion, Emma visited Vilnius. More frequently, her cousin came to Riga.

When Alec reached the booth, Emma already had the receiver to her ear and was raising her voice.

—Shura, she repeated, is that you? It's very difficult to hear. Hello?

Emma looked imploringly at Samuil and Alec.

—You can't hear her? Alec asked.

—Shurachka, can you hear me? Emma asked again. She paused and pressed the receiver tighter to her ear. There. Now I hear you. Yes, I hear you, she said.

In a letter they'd received in Vienna, Shura had written about the secondhand car her husband had purchased. It was two-tone, green and gold, and larger than a Volga. Her husband had a job half an hour's drive from their apartment. He was fifty-six years old and, in his entire life, had never operated a car. But he had passed for his license on the first attempt and was now driving on an eight-lane American highway. Shura was also learning to drive the car. Because of the car's size, her husband had fashioned blocks for the pedals and she sat on a feather pillow, which she stored in the trunk along with the spare tire.

She's been in America only four months but look at what she's done, Emma had said after reading the letter. It's hard to believe that she's the same person.

Alec tried to imagine his mother in similar circumstances. In Riga, his father had owned a car, a Zhiguli, which he drove poorly and infrequently. Arturs took him to work and, when the need arose, Samuil expected either Karl or Alec to drive him where he wanted to go. Otherwise, the car sat in the garage, halfway across town. Samuil recorded the mileage on a pad to ensure that neither Karl nor Alec took the car out for their pleasure. It never occurred to anyone that his mother might also want to drive it.

Some of the photos that Shura sent depicted her and her husband in the parking lot outside their apartment building, smiling in front of their car. Other photos showed them in downtown Chicago, set against a formidable panorama of receding buildings. There were also photos that they'd taken inside their apartment. One was of Lyona, Shura's husband, with a bottle of beer at the kitchen table; another was of Shura, her hand resting on a velour sofa, flanked by a floor lamp taller than she.

—For God's sake, don't bother with trivialities, Samuil hissed when Emma asked Shura about the weather.

—Other than Rosa and the children, we are all here. In a moment I'll let everyone say hello, Emma said.

The conversation proceeded for a minute or two along typical lines until Emma came to the point and asked her cousin about sponsorship.

—What happens, Emma asked, do you send your form to HIAS, or do they send something to you?

After this, there was a lengthy pause, during which Emma nodded her head and said nothing. Then she said, Yes, I'm still here. I hear you. I hear you. I understand. No need to apologize, I understand. Yes, of course, I understand. Naturally. All right. Would you still like to say hello to everyone?

—What is she saying? Samuil asked.

—Spin the globe, Karl said.

—Another time then, Emma spoke into the phone. Of course. Of course, I will write you. Yes. Certainly. Send my best to everyone.

Emma replaced the phone and tried to put on a brave face. The way she looked, Alec feared she would crumble if Samuil started to berate her.

—Well, Samuil said.

—Let her at least step out of the booth, Alec said.

—They got a letter saying that Lyona's brother's visa was approved, Emma said. They'd been under refusal for two years. What could she do?

—What could she do? She could keep her promise, Samuil said.

—It's Lyona's brother and his family. He's a brother. How could they deny them?

—I didn't know you had your heart set on Chicago, Alec said.

—What do I care about Chicago? Samuil said. Where I want to go, the door is closed. This is about principle.

—She feels horrible, Emma said.

—Not so horrible that she wouldn't betray you.

—We already shipped the furniture, Karl said, shaking his head. She doesn't have anyone else in Chicago who could sponsor us?

—I don't know, Emma said. She didn't say. I didn't think to ask.

Emma was still halfway inside the booth when she said this, and as Samuil, Karl, and Alec started to walk back to the counter, she remained rooted in place.

—What are you waiting for? Samuil asked, either not noticing or ignoring that she had started to cry.

For all his mother's agonizing and worrying, and for the harsh treatment she often received from Samuil, Alec rarely saw her cry. As a boy, after an argument with Samuil, he would often hear the unmistakable sounds of her crying behind his parents' bedroom door. Later, by the time Alec was old enough to understand the reasons for those arguments, they had subsided. New arguments replaced them, the subject typically concerning his and Karl's questionable behavior and misdirection. These arguments were conducted in the open, and didn't merit tears. They participated in them as a family and, in time, the arguments standardized into the routine that represented life at home. It wasn't until the talk of emigration that his mother found reason to cry again. If one of these arguments escalated beyond a certain point, she would leave the room. Karl and Samuil and Alec would then fall silent, temporarily chastened by her muffled sobs.

Now, in the telephone booth, with no place to hide, Emma cried openly. At first, she allowed only a few quiet tears, but after Samuil barked at her, she dropped her shoulders and covered her face with her hands.

A long interval followed during which nobody moved. They remained in this awkward standoff until Polina rose, walked over to Emma, and gently placed a hand on her elbow.

She leaned close to Emma and Alec heard her whisper, Emma Borisovna, come and let's sit for a minute.

Emma kept her hands over her face but allowed Polina to lead her to the seating area. Polina sat down and eased Emma into the chair beside her.

—It's nothing terrible, Polina said as she stroked Emma's shoulder.

The dramatics had attracted the attention of the phone operator and the Arab laborer, both of whom turned their heads to observe her—the phone operator with evident concern. Karl and Samuil, meanwhile, stood several paces away, in the neutral space between the seating area and the operator's counter.

—What are you crying for? Samuil demanded.

—It hurts, so I cry, Emma said, lifting her eyes above her hands.

—Cry, then. For all the good it will do.

—It's like a bad dream, Emma despaired. I can't believe it has happened.

—What's not to believe? Samuil countered. It's your own dream. You wanted it. You got it. So don't complain.

—Now we have nowhere to go, Emma said, wiping her cheeks with the base of her hand.

—Why? On the contrary, now we can go anywhere, Alec said.

—It's possible, Karl said, that we could still get into Chicago. Anyone can apply. We could explain our situation to HIAS.

—I will not live in the same city as those people, Samuil decreed.

—Chicago is a big place, Karl said.

—They have spat in our faces. I will not associate with them.

—Oh, for fuck's sake, Karl fumed.

—Don't you curse at me, Samuil thundered.

—Louder, Alec said, they can't hear us across the street.

Samuil strode indignantly ahead on the return trip to the train station, where he announced that their straggling had cost them one train, with the next one not due for another forty-five minutes. At this rate, he assured them, they would miss dinner.

To their mutual displeasure, he was correct.

7

I n the morning, soon after Karl had departed for Ladispoli to renew the search for an apartment, a doctor from the Joint arrived with, to everyone's surprise, a young Italian man who spoke a very passable Russian.

—I am studying Russian at university, the young man said and added proudly, I am a Communist.

—Then it may interest you to know, Alec said, that my father, the very man you see before you, once caught Molotov's hat when it was blown from his head by a gust of wind.

—I don't need a doctor, Samuil said.

—I'm sorry, comrade, the interpreter said, running his finger along a column in a file. It is mandatory for persons over sixty years of age or for those who have an illness.

—What does it say there about me? Samuil asked.

—It gives your year of birth as 1913 and your age as sixty-five. Is that correct?

—You can tell your doctor that there is nothing wrong with my health, Samuil said. Tell him that I was already poked and prodded in Vienna.

While the doctor examined Samuil, Polina and Alec left the room.

With Chicago a dead issue, Rosa seized the moment to advocate for Israel, where, she did not need to remind them, her parents and brother were enjoying a comfortable life surrounded by their own people. And unlike Emma's relatives, her family would not spurn them. How many times had they already extended invitations? The Israeli government would provide for their basic needs. They would not be guests in a foreign country, but rather valued citizens residing in their ancestral homeland. When Rosa uttered the words "ancestral homeland" she managed, pointedly, to avert her face completely from Polina.

—The ancestral homeland will always be there, Karl said.

—I wouldn't be so sure, Rosa said.

—Well, it's not going anywhere anytime soon.

—No thanks to the likes of you or your brother, Rosa said.

—Why bring me into this? Alec said. I said before that Polina and I were willing to go to Israel. Or at the very least Egypt. I hear good things about Cairo. Especially now that there will be friendship among nations.

—Everything is a joke to you, Rosa said.

—Who's joking? I expect Sadat and Begin, arm in arm, to personally greet us at the airport, Alec said.

Throughout the discussion—*Zionists!*—Samuil's unspoken epithet swelled above them like dark wrath.

—What do you think, Polina? Rosa asked. Alec does all the talking. We never hear from you.

—I don't know enough to feel strongly one way or another, Polina said.

—You understand that you're talking about your own life, your own future, Rosa persisted.

—Thank you, I understand that, Polina said.

Nothing was resolved. The word "Queens" was uttered and New Jersey was referred to several times. A fledgling community of acquaintances from Riga had settled in a town called *Fehr-lon*. If all else failed, they could say "Fehr-lon" and be no worse off than anyone else. Nobody expected an answer today, tomorrow, or the next day. More pressing was getting out of the pensione and finding an apartment, Karl said. Or two apartments, Alec offered, and received no argument.

There had been signs up at the pensione, and, evading the Krasnansky surveillance ring, Alec had also taken down the phone number of the listing at the Joint offices. Before the family conclave he had descended to the lobby and called the number. Another refugee had been in the phone booth ahead of him and, out of the goodness of his heart, he had shared with Alec his *gettone*. The man had drilled a tiny hole at the top of the *gettone* and tied it to a length of black thread. To make a phone call, he dropped the coin into the slot, listened for the click, and then—like toying with a cat—yanked it free of its grasp. He had performed the same operation on another coin, he explained, which he used in elevators.

The phone moaned twice before a man said, *Pronto*.

—*Buonasera*, Alec said, consulting a slip of paper on which he had copied out words from a phrasebook.

—*Buonasera*, the man said.

—Luigi? Alec inquired.

—*Si, sono Luigi.*

—*Appartamento*, Alec began, and then attempted to string his words together.

The man listened to him for a few moments before he interrupted, chattered very quickly in Italian, and then fell silent. Disoriented and intimidated, Alec stared at the telephone booth's scarred wooden panel. Gathering himself, he tried again. *A-ppar-ta-men-to*. There was another pause, after which the man laughed. His laughter was ringing and hysterical, as if Alec had just told him the greatest joke. Still laughing, the man said, in what Alec was almost certain was a mocking tone, *Appartamento*?

—*Si, appartamento*, Alec said, now angry and humiliated.

—What kind of apartment are you looking for? the man asked, this time in fluent Russian.

Only seconds earlier, Alec had wanted nothing other than for the man to miraculously speak Russian, but now that he had, Alec had to restrain himself from hanging up in fury.

—I was calling for Luigi, Alec said.

—I'm Luigi, the man said.

—You're Luigi? Alec asked.

—In Kishinev I was Lyova. In Netanya I was Arieh. Here I'm Luigi.

—And you have an apartment, Luigi?

—*Si*, the man said, and laughed again.

—Listen, just because I'm desperate for a place doesn't mean I'll deal with any lunatic, Alec said.

—Take it easy, Lyova-Luigi said. It's a miserable world. Can't a man amuse himself?

The price Lyova-Luigi quoted was almost reasonable and, speaking in the Soviet conspiratorial tone, he suggested they could possibly negotiate once they met in person. Alec considered this sufficient to propel him and Polina through the labyrinth of Rome. Wide, reassuring boulevards gave way to serpentine streets that seemed to double back on themselves or to terminate at the steps of gloomy churches. Sometimes teeming streets led to teeming squares, other times to courtyards occupied only by laundry and flower boxes. Often Alec suspected that a tiny street they had accidentally stumbled upon was a shortcut known only to locals, though, his being lost, the discovery was naturally of no use. Different blocks bore the marks of different centuries. Neighborhoods changed, but he could not interpret the changes. He could not have said with any conviction what kind of people lived where, or when a place should be visited or avoided.

Eventually they came to the river and crossed a bridge to the opposite bank. More stumbling and they began to see the names of streets Lyova-Luigi had mentioned. Trastevere, what the neighborhood was called, bore a distinct resemblance to Old Riga: dignified and ramshackle; three-story buildings; medieval streets, narrow and constricted, conducive to the spread of plague.

On Via Salumi they found the designated house: green shutters and a tangerine, peeling stucco exterior. Beside the frame of a wooden door, built to withstand marauders, was a line of buzzers. Alec depressed the little black nipple on the uppermost buzzer and then, through the door, heard the bolt and hinges of another door opening above and within, and then rapid footfalls beating the rhythm of staircase, landing, staircase, landing, staircase, landing. The door was pulled open; Lyova-Luigi stood before them and extended a long freckled hand.

—Lyova, he said. Welcome.

He was at least a head taller than Alec. His red hair and sideburns were chaos. His features were a series of conflicting planes: sharp, skeletal cheekbones; his nose a high, thin ridge; an Adam's apple that was like a second nose in his neck. He wore steel, large-framed eyeglasses that magnified his blue eyes and their pink rims. When he spoke or smiled he exposed long teeth and the flesh of his upper gums. He was the kind of ugly man women found attractive. Alec had often seen very beautiful women clinging to men like Lyova. Speaking as if under the influence of some narcotic, women described these men as "interesting." What the women meant was that they had faces that made you want to keep looking—which, for all practical purposes, was the same as handsome.

Alec and Polina followed him up the marble steps. On the third floor they went through the door which Lyova had left ajar. From the entrance, and to their right, they could see one large room that had been divided in half by a brocade curtain of green leaves on a black background. The far half of the room had windows, a single bed, an armoire, and a small television; the near half had a simple walnut table, four chairs, and a bookshelf with books and a telephone. To their left was a small kitchen, a door to the bathroom, and a third door, which was closed. Lyova walked ahead and opened it to reveal a larger bed with a headboard, a window, and a closet.

—I sleep here, Lyova said, and indicated the single bed behind the curtain. The other room would be yours. The table, the kitchen, and the washroom are shared. As you can see, it is clean. Everything works.

With a chivalrous gesture, Lyova invited Polina to inspect the place.

—Open anything you like, Lyova said.

When Alec didn't give any sign to the contrary, Polina stepped into the kitchen and glanced at the cupboards and the stove.

—Where are you from? Lyova asked.

—Riga, Alec said.

—And where are you going?

—We're still deciding, Alec said, and offered a summary of their recent reversal.

—It's difficult to travel with a large Jewish family, Lyova said. Too many opinions. Like the joke about the couple that has sex on the street in Israel. Everyone who passes by tells them they're doing it wrong.

—And what about you? Alec asked.

—Me? Lyova said.

—Where are you going?

Lyova raised his palms and exhaled contempt mixed with resignation mixed with despair.

—You've heard of Prisoners of Zion? Jews punished for Zionism? I'm the other kind of Prisoner of Zion. No country will take me. I lived in Israel, so I'm no longer a refugee. There is only one option: back to Israel.

—How long have you been here?

—Fifteen months.

—You won't go back?

—I haven't yet given up on the idea that I'm a free man in the free world. I lived in Israel. I worked. I paid taxes. I served in the army. I repaid my debt. Now I'd like to try somewhere else. Why not?

Polina moved from the kitchen to the bathroom. From the doorway, she peered into the bedroom.

—What do you think? Lyova asked.

—It's fine, Polina said.

—You haven't seen anything else yet, right? Lyova said. I understand, you have nothing to compare it to. But let me say, you won't find a better arrangement in Rome. Within walking distance are cathedrals, parks, monuments, galleries. Also the Porta Portese, the Americana market. I never have trouble renting the space. Normally, tenants leave, I know in advance and the day they leave I have already replaced them. This time, I was giving a tour of Florence, Venice, and Milan, and so the place has been vacant three days. But already I have had seven calls. I try to be selective. I live here, after all, when I am not giving tours. Generally, I can spot an honest face. Your wife, for instance, has an honest face.

—I've always felt that, Alec said.

—About you I'm not so sure, Lyova said and smiled.

—She will vouch for me, Alec said.

—In that case, Lyova said.

8

My dear Brigitte,

I hope you received my last letters. I sent two from Vienna. I send this one from Rome. I am writing it at the table of our new apartment. When I look out the window I have a view of the street. Actually, it is a view across the street of another building. I can see into the window of an apartment where a bald Italian man is reading his newspaper and drinking his coffee. Not very exciting, I suppose. I realize I could have looked out the window and seen essentially the same thing in Riga, and it certainly wouldn't have interested me or seemed like the sort of thing to include in a letter. But already I've looked up half a dozen times to see what he is doing. He's caught me looking twice and smiled. He may think I'm in love with him, or he may be used to this sort of thing. The apartment that we're living in has been rented by a continuous stream of émigrés. There must be different Russians staring at him each month. In New York and Melbourne and Miami there are people from Leningrad and Baku and Kiev whose memories of Rome include this man drinking coffee. Now mine will too. Wherever I end up.

This is what I wanted to tell you. It appears that we are not going to Chicago. Zoya's cousin can no longer sponsor us. They have to take her husband's brother instead. That was the reason she gave, in any case. There's a joke that if you want to make an enemy for life just sponsor a relative. So maybe it's for the best?

Now we must decide on some other city or country. Igor's family can't agree. I don't see that it matters, wherever we go we will be among strangers.

So you see, I do not know how long we will be in Rome. Even if we are here a short while it will allow enough time for this letter to reach you and for your reply to get back to me. But you will have to write quickly. I'm eager to hear from you. It would make me so happy to receive a letter from you. It's already been nearly a month since we last saw each other. I think about you every day and wonder how you are getting along and about how Mama and Papa are behaving toward you. So write to me and don't go off daydreaming and delay. Your sister misses you.

There was more I wanted to tell you, too. I wanted to describe the new apartment—although there isn't all that much to describe. It's really just two rooms that we share with a man from Kishinev who has trapped himself in Rome because he doesn't want to go back to Israel and no other government will take him. In Israel he has his parents, his wife, and a young son. He has been in Rome for more than a year. I don't entirely understand why he won't return, but I couldn't even begin to list all the things I haven't understood about some of the people we've met. But our roommate is otherwise perfectly fine. I think you would like him. We have been warned many times to be wary of people, but he seems honest. Or at least as honest as a person can be under the circumstances . . .

9

I t was bad enough, Samuil thought, that he'd been forced to listen to Alec voice his decision to take an apartment separate from the rest of the family; it was worse that Emma, after acceding to Alec, underwent a complete and total conversion that manifested itself in a pressing need to see this new apartment. That was the way it was with his wife. She was a simple creature. He had always known this. She had been simple when he married her, but he had attributed her simplicity to the fact that she was hardly more than a girl. However, over the years, rather than acquire shadings and complexities, she had become simpler still. Her brain was in her womb. But if he was to be honest with himself, he hadn't sought much more in a wife. He had believed that a household should have one head. When Samuil's division had been driving the Germans from villages around Minsk there had been a woman partisan who had mounted an ammunition crate and harangued the soldiers. *You fight as if you fear death more than you love your country!* People said such things then. She was a bold and electric woman. In the ensuing battle Samuil had seen her charge a self-propelled gun and not die. But what sane man would want such a woman for a wife? Better Emma, one moment treating their grown son like a boy leaving Mama for the first time, the next gushing as if he were establishing a new home for himself and his bride.

—Of course, while the tsar and tsarina cozy up in their apartment we stay in the pensione, Rosa said during dinner.

—We leave the day after tomorrow, Karl said, not bothering to look up from his plate.

—Boys, Emma said, a dacha near the beach. Just like we had in Jurmala. Do you remember the dacha in Jurmala?

—Will there be bugs in my bed? Zhenya asked.

—Grandmother will make sure that there aren't any bugs, my dear heart, Emma said.

—There were bugs in my bed in Jurmala, Zhenya said.

—In mine, too, Yury said.

The dacha in Bulduri had cost Samuil plenty. He had had to threaten, to cajole. It was a quarter of a kilometer from the beach, yet all his grandsons could remember were bugs in their beds.

Two days later, one of the Jewish agencies—HIAS or Joint, why bother keeping track?—sent a truck for their belongings. Alec, always an eager candidate for a joyride, volunteered to remain at the pensione to oversee the loading. The rest of them took the train. From the station Karl led them left and right until they reached a street of wooden bungalows and larger apartment buildings. Fruit trees grew in the yards. Hedges were manicured. Samuil had to concede that the street seemed altogether respectable. The apartment buildings were well maintained. On the balconies, Samuil saw potted plants, beach umbrellas, tables, and chairs. Through an open balcony door, he saw a woman contentedly sweeping. Passing them on the sidewalk were not only Italian children on bicycles, but also older Russian men, his coevals, promenading in leather sandals, looking the part of vacationers. They nodded at Samuil in greeting, as though recognizing one of their own.

Karl stopped in front of a bungalow the yellow of rancid butter. He lifted the metal hasp on a chain-link gate and proceeded down a short stone walk to the front door. He knocked and the door was opened almost instantly by his friend Boris the Bodybuilder. Boris looked over Karl's shoulder at the agglomeration of the family Krasnansky and grinned beatifically, like the world's master of ceremonies.

—Did I not promise you a suitable place?

The door was pushed open yet further so as to allow a darkhaired Italian woman with a baby in her arms to join Boris and Karl at the entrance. With the least shift of her eyes, Samuil saw the woman make a rapid assessment of her new tenants. Using an inquiring lilt, Samuil heard Boris utter what sounded like the Russian letters *veh, beh*. The woman nodded and repeated *Veh beh, veh beh*. She then handed Karl a silver key.

With a sweep of his hand, Boris beckoned everyone inside to acquaint themselves with their new home. The boys darted past Samuil's legs, competing with one another to be first. The front doors led to a kitchen, with a gas stove and a narrow refrigerator, both of which would have been antiquated by Soviet standards. At the feet of the appliances and at the edges of the room, the linoleum floor bore some kind of pattern or relief, but it was worn smooth everywhere else. Through the kitchen, in the sitting room, Boris was demonstrating how the sofa unfolded to become a bed.

At the doorstep, Samuil observed Karl handing Boris a thin stack of bills. Boris went through the motions of protesting and trying to press the bills back onto Karl before he counted them out, returned one, and pocketed the rest. He then withdrew his hand from his pocket, waved goodbye, and bounded out into the yard.

—Some friend, your friend, Samuil said.

—I gave him what was rightfully his, Karl said. He didn't ask for it.

—And what did his valuable services cost us? Samuil asked.

—Less than the going rate. But don't concern yourself. I'll answer for the money.

—If we both live in this palace, I'll pay my share. I've not sunk so low as to depend upon my children's charity.

—It has nothing to do with charity. I'll answer for the money now. When the time comes for us to leave, I'll find our replacements and get the money back with profit. It's the way things work.

—Well, if that's the way things work, Samuil said acidly.

Out on the street, there was the squeaking of brakes and the sound of an engine coming to rest. A truck door slammed and Alec jogged into the house, smoking a cigarette.

—The truck driver, eighteen years old, listens to Vysotsky. He has samizdat some émigrés have sold him and also recordings made in France. Doesn't understand a word of Russian but sings all the lyrics to "My Gypsy Song."

The young man kept his cassette player on and Vysotsky, whom the authorities had rightly censored for his cynical anti-Soviet attitude, rasped hoarsely as they, yet once more, unloaded their belongings. Once the truck had been emptied, Samuil went out the front door without a word of explanation and walked in what he determined to be the direction of the beach. He crossed the highway that ran the length of the shore, and removed his shoes and socks on a slab of concrete not far from an array of changing booths. It was the late afternoon on a weekday, if he could remember correctly (the days of the week bore little significance anymore), and the beach was not crowded. At random intervals, often with large gaps between them, people had laid out their towels and staked their umbrellas.

Samuil plunged his feet into the warm black sand, which he found to be pleasant, not scalding as it surely must be at midday, and pressed ahead to the firmer footing at the edge of the surf. A girl and a boy, dressed only in white underpants, crouched not far from him, digging at the wet sand with tin shovels. The boy wore a blue cap; the girl had a pink kerchief tied onto her head. Nearby, Samuil saw the children's corpulent minder—a triangle of torn newsprint adhered to her nose. She wore a green woolen bathing suit, her stomach balanced like a watermelon in her lap. Substitute the color of the sand, and these same children, this same grandmother, could have been in Jurmala or Yalta. They looked and acted as if nothing had changed for them. One beach, one seashore, was as good as any other.

The same sun shone down on their heads and shoulders. What did it matter to them where they were? How were they different from the birds who landed in one place or another, unmoored by allegiances or souls? What troubled them? That they might come home after a day at the beach to discover that there is no sour cream for their sun-burned backs? After a life such as mine, Samuil thought, this is where I find myself. Somewhere I went wrong. But where? He looked up from his horned feet, along the retreating peaks of the sea, to the flat line of the horizon beyond which was France or Spain. This was the Mediterranean. From here one could sail to Greece or Israel. His own father and grandfather, trapped and murdered in their Ukrainian shtetl, had only dreamed of such a wonder. He would have gladly gone to his grave without ever having seen it either. After everything I sacrificed, Samuil thought, where did I go wrong? And then he allowed himself to submit to sentiment and grieve: Reuven, Reuven, look how I failed you.

Outside the Joint and HIAS building, a primly dressed middle-aged woman approached Alec and Polina. Alec had watched her and another man circulate through the crowd of émigrés, offering pamphlets.

—Do you speak English? the woman asked.

—A little, Alec said.

—And your wife?

—No.

—Well, perhaps we can be of help. The woman beamed, handing Alec a pamphlet. I am with an organization offering services. Free English classes and assistance with immigration processing, for example.

—What is your organization?

—We are with the Baptist Church.

—What is she saying? Polina asked.

—Jesus Christ wants to solve all our problems.

—That's a relief.

As the woman filtered into the crowd of émigrés, Alec saw Karl, Rosa, the boys, and his parents advancing down the street. Before they could reach them they were intercepted by the woman's associate, the other missionary. Shielding her children, Rosa refused his pamphlets and brushed the poor idiot aside. Alec hoped he wouldn't try his appeal on Samuil. Alec remembered the day in the spring of 1961 when it was announced that Yuri Gagarin had become the first man in space. At nine years old, he'd been dizzied by the thought that a human being had traveled beyond the limits of the sky and, hovering in the blackness, had watched the clean blue globe of the planet rotate below. His father had repeated with great satisfaction Gagarin's comment that he hadn't seen any God up there. In his father's presence, only a fool or a masochist would dare question the nonexistence of God.

—So I see you're converting, Rosa said when she drew near.

—I'm keeping my options open. Besides, they're offering free English classes.

—In a church? I'd rather pay.

—Karl might disagree.

—He's right, I might disagree, Karl said.

—You see, Alec said.

—I think it's disgraceful.

—I already speak English. I was holding them for you, but suit yourself, Alec said, and let the pamphlets drop to the pavement.

They had gathered at the office that morning to present themselves before a caseworker. The Joint would not furnish them with their stipend if they didn't file papers for a destination. Rosa continued to agitate for Israel, even though two days before, Begin had officially rejected Sadat's latest peace proposal. While in Beirut, the Syrians were shelling the Christians, and Israel was massing troops on its northern border. Alec, having successfully avoided the worst of Soviet military service, wasn't aching to go from Ben Gurion Airport to boot camp. Getting killed or maimed in Lebanon, or Egypt, or wherever the bullets were flying, seemed to defeat the whole point of leaving the Soviet Union. Karl felt the same way and Rosa knew it. But when a man nearby loudly opined that Begin was allowing himself to be led down the garden path, that even Brezhnev would never be played for such a fool, Rosa interrupted and deflected the conversation onto the subject of the Shcharansky show trial.

—While the rest of the world condemns Brezhnev for Shcharansky you dare to compare him to Begin?

—One has nothing to do with the other, the man said.

—What are Shcharansky's crimes? Being a Jew. Wanting to go to Israel. Tell me how the two are not related?

—He wants to go to Israel not because of Begin's ridiculous peace with Egypt. If you want my opinion, he is willing to go in spite of it. He's a true believer. If Israel was run by a group of half-wits who bayed at the moon—so long as they were Jewish—Shcharansky would go.

—Are you suggesting that Begin is a half-wit?

—Show me the proof he isn't.

—Brezhnev is an anti-Semite. Begin is a Jewish hero.

—Tell me, please, if you're such a patriot, what are you doing in Italy? As I recall, the plane for Tel Aviv departs from Vienna.

—My reasons are my own.

—All right, fine, the man said. *Shalom aleichem.*

In the crowded HIAS waiting room, Alec stood with Polina until he heard the name Krasnansky pronounced once and then a second time above the din. Alec looked around and saw Syomka Bender stepping over feet and picking his way through the room. Syomka wore a denim jacket, clearly a recent acquisition, but was otherwise unchanged. His face, intelligent and reserved, allowed the trace of a smile.

—I saw your name on the list, Syomka said, and got myself assigned to your file.

—I forgot, Alec said, Iza told us you worked here.

—That's right, Syomka said, you saw my brother.

—We did.

—The less said about that the better, Syomka said. Follow me into the hall; it's impossible to talk in here.

—Just me or all of us? Alec asked.

—All of you is probably best, Syomka said.

Karl and Alec had both been friendly with Syomka in Riga. They came across him at parties and at the beach in the summer. For a long time Syomka had dated the same girl. She was from a good family and was studying piano at the conservatory. There was general consensus that the two were ideally matched. At parties, everywhere, you never saw one without the other until it became impossible to imagine them apart. They shared the same disposition, quiet, clever, vaguely aristocratic. Even to each other they spoke little and yet seemed, as if by telepathy, to communicate and agree. More than once Alec had met them after a movie or a play and, just by the measured way in which they listened and considered what he said, he became convinced that they had understood the movie or the play at a level far deeper and better than he. Alec would walk away from these encounters slightly embarrassed but basically full of admiration. Almost everyone held the same opinion of them. Which was why their breakup, unremarkable for any other couple, acquired the level of scandal. Nobody could have predicted that Lilya Gordin might be discovered, unapologetic, in the arms of a cellist two years her junior. For two days afterward it was said that Syomka trailed the cellist. He didn't confront him or say anything, he just waited outside his building and then shadowed him like a KGB agent. Alec never spoke of the breakup to Syomka. He didn't know anyone who did. Syomka continued to show up at parties and at the beach, sometimes with his brother. Women treated him with kindness and uncertainty; his longtime unassailability and his eminent devastation conferred upon him the aura of the exotic. A girl explained that it was as if there was something monastic or virginal about Syomka, profoundly magnetic. But Syomka seemed to keep to himself until, very late one night, at Dzintari, after much drinking, a girl wanted a swimming partner and Syomka brushed the sand off his pants and volunteered. After that he was no different from anyone else.

In the hallway, Alec explained their predicament.

—We have contemplated New Jersey, Los Angeles, Miami, Atlanta, and Seattle, Alec said.

—Do you want my advice? Syomka asked.

It was understood that the question was purely rhetorical. They lived in a fog of doubt and apprehension. Nobody refused advice.

—My advice, Syomka said, is Canada. Safer, cleaner, and in climate not all that different from Latvia. They have just increased their numbers. They want young, professional families.

—And our parents? Karl asked.

—Any serious health problems? Syomka asked.

Emma started to speak when Samuil cut her off.

—Nothing extraordinary for people our age, Samuil said.

—I can give you the forms for the United States, just in case. But now is a good time for Canada. I'd consider it myself but I've been waiting on Australia for so long I already feel Australian, Syomka said.

—Do we have to decide this second? Karl asked.

—No, you can think about it, Syomka said.

—We'll think about it, Karl said.

—You can use the stairwell. It's quiet. I'll come and fetch you in ten minutes, Syomka said, and opened the door that led to the stairwell.

In the stairwell, Karl's sons, sensing the gravity of the situation, hooted once to hear the echo, and then were silenced. Karl remained standing and leaned his back against the door.

—This is how you decide your family's future, ten minutes in a stairwell? Samuil asked.

—Are we talking seriously about Canada? Rosa asked.

—I am, Karl said.

—Just like that you're prepared to go and say Canada? What do we know about it? Rosa continued.

—What do we know about anyplace? Karl said. You watched the Olympics. You liked what you saw of Montreal. And in 1972 they also showed something of Toronto, Winnipeg, and Vancouver.

—You're talking about the hockey games? Rosa asked incredulously.

—*Da, da Canada; nyet, nyet Soviet*, Alec said.

—If you have nothing intelligent to add, Rosa said.

—It's more European than America, and more American than Europe.

—What does that mean? Rosa asked.

—It means, Alec said, that a person can eat and dress like a human being, watch hockey, and accomplish all this without victimizing Negroes and Latin American peasants.

—Basically, Karl said. Their dollar is also strong.

—It doesn't concern you that we will have to stay for months in Italy? Rosa asked.

—That's a reason against Canada?

—It's something to take into account.

—Very well. I take it into account. We won't be the only ones. We'll manage. The boys will spend the summer at the beach. In the fall we'll leave and they'll start school.

—Now I'll have to explain to my parents that we're going to Canada, Rosa said, essentially to herself.

—What's there to explain? Karl said. They understand how it is. One door closed, another door opened.

At this moment, Syomka reappeared. As he ushered Alec and Polina toward one of the small HIAS offices, Alec heard Syomka say to Karl, Now, for the rest of your lives you'll remember me.

—For good or ill, it remains to be seen, Rosa said.

And then Alec and Polina were alone with their caseworker. The nameplate on her desk read Matilda Levy. She was a woman of a certain age whose hairdo, perfume, and bulky rings identified her as a fading continental beauty. Though Alec was certain that they had never met her before, she didn't bother with the formality of introductions. Almost before he and Polina sat down Matilda recited what she believed to be the pertinent information.

—Riga, Matilda said, I knew it before the war. My father had business there. A European city. That works in your favor. The Canadian government prefers people from the Baltics. They took enough of them after the war, not a few of them Nazi butchers. You speak English?

—Yes, Alec said.

—Your wife doesn't.

—No.

—But you we could use. Semyon said your English is as good as his. It could take six months or longer to process the papers for Canada. Meanwhile we could use you as an interpreter. It would mean eighty *mila* lire more for you each week. Come back tomorrow and I will explain everything. It isn't very complicated. Now, we will have to make some appointments for you and your wife to see a doctor. You don't have tuberculosis, do you?

—No, Alec said.

—They will x-ray you anyway. You both look healthy enough to me.

The woman proffered a document for them to sign.

—This is to confirm that you want to go to Canada. You will get a notice in the mail for the doctor's appointment and for your interview with the Canadian consulate. A word of advice: if you want to go to Toronto, don't ask for Toronto. Good? Good. Now, if you could call in your brother and his family.

Like that, Alec and Polina left the office. Karl, Rosa, and the boys entered in turn, then Samuil and Emma. Later, when Alec and Karl reconstructed the first meeting with Matilda Levy, neither could recall having ever told her that they had decided to change their destination from America to Canada.

AUGUST

1

There had been a point—once it became obvious that his sons would leave Riga, that no manner of threats or appeals would deter them, and that his family and his reputation would be destroyed—when Samuil had, for the first time in his life, contemplated suicide. The idea plagued him for weeks. He sought a reason to keep living, to justify his waking-and-breathing participation in the future. Almost certainly he would be expelled from the Party. And then what kind of life would he have in Riga? At best, the phone would ring occasionally when a former colleague's wife would take pity and invite him for dinner. But could he even see himself accepting such invitations? What could he possibly say to people and what could people possibly say to him? And as for the other alternative—emigration—it was, in its own way, equally bad. But after a lifetime spent eluding death, the habit of survival was deeply ingrained. He could not separate the image of putting a revolver to his head or jumping into the Daugava from the image of the White thugs who murdered his father—themselves doubtless long cold in their graves—dancing, singing, and drinking in celebration. He was not prepared to give them the satisfaction.

In Ladispoli, thoughts of suicide returned. There was nothing here for a man like him. The young men, like Karl, packed their bags of trinkets and laid them out on blankets near the beach. When the police came, they scattered. When the police left, they returned. To see such things brought back to memory his first lessons in the Soviet Yiddish school in Rogozna. Their teacher had instructed them in the alphabet:

Is "komets" and "alef" O?
O!
Is "komets" and "beys" Bo?
Bo!
Is there a God?
No!
Is there a shop owner?
No!
Is there a landlord?
No!

Men his age he saw tending to their grandchildren, pushing prams, shaking rattles. Emma encouraged him to take the boys. Somehow, it had not occurred to her that this would offend a man's sensibilities. More than offend. To be a useless old man was bad enough; to transform himself into an old woman was worse.

To break the monotony, Samuil walked. Most mornings he would start by going to Club Kadima, where he could listen to the radio or read the weekly émigré newspaper, *Jews in Transit*. Then he would walk to the beach and skirt Piazza Marescotti. There, among the other peddlers, he would see veterans with medals pinned to their blazers and shirts. There were only several who were more decorated than he, although Samuil would have been hard-pressed to prove this claim given that his medals had been confiscated at Chop by a smug, acne-faced customs clerk.

—Not permitted, the clerk had said offhandedly.

—I shed my blood for those, Samuil had said.

—So you say.

—Here are the papers, Samuil had said, and presented the old typed documents.

—This is of no interest to me. I am not an expert in forgery. The directives are plain: the medals belong to the Soviet Union.

—Look me in the face when you speak, Samuil had commanded.

—What for? You think I don't see enough traitor Jew faces every day?

The customs agent swept the medals like scraps from the table into a bin containing other items designated as contraband: silverware, medical instruments, brooches, rings, and bracelets. His medals landed with a clatter, and he saw, burning like embers at the top of the heap, his Order of the Red Star and his Order of the Patriotic War—the so-called Officer's Set. Because of this, Samuil paid close attention to the decorations he saw other men wearing. He saw one man with an Order of the Red Banner, extremely rare for a Jew if it was authentic. He saw another man with a chestful of campaign ribbons, attesting to a prolonged, near-miraculous frontline tenure. Most, however, possessed the standard commendations that accrued to anyone who survived the war: combatant medal, bravery medal, victory over Germany medal, and the commemorative decorations issued to mark the jubilees of triumph: one decade, two decades, a quarter century. Samuil's eyes were always primed. He saw a small, one-legged man with an Order of the Red Star. This same man seemed to be everywhere. He saw him mixing with the others at Piazza Marescotti, and he saw him also wearing his Red Stars and playing the violin for spare change in front of a café at the beach. He felt, too, as if he had also seen him at Club Kadima, reading the newspaper. This was confirmed when he saw him at Club Kadima a second time, sitting, his crutch propped against his chair, at the table beside Samuil's. The man was laughing at something he was reading in a way that denoted a prelude to conversation. Peripherally, Samuil saw the man look up from his paper and turn his face this way and that in search of an interlocutor. As there was nobody else nearby, Samuil did not doubt that he would be singled out.

—Are you a chess player? the man asked.

—I wouldn't call myself one, Samuil lowered his newspaper and said.

—Do you follow the game at all?

—No more than anyone else.

—But you're aware of the championships in the Philippines?

—Naturally.

—Do you side with Karpov or Korchnoi?

—Korchnoi is a defector.

—Perhaps I misunderstood you, but you sound as if you disapprove.

—You didn't misunderstand me.

—Ah, I see, the man said. But I like this Korchnoi. Even if he did beat Tal.

—Are you from Latvia?

—No, Kiev.

—I thought since you mentioned Tal.

—Only as an admirer. Besides, he is one of ours. Though so too is Korchnoi, on his mother's side.

—I happen to know Tal. After he became world champion in 1960 I helped organize his heroic return to Riga.

—Wonderful man, Tal. A true genius. Although he is in Karpov's entourage in the Philippines. What can I say, it's hard to be consistent with one's allegiances.

—For some, yes.

—It's certainly been true of me. If I settle on an allegiance it is guaranteed that new and compromising information will emerge. I revere Lenin, I learn he's a German agent. I venerate Stalin, Khrushchev tells me he killed Mandelstam and a few million others. I tell you, if I worshipped the sun, we'd all end up in the dark.

—During a turbulent revolution some mistakes are inevitable. But Stalin was a great leader.

—Believe me, I understand how you feel. It's not my intention to start a debate. It remains a delicate subject for people. My tongue, once it starts walking, sometimes wanders where it shouldn't.

—Criticism is easy. The young generation is quick to criticize. It is easy to criticize if you never experienced life before communism.

—Of course, anything is better than a pogrom.

—That is your commentary on communism?

—I consider it no small compliment. In 1920, the Poles came through our shtetl and behaved like animals. You don't think my father greeted the Red Army like liberators, even if they took our last crust of bread?

—You said you were from Kiev?

—I lived there since after the war. Before that I was from Olebsk. Not far from Zhitomir. Not that far from Kiev, either. In Volhynia.

—I know it. I was born in Rogozna. Though my mother moved me and my brother to Riga when I was still a boy.

—Yes, I know Rogozna as well. I said goodbye to my leg in western Poltava. I imagine it is still there.

—I have seen you wearing your Red Star.

—Yes? They gave it to me in exchange for my leg.

—Who did you serve with?

—First Ukrainian Front. I was a sapper with the Twenty-third Rifle Corps. As you can see, I am a small man. When they needed someone to crawl ahead, I volunteered. I didn't want them to say that a Jew was a coward. *There are mines to be cleared. Who will do it? Corporal Roidman requests the honor, comrade Sergeant!*

—You're called Roidman?

—Is the name familiar to you?

—I don't believe so.

—I'm actually a relation of a famous person. Only by the time she became famous she had already changed her name.

—Whom do you mean?

—Do you recognize the name Fanny Kaplan?

—Fanny Kaplan? The one who shot at Lenin?

—History remembers her as Fanny Kaplan, but she was born Feiga Roidman. We're *mishpucheh*. My father was her cousin.

—I don't suppose this was the sort of thing you publicized in Kiev.

—You're right, of course. But I am a musician. I play the violin. I am an amateur, no formal training mind you, but I have been told that I have a certain knack. For some time now, in secret, I have been composing the opera of Fanny Kaplan. Her story is a modern tragedy. Do you follow music?

—No more than I follow chess. My brother played in a military band, but I never took it up.

—Ah yes, chess, Roidman said. Which is where we started. Now I am back to what I wanted to tell you originally about the curious incident at the chess match. The game was played to another draw, you see, but Korchnoi lodged a formal protest because, during the match, Karpov's supporters brought Karpov a cup of blueberry yogurt. Korchnoi claims that this could have been a signal agreed upon by Karpov's team. A secret tactic. They bring a cup of blueberry yogurt and it means: accept the draw. Or they bring strawberry and it means: knight to rook four. It's wonderful. There is no limit to human intrigue, is there?

2

The room where Lyova slept was always inundated with sunlight. At first Polina was reluctant to venture out in the morning for fear of disturbing him, but she soon discovered that Lyova didn't sleep much and always rose before they did. If he was still home when she and Alec awoke, Polina would most often find him reading at the table. He had collected a great number of books that he stacked up near his bed. He also had a large archive of an English-language newspaper that he purchased once a week. It was from Lyova that they heard, on the morning of their medical examination, about the testimony of Shcharansky's neighbor.

PROSECUTOR: Did Shcharansky arrange meetings with the American journalist by telephone?
IRINA: We do not have a telephone at the apartment.
PROSECUTOR: How would you describe Shcharansky's character?
IRINA: He was a polite, well-mannered, cultivated man—though not a careful dresser.

At the doctor's office, the anteroom was occupied mostly by Italians. The office was a regular medical practice, though the doctor had an arrangement with the Canadian embassy. Polina and Alec were the only Russians there with the exception of one other couple and their eleven-year-old son. They didn't need to speak a word of Russian to identify one another. In a doctor's office, where everyone is wary and secretive, they were more wary and secretive. Still, it didn't take long for Alec to strike up a conversation. The husband was a metallurgist. He was acquainted with Canada primarily on a subterranean level. Alec asked their son if he was eager to go to Canada. The boy shrugged his shoulders and started to blink spasmodically. "Calm yourself, Vova," his mother said to him. Polina saw the husband set his jaw bitterly at his wife. "He's a good boy," the mother said, defending herself as much as her son, "it just happens to him when he gets nervous." Under the weight of his parents' scrutiny, the boy lowered his head, gripped his chair, and blinked harder.

The metallurgist and his son were called first. They reappeared half an hour later, the boy blinking as vigorously as before, the metallurgist smoldering.

—He made him hop on one foot and touch his nose, like in a circus show, the metallurgist said.

—Did he do it? the mother asked with sincere, desperate concern.

—Of course he did it, the metallurgist barked. Why not? There's nothing wrong with him.

After the metallurgist's wife returned from her examination, Alec was called in by one doctor and another doctor materialized and beckoned Polina. She and Alec walked down the same short hallway which branched off in two directions. Polina's doctor turned right. He opened a door to an examining room and motioned for Polina to take a seat on a padded table. The doctor was very well groomed— clean-shaven, but for a tightly clipped mustache. He looked not so much professional as prim, even prudish. He removed his gold wristwatch and deposited it on a metal dolly beside the door, about as far from Polina as possible given the dimensions of the room. He then indicated that Polina should unbutton her blouse, and once she had, he commenced the examination, touching her gingerly with dry hands, tapping her here and there, applying the stethoscope, and performing all this in such a way as to make Polina feel ashamed of her body.

After he had completed this first stage of the examination, the doctor turned his back and made notations on a form, at the top of which Polina discerned the emblem of the Canadian flag. When he turned in her direction again he gestured for Polina to put her legs up. With a quick movement he reached under the table and snapped two stirrups into position. All of this, from the very first, he conducted without uttering a single word. Without, Polina realized, even so much as a sound. It was this antiseptic silence combined with the physical humiliation of being touched with such disdain that made Polina feel as if she were once again back in the green-walled hospital clinic.

The doctor there had been a woman. She'd walked into the surgery and parted Polina's knees without quite looking at her. She'd offered no explanation of what she intended to do or when she intended to do it. She said nothing at all until a nurse walked in and then she berated her for not having already prepared and sterilized the patient.

Like a magician's assistant, Polina had felt as if she had been split in two. The doctor and the nurse pretended her top half didn't exist and dealt only with her bottom half. Polina relinquished it to them. She concentrated on her top half. She tried to retain this focus in spite of the pain, refusing to cry out, as though what was happening below was incidental and remote. She imagined that the pain was coming at her from a vast distance, as from the unseen bottom of a gorge.

When they were finished, the nurse transferred her onto a gurney. She was rolled out into the hallway and left there, once again, without explanation. Polina thought that she could still feel blood seeping. The loss of blood, the pain, and the cold metal of the gurney chilled her and she started to shiver. She was exhausted and drained, too weak to call out, and yet the tremors became so violent that her gurney creaked from side to side on its rubber wheels. Time and again people rushed by and ignored her. When she saw her doctor hurrying past, she reached out and caught her by the arm. Through chattering teeth, she told her she was cold, that she wanted a sheet for her gurney.

—How old are you? the doctor asked.

—Twenty-one, Polina said.

—You're not a child. Pull yourself together, the doctor said.

—Please, is there a sheet? Polina asked.

—Who are you to make demands? You don't like it here? Don't fuck so much next time.

When they released her that evening, Maxim was waiting for her outside. She wasn't really in any condition to take the bus by herself, so, in a way, she was grateful to have someone help her. She only wished that it were someone else. Who exactly she couldn't have said, even a stranger, anyone but Maxim. She saw him through the square wire-reinforced windows of the hospital doors. He was at the bottom of the stone steps, bent slightly at the waist, listening to another young man who smoked and talked. When Polina opened the doors, Maxim looked up and mounted the steps as if to help her with it. But when he reached the top, the door was already swinging shut behind her. He looked lost for a moment. Polina expected that having missed the door, he would offer her his arm. She looked forward to refusing him, only he didn't offer his arm. He also didn't do or say any of the unwelcome things she expected him to do or say, which, curiously, irritated her even more. She looked at him and saw penitence and relief vying for dominion in his face.

—Did you happen to see a kind of chubby girl in a blue cloud-pattern dress in there? a young man asked when Polina and Maxim reached the bottom of the steps.

—I don't think so, Polina said.

—Raisa is her name. She has shortish brown hair and sort of a dimple in her chin.

—I really don't know, Polina said.

—Her girlfriend brought her in this morning. That's a long time. Let me ask you, and please be honest: What do you think, should I keep waiting?

Polina allowed Maxim to escort her home on the bus. From the bus stop they walked the two blocks to her building without speaking. It was only when he had to say goodbye that Maxim delivered his line.

—It's better for our future, Maxim said.

The following day Maxim brought her carnations and inquired after her well-being. Several days later, he brought carnations again. In a week's time he returned with more carnations, now on account of the fact that he had, before the abortion, established the habit of bringing her flowers once a week. He presented these to Polina in such a way as to communicate that he believed things had returned to normal. Though she had an indefinable urge to protest, she admitted that things had indeed returned to normal. She couldn't justify her lingering resentment. Her experience at the clinic had been horrid, but she'd had no reason to suppose that it would be otherwise. Almost everyone she knew had had at least one abortion. Some had gone to hospitals; others, hoping to conceal the pregnancy from their parents, had had their boyfriends pay twenty-five rubles and submitted to the procedure at the apartment of a nurse or a doctor. Not a few of them ended up in the hospital anyway with infections and complications. Compared to these, her ordeal hardly ranked.

In their own way, Polina and Maxim had kept the abortion to themselves. Maxim had given a tin of caviar to the doctor at the regional polyclinic who had referred Polina to the hospital. It was understood that the doctor wouldn't say anything to her parents. Polina also didn't share the information with her sister. Which was why, since they did not know otherwise, her mother and her sister each made a point of commenting on Maxim's extraordinary romantic display.

—Three bouquets in one week. It's a very refined and thoughtful gesture, Polina's mother said.

—He's probably going to propose, Nadja said.

Maxim had already talked seriously about marriage. But he'd refrained from making a formal proposal because they were at a "crucial point in their lives." To make a major life decision before graduating from the institute would be rash. They would both have to pass their exams and, ideally, finish near the top of their respective classes. After that, Maxim would have to perform his military service. He would be gone for two months and be obliged to pass another exam. Neither of them yet knew where they might be posted for work.

Much later, when Polina became involved with Alec, she looked back upon her younger self, the girl who at twenty-one had allowed Maxim to dictate the terms of her life. She understood that she had made a mistake. But she also understood that, at the time, she had been incapable of acting differently. Unlike her friends who descended into infatuations, she had never had a great love. Some people's conceptions of what was available to them coincided with what was actually available to them, other people's conceptions did not. There were men whom she found more engaging than Maxim but they didn't much pursue her. They found her too serious. There were many other pretty girls who fawned and laughed more easily. What put those men off drew Maxim to her.

She met Maxim at a party in her friend's dormitory room. Polina had been sitting and talking to one of her friend's roommates when she turned her head and saw Maxim standing beside her. Maybe she smiled at him, maybe she didn't. As if reading from the pages of a courtship manual, Maxim asked if she would care for a drink of any kind. Polina couldn't think of a reason to decline, and so he returned with a glass of lemon soda and installed himself at her side for the rest of the evening. He ascertained her name, where she lived, what she was studying, her opinion of her program, her career aspirations. Next he proceeded to cultural and recreational interests: movies, books, ballet, musicians, figure skating, volleyball, rhythmic gymnastics. To be polite, Polina answered his questions, and when Maxim asked to see her again she said yes because she didn't want to say no. She then forgot all about him until he appeared one evening at her door. Her mother told her that she had a gentleman caller, and she couldn't imagine who it might be until she saw him waiting there. Worse still, she felt panicked because she couldn't remember his name. But she experienced her first affectionate feeling for him when he rescued her by reintroducing himself. He didn't appear to do this because he'd inferred that she had forgotten his name, but because a person was well advised to repeat his name upon meeting someone for only the second time.

That night he took her to see a figure skating competition at the Palace of Sports. He recalled, he said, that she had expressed an interest in figure skating. She recalled having expressed only the same generic interest in figure skating as in volleyball and rhythmic gymnastics. But tickets to the figure skating competition were hard to come by, even two at the very back of the arena. After the competition he took her to a café. He opened the door for her and held her chair. He did everything with precision and earnestness. At some point someone had taken him aside and informed him that, in the civilized precincts of planet Earth, there existed certain protocols. At some point, everyone heard a variation of this same speech, but not everybody took it to heart. Maxim had. In Polina, he sensed that he had found someone who also possessed a respect for the protocols.

Polina didn't encourage him, but he didn't seem to require encouragement. He courted her with the measured discipline of a person climbing a long flight of stairs. There was something endearing about Maxim's doggedness as, step by step, he insinuated himself into her life. He asked to be introduced to her parents. He brought flowers and a bottle of cognac. He also brought a gift for Nadja and subsequently invited her along on outings. She was then only twelve or thirteen. They went to the zoo. He hired a boat and rowed them on the Lielupe River. Nadja teased him in a playful way. When they were in the boat, she hopped up and down in the bow, leaned over the edge, and made a theatrical speech about the cruel, cruel world and the weedy river's irresistible call.

—I'm going to do it, Maxim, she said. Are you going to jump in and save me?

—Don't be silly, Maxim said.

—I'm going to do it, Nadja said.

—Polina, Maxim appealed.

—Nadja, Polina cautioned.

—Oh, it's all just too too much for a delicate girl to bear, Nadja said, and flopped over the side.

The green water closed over her like a curtain. Polina looked back at Maxim with apology and exasperation. They watched the water and waited for Nadja to part the curtain again. Polina stole glimpses at Maxim. Just when Maxim seemed ready to plunge in, Nadja thrashed to the surface, gasped for help, then disappeared again. Maxim waited a few moments longer and then, stalwartly, as if complying with an order, removed his shoes and jumped in after her. A lesser man, Polina thought, would have let Nadja flounder until she grew bored. Another kind of man, however, would have embraced the game.

After some requisite diving and searching, Maxim found Nadja peeking out from under the keel. When they floated back into view, Nadja had her head tipped back and one arm around Maxim's neck. Her free arm swayed dramatically above her head. My hero, Nadja sighed, her eyes half closed. Maxim endured Nadja's performance with the consummate face of the adult: distaste subjugated to obligation.

Reason, or its pale ambassador convention, ordered their time together. It extended to everything, including sex. Before Maxim, Polina had had three encounters that had approached but never crossed the line. On two of the occasions she had halted things before they went too far. The other time, at a Komsomol retreat, she had been willing but, at the critical moment, another couple entered the barn and started climbing to the hayloft.

Polina couldn't say that she was eager to take the next and inevitable step with Maxim, but she did wonder when he would grant himself the permission to do it. During their gropings and fumblings, she felt like a spectator, watching Maxim as he denied himself for the sake of her honor. These preliminary bouts always ended with Maxim apologizing for the liberties he had taken. Polina either pardoned his liberties or said nothing at all. They would then sit or lie together on a bench in the public gardens, or on the embankment of the river in the industrial quarter, or in the cold, shadowy entrances to public buildings, and share momentous and ostensibly soulful silences. Eventually, Maxim interrupted a bout of groping to ask Polina for her opinion and her permission. She consented with a simple All right, and waited as Maxim scrupulously tore the edge from the yellow paper wrapper she had heard about but never actually seen. Inexpertly, he put the rubber on himself and then spat on his hand and pawed Polina clumsily in preparation. Polina shifted her weight from one hip to the other so as to help him and then put her hands on his chest to resist his weight. She said, Careful, because she wasn't quite ready and she didn't know how to explain that to him. It was the only word that passed between them. Afterward, Maxim acted as if something significant had transpired and Polina didn't contradict him.

From then on, they repeated the act with some regularity. Polina saw that Maxim liked it and wanted it, so she obliged him. What they did, they did with no variation. For Polina, intercourse began when Maxim tore the edge from the yellow paper wrapper. She assumed that it was the same for everyone until she overheard other girls speaking about their experiences with their mainly drunken boyfriends. That was when she learned that most men went to great lengths to avoid having to deal with the contents of the yellow wrapper, and that, despite the risks, most women relented. They rationalized their actions by maligning the quality of Soviet condoms, which were known to rupture or slide off. It made little sense, they said, to put one's faith in something so unreliable. In Polina's experience, the condoms had never ruptured or slid off. She also thought the alternative measures the women cited—hot water, wine vinegar, urine—sounded dubious, but several weeks later, when they were alone in Polina's apartment, her parents having gone with Nadja to attend a choral recital, Maxim found that he did not have any condoms, but Polina insisted that they do it anyway. It was not something she had planned in advance, but neither was it entirely spontaneous. It was the first time she had ever challenged Maxim's authority, and she was as aroused by the prospect of luring him into temptation as by the recklessness of what they were doing. Maxim was sitting up on his knees when she told him what she wanted, and he wavered for a few seconds, a look of fear and doubt on his face, before Polina reached out and took him into her. After that, the fear and doubt left his face and were replaced by something insular and fierce. For as long as it lasted, Polina felt florid reverberations, as if from dense and cumbersome things thrown against her body. Gothic thoughts took shape in her mind, some of which momentarily surprised her and then mocked her surprise. Shortly before it ended, Polina hissed in Maxim's ear that she wanted him to do it inside her. It was a sentence that had been circling malevolently in her head from the moment she had insisted that they have sex. As she said it, she knew it couldn't have had less to do with a desire for children. And as soon as Maxim finished, Polina slid out from under him and went to the kitchen for a basin and a purple, thin-necked vase from which she had to first remove three of Maxim's carnations. She returned to the bedroom, set the basin in the middle of the floor, and urinated into it. Carefully, under Maxim's silent gaze, she transferred the urine from the basin into the vase, spilling several drops onto the floorboards. She then stretched out on the floor, arched her pelvis, and instructed Maxim to pour the urine into her from the vase. What they were doing was disgusting and sordid, and Maxim avoided Polina's eyes as he carried out her instructions. He was pliable then in a way that he had never been before and never would be again. She had made him complicit in something depraved, and she expected that, in some way, she would be punished for this. Later, when her punishment was meted out, Maxim never once blamed her for what she knew was exclusively her fault.

3

On his third day at the briefing department, standing before the newly arrived émigrés at their cafeteria orientation, Alec felt like a fraud. He felt tempted to confess that, not one week before, he had been sitting in their place, and that he knew no more about Rome than they did. But he was aware that this kind of revelation would only sow panic.

After the orientation Alec made the rounds of the émigrés' hotel rooms. He distributed U.S. emigration forms, priming people for their Persecution Stories and, if necessary, their Party Stories. Some people came prepared with a vast catalog of grievances that they had been compiling their entire lives; others needed some interpretive assistance.

A couple from Berdichev found the concept particularly boggling. The wife looked at Alec like he was obtuse.

—What do we need this for?

—Nobody's saying you need it. The Americans need it. You're claiming refugee status. To be a refugee you need to have been persecuted.

—The entire country was persecuted.

—Did you and your husband attend university?

—Yes. Both of us.

—Was it the university of your choice?

—I was not an exceptional student. I had no grand designs.

—And your husband?

—He has a good head for academics. He had wanted to study history.

—He wasn't accepted?

—Not into that faculty.

—How come?

—What do you mean how come? Look at his nose.

Alec had landed in the briefing department after a brisk evaluation by Matilda Levy. She had walked him through the HIAS offices while rattling off the various positions and personalities.

—Konstantin is our messenger, Matilda said when they passed the table reserved for the messenger. He is going to Canada. After one month he could find his way without the aid of a map not only in Ostia and Ladispoli, but also in Rome.

At the doors of the transportation department, a room that smelled strongly of body odor, cigarettes, and fried food, Matilda Levy introduced Alec to three of the four men who worked there. They looked up from their particular stacks of documents and submitted to the introduction in a cursory way, disguising not at all their displeasure at having to engage in the formality of greeting a superfluous person. The fourth man, Matilda explained, was at the dockyards coordinating the movement of freight. The slightest mistake and you had disaster—a family lands in New York but their dining room set lands in Melbourne.

—You do not seem to me an imposing man, Matilda said.

—Imposing? Alec asked, not understanding.

—A man to give orders to other men, Matilda said. No, they would eat you alive on the docks.

As neither the docks nor the musty office held any appeal for him, Alec saw no reason to contest Matilda's perception of him. Besides, she was essentially right. His father was imposing and enjoyed issuing decrees and orders. Karl had this capacity as well, although he didn't derive the kind of pleasure from it that their father did. Whereas the only thing Alec detested more than being ordered around was having to order someone else around. Basically, he was of the opinion that the world would be a far more interesting and hospitable place if everyone—genius and idiot alike—was allowed to bumble along as he pleased. "More freedom to bumble" neatly described his motive for leaving the Soviet Union.

—You are the type that prefers the company of women, Matilda Levy said as they stepped away from the Transportation Department. Is this correct?

They stopped in the hallway and Matilda Levy peered boldly into Alec's eyes, squinting slightly as if in this way to achieve a better vantage into his innermost character.

—Yes, it is correct. I have always preferred the company of women, Alec said and, after hesitating one instant too long, smiled.

The smile, Alec immediately felt, was a mistake. Under Matilda Levy's peculiar scrutiny and under the demands of a foreign language, he had momentarily been unable to act like himself. He had intended only to deliver a simple statement in the English language and season it with a little charm but had instead, because of the yawning gap between his words and his smile, presented for Matilda Levy's consideration a man who was either licentious or deranged or some combination of the two.

Matilda Levy seemed to regard him ruminatively.

—Yes, she said, I believe it is so.

Alec wasn't sure what she meant: What was so? He had temporarily lost track of what they had been talking about. Matilda Levy appeared before him transformed, as though she had stepped out from behind some scrim that had been obscuring a more vital Matilda Levy. Alec sensed that she was now differently disposed to him. They were no longer administrator and prospective employee, but rather woman and man—with complementary desires and bodies. For Alec's consideration Matilda Levy presented the physical Matilda Levy: hips, breasts, legs, hairdo—adorned with nylons, necklaces, bracelets, bulky rings, and lipstick.

Saying nothing further, Matilda Levy swept around and, wielding her bosom like a prow, sailed down the hall, to the stairwell and beyond. Alec followed in her wake. It had been a long time since he had found himself in this position. More often, he led the way. Other times, the act of seduction was performed in a spirit of mutuality. Nobody led. Hand in hand, both tumbled together. But Alec couldn't imagine himself tumbling hand in hand with Matilda Levy. He could imagine other scenarios, though these, even cast in the most favorable light, were either comic or absurd. Nevertheless, as Matilda reached the bottom of the stairwell and crossed four lanes of traffic, Alec felt that he had to seriously consider the possibility. Could it be that his job with HIAS was conditional upon becoming Matilda Levy's lover? Far stranger things happened with astounding regularity. His mother's cousin, raided by the police, once tried to swallow an inventory list. When one of the officers attempted to pry it out of his mouth, he bit off the policeman's finger. Compared with that, sleeping with Matilda Levy for a middling job at HIAS seemed perfectly reasonable. And with every successive step Alec took he asked himself: Should I do it? The answer, of course, resided in the question. If you asked yourself if you should do it, you shouldn't do it.

Matilda Levy inserted a key into the lock of a nondescript building and stepped inside the shadowy lobby. She did not look back to check whether Alec was behind her. She pressed ahead with implacable resolve, as if everything was foregone and settled, as if she and Alec had come to an agreement. Alec supposed that maybe he had agreed to more than he'd suspected. Between a man and a woman, the merest look has sexual implications. For all he knew, Matilda Levy could have taken his smile for a marriage proposal. He thought to say something, to clarify his position in some diplomatic way, to alter the tone, but Matilda Levy's silent determination discouraged talk.

In spite of all this, Alec found himself inspecting the lobby for suitably concealed corners where the act could be consummated. This was purely reflexive, a consequence of Soviet privation. It was one thing to attract a woman, quite another to find a place where you could be together undisturbed. One time, in a bind, he had convinced a girl to climb up onto the broad bough of an oak tree. She'd feared falling, tearing her dress, losing a shoe. He'd had to reassure her, and also hoist her up on his shoulders. She was not a large girl but neither was she a natural climber. "What are we, squirrels?" the girl had complained. "If only," Alec had said.

But this was the way it was with any human endeavor, great or small: one had to be blessed with a skill for it. Some people were good with numbers, others never forgot a face, others still had perfect pitch—as for himself, he could usually find a decent, serviceable place to copulate. Naturally, if you had such a skill, you couldn't simply turn it off. In this respect it was like being a thief or a spy, habitually taking stock of your surroundings. Even in the presence of Matilda Levy, Alec still couldn't help but notice that there was, to the left of the mailboxes, a narrow hallway that branched off at an obtuse angle and led to only two apartments. In his estimation, at this time of day, that hallway represented better-than-average odds. And, like a thief or a spy, Alec felt the nagging temptation to try his luck just to see if his instincts were still sharp.

Matilda Levy stepped to the elevator and pressed the call button. An instant later, a light blinked, and Matilda pulled open the iron accordion door. She waited imperiously for Alec to join her. Once he was inside, she dropped a coin into the mechanism and pressed a button for the fourth floor. The door glided back into place, clicked shut, and the elevator crept dramatically up. As it made its slow ascent, the compartment grew dense with Matilda Levy's cosmetics and perfume. The air became constricting, intimate, and glandular. The elevator felt less like an elevator than like Matilda Levy's laundry basket. Just standing there, Alec felt compromised. In his mind, in spite of himself, he began to envision it happening. He unclasped her necklace, unbuttoned her blouse, asked her to stand at a short remove, and watched her unzip her skirt and step clear in garters, nylons, and heels.

At the fourth floor, the elevator lurched to a halt and Matilda Levy reached out and retracted the door.

—Your hand, please, Matilda said at the threshold of the open door.

The elevator had stopped some thirty centimeters short of the landing, creating a visible, though far from insurmountable, obstacle. It was, in actuality, no higher than a normal step, but Matilda Levy stood arrested before it, with one hand outstretched, awaiting assistance.

Alec wondered if they had now reached the decisive point at which, in no uncertain terms, the sexual proposal was slapped down on the table like a fish. It was when one person asked the other to do something unnecessary. For instance, to leave a party, to climb a tree, to gratuitously lend a hand out of an elevator.

But what to do? Alec thought. He couldn't tell Matilda Levy that he believed she could get out of the elevator by herself.

Alec gave her his hand.

—The machine is not perfect, Matilda said, but what it lacks in function it makes up in character.

Using Alec's hand for support, Matilda Levy climbed out onto the landing and took several steps down the corridor and again waited for Alec.

With every apartment they passed, Alec resigned himself more and more to the inevitability. It would be a charitable act, no crime against Polina. Behind the door of the first apartment, Alec heard the voice of an Italian broadcaster either on the radio or on television. The next apartment they passed was silent. Behind the door of the third, he heard the clink of plates. Matilda Levy stopped at the fourth door and withdrew her keys. From the beginning, Alec had considered it oddly coincidental that she would have her apartment so close to the HIAS offices. On the other hand, it was quite possible that this was not her primary apartment. Unlike Riga, Rome had no municipal commissions dictating how many residences a person could have. It was a free country. A person could have as many residences as he could afford. It was completely within the realm of possibility that Matilda Levy might keep an apartment across the road from HIAS for the sole purpose of conducting trysts with Russian émigrés.

Matilda Levy turned the key and opened the door. Alec looked inside, expecting to see one thing, but saw, instead, several young Italian women reading documents, organizing files, and using a large photocopier. Among them were two middle-aged Russian men, one of whom wore impressively thick eyeglasses.

—This is the briefing department, Matilda Levy said, responsible for intake and processing. The work done here is very important. Most people consider it a desirable position. But the last man we hired was very rude to the girls. He had some kind of complex. A very difficult character. I don't tolerate rudeness to the girls. They are sweet girls and work very hard. But I don't expect such a problem with you. I can see that already. A woman knows. Now, as for what you need to learn, ask Oleg in the glasses or Lucia in the white skirt.

The office looked fine, and the prospect of working with ten Italian girls was pleasing, but mainly Alec felt like a man reprieved. The day's report would remain unblemished. *What happened today? Nothing bad.* Which was the way of the world, between misunderstandings, bankruptcies, and stomach cancers.

—Matilda is right, Oleg said later, peering through the ophthalmological achievement of his glasses, the job is desirable. It also presents certain opportunities. But I do not advise pursuing them. At least not without great circumspection.

It was these very opportunities that precipitated Iza Judo's appearance outside the briefing department building two days later. When Alec bounded out the door, Iza reacted as if he were the unsuspecting beneficiary of a happy accident. The look on his face was intended to convey simple, good-natured incredulity: there he'd been, Iza Judo, innocently taking a break from the heat in front of some random building, when who should emerge but his old pal Alec Krasnansky!

—You wouldn't believe it, Iza said.

—Is that right? Alec said.

—Not five minutes ago, I was telling Minka here about you, Iza said, motioning to a young man leaning against the wall. The man was very fair, practically, if not clinically, an albino. His gray T-shirt exposed arms that were liberally adorned with prison tattoos.

—I believe it, Alec said smiling.

—He believes it. What a guy! Iza crowed. Minka, didn't I tell you he was sharp?

—That's what you said, Minka affirmed, looking up and shielding his eyes from the sun.

—The sun's murder, Iza said, how about we find a shady place for a drink?

—I'm expected across the street, Alec said.

—Your job, right? Iza said. I understand. But what's fifteen minutes here or there? Carter won't change the immigration policy because you stopped for a coffee with a friend.

—And for a beer? Alec said.

—He won't change it for a beer either, Iza said, putting his arm around Alec's shoulders and propelling him down the street toward a place with an awning.

Minka edged himself away from the wall and fell into step just behind them.

—Crazy heat, Minka muttered.

—It's hot like this in Israel, Iza said.

—All the more reason to stay out of Israel, Minka said.

—Minka's having a hard time getting into America.

—I'm a qualified mechanic, Minka said. Specialize in diesel engines. You tell me America can't use another mechanic. All those highways. All those trucks.

They walked into the café, where Iza ordered three beers at the bar.

—You don't want to sit? Alec asked.

—It costs extra to sit, Iza said.

—Is that so? Alec asked.

—It's their system. The entire country. Go figure why.

—The best is in the mornings, Minka said, when they're all crowded like cattle around the bar, drinking their coffees, empty tables everywhere, not one single ass in a chair.

—So who are the tables for? Alec asked.

—Tourists, Iza said.

He raised his beer and toasted *l'chaim*.

—Next year in Los Angeles, Minka drawled, lifting his beer in his tattooed hand.

As a boy, Alec had had a friend whose older brother, Vanya, had spent time in jail and returned home proudly displaying his prison tattoos. He seemed at the time like a heroic and exotic character, even though he was really just a petty crook who enjoyed the sound of his own voice. Later, he got into more trouble and was shipped to a prison where he was cruelly disfigured. The rumor went that his attackers held him down and nailed his tongue to the floor. But while his tongue was still intact, he'd taught Alec and the other neighborhood boys how to decipher the arcane symbols of criminal tattoos. The initiation cost a pack of cigarettes, which each boy was supposed to acquire by dishonest means. For his part, Alec stole the money from his grandmother's purse while she napped. Scrupulous about such things, his grandmother noticed, and fretted terribly about her absentmindedness. She never thought to accuse Alec, but Samuil wasn't so easily deceived.

In the days after his beating, Alec swaggered around, streetwise and cocky. He felt as if he had drawn nearer to the ranks of men. On buses, in streets, cafeterias, and kiosks, he read the coded biographies inked on people's skin. *This one's a thief. This one's a high-ranking thief. This one's a common hooligan. This one served eight years. This one's a lackey, an errand boy, a "sixer." This one was booked for a military crime. This one did solitary. This one's a "waffle eater," a cocksucker.*

Judging from what he saw on Minka, the man had done his share of time. A barbed-wire tattoo on his forearm gave 1962 as the date of his first incarceration. A ring tattoo of a black diamond with a white stripe attested that he'd moved from a juvenile to an adult offender.

A grinning cat on the back of his hand identified him as a member of the brotherhood of thieves. A second ring tattoo spelled the acronym MIR: "Shooting will reform me." Another ring tattoo, a tiger's head at the intersection of two strands of barbed wire, meant that he'd committed a crime while in prison.

—Not as good as what we had in Riga, but not bad, Iza said, setting his bottle on the bar.

—I'd drink horse piss to get out of this heat, Minka said.

—Minka's had enough of Rome, Iza said.

—If only the Yid sons of bitches let me, I'd get on a plane tomorrow, Minka said.

—Syomka tried and talked to someone at HIAS on Minka's behalf, Iza said, but of course he can't help everybody.

—Shitocracy, you know, Minka said. Put a guy behind a desk and he starts looking down his nose.

—He doesn't mean you, Iza said.

—Naturally, Alec said.

—Iza claims you're a good guy, Minka said and wagged a cautionary finger. Don't let them turn you into a shitocrat, is what I'm saying. Don't become insensitive to human beings.

—I'll keep it in mind, Alec said.

—That's good. You do that. Minka nodded. A man in a position to help people should help people.

—The immigration puts people under a terrible strain, Iza said. I don't have to tell you, you've seen. And not everyone is equipped to handle it. Old people. Sick people. Virtuous people. They need to be protected.

—Iza, you know what my job is? Alec said. I go with a few others and we give the welcome speech and help people fill out their forms. Sometimes we suggest, "Write this; don't write that." Then we pass the forms to another department. From there I assume they go to the embassies. But I've been on the job three days. I know next to nothing. I'm still deciding if it's for me.

—Of course, Iza said. I hope you didn't misunderstand me. I know what the briefing department does. This isn't about Minka's case. This isn't for me or for Minka.

—No? Alec asked. Who, then?

Fleetingly, he wondered if Iza might have been gripped by some altruistic impulse.

—It's known that the briefing department is informed in advance about the new arrivals—how many and when. But then what happens? Almost as soon as the people arrive, before they can get their bearings, the vultures descend and try to exploit them. This isn't right, is it?

—No, Alec replied, knowing that it was completely immaterial what he said: *No, Yes, Tomato.*

—Someone should protect them. But who?

—You? Alec ventured.

—Me? No, not me, Iza said. You.

—Me?

—Sure, why not? Iza said. Why couldn't you protect them? You think it would be hard? It would be easy.

From there Iza outlined the standard scheme. It deviated in no significant way from what Oleg had described. In exchange for giving Iza advance notice of the arrivals and their location, Alec would receive a certain retainer. With advance notice, Iza and Minka could be the first to solicit the new arrivals. They would pay them fair prices for their goods, and thus protect the weak and innocent from the venal and corrupt.

—I'll think about it, Alec said.

—What's there to think about? Minka asked.

—If HIAS found out, it could be more than my job. It could be real trouble. Maybe a negative report to the Canadian embassy?

—For trying to help people? Minka said.

—You said yourself. Shitocrats. Not everyone is sympathetic like you.

—That's true, said Minka with surprising delicacy, there are a lot of nasty people in the world.

It then occurred to Alec that everybody had a rough time in the emigration, including a thief like Minka. He too was vulnerable and confused. He too had been cast into alien surroundings and was now obliged to compete with thieves and hoodlums from the disparate corners of the Soviet Union. He was no longer a boy, and he would have to start from scratch to establish himself like anybody else. You'd think that a thief could prosper anywhere, but Alec saw that thieves suffered too. And if it was true that the emigration turned honest men into thieves, why not the reverse? Looking at Minka, it seemed that he was not immune; he mourned the loss of his old, familiar larcenous life.

Samuil had not sought a friend or confidant in Josef Roidman, but Roidman was an irresistible force. Samuil discovered that when he approached Club Kadima to read his newspaper he wondered if Roidman would be there. In fact, he came to look forward to seeing him. He was a man to whom one could speak in a forthright way. Between Samuil and his family there was no longer a subject that remained unbarbed. Roidman may have suffered from an excess of Jewish irony, and he entertained some misconceptions about the Soviet Union, but at heart he was not a subversive or a reactionary. And even his operatic tribute to the terrorist Fanny Kaplan—portions of which Roidman periodically foisted upon Samuil—could be excused as little more than dilettantism and sentimentality.

(Outside the doors of Club Kadima, Josef Roidman flourished an introduction on his violin.

—Imagine: The year is 1905 and I am Mika, a young anarchist, nineteen years of age. Rakishly handsome. A recruiter and provocateur. In your mind, Samuil Leyzerovich, pretend that it is not me that you see and hear but a strong and striking tenor. Now, as for the set, picture that we are in the shtetl. Here, Mika approaches the modest

house of Chaim Roidman, a melamed, a humble Jewish teacher. This
Mika lights a cigarette, and a pretty, dark-haired maiden emerges
from the house. She is a girl of sixteen. She is shy as young village
girls are shy. And yet, that is not the whole story. Behind this shyness
lurks a keen intelligence and a bold and courageous heart. With soft,
almost soundless steps, she approaches.

Here Roidman played a new theme.

Kind sir, please forgive me, but do you not know that you trans-
gress? Today is the Sabbath. One should not kindle a light.

Roidman alternated the pitch of his voice, high and low, to assume
the different roles.

Girl, do you wish that I extinguish this light?

Once you have lighted it, to extinguish it is also a sin.

Girl, do you know whereof you speak?

I speak of the Sabbath.

No, my dear, you speak of the Revolution.)

Josef had a son in Winnipeg. The son, with a wife and two children, had emigrated from Kiev two years earlier. Josef had remained
behind with his late wife, who was at the time gravely ill with a
female condition. The surgeons had cut out all there was to cut out.
It was all very dismal. His son didn't want to abandon his mother at
such a time, but there was the danger that his visa would expire. It
was only when Josef's wife commanded him that he consented to go.
The living should not arrange their lives around the dying, she had
said.

—I do not need to describe for you the parting scene, Josef said.
How to put it into words? I watched my son kiss his mother goodbye.
It was like he buried her. Then, four months later, I buried her again.
Like with all things, the second time was easier.

After his wife died, Josef applied for a visa. He traveled alone,
carrying only his violin case and one other bag. He had already been
in Italy for three months and there was still no telling when Canada
might accept him. Letters were being sent; well-intentioned Jewish
ladies were placing phone calls to Canadian ministers. As for how
effective all this was, Josef had his doubts. But, if you listened to his

son, you were liable to believe that Pierre Trudeau's greatest concerns were what to do about Quebec and what to do about Roidman.

—By the way, Josef said, did you know that the Soviet Union was financing the Quebec separatists?

—That's nonsense, Samuil said.

—During the Montreal Olympics they held secret meetings. Members of the Soviet contingent arrived with briefcases packed with money. They also revealed classified information, of an intimate nature, about various Canadian politicians.

—Where did you hear this? Samuil asked.

—Here. From a man from Moscow. He said he had it on good authority. To be honest, I feel as if I have learned more about the Soviet Union during my three months in Italy than in my sixty-three years in the Ukraine.

—What you're learning is capitalist slander, Samuil said.

—Also a possibility. Still, one can see how it could make sense. Strategically speaking. This Quebec could become the "Cuba of the North."

Waiting in Italy, on the seashore, in the summer, was not exactly a tragedy. Josef was prepared to wait a while longer, a few more months—but if nothing transpired he would apply to the United States. In New York, they accepted everybody. One leg, no legs, three arms: they took you anyway. His son could come to New York in his car and then simply drive him across the border. Once he was in the country Josef doubted the Canadians would notice that they'd gained another elderly invalid.

He recommended that Samuil also prepare a contingency plan.

—Contingency plan, Samuil said. What is my contingency plan?

—America, Josef said.

—America, Samuil snorted.

—Well, where else?

—Where else? The other place.

—What other place? Israel?

—The grave.

—I understand your perspective, Samuil Leyzerovich, Josef said.

But please remember that I speak to you as a friend. It is not too soon to start making preparations. Half an hour. An hour. You fill out some forms, saying you weren't a member of the Party, and that's it.

—My youngest secured himself a job with HIAS. I'm acquainted with these forms.

—So, then.

—My hand would turn to stone before I wrote such a thing.

—Yes, I understand, Josef said, it's a problem. But the Americans regard Communists the way the Canadians regard invalids.

—Stone, Samuil said.

—Samuil Leyzerovich, these are not your memoirs. In one's memoirs—which are, so to speak, between one's self and one's soul—one must be truthful, but not, I would suspect, on an immigration form that is only between one's self and the American immigration service.

—It is not a question of where one writes it, Samuil said. Apostasy is apostasy. It is always between one's self and one's soul.

Samuil felt that this statement possessed finality. It was as solid and imposing as a fortress. He identified himself with this fortress. His argument was himself. He felt as if aglow with moral satisfaction.

He left Club Kadima still aglow. However, before he reached home, the glow began to fade. He thought more about what Josef had said about the Party Story document. It disturbed Samuil to think of the dozens, the hundreds if not thousands of Party Stories being written by traitors and prevaricators to please the Americans. Samuil envisioned the dossier the American diplomats were compiling, full of false testimonies. In the end, it would lead to a gross distortion of the historical record. Samuil recalled life before the Communists and life after the Communists. He remembered the excesses of the bourgeoisie and the abject existence of the proletariat. He remembered hunger, cold, filth, penury, and, worst of all, the smothered hopes of gifted, honest proletarian youth. No one who had not experienced these things could legitimately judge the Communist state. Of course, he acknowledged that, at times, mistakes had been made, that opportunistic elements had wormed their way into positions of power, but the system could not be judged on the basis of rogues and impostors. Rogues and impostors could not be allowed to qualify the essential Communist picture. In order to see this picture, a person would need to take up residence inside Samuil's head, where the real events of proletarian struggle and triumph were housed like a breathing archive.

In the weak light, Samuil saw the smudged face of his brother and of the other bookbinders, bent over the lathes in the chill of Baruch Levitan's miserly home workshop.

He saw himself and Reuven stepping briskly through the dark streets of the Moskovsky district, risking beatings and arrests, to collect copies of *Der emes* and *Der apikoyres* that Hirsh Kogan had smuggled in from Russia and dropped in a barrel behind Ozolinsh's blacksmith shop.

He saw the burning and undernourished faces of the girls on the education committee, folding pamphlets into the night after twelve hours at their sewing machines. Their pale, quick hands, their frayed coat sleeves, their serious expressions: Chaverte Rivka Shapira, Chaverte Shulamis Garber, Chaverte Malka Averbukh, and the great beauty, Bluma Fabrikant. All dead.

Where were they in the record of history? None would be found in the revisionist volumes of the émigrés' Party Stories. In their place would be complaints over congestion in communal apartments, shortages of chocolate and of denim pants, repression of Zionist-nationalist organizations, and holy outrage over an anti-Semitic taunt shouted by some drunken bus driver.

5

Before they left Riga, Alec arranged for Polina to take a three-day immersive course given by an old classmate of his from the English school. The class was conducted in secrecy in the man's apartment. There were six students, none of whom spoke any English. But for those three days, they were forbidden to speak any other language. The only Russian they heard came from some Soviet instructional recordings. Of those three days, Polina retained little more than two phrases. One was:

Did you go on a motoring tour of England?

The other was:

Why not visit the exhibition of national economy achievements of the USSR?

In Rome, she enrolled in a language class offered by a Jewish vocational agency. A young American girl taught the class, and she spent the first lesson demonstrating the differences between British and American English. At the end of the class, everyone came away feeling like they knew even less than when they went in.

To help her with her studies, Alec and Lyova took to speaking English in the mornings before Alec left for work. Lyova had learned some English in Israel because his civil engineering firm had had a

German client. In Rome, he read the *Herald-Tribune* and *The Times* of London.

Good morning, Al.

Good morning, Leo.

Good morning, Paula.

Would you like a cup of coffee?

Yes, thank you.

It is a nice day.

The sun is shining.

Please open the window.

There are many people in the street.

There are men, women, and children.

There is a cat.

Rome has many cats.

Rome has many beautiful women.

But they are not more beautiful than Paula.

Polina had always been a good student, but she found herself struggling with the language. Alec encouraged her, saying that even his mother's cousin in Chicago, barely five feet tall, was learning the language. Everyone learned it. Millions of imbeciles spoke it every day. Lyova said that, in his experience, the most important thing in learning a language was confidence. Intelligent people who doubted themselves often had it the hardest.

—How were you in school? Lyova asked.

—In what sense?

—Did you worry very much?

—Only at the very end.

—The exams? That's nothing. Everybody worries about those.

—I might have worried more.

—Why?

—I didn't want to be separated from my boyfriend.

—And what happened?

—I scored well. We weren't separated. Instead we got married.

—Later divorced.

—Yes, it might have been better if we'd been separated. But I didn't think that at the time.

The truth was that, at the time, she'd wanted desperately to fail and be sent away to some far-flung region where Maxim would never be expected to visit, but she was disgusted with that part of her and wanted to renounce it, smother it, seal it inside a vault of constancy. And so she'd worried about scoring well enough to secure a placement in Riga. As she waited for her grades, she resolved that, if they were insufficient, she wouldn't simply abide by the decision but would do whatever she could to steer her life onto its proper course.

She went to her father, something she'd never done before. He had just then returned from Gdansk. She waited until her mother and sister were away from the apartment and then told him—careful to keep any hint of plaintiveness out of her voice—that there was something she needed to discuss.

Her father sat at the kitchen table in a wash of afternoon sunlight. He had covered the table with newspaper and spread out upon it the disassembled parts of a hair dryer that had recently stopped working. He'd brought the hair dryer back from East Germany several years earlier as a present for Polina's mother and it had become one of the family's most prized possessions. They didn't know anybody else who had one. Polina's mother used it sparingly for herself and for the girls, and, occasionally, she loaned it to some of their neighbors. Every now and then Polina would answer the door and discover a woman with her head wrapped in a towel. Another family might have turned this into a small venture and charged for it, but in their home even to intimate such a thing was an abomination. Sometimes a neighbor brought a jar of preserves or a tin of sprats, but only out of the goodness of her heart. When the dryer broke down, another neighbor, an electrician, would conjure the necessary resistor or fuse for which Polina's father paid the designated market price—not a kopek less—always in front of witnesses and always with a signed receipt. Her father would then go about fixing the dryer himself. Tinkering with devices and gadgets was the closest thing he had to a hobby. Like others of his generation, he possessed a deep reverence for mechanical things. With Polina's graduation approaching, her mother had hoped he might get the dryer back into working order so that she could set her own and the girls' hair for the ceremony.

The hair dryer and the graduation ceremony provided Polina with a convenient way to broach the topic. She tried to frame her words as directly as possible. At first, it seemed as if her father didn't quite hear her, as if he was too immersed in the coils and circuits of the hair dryer, but eventually, as she persevered, he turned his attention to her.

—You have always been an excellent student. You will do fine, he said.

—I don't think so.

—Nothing comes of this sort of talk.

—I don't want to be separated from Maxim, Polina said, conviction trailing a half step behind her words.

—Nobody is forcing you to separate.

—If we're sent to different places we won't be able to get married.

—This is a pointless conversation, her father said evenly. I'm surprised at you.

His attention drifted back down to his repair work. He had issued what amounted to his harshest rebuke: the suggestion that Polina was behaving in a way unbefitting "her father's daughter."

—I just thought if something could be done, Polina said.

—I've heard enough.

Polina knew not to raise the subject again. In the succeeding days her father acted as if the conversation had never happened. When he was home, he kept tinkering with the hair dryer until, one morning, Polina awoke to the sound of its shrill whine. Later that same day, as her father was heading out the door, he called Polina over and somberly told her that there would be a position for her at the VEF radio factory. Before Polina could collect herself to thank him, he was already down the hall.

In the end, both her panic and her father's intervention proved unwarranted. When the grades were announced, Polina discovered that she had finished in the top quartile. Her results guaranteed her a position in Riga. Now, if VEF hired her, nobody could challenge the impartiality of their decision. The outcome suited everyone. With her grades, she had vindicated herself before her father; meanwhile, without suffering any adverse effects, her father had been able to demonstrate his love for her.

On the day of her graduation ceremony she sat with her parents and Nadja under the glass roof of the university's great hall. According to custom, her father held a bouquet of flowers—white, fragrant calla lilies. Polina's hair, freshly shampooed and styled by her mother, shone brilliantly, as if radiating intellectual light. She wore a new dress of luminous green cloth—the material purchased by her mother and then sewn by a seamstress after a French pattern. Polina was the first in their family to receive a university degree. Anything her father had learned after eight grades of primary school came courtesy of the Soviet navy. Her mother had come from a small Byelorussian town where the pursuit of higher education was rare for anyone, and particularly for women. When Polina heard her name called, she rose from her chair and felt herself propelled to the stage as if by the cumulative force of her parents' dreams.

In the evening, Polina joined her classmates for a party at Café Riga in the old city. All over town, graduates were dancing and toasting their student days goodbye. A number of her classmates brought their instruments and played the songs of the Beatles, Raymond Pauls, and Domenico Modugno. Glasses of champagne were circulated, and they all dropped the diamond-shaped lapel pins they'd been awarded into them, then downed the contents in one swallow, leaving the shiny blue enamel glinting between their teeth. At around ten o'clock, Maxim left his class's party and joined Polina at Café Riga. When she spotted him in the crowd, she was surprised by how glad she was to see him. A warm, proprietary feeling bloomed inside her. This man—blinking through the haze of cigarette smoke, intently searching the room for her, rubbing absently at the scar above his eyebrow, where, as a boy, a schoolmate had hit him with a badminton racquet—this was her man. Out of the many, he was hers, and this simple recognition was enough to endear him to her. Flushed with optimism, alcohol, and affection, Polina fell into his arms and swept him onto the dance floor. Her classmates offered them a steady flow of champagne, vodka, and wine. Before long, Maxim forgot his usual reserve, loosened his tie, and danced with uninhibited, clumsy exuberance as the band played the Beatles' "Get Back."

At dawn, as they weaved together along the cobblestones of the old city, Maxim proposed and Polina accepted. Their future seemed as assured as a future could be. Like Polina, Maxim had scored well on his exams and had his choice of prestigious factories. She would take the job at VEF, while he would take a position at the highly regarded Popov Radiotechnika. They would marry, move in with his parents, file a request with the municipal housing authority for a separate apartment, and start a family. They would embark upon productive and satisfying adult lives.

6

When he was not taking his walks or reading the newspapers at Club Kadima, Samuil busied himself with writing the true account of his life and times. He began with the private intention of having Alec translate and submit his biographical statement to HIAS and the American embassy. As he wrote, he clung to the guiding principle that his work would have corrective and instructive value, and in this way he granted himself license to dwell upon his personal history. For hours each day he settled conspicuously at a card table in the sitting room and demanded not to be disturbed. Nevertheless, his grandsons scampered through the room with impunity and his wife and daughter-in-law often interrupted him with their comings and goings between the bedroom and the kitchen.

To his wife's inquiry about what he was doing, he said, I'm doing what I'm doing.

While he wrote, he could almost fool himself into believing that he was again in the company of the beloved dead. For those hours, he strongly felt their essence. The feeling evoked in him the deepest regret. It wasn't that he wanted to join them in the grave or return to the past so much as he wished that they were still living. Had they lived, Samuil thought, things would have been different. But the best and the bravest never lasted long. This was a natural law, like gravity or the seasons, and he had seen it confirmed thousands of times at the front. As the *frontoviks* liked to say: Our lives are like a child's shirt, short and covered in shit.

Aside from writing his biography, taking his walks, and reading the newspaper at Club Kadima, there was nothing else Samuil cared to do. Every day, Emma took the boys to learn Hebrew songs. At Club Kadima, a young American with a guitar led a children's choir. Emma also went with Rosa to hear lectures, mostly by representatives of Sachnut, the Israeli agency. Rosa returned from these lectures spinning Zionist fairy tales. *Only in Israel would they be able to work according to their professions. Only in Israel would they receive decent housing. Only the Israeli state would provide for their welfare. Soviet media exaggerated Israeli hardships, when in fact Israel was an immigrants' paradise.*

From time to time, Emma would try to interest him in some activity or event.

—I am worried about you, she said. Always by your lonesome.

—Do you hear me complaining?

—It's not healthy.

He felt healthy enough. And he certainly couldn't see how sitting for an hour listening to some pampered American strumming Hebrew songs on his guitar would be beneficial to his health. The same applied to a lecture encouraging Jewish religious practice by the resident Lubavitcher, imported kosher from Brooklyn, a pale young man with a patchy, wispy beard.

—A very intellectual and pious man, Emma said preemptively, in the rabbi's defense.

In the end, he had surprised her by announcing that he would like to attend the screening of the American movie based on Sholem Aleichem's *Tevye der milkhiker*. He had seen the postings up at Club Kadima as he was in the early stages of his biographical statement, very much at the point in his life when he would have gone with his mother and brother to see the Tevye play performed by Rogozna's amateur Yiddish theater troupe. This was in 1919 or 1920, when he was six or seven years old. But he remembered the experience very clearly. Once a month, as a treat, his mother would take him and Reuven to the theater. The old synagogue, converted by the Jewish Section of the Communist Party into a social club and theater, was always filled to capacity. It was the only place where he could see his mother smile and hear her laugh. During the performances he watched her as much as he did the stage.

At the end of the evening, Rogozna's principal actor, Zachar Kahn, the former ritual slaughterer, would make a point of coming up to Samuil's mother and asking her opinion of the show. He always referred to her respectfully as "the widow Eisner."

—If I may inquire, how did the widow Eisner enjoy the show?

He struck a memorable figure, Zachar Kahn, a tall man, almost two meters, with a black eye-patch, a slashing scar down his right cheek, and the sleeve pinned where his right arm used to be.

Before the Civil War, Zachar Kahn's slaughterhouse had been located a few doors away from their house. Because the light in the slaughterhouse was not always adequate, he would sometimes use the Eisners' kitchen to inspect the lungs of a cow or a sheep he had butchered. The sight of Zachar Kahn on their snowy doorstep, a giant man holding a steaming wax-paper bundle, was one of Samuil's earliest memories. He and Reuven had both been fascinated by Zachar Kahn, and scurried around him as he unwrapped and scrutinized the glossy, brownish organs. He would let the boys draw near so that they could peer at the grotesque and otherworldly things that made life possible and which everyone—from a mouse to a man— had pumping and sloshing around in the dark hollows under his skin. Grotesque to the untrained eye, the organs were in actuality perfect in aspect and form, Zachar would explain. They were the handiwork of God Himself. If flawed, the flaw, too, was part of His design. Though if they were flawed, then the animal's flesh could not be eaten. Lifting the lungs to his mouth, Zachar Kahn would blow to see if they would inflate.

The American movie of *Tevye der milkhiker*, though set in a Russian shtetl, didn't have a single word of Russian and hardly a word of Yiddish. Americans with Semitic features had been dressed in caftans and shawls while, on stiff wooden chairs, sweating and fanning themselves in the Italian heat, a roomful of Russian Jews goggled at the screen.

—This is what the commotion is about? Samuil asked Emma.

—It's a wonderful production, a middle-aged woman behind them offered. Believe me. This is my eighth time watching. I'd watch it another eight times. In Russia, God forbid they should ever have a Jewish character in a film. But in America they made a whole movie about us.

At the front of the auditorium, to the left of the screen, a paunchy, hirsute, mountain Jew held a microphone, and provided a simultaneous translation.

A fiddler! On the roof! Strange? Sure. But here in our little village of Anatevka every one of us is a fiddler on the roof, trying to play a song without breaking his neck. It isn't easy. No, it isn't easy. So you may ask why do we stay if it's so dangerous? Well, we stay because Anatevka is our home.

—They could only get a mountain Jew for an interpreter? an elderly man near Samuil complained. That accent. You'd think there was no one available from Moscow or Leningrad.

And how do we keep from falling and breaking our necks? That I can tell you in one word: Our traditions!

On the screen Samuil watched a lurid, fetishistic montage of Jewish symbols: a Star of David, a menorah, Hebrew letters, the worn burgundy velvet cloth covering the bimah. He looked around and saw that his wife, his daughter-in-law, and many others were entranced by it. Somewhere in America, Sholem Aleichem was spinning in his grave. The filmmakers had taken his "goodbye" and turned it into "hello." What Sholem Aleichem had meant as an acceptance of a new reality and a critique of the outmoded ways had here been transformed into sentimental Jewish burlesque. The movie encouraged a wistfulness and a mourning for the past, but what past? The filmmakers had no idea, but Sholem Aleichem could have told them. The old man had seen enough, even if he'd left for America and died there before the worst of the horrors.

Samuil had no appetite for the movie, but he stayed out of curiosity. He wanted to see, for the sake of comparison, the actors who played Tevye, Motl, Perchik, and Hodl. He remembered these characters well. Zachar Kahn had naturally been Tevye. Motl had been played by a real tailor named Froim Goldstein. Eudis Fefer, a young schoolteacher, admired for her looks, had the role of Hodl. Aron Zweig, the secretary of the local Komsomol, took the coveted role of Perchik, the fiery revolutionary.

These characters had captured Samuil's childhood imagination. Months after the performance, he and Reuven were still reenacting what they'd seen, with Reuven assigning the parts. For himself he took that of Perchik and pretended accordingly that Eudis Fefer, as Hodl, was his wife. Samuil became Motl, the tailor, and Reuven allowed him to take Rochl Lieberman—a second cousin who hadn't actually been in the play—for his imaginary wife. In their games, Reuven would typically set off to attack the bourgeoisie and launch the revolution. At the door he would have an impassioned exchange with Hodl/Eudis. She would declare her love and plead with him to stay, but he would resist heroically and fly out the door. Samuil would hear the *piff-paff* of rifles and he would rush out in pursuit. He would find Reuven mortally wounded, lying in the street or on a patch of grass beside their house. He would drag him back inside and lay him on their bed, whereupon Reuven would clutch a feather pillow to his chest and rasp his dying words to Hodl/Eudis. With his final breath, Reuven would exhort from Samuil a promise that he would take care of Hodl/Eudis and carry on the struggle for revolution. Then Reuven would expire and Samuil would run outside to exact revenge and tumble to his death in a hail of tsarist bullets. Sometimes, for variety, Samuil would get shot as he went looking for Reuven, and he would fall down beside him so they could die together.

In all of their doings, Reuven took the lead. One day he returned from Pioneers with a small oak-handled penknife and taught Samuil how to play "knives," instructing him how to throw the blade between his feet so that it stuck in the ground. Another time he taught him the words to a dirty Russian song.

Hey, hey! Fuck your mother!
You're a colonel, I'm a soldier,
Fuck your mother,
Hey, hey, I'm a soldier!

He remembered the conversation he had with Reuven after his kindergarten class was taught about class distinctions.

—Have you talked about this with anyone else? Reuven asked.

—No, Samuil said.

—Don't.

—I won't, Samuil said. Only with you.

—The Whites are *burzhoois*, Reuven said. They are the class enemy. The Whites killed Papa. In war you do not kill your own, you kill your adversary. So, since the Whites killed Papa, it means he was against the tsar and in favor of the revolution.

Samuil always found it hard to connect the word "White" with the men who had murdered their father and grandfather. When he thought of the men who had done the killing the colors that sprang to mind were the pale yellow and the cornflower blue of the rugs they wore across their shoulders. He had never seen anyone dressed this way before and, in spite of his fear, he had been impressed by how brash and adventurous it made them appear.

Before the soldiers came, their mother had hurriedly set the table with bread, sour cream, smoked fish, fruits, and vegetables. It was summer, and they had fruits and vegetables growing in a plot not far from their house. Their mother bustled about, gathering items from the cupboards and putting them out on the table. Meanwhile their father and grandfather frantically collected their dearest valuables: a leather pouch with gold coins, a fold of banknotes, and several pieces of jewelry that had belonged to their grandmother. They wrapped everything in a rag and concealed it behind a loose brick in the stove. From the street came fiendish, terrifying shrieks. When the soldiers burst through the door, a pot had been set to boil.

Samuil remembered their caps and their drooping mustaches. He remembered their drawn sabers. He remembered how the one wearing the yellow rug brought his saber down across his grandfather's chest in a blur of violent force and the surprisingly feeble noise his grandfather made in response. He remembered quaking and then wetting himself as his mother shielded him and Reuven from the soldiers. He remembered his father's groans and wheezes during the torture. He remembered his father's face, and how he kept opening his eyes to gaze at them.

7

After her English class one afternoon, Polina came home to find Lyova at the kitchen table, hunched over the telephone. She heard him say, It's good you can hold your breath for a minute and twenty seconds, but don't upset your mother. Practice in the bathtub, not the sea.

Lyova raised his eyes and smiled weakly when he saw Polina enter.

—I don't know how long I can hold my breath, he said. Probably not that long.

Polina crossed the apartment as quietly as she could.

—All right, I promise, Lyova said. I'll try today and write you with the result. If you don't hear from me, it's because I burst.

Polina made to sneak into the bedroom, but Lyova gestured for her not to bother. She saw him glance down at the tabletop, where he'd laid his wristwatch.

—Okay, there's thirty seconds left. I miss you. I kiss you. Let me say a few words to Mama.

Not knowing quite where to go, Polina went into the kitchen and began to carefully unpack the vegetables she'd bought at the round market.

She heard Lyova say, I'm glad he likes the shirt. And what about the shoes? Give me your honest word. Because if you don't like them, you should sell them. They're Italian leather, and many women wear your size.

There was some silence, and Lyova fiddled with his watch.

—All right. All right. Give my best to everyone, Lyova said and laid the receiver into the cradle. He rested his chin in his hands as if after a great exertion.

—I look forward to these calls all month, but they're costly, and not just in money.

Then, instantly, as if he had thrown a switch, he flattened his palms on the tabletop and thrust himself up.

—I could use a walk, Lyova said. What do you say?

On the street, shop owners were beginning to open their doors after siesta. Lyova took Polina to a bakery in whose windows were trays ladened with assorted biscuits. The woman at the counter greeted him by name. Lyova filled a white paper bag with biscuits, and they walked along the streets, taking turns reaching into the bag.

—When I left, Lyova said, I thought everything would get sorted in a few months. You can say a few months to an eight-year-old boy without terrifying him. You turn three or four pages in the calendar. But after a year, he gets used to you not being around. For now he still lets me behave like a father for five minutes once a month on the phone.

On their way to Piazza Santa Maria in Trastevere, Lyova described, as he hadn't before, the balancing act that was his life in Italy—the tours he gave to cover his expenses, to send money to Israel, to buy gifts, and to pay for the monthly overseas phone calls.

In the piazza, they found places on the steps that surrounded the central fountain. The crowds hadn't yet arrived. The white paper bag stood open between them. Polina kept her shoulders square, but her bare knees, exposed below the hem of her skirt, were turned casually toward Lyova. Sitting this way, unhurriedly, on marble steps, reminded her of her student days, when she would unexpectedly fall into conversation with a male classmate. A fleeting, platonic intimacy would arise, and they would wind up speaking frankly and seriously about themselves. Then they'd go their separate ways and never speak like that again, or need to. She'd forgotten all about these conversations.

—You love your son, Polina said. Why don't you go back?

—It's for him that I left Israel, Lyova said. I want him to grow up in a different sort of country.

—What sort of country?

—A psychologically easier sort.

—My sister-in-law's parents and brother are in Israel. She says they're happy.

—I'm sure they are. Many people love it. To live there, you need to love it. The country asks a lot of you. If you don't love it, you should leave. That's me. I also loved it, but then I saw some things and I didn't love it anymore. I said to myself, Time to go. I didn't want to have to see those things again, and, even more, I didn't want my son to have to see them.

—A year away from your wife and son is a long time. You must be sure that America doesn't have those same things. Or other things just as bad.

—"Those things." Lyova smiled. I don't mean to be cryptic. How to explain it. I know it's hard to believe, but I was a military man, a tank officer. I grew up on my father's war stories and I also wanted to be a hero. But instead of a war, I drew Czechoslovakia. I was one of those poor bastards on top of a tank in Prague, pointing a submachine gun at a bunch of students. Pretty girls in raincoats spat at me. After that, I was done with the army and the Soviet Union. And when people started applying for exit visas, I didn't think twice. We lived a very good life in Israel for three years. I had a job and a car. And then in '73 I even got my war. If you remember it.

In 1973, Polina hadn't had any reason to pay attention to Israel. To the extent that she'd been aware of the country, it had seemed a tumultuous land forever at war.

—Well, there's nothing good to remember about it, Lyova said. I was almost thirty then, with a wife and son. I no longer had any desire to be a hero. All I wanted was to get out in one piece. I was a tank man in the Sinai. I served with young boys from the kibbutzes who had never been anywhere. They'd never been on a train. They'd never seen a museum. They left life having barely tasted it. When the war ended, they sent us to Gaza. Once again I found myself on top of a tank pointing a gun at civilians. When they saw us coming, women clutched their children, and the men turned to face the walls. In Czechoslovakia, I had consoled myself with the thought that my people weren't responsible. The Russians were doing it, and I was a Jew. In Gaza, I couldn't think this. With me was an Israeli, another reservist with a wife and kids. He said, *It's shit, but it's our shit.* For me this wasn't the excuse, this was the problem. I'm sure there's much I don't know about America, but I know that their sons don't have to go and do this.

They left the piazza and headed back to the apartment. As they went, it occurred to Polina that she had never seen a photograph of Lyova's wife and son. He hadn't any up in the apartment. Early evening was approaching, and they were in the narrow Via Della Lungaretta with the growing ranks of tourists who loitered in front of the souvenir shops that lined both sides of the street. Lyova stopped in the middle of the street and withdrew a snapshot from his wallet. He showed it proudly to Polina.

—One month ago, he said.

His wife and son were side by side in front of an ice cream parlor, each holding a cone. Some distance behind them could be seen the crowns of palm trees. There was, in the light and the architecture, the intimation of a beach. Lyova's wife stood not much taller than his son; in a sleeveless dress, her upper arms were soft, her shoulders round. She wore her brown hair cut short and she peered into the camera defiantly, her expression at odds with the backdrop and the ice cream. The boy, lanky like his father, but otherwise bearing a closer resemblance to his mother, beamed.

—People say he looks like his mother, Lyova said.

—The smile is yours.

—He's a handsome boy, Lyova said. Good that he didn't get my face.

—What's wrong with your face? Polina asked.

—Mine is the archetypal Jewish face. Like something formed on the run and in a panic. Nose, eyes, ears, mouth: finished. He has a face for a new age, I hope. No more running, no more panic.

8

My dearest Lola,

Now I can finally reply! I will write you at least one letter a day
for the next week. Just watch, you'll get so many letters from me
you'll dread going to the mailbox. "Oh God, her again. How she
babbles on." You see, this way it will feel like we were never
separated at all.

In case you were wondering, I think I've received all of your
letters. I have four so far. Two from Vienna and two from Rome.
I've read each of them a thousand times and could recite them by
rote like verses from Eugene Onegin. It all sounds like a fantastic
adventure, including the miserable parts. Not that you asked for
my advice, but I'll give it anyway: enjoy yourself and don't spend
any time worrying about me. I miss you terribly, but other than
that I'm just fine.

It felt very strange waking up the morning after you left. I
didn't sleep well and when morning came I looked out my
window and saw that it was raining. I thought that was fitting.
It seemed perfectly reasonable that the weather should reflect how
I felt. But after breakfast the sun came out and it turned into a
brilliant morning. I thought that this had some kind of

*significance too. Maybe it meant that everything would turn out
for the best? And then, when I went out, the sky darkened again
and I was caught in a thundershower. It lasted no more than ten
minutes and then cleared completely. So I read something into
that as well. This was the way I felt all day—everything had to
do with you and me. Outside our building, a boy rode past me on
his bicycle, shouted something, took his hands off the handlebars,
and plowed into a parked car. Going to meet a friend, I thought I
would miss my bus; it passed me on the way to the stop and I
didn't even bother to run after it. But then, conveniently, it
delayed at the stop for a long time. When I got there, the ticket
taker was arguing with a drunk. People were shouting at the
drunk and several men rose from their seats to physically remove
him. When they put their hands on him he started to wail that
they should have pity on him seeing as how he was a veteran
who'd been heavily wounded in the battle for Berlin. As they
pushed him out the door he struggled to undo his shirt and show
everyone his scars. I'd never seen this drunk before, but people on
the bus said they were familiar with his act. Other times he'd
claimed to have received his wounds in Stalingrad and in Kursk.*

*And finally, the strangest of all. When the bus reached the city
center, at the stop across from the store, Children's World, who
should get on but Maxim? I could scarcely believe my eyes. I
couldn't have been more shocked had it been Jesus Christ
himself. It had been so long since I'd seen him last and I was
amazed by the coincidence. The bus wasn't very full and so there
was no way we could avoid seeing each other. But he said
nothing to me and so I said nothing to him. All I could think
about was whether or not he knew that you had left the previous
day. I was so uncomfortable being on the same bus with him that
I got off three stops early. Since we'd not said hello to each other,
we also didn't say goodbye. Not that it matters, but he looked
well. It seemed like he'd gained some weight and, if I'm not
mistaken, I think he was wearing a new shirt.*

In other matters, the weather is fine. I go to Jurmala when I can. I've become friendly with your mailman, who is very courteous, funny, and energetic. I'd always thought someone in his position would be depressed, but he seems to be in better spirits than most. It could be that he's just a happy idiot.

Mama and Papa are about the same. Papa spends more time reading the newspapers and has taken to clipping certain articles. He leaves these lying around the apartment for me to find, as a precaution, to discourage me from also committing a terrible mistake. Mama is as before, except that she's started going on long walks in the morning. In short, we are managing. There isn't too much more I can say on this subject . . .

9

A t six o'clock on Sunday morning Alec and Polina walked briskly
along the Lungotevere. The morning was cool and clear. Across
the opposite bank, the rising sun spread more color than heat
as it crept above the marble and terra-cotta of the Palatine
Hill. Traffic was almost nonexistent on the Lungotevere, and down
below, on the paved paths that ran along the river and under the
vaults of bridges, Alec saw the slumped forms of drunks and heroin
addicts, stirring groggily.

It was a great morning for a stroll. The sort of morning where he
and Polina could walk linked arm in arm, but in this instance both of
Alec's arms were weighed down by merchandise. In one hand he
held the notorious plywood suitcase that contained stereo LPs of
Tchaikovsky, Mozart, and Beethoven—pressed by the Melodiya label
in Leningrad, an "All-Soviet Gramophone Record Firm." In his other
hand he carried a satchel filled with the Latvian tooled leather
goods, lacquered boxes, ballet shoes, and various toys and plastic
knickknacks meant to appeal to children and imbeciles. Polina was
similarly encumbered. With both hands she clutched the handles of a
duffel bag packed with linens. Alec had tried to dissuade her from

loading herself down this way, and from making this early-morning hike in general, but Polina had been resolute.

As Lyova had said, their apartment put them in ideal striking distance of the Americana market. While others were racing down from Ostia and Ladispoli, rushing to catch trains, loading and unloading their wares, then sprinting from Trastevere Station, Alec and Polina were a short walk away. They could stop and rest when they chose, knowing that they would still be among the first to arrive. Karl had set them the task of claiming two well-situated tables in the Russian section of the market.

Alec and Polina arrived at the market at half past six as the first vendors were starting to unload their goods onto the broad wooden tables. Most traded in clothing, either new or used: jackets and sweaters, pants and hats, shoes and bikinis, formalwear and army surplus. The vendors were mainly Italian, although there were also Arabs, assorted Bulgarians or Romanians, and Gypsies, who laid their miscellanies on blankets on the ground. More arrived with every passing minute, turning in from Viale Trastevere in trucks, sedans, motorized rickshawlike contraptions, bicycles, and scooters— many loaded to excess with goods lashed into place by methods that ranged from ingenious to hazardous.

For a long time, as the market took shape around them, they saw nobody who could have been confused with a Russian. Vendors went about the mundane business of preparations, like actors before a performance, talking little, working automatically, making silent calculations. Alec thought to study them for pointers. It was possible that good looks and charisma were not enough. Or a disadvantage, even. In Riga, the most successful black marketeer he knew was a seventy-year-old Jew named Alter Schlamm, a head shorter than Alec and with the face of a dour picture-book dwarf. He'd seen Schlamm on occasion at the apartment Karl shared with his in-laws. Schlamm dealt in various commodities, and Rosa's father, though timid in business, would now and again buy fabric from him. Alec had seen him arrive one evening and remove his oversize raincoat. Underneath, he'd wrapped himself in several meters of fabric.

—This here could make a nice dress. Short at the hem, how they're wearing it now. And here could be a dandy little suit for the big brother with still enough left over for the baby.

It was said of Schlamm that he had an iron pail full of gold coins. It was said he had a woolen sock stuffed with rubies and diamonds. It was said he'd anticipated the last currency devaluation and made a million dollars.

Alec saw in the eyes of the vendors at the market the same thing he had seen in the eyes of Alter Schlamm: the fire of inventory.

When they had walked nearly the length of the market, Alec noted the first, unmistakable Russian. A wide-shouldered, bearded man was building a pyramid out of packs of Soviet cigarettes. Laid out beside these were the familiar linens and, strangely, cans of Soviet coffee.

—I take it we've found the place, Alec said.

—You've found it, all right, the man replied. I've got these two tables.

Alec put his records down on the nearest table but one. The other bag he set as a placeholder for Karl. Polina dropped her duffel bag behind the first table and started to unpack.

—Can I ask you, Alec said to the man, does the coffee sell?

—I have three customers. Italians. They come every week. Don't ask me what they do with it.

Just before seven o'clock, as Polina was putting the final touches on their display, Alec saw the unmistakable figure of his brother lumbering up the path. He carried two large duffel bags, immensely heavy, their canvas skins stretched taut. He plodded ahead, betraying no hint of struggle or pain. He'd always been like this. They had lived in Teika, not far from VEF, a predominantly blue-collar area with few Jews. While Alec had been sent to the Number 40 School, specializing in English and located in the center of the city, Karl had been enrolled at the local school. If somebody said *Yid*, Karl went after him. Though sometimes he also went after people who said *Hey, you*, or who, he felt, had looked at him the wrong way. There were many afternoons when Alec returned home to find their mother patching Karl up, her doctor's bag agape on the kitchen table. Karl never cried or complained, only sat broodingly and tolerated their mother's lectures and ministrations. At night, in their room, he recounted the details of the fights and methodically planned his strategies for attack and revenge. Alec had been thrilled by the stories, and amazed by Karl's fearlessness, or his ability to suppress his fear. Secretly, though, he worried that Karl's battles would spill over from the schoolyard and follow him home.

Not surprisingly, Karl earned the respect of his foes, who then became his friends. Up until his graduation, Karl preferred them to people whom he hadn't punched in the face. They drank together, played soccer, beat up other people, and in the winter went on marathon cross-country ski excursions. Later, Karl became infatuated with physical culture, and started doing push-ups and sit-ups by the hundreds. That led to Roman Berman's bodybuilding class at the Dynamo gym and Karl's pride in developing a neck almost fifty centimeters around for which he had trouble finding suitable shirts. Since the official Party line on bodybuilding was that it was a vain and decadent bourgeois activity, their father condemned it. But Karl, who loved dumbbells more than the Party, continued to train until marriage and fatherhood put an end to it. Alec naturally assumed that such a love never completely died.

He thought something along these lines as he watched his brother come to a stop and lower the bags in the middle of the path. Karl was still some twenty-five meters shy of their tables, but he remained in place, his expression incredulous and sour.

—Unbelievable, Karl said when Alec came over.

—What? Alec asked.

Karl kicked one of the duffel bags, which received the blow inertly, like a fat, sleeping drunk.

—What? Karl sneered. You'd think I was carrying them for your amusement.

—You carried them this far, I thought you'd want to finish.

Karl shook his head disparagingly.

—When they make it an Olympic event, I'll finish. For now, give a hand.

Alec nodded casually and heaved the bag onto his back. He followed Karl to his table and slid the bag onto it. Karl did the same.

Relieved of the bag, Karl's mood improved.

—I dreamed of shit last night, Karl declared. Means we're due to come into money.

In short order he unpacked his bags and spread out his almost identical wares. By nine o'clock all the stalls were filled and buyers congested the paths. From every side came the calls that Alec immediately learned and imitated: *Una pezza, una lira!* and *Per bambino! Per bambina!*

Early in the day, Alec fell in among the crowd to see what prices others were charging for comparable goods. Nobody was eager to reveal their prices to competitors, but it didn't take much to realize that the prices didn't vary greatly. The trick, Alec saw, was to use any possible means to attract a buyer to your stall. A man selling Soviet cameras—Kiev, Zorki, and Mir—demonstrated his products by pretending to snap a photo of the buyer and then, with primitive sleight of hand, producing a small photograph of Stalin. If he received a cool reaction, he shook the photograph as if to erase and develop it anew. He then showed the customer the corrected photo: Mussolini. If that failed to please them, he shook it again until it bore the likeness of Sophia Loren. Another Russian, selling pantyhose, waved a cardboard cutout of a shapely woman's leg. A good-looking young man from Kaunas, in a smiling courtly manner, lavished his Italian customers with Yiddish curses. *Ale tsores vos ikh hob, zoln oysgeyn tsu dayn kop!* He was very popular. His customers smiled resplendently as they handed over their money.

There was every kind of distraction at the market. Gypsy women with small children roamed through the thick crowd begging and clasping on to people. Shoppers batted the children's hands away like gnats. Alec saw a Gypsy woman pinch her infant to make it wail, then look imploringly at passing tourists. Like rocks in a stream, some vendors planted themselves in the middle of the path and brandished small items for sale: wristwatches, utility knives, cigarette lighters, batteries. At intervals, trucks were stationed from which sausages and pizza could be bought. More humble operators roasted corn on the embers of blackened iron grills. Lugging big aluminum coolers, boys sold ice cream and soda. Where a lane intersected the main path, a heavyset man with a gourd-shaped head, wider at the jaw than at the temples, presided over a shell game.

When Alec returned to their stall, Polina was calmly watching people sift through their goods. It seemed to Alec that there was a lot of touching but not a lot of buying. At Karl's table, Karl was clapping his hands and boisterously calling out to every passing *signore* and *signora*.

—Anything so far? Alec asked.

Polina smiled a sketch of a smile.

—You sold something? Alec said.

—You can't tell? Polina replied.

Alec scanned the table to take stock but he couldn't identify what might have been sold.

—Three windup plastic chicks, Polina said proudly. A woman bought them for her grandchildren.

Polina reached into her pocket and drew out several bills.

—Our first sale, Alec said. We should spend it on something memorable.

—It's only six *mila* lire, Polina said. I didn't know how much to ask. Karl said ask for five and you'll get two. So that's what I did.

—Not bad, Alec said. Next we should try to unload something heavier.

As the day wore on, Alec discovered that he could concentrate on selling only for short periods before his mind wandered. There was so much activity, so much curious human traffic to contemplate. There were also many girls and housewives demanding to be noticed and admired. Even standing beside Polina didn't deter him or inoculate him against a consuming interest in other women. Each time a new one appeared she temporarily obliterated the rest of the world.

Everything blurred and receded, leaving only the tantalizing possibility. If she walked away unknown, mystery and regret trailed after her like the tail of a comet. The consolation was that she was almost immediately replaced by another woman. Who vanished trailing mystery and regret. And then again and again. It was repetitive but never dull. However, it made it hard to focus on selling windup toys, linens, and hand-tooled leather goods.

10

Samuil hadn't felt any apprehension when their mother told them that they would move to Riga, he'd felt only the excitement of traveling to Kiev and riding on a train.

Reuven wanted to know if he would still be a Pioneer in Riga. When he learned he would not, he wondered what he should do with his red neckerchief. Their mother suggested that he wrap it nicely in newsprint and leave it behind as a present for the neighbors' youngest daughter. Samuil had watched as their mother helped Reuven fold the neckerchief into a compact triangle. Like this and like this, she said, guiding his hand.

In the morning they climbed onto a hired wagon. Their driver was a burly Jew who wielded a long whip and kept a loaded pistol under an empty burlap sack. He uncovered it to show their mother before they left town. For the brigands in the forest, he said. They encountered no brigands, only Ukrainian boys who jeered at them as they rumbled past and pelted them with fist-size clumps of frozen earth.

In Kiev he saw his first tram. He saw golden spires and smokestacks taller than any tree.

In Kiev's great stone railway terminal, he saw more people than he had ever seen in any one place and it had seemed to him that every other man was in uniform.

Three Red Army officers slept in their railcar. They let him and Reuven polish their boots and gave them a silver teaspoon.

—Don't forget your native land, their mother said as the locomotive rattled through the towns and fields of the Ukraine. In this land your father is buried.

In Riga, their uncle Naftali had three small rooms on the second floor of a building in the Moskovsky suburb. The railway tracks separated the Moskovsky from the center of the city; Samuil heard the steam engines come and go in the night. They were eight people in the apartment; his uncle's children were aged three, two, and a few months. His uncle had seemed old to Samuil, but he could have been no more than twenty-four. On his left foot, he had only three toes. In the mornings, he balled up old newsprint and stuffed it into his boot. When he saw Samuil and Reuven gawking, he called them over.

—Frostbite, he said. Nothing to fear. It's a lucky man who goes to war and loses only two toes.

He had lost his toes serving in the tsar's army. He still had a photograph of himself wearing a private's uniform.

Trotsky had signed the armistice at Brest-Litovsk while their uncle was recuperating from his injury. He returned to Riga, opened his bookbinding shop, and had a second child before the next wars. From the next wars, their uncle also had photographs. He wore the same uniform, only with different hats. His uncle's war stories were confusing. He fought with the tsar against the Germans, then with the Germans against the Bolsheviks, and then with the Latvians against the Germans again.

—I fought with the tsar because I was young and foolish. I fought with the Germans because the Bolsheviks tried to close the shops and the synagogues. And I fought with the Latvians because the Germans wouldn't leave.

After a year, their uncle found them a two-room apartment in the neighboring building. Not since the murder of his father and grandfather had they had a place to themselves. It had been good to be alone with his mother and brother where he no longer needed to mind his every move.

Their mother took a job as a seamstress in a coat factory. He and Reuven were enrolled in a Yiddish school and in the Zionist youth group, Hashomer Hatzair. In the evenings, after their studies, their uncle took them to the bindery and showed them the trade. When they were older, he planned for them to join him.

—Books are the future, he said. Even the lowest peasant is learning to read. Novels, poems, textbooks, manuals: someone has to bind them all.

Samuil had liked the bindery. He liked the acrid, moldering smell of paper and glue—the smell of knowledge. In one corner of the shop sat two old bookbinders, pious Jews, who bound and repaired Hebrew holy texts. Everywhere else were books in Yiddish, Latvian, German, Hebrew, French, English, Russian, and Esperanto.

Sometimes their uncle would bind an extra book for himself. In his apartment, he kept a small library. He encouraged Reuven and Samuil to read these books, and it was the only one of his uncle's prescriptions that Reuven accepted willingly.

For a long time, Samuil did not understand why Reuven behaved the way he did. He excelled in his studies, he had many friends, but he never seemed happy. One time, after Samuil had won a prize for reciting a Hebrew poem, Reuven scolded him. Samuil had been too self-satisfied. As they walked home, Reuven asked if he knew what day it was.

—No, Samuil had said.

—Today is three years since the Whites murdered Father and Grandfather.

Samuil fell silent with shame.

—Do you remember how Grandfather said the Shema when they killed him?

—No, Samuil said weakly.

—A Hebrew poem never saved a Jew from a pogrom.

After that, Reuven came less and less to the Hashomer Hatzair club. He said he was having difficulty learning Latvian and he couldn't spare the time from his lessons. Samuil went alone to the meetings. It was the last time they were apart until the war separated them permanently.

Reuven took his lessons at their next-door neighbors. They were a Latvian family, headed by a tall, bald, friendly man named Eduards. Because their mother was without a husband, Eduards offered to help with masculine chores. When he drew water from the well, he also filled a pail for them. In winter, he went with Reuven and Samuil to bring up their coal. And his eldest daughter, a school-teacher, tutored Reuven in Latvian at no cost. Samuil would watch Reuven gather his books to go across the hall, promising their mother that he would behave himself and decline politely if they offered him *treyf* food.

One time, their uncle was at their apartment as Reuven prepared to leave.

—What do you know of these neighbors? he asked their mother.

—Only that they have been very generous.

—Where did the man learn to speak Russian?

—I don't know, their mother replied. But his wife barely speaks a word.

—I would be careful, their uncle said.

—Reuven is doing better. Do you suggest I stop him from going?

—I suggest you take no chances, their uncle said.

Once home, Reuven quarreled with their mother and said that he would continue with the lessons. About their uncle he said: If I like something, he doesn't.

Samuil sensed that there was something the matter with his brother. At times he felt very close to him; other times he felt as if he did not know him at all.

Just when he thought his brother wanted nothing more to do with Zionism, Reuven took him to hear Ze'ev Jabotinsky give a speech to a hall full of Jewish youths. On the walls, Samuil saw posters of the one-armed martyr Joseph Trumpeldor, his feet planted firmly on the land of Palestine, his good arm gesturing for the Jewish youth to join in the struggle. At the bottom of the poster were printed his parting words: Never mind, it is good to die for our country.

He and Reuven had squirmed to the front of the stage. They saw up close Jabotinsky's jutting chin, stern mouth, and piercing eyes, and they heard his cry: Jewish youth, learn to shoot!

Afterward, many of his friends quit Hashomer Hatzair and joined Jabotinsky's Betar. To the songs and the scouting lessons, they now added classes in hand-to-hand combat. A veteran of the Jewish Self-Defense Organization instructed them in the use of "cold weapons." He had a suitcase filled with brass knuckles, wooden batons, and lengths of iron pipe. In the spring and summer, there were retreats to the countryside where they slept in tents, did calisthenics, and learned how to handle rifles and pistols.

Reuven became one of the most active members. He attended all of the meetings, gave lectures, and became a crack shot. But, after one year, just as he drifted away from Hashomer Hatzair, he also drifted away from Betar. This time, when Samuil asked him why, Reuven took him aside and confided in him. Samuil was twelve years old—old enough to be trusted.

When Samuil learned the truth, he was astounded by his brother's self-discipline.

After that, Samuil joined Reuven at Eduards's apartment, where they were given their Latvian lessons from Communist pamphlets. The seeds that had been sown in Reuven in the Pioneers of Rogozna, Eduards cultivated in Riga.

In his apartment, Eduards had a radio that he tuned to a Soviet frequency. It was at this radio that Samuil listened to the trials of Kamenev, Zinoviev, and Bukharin. And it was at this radio, unbeknown to Samuil at the time, that Reuven had listened to the broadcast of Lenin's funeral. He spoke of it later to Samuil and their other comrades in a hushed, reverential tone. Though he had only been listening to a radio in Riga, it had seemed to everyone as if he had been much closer to the event—if only because, just listening to the radio, he had been much closer than anyone else they knew.

When Samuil thought of his brother, he pictured him in Eduards's apartment. He saw the darkened corner where Eduards kept the radio, with its gilded dial, which, when dormant, rested on an unincriminating Latvian frequency. He saw Eduards's heavy damask armchair, the haze of pipe smoke, and the faded green rug at the base of the radio cabinet where Reuven and his daughters sat. He saw Eduards lean intimately toward the radio and turn the dial. How weighty and faraway the radio announcer's voice must have sounded that afternoon. Emerging from the fading strains of the "Internationale," the announcer had boomed: Stand up, comrades, Ilich is being lowered into his grave!

In Eduards's apartment, his brother rose from the green rug and stood solemnly at attention beside Eduards, his wife, and their daughters. A vast primordial quiet descended and hovered like a soul above a body until the announcer's voice returned and proclaimed: Lenin has died—but Leninism lives!

11

Going to see his family felt to Alec like doing penance for any enjoyment he derived from life. They fundamentally disagreed about everything important, and also unimportant. Whenever Alec said anything, Rosa and his father found common cause in his idiocy. Their conversation was a series of digs and ambushes.

Alec and Polina arrived in the late afternoon and found his family gathered in the small garden behind the house. The Italian owners had provided a table and several iron chairs for tenant use. In among his family, Alec saw a short, one-legged old man with medals pinned to his blazer.

—I come now and again to disturb your father, Josef said.

—A guest is never a disturbance, Emma corrected.

—No, no, Samuil grumbled in a noncommittal way.

At the back of the garden, Yury was kicking a pink rubber ball at his brother, who was playing goal, defending the garden gate. A hollow resinous twang accompanied each kick.

—Boys, come over and say hello to your uncle and aunt, Emma called.

—Did you bring us anything? Zhenya asked.

—Greetings from the late pope, Alec said.

Polina extracted a small bag of caramels from her handbag. They had melted in the heat and needed to be refrigerated. She gave them to Emma to give to the boys.

—For later, Polina said.

—How very thoughtful, Emma said.

—Yes, thank you, Rosa added.

—Afterward, Emma said, when they sing the songs they learned in the Hebrew choir we'll give these as a reward.

The boys, Rosa explained, had been going daily to Club Kadima to learn songs for the High Holidays, Rosh Hashanah and Yom Kippur. Rosa, who actually possessed an excellent singing voice, was part of the adult choir. Karl, regrettably, was not. He was a true bass, and they could have used him. In Riga, Rosa said for the enlightenment of the one-legged Josef Roidman, Karl had belonged to a choir. It was where the two of them had met.

As Rosa spoke, Alec glanced at his father, who sat stonily in his chair.

—Normally, they don't accept children so young, but the boys learned the Hebrew very fast, like a mother tongue.

Alec could only imagine his father, at his most saturnine, his eyes like mineshafts, enduring the Hebrew singing of his grandchildren.

Rosa mentioned the date of the concert.

—Of course they will come, Emma said.

—They have a very capable conductor, Roidman volunteered. It promises to be a very memorable show.

—Maybe it will sell out? Alec asked.

—Don't you worry, Rosa said. Nobody who wants to come will be turned away.

—Very good. Alec smiled. We'll come, so long as it doesn't conflict with the inauguration of the new pope.

—Well, naturally, Rosa said, you have your priorities.

Since they had already started in this direction, Alec said that he and Polina had in fact gone to St. Peter's, where Pope Paul VI was lying in state.

The excursion had been Lyova's idea. At first, Alec hadn't been enthusiastic about it.

—I prefer to remember him as he was in life, he'd said.

—You saw him in life? Lyova asked.

—I saw pictures.

—You don't want to go?

—I'd just as soon not go out of my way to see a corpse. Even a famous one. In the end, every corpse has the same face: your own. It's depressing. My policy is to think about my own death as little as possible.

—Did you know this about your husband? Lyova asked.

—Not in so many words, Polina said.

But in the end he had come along and joined the line of mourners. Some were interlopers like themselves, others fingered rosaries and murmured prayers. There were those who wept quietly. The crowd numbered in the thousands and flowed forward at a surprisingly brisk pace. Unsentimental Roman policemen shouted, *Andare! Andare!*

They shuffled forward and through the doors of St. Peter's Basilica, where the pope was stretched out on a catafalque, under the cathedral's towering cupola, designed to reduce a man before God's grandeur. Mourners were instructed to pass four abreast. Alec, Polina, and Lyova formed a group with a bald Roman man who remembered an act of kindness this pope had performed during the war when the Americans bombed San Lorenzo.

Two fans rotated above the catafalque, where the pope lay draped in purple velvet. A black-robed attendant stood at his side, his face composed for the occasion. Candles and incense burned, but not sufficiently to cloak the scent of rot. Alec heard people gasp in shock. Some crossed themselves and averted their eyes. When his time came, Alec looked upon the pope's ghastly face. It should have come as no surprise in such heat, but he, too, had expected that, for the pope, death might take the form of a benevolent hand, leading immaculately into heaven. As they moved away, a fly settled on the pope's forehead, which the attendant immediately and impassively brushed aside.

The world's multiplicate attentions were now focused on this one corpse. Presidents and potentates would fly in from all over the globe for the official funeral.

—What kind of presidents? Roidman asked. Carter? Trudeau?

—Possibly, Alec said.

Roidman waggled his head appreciatively.

—What is this to us? Rosa interjected. We have our own problems. There is more important news in the world.

—For instance, Karl said, Christina Onassis, the world's richest woman, married a one-eyed Russian and plans to live in a cooperative apartment in Moscow.

—For instance, scolded Rosa, Begin said he will meet Sadat in Washington.

—She has five hundred million dollars. He has a glass eye, Karl said.

On their way home, to reward themselves for having made the trip, Alec took Polina to the Ladispoli movie theater that showed pornographic films. Ladispoli had only one, although there were a number of them in Rome, mainly in the vicinity of Termini Station. Lyova, a connoisseur of all things Roman, had been the first to introduce Alec to the theaters.

—Something else communism denied us, Lyova said.

Together they had gone to one of the theaters near Termini to catch a show. Lyova had extended the invitation to Polina as well, but she had demurred. So they had gone without her one evening, and sat with other men in a theater half filled. Lyova didn't distinguish particularly among the movies showing, and just picked one he hadn't seen before. The lights went down, immersing the theater in total darkness—a darkness so complete that it was no longer possible to see the person sitting beside you. Then the screen came to life, flashing images of a beautiful young woman in an urbane setting. Some American dialogue followed and soon the woman was naked and being licked and caressed by two other naked women, a Negress and a Chinese. Already, this exceeded Alec's expectations. For all his experience with sex and women, he was seeing on the screen combinations, situations, and acts that he'd never before seen, engaged in, or even conceived of. Images of happy, coy, compliant women were projected. The camera traveled languorously over breasts, buttocks, and open thighs. A man dropped his pants and the leading actress readily took his cock into her mouth. The screen filled with her bobbing head and her big, intent eyes. Later, on a huge, gleaming, candlelit dining-room table, she was ravaged simultaneously by two men and another woman. To a syncopated soundtrack, they squirmed around and inserted fingers, tongues, candles, and cocks into every available orifice. When it ended, Alec grasped the full extent of Soviet deprivation. If Russian men were surly, belligerent alcoholics it was because, in place of natural, healthy forms of relaxation, they were given newspaper accounts of hero-worker dairy maids receiving medals for milk production.

The afternoon Alec took Polina, a French film was playing at the theater in Ladispoli. The film was already in progress when they arrived. The theater was as dark as the one in Rome and they were able to find their seats only with the help of a dreary-looking usher. On the screen, as they sat down, was a scene in the countryside, where the leading actress was being mounted from behind by a strapping country lad, who was naked but for a pair of leather riding boots. Standing obliviously behind them, nibbling the occasional clump of grass, was a muscular white horse. The actress was blond and very attractive, but what aroused Alec wasn't so much the way she looked but the sounds she made. To hear her cry out using her French words and inflections heightened the experience. Silent, she could have been any woman. But crying out, she became a Frenchwoman. Sexual pleasure resided in adjectives. Nobody ever just fucked a woman. Fat, skinny, young, widowed, rich, poor. Or, more resonantly: Armenian, Kalmyk, Estonian, Gypsy, Polish. Watching this one Frenchwoman, Alec felt as if he had been given carnal insight into all Frenchwomen. In fact, into the entire French nation. If he ever traveled to France he would no longer be intimidated by the culture. He now knew the French. He reached over and slid his hand under Polina's skirt. She didn't rebuff him, but clenched briefly to assert her personality, before parting her legs and letting him do what he wanted. Then, as if interpreting the pulsing signal of his hand, Polina reached across the armrest and lowered her hand into his lap. Instantly, Alec was reduced to the part of him that existed under the play and pressure of her fingers. Around them, the darkness assumed the geometry of a chamber that separated them from the others in the theater, who occupied their own dark chambers.

It was like this, in the clandestine darkness of a Riga movie theater, that Alec had, at the age of twelve, entered into manhood. That time, not Frenchmen but Hindus had been on the movie screen and the girl beside him was Olya, Karl's ostensible girlfriend. Karl had decided he wouldn't go to the movie and forever changed Alec's life.

Karl was sixteen then, as was Olya. It was a Sunday afternoon and Karl had simply changed his mind. He'd already seen the movie with her and he didn't want to see it again. Instead, he said he would stay home and study. But since Olya had no telephone and lived in the center of town, he had no way of contacting her.

—Hey, dimwit, Karl had said, what are you doing?

And, just like that, Alec was riding his bicycle to the center of town to inform Olya that Karl couldn't make the movie.

Karl told him to look for Olya outside her building where Krisjan Baron met Karl Marx Street. Alec had never seen her before, he'd only heard Karl mention her in passing. But since Karl wasn't one to bare his soul, the only thing he knew about her was that Karl had described her as a little nuts. When Alec asked how he might recognize her, Karl said that it would be easy. She would be the only girl on the street wearing an Indian sari.

—What's a sari? Alec had asked.

—It's like a sheet. All wrapped around. You can't miss her.

True, as Karl said, Alec spotted her immediately as he coasted down Krisjan Baron. It was a warm spring day and, even though

there were very many people out on Krisjan Baron, Olya was conspicuous among them. It wasn't only because she had wrapped herself elaborately in a red sheet, but because Alec noticed that she was
very pretty. She had dark hair down to her shoulders, fair skin, a
thin, straight nose, and green eyes the color of bottle glass. As he
rode toward her, he tried to think up a reason that would allow him
to remain longer in her presence. He was still trying to come up with
something when he brought his bicycle to a stop beside her. Olya was
scanning Krisjan Baron and Karl Marx Streets and didn't immediately grasp that the boy on the bicycle had stopped beside her deliberately. She retreated half a step to let him pass, but when he didn't
budge, she fixed him with a wry smile, as if she knew better than he
did what he was up to. As she regarded him, Alec gazed wordlessly
back. He felt neither nervous nor awkward, only content. This was
love. It was his first experience and he was certain that the feeling
would never abate. There was nothing he wanted to do except look at
her. And he knew that as soon as he opened his mouth and delivered
his message he'd have to stop looking and pedal home.

—Didn't your mother teach you it's not polite to stare? Olya said.

—I'm Karl's brother, Alec replied.

—You don't look alike, Olya said, which, though he knew it to be
true, Alec was nevertheless disappointed to hear.

—Some people say there's a resemblance.

—No, not at all. You're completely different. The shape of your
face, your eyes, the nose, the mouth. Look at your eyelashes. You're
like a little doll compared to him.

—Karl sent me to tell you that he can't come to the movie, Alec
said brusquely, to show that he was no doll.

—Oh, Olya said, with a swell of sadness that caught Alec by surprise.

A quaver entered her voice that made her sound not like a
sixteen-year-old goddess but like a little girl.

—Why couldn't he come? she inquired.

To spare her feelings, Alec lied and said that Karl was sick. He
had a temperature.

—Oh, Olya said again, only this time with an upward lilt in her voice.

She seemed satisfied with the excuse. In an instant, as quickly as she'd been devastated, she recovered and showed no trace of having been hurt. She fingered a thin gold chain around her neck. It was fairly long, and it dipped into the folds of her sari and down between her breasts. Suspended from the chain was a small golden locket. Olya plucked it up and opened its case. Inside was a miniature clock face.

—The movie starts in ten minutes, Olya said.

She snapped the case shut and let the locket fall back down into her sari. Alec expected that she would go on her way and leave him, but she looked at him in an enigmatic way.

—Do you like movies? Olya asked.

—Sure, Alec said.

—Do you like Indian movies? Olya asked.

—I like every kind of movie.

—Have you ever seen an Indian movie?

—Of course, Alec said, lying instinctively.

—Which one?

—I don't remember the name. But it was full of Indians.

—Did it have Raj Kapoor?

—Maybe.

—Nargis?

—Who?

—Nargis. She's the most glamorous Indian actress.

—Well, then, probably, Alec said.

Olya cocked her head and flashed that same skeptical, amused expression.

—You're not a very good liar, she said.

—I'm not lying, Alec protested.

This only caused her to laugh.

—You know, you really are like a darling little doll, Olya teased.

—I don't like being called that, Alec said.

—No? Why not? What's wrong with being a darling little doll? Some people would say it was nice.

—Not me, Alec said.

—That's too bad, Olya said.

—Why? Alec asked.

—Do you like girls? Olya said.

—Of course I like girls, Alec said. I'm not queer.

—Well, there are lots of girls who like dolls.

—So what? Alec said.

—So, Olya grinned, would the little doll like to come with me to see *The Tramp* with Nargis and Raj Kapoor?

Before they set off, Olya safely stashed Alec's bicycle in the courtyard of her building. Then she took Alec by the hand and led him down Krisjan Baron Street to Perses Street and then over to Suvorova, where the Palladium movie theater stood.

Since Alec hadn't planned on going to a movie, he had almost no money on him, but Olya paid for him and also bought him an ice cream. On their way to the theater and also while climbing the steps to the balcony, Olya talked about her love of Indian movies and of *The Tramp* in particular. Already, she had seen it six times. Once with her mother, four times by herself, and once with Karl. She'd memorized nearly all of the dialogue and knew the lyrics to all of the songs. On Suvorova Street, as they had approached the Palladium, she sang one of the ballads, releasing Alec's hand long enough to demonstrate some dance steps—prancing backwards and making big, sweeping flourishes with her hands. Onlookers gawked at her, a few smiled, more raised their eyebrows disdainfully, but if Olya noticed she clearly didn't care.

The tickets Olya purchased were in the balcony, in the front row, at the railing, high above the gallery, from where they could peer down upon the scattered people below. In those moments before the movie started, Alec became aware of the magnitude of what he was doing. He still didn't know where it would lead, but even if nothing else happened he felt that he had crossed a boundary. His parents didn't know where he was. He was in a movie theater alone with an older girl—a girl who happened also to be his brother's girlfriend. He had lied to her, and he anticipated that he would lie to his parents and to Karl when he got home. He had a sense of all of this, an intimation of significance, but he couldn't have formulated it in words. Later he came to see this moment as the one in which he took his biggest stride out onto the promontory of life.

The movie, as Alec recalled, was incredibly long. For its entire length he concentrated far less on what was happening on-screen and much more on what was happening in the span of centimeters that separated him from Olya. He followed her silent example, and stared raptly at the screen while his hand, in incursions measured in fingerbreadths, crept up her arm and across into the folds of her strange garment. He didn't even know where his hand was going, but like an advancing army, it took whatever territory was conceded to it.

When Raj Kapoor performed the film's signature song, "A Tramp, I Am," Alec's hand gained Olya's breast. As Kapoor sang, Alec felt for the first time a nipple, like an independent living thing, grow rigid under his touch. This was part of the great tantalizing secret guarded by the adult world. It was the forbidden thing paraded around in plain sight. Parents or teachers would describe the function of a locomotive, a diode, or a molecule, but wouldn't say a word about what was going on between everyone's legs. This knowledge you had to acquire on your own. Often as not, in the dark—possibly even while an Indian actress executed a bizarre, jerky, melodramatic dance around the mast of a sailboat. *I wish the moon would look away / while I make love to him*, Nargis sang, which Alec took as encouragement to allow his hand to explore further, drifting down to Olya's thigh. Once there, he became indecisive, unsure if he could proceed. But then, with her own hand, Olya reached down and guided Alec through a gap in the fabric and onto the warm, faintly moist cotton of her underpants. She raised the elastic where it hugged her thigh, drew Alec's hand into the opening she'd created, and left him there to make sense of the soft, mossy, alien landscape.

When the film was over, they walked together back to Olya's building. Hours had passed and the streets had assumed their evening character. As before, Olya held Alec's hand and rattled on about the movie as if nothing more had happened. In her courtyard, she went directly to the spot where she'd stashed Alec's bicycle and wheeled it out for him. Alec kept waiting for her to acknowledge what had transpired between them, to utter some pledge or promise of a future meeting. But she gave not the slightest indication that this was on her mind, and instead made Alec wonder if she'd been in some kind of trance during the movie and couldn't remember what she'd allowed him to do. The thought that he might never be able to touch Olya again sickened and astonished him. Even though he knew he shouldn't, he couldn't stop himself from offering to return the following Sunday to see the movie a second time.

—Sorry, Olya said, today was the last day. Tomorrow they start *The Cranes Are Flying*.

And that was it. Olya went into her building and Alec cycled home in a state of anguish and reverie—the paramour's companion feelings. When he came home, he sensed that he was no longer the same person. Climbing the stairs to his apartment, he felt imbued with a new knowledge. And as he readied himself for the inevitable beating from Samuil, he consoled himself with the thought that no amount of beating could revoke what he'd learned or undo what he'd done.

12

My dearest Brigitte,

It was wonderful to get your letter and to hear your voice again,
if only on the page.

It's strange that you would have seen Maxim on that day,
though not so strange to hear that he's looking well. Perhaps he's
found a new woman to take care of him, someone more suitable
than I was. I'm sure there's more than one who would leap at the
chance for the apartment alone.

Here, we continue to wait for our interview with the Canadian
embassy. Everyone we've spoken to says that we should expect to
spend the fall and winter in Italy. And maybe even the spring. I
know that this doesn't sound like a horrible predicament to be in,
and yet I still haven't quite adjusted to the idea. There had been
uncertainty every step of the way getting to Rome, and I'd
somehow expected that once we got here everything would be
made clear. In any case, there's nothing we can do but wait, and,
as everyone tells me (including you), make the most of it.

You'd be surprised how I've made the most of it so far. For five
consecutive Sundays, Igor and I went to the Americana to try to
sell all the ridiculous things we'd brought with us. I've managed

*to sell nearly everything we brought, including a few things for
other people—apparently, I'd developed a reputation. Now that
everything has been sold, I have gone looking for other work. Igor
told me that I didn't need to, in fact, he encouraged me not to. He
thought I should just be a woman of leisure, a tourist in Rome.
He says that we can survive perfectly well on the money we get
from the Jewish Agency and from his job at HIAS.*

*For one week, I tried, but I just don't have the right
constitution for it. I went to beautiful tourist attractions and felt
strangely out of place. I felt like a solitary person in a crowd. For
the week that I was supposed to be a woman of leisure, I just
wandered around the city feeling idle and aimless. I told Igor
that he needed to recognize that he'd married an incorrigible
proletarian.*

*So, in short, I went looking for a job. Many Russians work
here. Men like Igor, who speak English, get jobs with the Jewish
agencies. Men who don't speak English sometimes get work at
construction sites. Others, like our roommate, give tours of Italy to
émigrés. There are cultured women who take émigrés through
museums and galleries in Rome. And there are also Italian
shopkeepers who hire Russian girls to cater to their Russian
clientele. The day before yesterday, Lyova introduced me and Igor
to a shopkeeper he knows in Piazza Vittorio.*

*We went at the end of the day, as the market was closing. I
was nervous, as you can imagine. Igor and I had made plans to
meet Lyova in the Park Borghese and we waited for a half hour
for him to show up. The Park Borghese is very big and we
thought maybe he'd gotten lost, or that we were waiting for him
in the wrong place. But just when I really started to despair, I
spotted him from a distance, jogging toward us with a picket
sign. He was coming from the Israeli embassy, where he and four
or five others occasionally stage protests. In Hebrew, Italian, and
English his sign read: "Israel, Let Your People Go!" Igor
contended that the English had a grammatical error.*

The two of them alternated carrying this sign from the Park

Borghese to Piazza Vittorio. It isn't a short walk and it leads through the middle of the city. I think people took us for avant-garde street performers.

The shopkeeper Lyova introduced me to is named Giovanni. He is probably in his fifties. His wife works with him. We were only able to exchange a few words, but they seemed like warm people. They sell leather goods for women and men—shoes and coats and even skirts. They'd hired a Russian woman once before, and Lyova has dealt with them and he says they are fair. Their shop is small and the salary they offered is modest, but I will get to keep a percentage of my sales. Honestly, I don't anticipate that I'll make much money. And Igor still believes that I'm foolish to take the job: Why would I choose to spend my days surrounded by cowhide when all the splendors of Rome are spread out before me? But it's hard to explain to him that I miss order and I miss routine. For that I am prepared to forgo splendors. When Giovanni offered me the job I was so happy and grateful and relieved that I nearly gushed like a little girl. All I could think was that now when I woke up I would have someplace to go.

Tomorrow will be my first day. Wish me luck! I will work in the afternoons on the days I have my English classes, and on the days when I don't have classes I will work a full shift.

And, by the way, since I know you're wondering, the things that Igor disparaged as cowhide are actually quite stylish. It is customary, Lyova says, for employees to be given a discount. So, if nothing else, I might be able to pick up something nice for myself—and maybe even for you.

13

I n the fall of 1942, when he was in hospital recuperating from a
fractured skull, Samuil had had as his neighbor a young man
named Srul Brunstein, a Yiddish poet dying of a lung wound.
From his cot, Brunstein would recite his poems. There was one
that Samuil remembered very distinctly because it captured his life
the year he turned seventeen, after his uncle spat blood, became an
invalid, and lost the bindery. He and Reuven went door to door, offering their services to anyone and everyone. They appealed to the relatives of boys they had known in Hashomer Hatzair and Betar. Most
listened with half an ear and gazed over their heads. Some made
symbolic gestures that consisted of a day or two of casual work,
sweeping the floor or delivering packages.

Kh'shlep arum a zak mit beyner, was how the poem went.

I drag around a bag of bones
In the streets to sell
No one, however, wants to buy my wares,
No one.
Sorry, I did encounter a buyer once

But he needs real bones, dead bones.

Not like mine, alive and still in the flesh . . .

Their uncle was confined first to his bed, and then, for six weeks, to a tuberculosis ward in Kemeri. Their cousins were still children, thirteen, twelve, and ten years old. Their aunt took in laundry, and their mother continued to work at the coat factory. Money needed to be found for food, for their uncle's medicines and treatments, and for rent.

For two weeks, in winter weather, using their bare hands, he and Reuven cleaned out the charred remains of a burned-down house. At night they returned to their cold apartment, covered in soot, their hands torn and numb, having eaten nothing all day but a piece of black bread. Their mother, herself exhausted from work, waited for them with a basin of water and a bar of soap.

From dawn to dusk, in the worst weather, they managed in thin spring coats. Alongside them worked other members of the Jewish proletariat.

The revolution was coming, nobody doubted this. The only question was when and what form it would take. The Zionist-Socialists believed in one revolution, the Revisionists in another, the Bundists in a third. Reuven and Samuil were careful to keep their views to themselves. They said only that the days of the old order were numbered.

No longer able to afford the rent on two apartments, they moved back in with their uncle. Quarters that had been cramped when they were children were more cramped now that they were adults.

For eight people, there were three beds. Samuil and Reuven shared a bed with Yaakov, their oldest cousin; their mother slept with the two girls, Rakhel and Fania; and their uncle and aunt had a bed to themselves. At one end of the apartment, farthest from the door, a corner was curtained off where a person could attend to his physical needs.

Like cattle, Reuven said. But they knew of comrades who had it worse.

Through one of these comrades, they eventually found their way to Baruch Levitan, who hired them as bookbinders for the workshop that dominated his apartment. Counting Baruch and themselves, there were seven bookbinders, squeezed together amid the Levitans' beds and household implements. They would arrive for work just after dawn, so as not to squander any daylight. Most workdays lasted twelve hours, the last of which were conducted in near-darkness, since Baruch refused to switch on the electric lights until you could no longer tell Stalin from Trotsky.

They spent no more time at home than was absolutely necessary. Only to sleep and to see their mother. Too proud, their uncle hadn't reconciled himself to his illness or to his dependence on his nephews. He still tried to assert his control. Nothing they did was right. They did not lay tefillin or join him in morning prayers. They refused to keep the Sabbath, or go to synagogue on the holidays. They broke with Betar. They dropped any pretense of minding him.

Instead, they spent many evenings with their old neighbor, Eduards. Through him they were able to meet non-Jewish workers, Latvian Communists. It was also there, through Eduards's daughters, that they continued their studies. The same daughter who had tutored Reuven in Latvian loaned them the writings of Thomas Mann, Maxim Gorky, and Romain Rolland. She also schooled them in the international language of Esperanto. She used primers in combination with issues of *Sennaciulo*, a weekly journal whose title meant "Nationless."

Later, they continued independent of her, and to the consternation of Baruch Levitan, they practiced the language at work.

Kioma horo estas nun, Reuveno?

Estas jam tagmezo kaj kvarno. Kial vi volas scii, Samuilo? Cu vi malastas?

Mi sentas etan malaston, jes.

Cu vi volas mangi ion?

Mangeti, jes. Mi certe ne deziras grandan tagmanon.

Kien ni iru, do?

La kafejon ce la stratangulo? Sanjas al mi, ke gi estas malmultekosa.

Ni iru tien. Verdire, mi tre malsatas! *

Many nights they slept only a few hours. But such was the life of the revolutionary. In biographical accounts of Lenin, it was said that he rarely slept more than four hours. This idea was reinforced in the speeches they heard given by Max Schatz-Anin, an old Bolshevik tortured and blinded by Denikin's men during the Civil War. Of the few authentic Bolsheviks in Riga, he held claim to the most illustrious past. There was the torture and mutilation, and there was also his personal acquaintance, not only with Peters and Lacis-Sudrabs, but with Voroshilov and Kaganovich. Sometimes, after a full day of work at Levitan's, they spent four or five more hours binding books and pamphlets at Schatz-Anin's publishing house, Arbeter-Heym.

He and Reuven were nearly always together—in the dreary confines of Levitan's workshop, at rallies, lectures, and cell meetings. They rose together in the morning and retired together at night—often falling into the bed already occupied by their cousin Yaakov. A cheerful young man, blessed with a head for numbers, he'd secured a position keeping the accounts for Vasserman, a successful linen broker. Vasserman paid poorly and rarely said a kind word to Yaakov, but their uncle believed that Vasserman would be Yaakov's salvation. Vasserman was in his sixties and had no male heir; certainly, their uncle believed, he was grooming Yaakov to succeed him in the business.

Their cousin had little faith in Vasserman's largesse, but he didn't particularly care. Whereas Samuil and Reuven rejected Zionism, Yaakov had ardently embraced it. As soon as he was issued a certificate to enter Palestine, he would bid Vasserman, and Riga, and the rest of it goodbye. And though Samuil and Reuven derided

---

*What time is it, Reuven?
    It is already a quarter after twelve. Why do you ask, Samuil? Are you hungry?
    I feel a small hunger, yes.
    Would you like to eat something?
    To eat a little, yes. I certainly don't want a big lunch.
    Where shall we go then?
    The café on the corner? It seems to me that it is inexpensive.
    Let's go there. To tell the truth, I am very hungry!

Vasserman as the epitome of the preening bourgeois, Yaakov noted the man's virtues. Once, for Purim, he'd presented Yaakov with a packet of Turkish cigarettes. Another time, he'd given Yaakov a bargain on an old phonograph. Yaakov loved music and, during his military service, he'd picked up the clarinet, just as Reuven had picked up the concertina. Samuil, who possessed no musical talent, had picked up only a high proficiency with the Browning M1919 machine gun.

Both Yaakov and Reuven were partial to American "hot jazz"—chirpy, upbeat music. In a small clearing of floor space in front of the phonograph, Yaakov and Reuven would teach Rakhel and Fania how to execute the modern dance steps. Samuil could still picture them, vivid as life, in the sepia glow of the kerosene lamp, dancing to "Mister Brown," one of his cousin's favorite songs. The song was inane, and consisted of only one line, which was repeated by different voices in different accents and registers. Because there was so little to it, it had lodged in Samuil's mind. For years, the words in the song were the only English words he knew.

How do you do do, Mister Brown?
How do you do do, Mister Brown?
How do you do-do, do-do, do-do, do-do, Mee-ster Brown?

Sitting on the bed, Samuil would watch his brother and his cousins, stepping happily and clumsily on the bare floorboards. Across the room, their mother and aunt would be watching as well.

—When the revolution comes, Yaakov asked, will it be permissible for me to listen to "Mister Brown"?

—There's nothing objectionable about the music, Reuven said. It is the legitimate cultural expression of the downtrodden American Negro.

—But the lyrics are decadent and would have to be changed, Samuil said.

—To "Mister Marx"?

—An improvement, Samuil said. But it would require something more to edify the workers and reflect the social ideals of the revolution.

—And dancing?

—Why not? Reuven said.

—So long as every step is to the left, Yaakov said.

—Naturally, Reuven replied.

In bed with the enemy, Yaakov would joke. But he knew better than to ask sensitive questions, just as they knew well not to inquire into the activities of his Zionist group. Not once could Samuil remember them arguing about politics; at most they made subtle efforts to persuade and reform one another. Samuil recalled once inviting Yaakov to go with them to a Yom Kippur picnic, an event organized by a number of Jewish socialist groups. Yaakov had declined and gone instead with his father to Gutkin's Minyan on Stabu Street.

Before the picnic, Samuil joined a group of provocateurs who interrupted services by flagrantly eating an apple or a boiled egg in the midst of the congregation. Others, who were yet more audacious, pelted the fasting congregants with raisins and crusts of bread. To the congregants' cries of *Pigs! Heretics!* the comrades answered with *Hypocrites! Exploiters!*

The Yom Kippur picnics, the Red Passovers: he never again saw such unity and purity of doctrine. All the serious, impatient, strident, blustery, desperate Jewish workers. Their need for revolution, their intense, maddening need for change. The endless, demoralizing, profitless toil from morning to night. And the murderous advance of the fascists. Grandiose, strutting Mussolini and his blackshirts. Hitler and his deranged lumpen proletarian thugs. Franco and his gang of reactionaries, confounding the will of the Spanish people. And, in their own country, if not an outright fascist, then the dictator, Ulmanis. They felt their lives, their youth, ticking away minute by minute. How insignificant, how expendable were their pitiful, singular lives. How to describe the nature of that despair? All the times when, for no particular reason, Samuil had been paralyzed by the thought, A life, such a tremendous thing, a life! What right did they have to deny him his life? What made his life, that of a simple worker, less valuable than the life of a factory owner's son?

THE FREE WORLD

Twenty-five years ago the working classes of Russia with the help of peasants searched for chometz *in their land.*

These were the words of the Red Haggadah. Every Passover, Hirsh Kogan would remove it from its hiding place, under a plank in his floor, and they would recite it together in his room, even as they heard, through the wall, the neighbors chanting the ancient liturgy.

They cleaned away all the traces of landowners and bourgeois bosses in the country and took power into their own hands. They took the land from the landowners, plants and factories from the capitalists; they fought the enemies of the workers on all fronts. In the fire of the great socialist revolution, the workers and peasants burned Kolchak, Yudenich, Vrangel, Denikin, Pilsudskii, Petlyura, Chernov, Khots, Dan, Martov, and Abramovich . . . This year a revolution in Russia; next year—a world revolution!

And then, three days after the Nazis rolled triumphant and unimpeded into Paris, Samuil, Reuven, and their comrades, waving red rags and banners, rushed to the tracks near the Central Station to welcome the Soviet soldiers and tank drivers.

14

Riga was two cities the day the Soviets came. Samuil remembered marching and singing along Elizabetes Street while stony faces gazed down from the windows. Come another year, and these people would be in the streets offering bouquets to a different army.

How quickly it all happened, and how astounding it seemed, even when the tide was in your favor.

The morning after the Soviets arrived, posters and handbills appeared across the city. Edicts were announced and meetings convened. In a matter of days, nearly every outward sign of the old regime was eradicated. New names appeared on streets and institutions. Everything that Samuil had considered imposing and intransigent shrank meekly out of sight. The state police, who had for so long pursued and harassed him and his comrades, now themselves scuttled for cover. Usually, to no avail. Measures were taken to eliminate them. The streets were patrolled by new men in new uniforms.

As for him and Reuven, they joined up with the new militia, the Red Guard. Reuven was twenty-nine and Samuil was twenty-seven. Their revolutionary credentials were impeccable. For patrons, they had Schatz-Anin—installed as editor of a Yiddish newspaper—and

Eduards, who was appointed to a position within the Gorkom, the municipal government. Among their tasks, they were entrusted with converting Levitan's workshop, and others like it, into cooperatives. Politely, in measured tones, they explained to the proprietors how their lives and the lives of their workers would be improved. They went from shop to shop, moving purposefully through the streets, aware of the eyes that followed them and the conversations that died at their approach. The vulgar allure of power was very strong, but they did not succumb to its temptations. In all of their dealings, they were mindful of themselves as representatives of the Party. They were encouraged to imagine themselves as physicians, and the revolution as an organism, beset by toxins and contagions. Some toxins the organism could tolerate and neutralize; others were lethal. These had to be purged. And it was up to them, as the physicians, to distinguish between the mildly disruptive and the noxious, and to err on the side of caution.

In the first weeks after the arrival of the Soviets, there were very many physicians like themselves, circulating among the population, issuing diagnoses. Goods wagons were prepared at the railway station to expel the contaminants. Among them was their cousin Yaakov. Reuven had seen his name on a list. This, they both realized, was the test of their revolutionary mettle. Samuil remembered how they had discussed the matter between them. They decided that they would be committing no crime by telling their cousin what he was bound to learn anyway in short order. This way, at least, he would be able to prepare himself for the journey.

That evening, in front of their family, Reuven delivered the news. There were six of them in the apartment then, the girls having married and moved out.

It was hardly unexpected. Conspicuous class enemies like Vasserman had been rounded up. The Zionist organizations had burned their membership rosters—as though, even without the rosters, everything wasn't abundantly known.

Folding his hands on the kitchen table, their cousin said, What's the point in making a fuss? This is the nature of our times. Samuil and Reuven bet on one horse. I bet on another. My horse lost.

—Don't spout nonsense. What a fool you are, their uncle growled. And turning to Samuil and Reuven, he commanded: You two heroes of the revolution, go to your commissar and have him remove Yankl's name from the list.

—It's not possible, Reuven said.

—You have no idea what is possible, their uncle countered. You think these people are pure as the driven snow? I fought with them and I fought against them, remember. For a liter of spirits they would denounce their own mothers.

He removed his wedding band and held out his hand for his wife's. Their mother volunteered hers as well.

—Here, their uncle said, offer these. Tell them it's a contribution to the revolutionary cause.

—If we said that, we would be shot. And with good reason, Reuven said.

—Then I'll do it myself, their uncle said.

—Then you'll be shot. And Yankl will have to say kaddish for you on the train.

—Can't you do anything? their mother asked.

—We can help him pack.

Their cousin observed the conversation as if it involved someone who was not him.

—Monsters, their aunt hissed, we took you into our home!

—Mama, stop it, please, their cousin said, and moved to console her.

At that moment, Samuil had felt his resolve weaken. Sympathy grabbed him as if by the lapels and thrust him toward his family. It was possible that their uncle was right, and that a word from him or Reuven to the appropriate person could spare their cousin. The temptation was immense. Samuil knew that he had to master it. Not in great battles or debates was the fate of the revolution determined, but in moments like these. The revolution's success or failure depended upon thousands upon thousands of tiny, individual moral dilemmas. To resolve them properly, clearly, and bloodlessly was the challenge facing every Soviet person.

Samuil presumed that Reuven was waging the same battle and arriving at the same conclusion, but his brother looked at their uncle, aunt, and cousin and said, They will come for him tonight. If he's here, they'll grab him.

Nobody mistook his meaning.

—What's the use? Yaakov said. Where will I go? The Germans are one way, the Russians the other. And in the woods, the Aizsargi and other nationalists.

—Never mind that about the nationalists, their uncle said. I fought side by side with them in 1919. We embraced each other like brothers.

—It's no longer 1919, Yaakov said.

That evening, they helped him pack his things. Their mother and aunt stripped the shelves bare and also appealed to the neighbors for dried fruit, tinned fish, and bread. Samuil and Reuven made a bundle of their warmest clothes—a wool sweater, a hat, gloves, and Samuil's one pair of sturdy boots. Whatever money was in the house they turned over to Yaakov, much of it sewn into the lining of his summer jacket.

Once they were finished, nobody went to sleep. They sat and waited for the guards to arrive.

—I leave you my phonograph and records, Yaakov said to Reuven, and added wryly, Play them at your peril.

Around three in the morning they heard footfalls on the stairs and then the knock on the door. Two comrades, a man and a woman, vaguely familiar to Samuil, delivered the order. They showed no surprise to find everyone awake, and their quarry packed and ready to go. After a brief exchange, Reuven succeeded in gaining their permission to accompany Yaakov to the rail depot.

—He is ours; we will take him, Reuven said.

That night, as the first tint of color seeped into the sky, they drew up to the railway depot, where the goods wagons stood waiting. Even before they reached the site they heard the susurrus of countless, unintelligible voices. At the depot, they saw a horde of thousands, massed together in disarray. Dozens of armed NKVD guards and members of the local Communist militia encircled them. Occasionally, there was the bark of an order. Samuil and Reuven watched carefully to make sure that their mother, aunt, or uncle did not get lumped together with the condemned. Samuil knew it could easily happen. There were, among the thousands, many women, children, and old people. If one looked, one could find many mild and careworn faces. The uninitiated might presume them to be innocent. Their cousin also appeared mild and innocent, yet he was a Zionist, a dangerous element. The same applied to the others. Latvian nationalists, capitalists, bourgeoisie, members of the former government, priests, rabbis, Hebrew teachers: every one a potential threat.

Because their aunt and uncle refused to leave while the train remained in the station, Samuil, Reuven, and their mother also stayed. They lost sight of Yaakov immediately after he took leave of his parents, and they didn't see him again until shortly before the train was set to move. As people were being forced up into the wagons, there was a loud confrontation at one of the doors. Samuil looked over in time to see Vasserman protesting something to an NKVD officer. Swinging his rifle butt, the officer knocked Vasserman down. Standing beside the fallen Vasserman was Yaakov. Samuil watched his cousin help Vasserman to his feet, and then into the wagon. When Vasserman was on board, Yaakov pulled himself up behind him. The NKVD officer bolted the door and Samuil never saw his cousin again.

15

On her first day at work, Giovanni and Carla, his wife, gave her posterboard and multicolored markers and gestured at the assorted merchandise. She composed signs in Russian and arranged them in the window display. That same afternoon she made her first sale to a young man from Mogilev. He and his wife came into the shop and wandered cautiously between the narrow aisles.

—His whole life he's had one dream, the wife said.

—A brown suede blazer, the man said.

Polina barely knew her way around the store, but she found a rack of suede blazers, some of which were brown, and one of which fit the man from Mogilev. They went through the motions of haggling; Polina conferred with Giovanni and Carla; the Italians wrote a figure on a piece of paper; and the man from Mogilev realized his life's ambition.

—That's it, now he can die, his wife said.

—If I die, bury me in it, he said.

She made her second sale not long after to an older Italian man, squarely built, dressed like a laborer. Carla greeted him familiarly and Giovanni saluted him from behind the cash register, but the man explained that he wished to speak with Polina. Polina didn't immediately understand what was being asked of her. There was an uncomfortable moment when everyone seemed ill at ease, but then the man addressed Polina in Russian and relieved the tension. He apologized for imposing upon her, and for his shaky Russian. Twenty-five years earlier he had been a university student in Leningrad. Since then, he'd had few opportunities to practice the language.

—I was there a long time ago, the man said. I was there when Stalin died.

He recalled the ranks of people in the street, old women and schoolchildren in tears. For the modest privilege of speaking to her in Russian, the man bought a belt and a pair of sandals.

Before he left, the man shook hands firmly with Giovanni, and Polina noticed two things that had previously escaped her. One was the collage of photographs and newspaper clippings that Giovanni had tacked onto the wall behind the cash register: a posed photo of a soccer team, above a small maroon and orange banner; newspaper clippings showing the faces of smiling men, whom Polina took to be politicians; other clippings showing grainy snapshots of younger men, whom Polina took to be either criminals or victims; and framed portraits of historical eminences. Of all these, Polina recognized only MarxEngels, the stern two-headed deity of her girlhood imagination.

The other thing Polina noticed was that the outer three fingers on Giovanni's right hand were misshapen, as from an industrial accident.

Back at the apartment, when she mentioned these things to Lyova, he explained that Giovanni and Carla were active in the Italian Communist Party. Communists and merchants—in Italy, the two were not mutually exclusive.

About his fingers, Giovanni told her himself. After she had worked at the store for several weeks, he saw her looking at his hand; he lifted it, turned it back to palm, and declared, *Fascisti*.

There was no other talk of politics. The Russian signs in the window drew people; others came from word of mouth. Polina and her employers settled into a comfortable rhythm. The hours blended together. She felt a contentment she hadn't known in a long time. Walking to and from work, she seemed for the first time to see the city. Details came to her peripherally, when she wasn't looking. Now when she came home she told Alec about a marble hand incorporated into the brickwork of a wall in San Lorenzo, or the statue of a king tucked under a palm tree in the Giardini Quirinale, or the graffiti on the store facing theirs that read *Hitler Per Mille Anni*.

16

After a day at the briefing department, Alec would also come home and recount one or another of the day's oddities for Polina and Lyova. One was a story about the man from Cherepovets who'd arrived with his wife and young daughter during a thunderstorm. As soon as they'd been assigned to their room, the man had gone in search of a HIAS representative. In the corridor, he'd stopped Alec. He insisted that he had to go immediately to the U.S. embassy because he had highly sensitive information to impart. Outside, the rain was coming down in torrents. Not bothering with an umbrella, the man raced out into the street, Alec trailing after him, calling out which way he should turn. By the time they reached Via Veneto, the man was drenched, his eyes glaring urgently, and his scalp, through sparse black hair, showing obscenely white. He looked like a lunatic, which explained why the marines held him at the door, one of them drawing his club. Alec did his best to speak for the man, but the marines cut him off. The sergeant lifted the receiver from his desk, and then they hustled the man upstairs. Three hours later, he emerged: dry, his hair combed, and with an American flag pin on his collar.

Another time, a commotion had erupted in the pensione after the arrival of a new batch of émigrés. Members of the briefing department hurried over to quell the uproar. At the door to one of the rooms, an old woman was shrieking at her neighbors—an elderly couple. The angry woman's adult son and daughter tried to calm her, but to little effect. Remarkably, it turned out that the old man was the woman's errant husband and the father of her now grown children. During the war, this man had been wounded at the front and discharged. At the time, his wife and two young children, having wisely evacuated from the Ukraine, were living in a kolkhoz in Uzbekistan. The man traveled there to reunite with them. Also living in the kolkhoz was the wife's cousin and her family. Depending on which version one believed, either the cousin seduced the husband or the husband seduced the cousin. Either way, the result was the same. One night, the two lovers vanished. They disappeared into the vastness of the Soviet Union, not to be heard from again. Until now, when, after all these years, fate had conspired to make them neighbors in a Roman pensione.

A different kind of story involved a fat man from Lvov traveling with his wife and teenage son, also fat. Upon their settlement into the pensione, the father drew Alec's colleague, the myopic Oleg, into his confidence and asked how he might avail himself of the services of a reliable surgeon. In Lvov the man had flourished in the underground economy. When it came time to leave, he had been unable to find a means to transport his valuables abroad. Everyone had heard accounts of sealed railcars loaded with expensive goods, and of the astronomical bribes paid to high-ranking border officials. But he had failed to get to the right people. Desperate for a solution, he'd converted a great proportion of his wealth into gemstones and rich foods. In the year leading up to their departure he had himself, his wife, and his son on a strict regimen of eating. He gained forty kilos. His wife and son also put on a lot of weight. When they'd all attained a satisfactory size, a surgeon creatively implanted diamonds and rubies into their bodies. For the man and his son, he made incisions that mimicked appendectomies. For the wife, he created a caesarian scar. Now that they were safely in Rome, they needed someone to cut them open so that they could retrieve their fortune.

—It reminds me of something I read in Josefus, Lyova said when Alec told the story.

Besieged from without by Romans and their Arab allies, robbed, starved, and persecuted from within by rival Jewish gangs, scores of ordinary citizens had tried to escape the city. A small minority swallowed gold coins so as to avoid detection by the Jewish guards. One, who made it to the Syrian camp, was found picking coins out of his stool. A rumor spread through the Arab and Syrian camps that Jews were leaving the city stuffed with gold. Immediately, the Arabs and Syrians took to slaughtering the refugees and searching their bowels.

—A story like that makes you sentimental for the gentleness of the Soviet border guards, Lyova said.

—We crossed at Chop, Alec said. Not to get into specifics, but those bastards did everything except slice us open.

—Yes? Lyova said. And did they find anything?

—The same thing they'd find if they searched me yesterday or today, Alec said.

The crossing at Chop remained a sore point, one that Alec avoided bringing up. Unlike nearly all other emigrants from Riga, they had had to cross there instead of at Brest.

Rosa maintained that no comparable horror could have existed at Brest, but Alec had met any number of people who believed that what they had witnessed there was the height of savagery. A man, traveling with his wife and invalid son, described how an inspector had demanded the boy's prosthetic arm and, in an ostensible search for contraband, splintered it with a hammer. He heard about monsters who interrogated and terrified small children. He heard of an incident involving an old man who'd been denied access to the lavatory, and who'd soiled himself and then sat for hours in his own filth. And recently a woman had described how her son had been detained by the Brest customs agents, roughly handled, and then beaten by the police. Alec had gotten to talking with the woman after he'd taken note of her and her two children at the orientation meeting. Out of every group of new arrivals there were invariably some who caught his attention. Typically, these were attractive girls and women. He gravitated to them and offered his assistance. He wouldn't have said that it was because he had an ulterior motive, but simply because he saw no reason to repress a natural inclination. No matter how bad life got, the presence of a beautiful woman made it impossible to despair completely. Even Christ, in his crucified agony, had had the solace of Mary Magdalene's face, which—if the devotional paintings could be trusted—hadn't been bad to look at.

But beauty didn't decide all. In the case of this woman and her children, Alec had been acutely conscious of them while he delivered his rote orientation speech. Would someone else have been quite so drawn to the truculent hoodlum and the dark-haired girl at his side, with the dramatic, arched eyebrows and large, coltish eyes? As he spoke she played a game in which she sought his gaze, peevishly dismissed it, and then commanded it again.

They were from Minsk, the mother said. It was the three of them traveling together. She was a widow. Her husband had died when the children were still small. The children now appeared to be in their early twenties. The girl introduced herself as Masha, and her brother appraised Alec stonily and gave his name as Dmitri. Given Dmitri's appearance, Alec wasn't at all surprised that he'd been detained by the customs agents and then beaten by the police. Like those of Minka, Iza's albino friend, Dmitri's hands and neck were festooned with prison markings. It looked like he'd spent a fair portion of his young life behind bars. Alec had noticed that men like him passed through the halls of HIAS in no small number. The Soviet authorities had been only too happy to clear the jails and prisons of Jewish criminals. The unambiguous message from the Kremlin to the Knesset was: *You want Jews? Here, take these.*

Efforts were made to divert some of the convicts to places other than Israel. To spread out the criminal element. The criminals were usually more than happy to comply; the immigration offices less so.

It wasn't easy to get the criminals past the interview process. Short of wearing gloves, there was no way for them to conceal their ring tattoos, and one glimpse at these was usually enough to settle the issue.

—We would like to go to Boston, said the mother, who gave her name as Riva Davidovna Horvitz.

She was a lean, dark-complexioned woman, once appealing, Alec supposed. Now she had the severity of a person who had been marked by misfortune and did not wish to conceal it.

While Riva spoke about the rigors of their emigration, Alec found himself constructing fantasies and stratagems about her daughter. Masha had elicited in him the same feeling he'd had when he first saw Olya on Karl Marx Street. In the intervening years, for all his conquests, he'd rarely had that feeling again. There were very few women who possessed perpetual mystery—who revealed less than they knew and remained, at some level, mysterious even to themselves. Occasionally, Alec saw a woman and suspected that she was of this type, only to discover that he'd been mistaken. But there was something about Masha that compelled him. She looked to have what Olya had had—beauty like a long blade, carelessly held.

Polina's allure had been altogether different, she had been like the still point at the center of a gyre. He'd seen her, day after day at her desk in the technology department. Beside her was a stern old matron. Every time Alec thought to approach Polina the matron had been at her side, discouraging him with castrating looks. For at least a month he contemplated ways to breach the system of defense and get to Polina. At first, he wanted only a few words, just to see if he could elicit a smile. That was all. Nothing more. Just for a start.

Then finally, the afternoon he approached her with Karl in tow, her sentinel had vacated her post. Alec had made his silly, brash proposition, and succeeded in getting Polina to join them for a drink. She'd said little that evening; she'd let Alec entertain her. After she finished her drink, she discreetly checked her watch and rose to say goodbye.

—You can't leave yet, Alec had said.

—I can't? Polina had asked as if allowing that there might be substance behind Alec's words.

Alec had looked up at her from his place at the circular café table, hardly big enough to accommodate their glasses and ashtray.

—You see, Karl said, my brother can't bear to have a woman leave until she's confessed that she thinks he's the most desirable man on earth.

—Do many women say that? Polina asked.

—Surprisingly, Karl said.

—Or not, Alec offered.

—So this is the reason I can't leave?

—Only if you think it's a good reason, Alec said.

—Honestly speaking, I don't, Polina said.

—Then it isn't.

—So what is?

—There are many. Very important ones. To list them all would take some time. Please sit and I'll buy you another drink.

—Your reason to stay is to hear the reasons to stay? Polina asked.

—Not good enough?

She had gone home that night, but Alec had perceived an opening. Not long after the evening with Karl, on the day of the annual Readiness for Labor and Defense Exercises, Alec had finagled his way into Polina's group. The testing was done according to department, but Alec, in part because of his father's status, but mainly on account of his own gregariousness, moved fluidly throughout the plant. It raised no eyebrows when his name was included with those of the technology department. Broadly speaking, nobody cared about any of the official and procedural events. Celebrate the workers on the anniversary of the Revolution? Why not? Honor the Red Army on Red Army Day? Who could object? Either was a good excuse to avoid work. Lenin's birthday? Stalin's first tooth? Brezhnev's colonoscopy? Each merited a drink, a few snacks, and maybe a slice of cake. So, too, the Labor and Defense Exercises—only with less drinking and without the cake.

The morning of the exercises, Alec took his place among the

young workers of the technology and transistor radio engineering departments. Dressed in tracksuits and running shoes, they crossed the street from the plant proper to the site of the VEF sports stadium and target range. At the range, .22-caliber rifles awaited them, having already been retrieved from the armory. Members of VEF's athletic department—the trainers and coaches of the factory's various sports teams—had already prepared the field for the shot put, the long jump, the high jump, and for the short-distance footraces. The trainers and coaches roamed about with their stopwatches, measuring tapes, and the lists of the norms that had to be met. Somewhere, presumably in the Kremlin, a physical culture expert had determined the basal fitness level young Soviet workers needed to possess to establish their superiority over the Americans and the Red Chinese. Should these foes come spilling across the borders, they would encounter a daunting column ready to repulse them with heroic displays of running, jumping, shot putting, and small-arms fire.

Before the start of the events, Alec sought Polina out and tried to strike a bargain with her. He told her that he wanted to see her again.

—You're seeing me now, Polina said.

—One more evening, Alec said. All I ask. In the scheme of a life, what's one evening?

—Depends who you spend it with.

—A valid point, Alec said.

To reach the decision, Alec proposed a contest. If he scored better at the rifle range, Polina would grant him another evening; if she scored better, he would leave her in peace. Perhaps because she was beguiled by the prospect of a game, Polina agreed.

—I should warn you in advance, Alec said. Last summer, in the officers' training rotation, I placed eighth in marksmanship.

—Out of how many? Polina asked.

—Sixteen, Alec said.

—That doesn't sound very good, Polina said.

—No, it doesn't, Alec said. That's the idea.

—I don't understand, Polina said.

—Well, I was specifically trying for eighth place.

—Why is that?

—In the army, it's best to be somewhere in the middle. Trouble usually finds those at the bottom or at the top.

—So you mean to say that you're a good shot?

—Eighth place, Alec said.

—In that case, I should tell you that last year at Readiness for Labor and Defense, I finished second in my department. They awarded me a ribbon and printed my name in the factory newspaper. My husband pasted a copy of it into an album.

Alec noticed that Polina didn't brandish the word "husband" like a cudgel. She seemed to place the same emphasis on "husband" as she did on "ribbon" or "album." But Alec wasn't fool enough to believe that she'd included the word innocently. In a sense, since she hadn't unequivocally rebuffed Alec, anything she said about her husband verged on betrayal. Any information Alec had about him was information he could use against him. For instance, the fact that he was the kind of man who would preserve something printed in the factory's idiotic newspaper. Then again, it was possible that Polina found such a gesture endearing. It could be that she was implying that this was precisely the kind of man she wanted. A man unlike Alec, who, in his ironical sophistication, couldn't hope to access or appreciate such pure, sentimental feeling.

But whatever she meant, she'd tacitly agreed to the contest.

Refereeing the shooting range was Volodya Zobodkin, one of the company of young Jews with whom Alec and Karl played soccer on the beach at Majori. Zobodkin, like Iza Judo, was a graduate of the Institute of Sport, and now he coached the VEF soccer club. When Volodya distributed the rifles, Alec asked if he could get one with a reliable sight.

—Who are you, Zaitsev? Volodya chided. This isn't the Battle of Stalingrad. Just aim in the general direction of the target.

—Do you have one with an adjusted sight or not? Alec persisted.

—What's with you? Volodya asked. Have you been drinking? It's not even lunch.

Without much elaboration, Alec told Volodya what he'd arranged. Volodya glanced quickly at Polina, raised an approving eyebrow, and sorted through the stack of rifles for something suitable. He handed a rifle to Alec and then offered to find another, grossly inferior one, for Polina.

—There's one here that practically shoots sideways, Volodya said.

But that wasn't the kind of contest Alec wanted, largely because he sensed it wasn't the kind of contest Polina would accept. She seemed like the type who respected rules, including rules that dictated the breaking of other rules.

Alec shot first. For all his pride at having placed eighth, Alec had to admit that he couldn't compare the effort required to achieve mediocrity to that required to achieve excellence. Everything naturally flowed toward mediocrity; for this the world needed little in the way of your cooperation. Whereas total incompetence or extreme proficiency demanded some application.

To his credit and mild surprise, Alec shot well. Volodya called for cease-fire and presented Alec with his perforated target, a cluster of holes grouped reasonably close together, reasonably close to the bull's-eye. Even if Polina shot better, Alec felt that he'd performed well enough to warrant the date.

—Is this how you shot in the army? Polina asked.

—I've never shot so well in my life, Alec said. But then I've never had such motivation. As my teachers used to write in my school reports: Alec is personable and shows signs of intelligence, but is lazy, inattentive, and lacks all motivation.

For the sake of equity, Polina shot with the same rifle Alec had used. Alec watched her assume the prone position and take careful aim, the rifle's stock pressed correctly against her cheek, its butt in the crook of her shoulder. As she shot, Alec stood behind and slightly to the side and used the opportunity to evaluate her in a way he hadn't been able to before. Unchallenged, he let his eyes linger on her small lobeless ear, the creases at the corner of her squeezed-shut eye, the strong, sculpted tendons of her neck, and the fine symmetry of her profile. He watched her shoot with steady regularity, squeezing off a shot and then sliding the bolt to chamber the next round. It looked to Alec as though she were shooting to win, which he couldn't but construe as a bad sign.

Later, when things between them were better defined, Polina explained that she had shot the way she did not because she wanted to avoid seeing him again but because she couldn't perform otherwise.

—The graveyards and songbooks are full of people like you, Alec had remarked, a fact she had not disputed.

After Polina had finished shooting, Volodya collected her target and compared it against Alec's. Polina had shot well, but there was no doubt that Alec had shot better.

—Imagine that, Alec said, feigning bashfulness.

—Maybe it's not too late, Polina said. You could still make general.

—There's a disturbing thought, Alec said.

After this they ran, jumped, hurled the shot put, and killed time until the exercises were finished. As Alec was leaving the stadium, Volodya caught up to him and congratulated him again on his great triumph. He wanted to inform Alec that his shooting performance had earned him more than the date with Polina. It had earned him first place overall. As the top shooter, Volodya explained, Alec would be in line for a commendation as a Voroshilov marksman, and this would include official recognition at the Young Communists meeting and special mention in the factory newspaper.

—Come on, Vovka, Alec said, don't spoil the day for me. Write I came in eighth and give the honor to some other schmuck.

—Next in line is your girl, Volodya said.

—Perfect, Alec said. Her husband likes to paste articles from the factory newspaper.

The following week, when Polina's name was printed, an acquaintance spotted it and told Maxim. As before, he asked for a copy.

Polina described to Alec how she'd had to watch Maxim paste the silly article into the album. If only he weren't so foolish, Polina had told Alec, which he took as no ringing endorsement of his own appeal as a lover. But Polina always spoke plainly. If only Maxim weren't so foolish, she'd said, she would have remained faithful to him, never taken up with Alec, and lived a regular, quiet life.

17

I t was at the front that Samuil had become aware of the intersection between the dreamlife of the living and the afterlife of the dead. When he stole a few minutes of sleep under an artillery barrage, his fallen comrades had visited him. Later, when he had abandoned all hope of seeing his mother, uncle, and aunt alive again, they appeared too. For a time he couldn't sleep without encountering their ghosts. After he'd received notice of Reuven's death, he couldn't close his eyes without meeting his brother. In these dreams, Reuven was sometimes whole, the way he'd been when Samuil saw him last; other times he was disfigured, wounded in the legs or with a shattered face. But no matter what shape he was in, his brother seemed calm, at peace, either unmoved by or unaware of the fact that he was no longer among the living. Nights Reuven or his mother failed to materialize, Samuil felt disconsolate. To think that he would never see them again, not even in his dreams, filled him with sadness and apathy. He had known better than to share these feelings. He'd seen many of his fellow soldiers succumb to the same bleak and despondent feelings. These were men who'd received bad news in the field post—confirmation of a relative's death or of a wife's inconstancy. He saw his comrades mutilate themselves, commit suicidal acts in combat, attempt desertion, and make defeatist, ill-conceived statements. More than once Samuil referred these offenders to the NKVD and the military tribunals, having no illusion about the fate to which he'd consigned them.

Now again, all these years later, Samuil found himself regularly visited by his mother and his brother in his dreams. The dreams were like a precious gift and Samuil knew that if he spoke about them it would only cheapen them. Sometimes his mother and brother appeared as they had been when they died, still young. Other times, his mother and brother appeared as if they, too, had aged in the intervening years, looking nothing like themselves and yet remaining somehow intrinsically themselves. The one constant in all the dreams was that Samuil himself never varied. He was always an old man.

When Samuil started writing the account of his life, it hadn't occurred to him that this concerted effort at remembering would summon his mother and brother back into his dreams. In many ways, the project no longer resembled the original design. It had become an excuse to immerse himself in the past. There were certain things he wrote down, things that he felt suited the original purpose, but there were many other things that he didn't write down. These things he simply turned over in his mind.

He thought of Emma's grandfather as he'd been in his waning days. Samuil and Emma were then newly married. They were living with Emma's parents in the small Latgalian town of Baltinava. Emma's father, Yasha Aronovich, a formidable military man, had been posted there to impose order. Aizsargi, collaborators, Hitlerites, Latvian nationalist rabble camped in the forests, defying Soviet power. Samuil served under his father-in-law, patrolling the streets, fielding denunciations, and leading troops into the forest to flush out the bandits. Meanwhile, Emma's grandfather, Aron Moiseivich, her father's father, spent his days at home. Samuil would return in the evening to find him exactly as he'd been in the morning. It seemed that he did nothing but gaze off into space. What are you doing?

Samuil had once stopped to ask. Old Aron had languidly turned his head and replied with one word, Remembering.

How sad, Samuil had thought at the time. What a dreary existence. And now that he'd arrived there himself, he saw that he'd been wrong. Everyone and everything was in the past, his entire life, bustling and crowded with people whom he wished to meet again. What he wouldn't give just to speak once more to even the supporting players. To see in the flesh a man like Zachar Kahn, Hirsh Kogan, his cousin Yankl, or even Baruch Levitan. How had it happened that the people in the past, all long dead, now seemed to him to be the real people, and the people in the present, including his own children, seemed to him evanescent, so nearly figments that he could imagine passing his hand through them?

Still and all, the present wouldn't leave him be. Daily it interrupted his excursions into the past. Always, it seemed, with a new annoyance.

Under the influence of the Lubavitch rabbi whom his wife so adored, she and Rosa had taken to lighting candles of a Friday night. The rabbi had provided them with a set of flimsy tin candlesticks, a box of ceremonial candles, and a sheet of paper upon which were printed out, phonetically in Russian, the words to the appropriate prayers. Neither his wife nor Rosa understood a syllable of what they were saying, but they gibbered on anyway. The rabbi and his local accomplices also distributed, free of charge, a challah bread and a bottle of kosher wine to complete the spectacle. At first Emma had made the tentative overture to Samuil, but he had categorically refused. She then went down the ladder to Karl. If he was home when the sun set, Karl, for the sake of domestic harmony, consented to wear the yarmulke and mumble the *Boruch atohs* off the sheet of paper. But if Karl wasn't there to oblige, Emma and Rosa conscripted the boys.

—Perfect little yeshiva *bochers*, Samuil observed.

—And what would you have them be? Rosa countered.

She had already gotten them into the traditional costumes. She'd

outfitted them with little tzitzis so the fringes peeked out from un-
der their shirts, and with black yarmulkes, too big for their heads.
Eagerly, in their singsong voices, his grandsons chirped away in
Hebrew, and turned back two generations of social progress.

—Why stop at the bread and the wine? Samuil said. There are
more blessings. There are blessings for everything. God forbid you
should skip any.

—If you know them, by all means.

—That train left long ago.

—Very well, Rosa said. We're doing what we can. We're only just
learning. Look at your Soviet Union. Sixty years and they're still
building communism.

—Some are building; others are wrecking. Then there are those
who will say anything for the price of a kosher chicken.

Rosa turned to her dinner and knocked her cutlery emphatically
against her plate. I do what's best for my children, she said.

—You set a fine example, indeed, Samuil retorted.

—You disapprove, Samuil Leyzerovich, but you have no trouble
eating.

—My dear, these days I have trouble with everything from the
moment I open my eyes. What would you suggest I do?

Everyone had passed the medical examinations except for
Samuil. The Italian doctor hadn't failed to note Samuil's elevated
blood pressure, his arthritic back, the shrapnel wounds to his shoulder and side, and the scarring in his lungs from the tuberculosis he'd
contracted either from his uncle or at boot camp in 1941. His passport gave his age as sixty-five, but his time at the front had added at
least another decade. Soldiers in their twenties went gray in a matter of days. Sometimes, it seemed, overnight. Only those who fell
immediately died young. In the end, Samuil believed, fast or slow,
the war took them all.

—Your son works for HIAS, Roidman had said when Samuil told
him what had transpired. In his position, I'm sure he can find a
route.

—You don't know my son, Samuil said.

—So what will you do?

—It's of no consequence to me. My existence will be the same wherever we go. But my sons have become fixated on Canada. Two months ago they hadn't even considered it, and now they've convinced themselves that it is the only place on earth. And, if not for me, they could be there tomorrow. Naturally, they've forgotten that they started this mess. They did this to their father and now he is a weight around their necks.

—I'm certain it will turn out for the best, Roidman said.

—On what do you base this certainty? Samuil asked.

—On nothing, Roidman said, his eyes twinkling. I'm an optimist. A short, old, one-legged, stateless Jewish optimist.

Roidman did look particularly optimistic that morning. Under his blue blazer he wore a freshly laundered shirt. There was a smart crease in his trousers, and the fold at his missing leg was neatly and precisely pinned. Over his left breast gleamed every one of his medals and ribbons.

The occasion, Roidman explained, was a trip he was making into Rome.

—An immigration interview? Samuil presumed.

—Bigger, Roidman said, rising with the word. Recently they held the funeral for the old pope, *alav hasholem*. Today, they crown the new one. As your son said, many important people will attend. Mondale with Carter's wife. The king of Spain. Waldheim of the United Nations. The duke of Luxembourg. And our friend Trudeau. I want to see if he will recognize me.

—Trudeau?

—Who else? From the crowd I will wave with my crutch. "Pierre, I am here; it is me, Josef Roidman. Perhaps you remember my case?"

—You're an unusual man, Josef.

—These are unusual times.

And when had the times not been unusual? Samuil wanted to say. But he could see that Roidman was eager to get to his train station and his funeral.

Only in the summer of 1940, when the Soviets annexed Latvia, had he thought that the world was getting sorted out. Caught up in the spirit of the times, he and Reuven had assumed noms de guerre. In their new Soviet passports they were no longer Eisner but Krasnansky, the name chosen by Reuven because of its evocation of the Communist color.

—The Krasnanskys make the revolutions but the Eisners pay the bills, their uncle had sneered.

Within the Party they were trusted and respected, but at home they were held in contempt. Their uncle and aunt wouldn't look them in the face, and their cousins spurned them. They never forgave them for Yankl.

—Explain to me Ribbentrop-Molotov, their uncle said. Has Hitler stopped using your Communists for target practice?

—There are higher considerations that we do not understand, Samuil said, though he had asked almost exactly the same question at a Party meeting.

—It is a painful sacrifice, Reuven said, but Stalin has a plan. It is possible that the fascist invasion of the capitalist countries will inspire the masses to rise up.

—If you believe in such nonsense, Hitler will be on our doorstep tomorrow, their uncle said.

Samuil had thought their uncle a fool. Then, one Sunday, they attended a regular meeting of the Komsomol, where a Red Army major informed them that Hitler and his fascist vermin had, that very morning, mounted an unprovoked attack upon the peaceful citizens of the Soviet Union. The shameless, cowardly enemy had advanced into eastern Poland and was pressing the offensive into the Baltic republics. The German gains, the major assured, were temporary, the result of their criminal and underhanded tactics. In a matter of days, the forces of the Red Army would counterattack and force the enemy to retreat. Nevertheless, preparations needed to be made for the defense of the city.

That same night he and Reuven were each issued a rifle and a box of rounds, and posted to guard the entrance to the rail bridge over the Daugava.

Samuil remembered well the oddity of their assignment. He and Reuven stood at the mouth of the railroad bridge, the broad, unperturbable Daugava flowing beneath them, and wondered what they might do should the enemy appear.

—Two men with rifles cannot hope to do much against the German army, Reuven said.

—Then why put us here?

—There are always the local saboteurs, Reuven proposed.

They remained at their post for the next three days, during which an unaccountable calm reigned over the city. These were the last easeful hours he spent with his brother, the two of them reclining against the girders of the bridge, smoking cigarettes, watching the trains pass and the men fish on the banks of the river below. Even the weather was calm. Members of the Workers' Guard were deployed at crucial positions, but otherwise the city's inhabitants continued about their business. On the second day, when the Germans were reported to have taken Vilnius and surrounded Liepaja, Samuil saw the first columns of evacuees trickling east. On the third night, the government made the drastic decision to relocate to the border with Estonia. And the next day, the commander in charge of their Workers' Guard company ordered them to undertake a more mobile defense.

Walking home they saw, in the more affluent neighborhoods in the center of town, people loading automobiles and hired carts for the evacuation. Among them were many Jews, racing about in a state of agitation. In Moskovskaya, windows and doors were thrown open, and people lowered their belongings onto the street. Elderly men and women sat among the bedding and the battered household items, keeping a lookout for thieves.

At home, they discovered their mother, uncle, and aunt pretending that nothing out of the ordinary was happening. Their uncle was sitting at the window, skeptically watching the havoc below. Their aunt was sweeping the kitchen floor, and their mother was sewing a button onto one of their uncle's shirts. When Samuil and Reuven came through the door only their mother looked up with a penitent expression.

Reuven inquired why they'd done nothing to prepare for evacuation.

—Because we have no intention to evacuate, their uncle said.

—The Germans could be here tomorrow, Reuven said.

—We had Germans in 1919, their uncle said. They behaved better than your Communists.

—Have you heard nothing about Hitler?

—I've heard, their uncle said. He's no friend to the Jews, but it's the Bolsheviks he's after. Everybody who knows me knows how I feel about the Bolsheviks.

Their aunt looked up from her sweeping and said, How can we leave? If we go off into God-knows-where, how will Yankl ever find us?

Their own mother, Samuil still believed, had remained as recompense for Yankl.

—Boys, their mother said. Even if he wanted to go, your uncle, in his condition, could not survive such a trip. And if he stays, I must stay also. The girls have their families and your aunt could not manage to care for your uncle on her own. They need me.

—They, and we? Reuven asked.

Reuven had been thirty years old then, but he had spoken the words as if he were a child.

He and Reuven should have dragged her from that apartment, forced her to go at the points of their rifles. Anything they would have done would have been justified. The condemnation never left him: he had not done enough to save his mother's life.

That same night they boarded trucks that drove them east to Gulbene. They traveled with the other members of their Workers' Guard company and also Eduards and his family.

From Gulbene they proceeded on foot, mixed among the columns of dazed and exhausted refugees. Some had already been walking for days, sleeping in the fields, eating whatever they could scrounge.

Without warning, as if for sport, German aircraft would bombard the road. People would scatter and throw themselves into ditches and furrows. When the danger passed, a feral howling would arise from those who discovered their own among the dead and the dying.

The next morning, they reached the Russian border. Several NKVD officers, mounted on horseback, trotted past in a summary inspection. At the border, a cordon of NKVD soldiers passed swift judgment. A clutch of suspects waited under armed guard beside the wooden border station. Others knelt before the NKVD, pleading not to be turned back.

When his and Reuven's turn came, they presented their documents to the NKVD guard, an older man, easily in his forties, heavyset, with grease stains on the front of his tunic.

—We are Communists, Reuven said, members of the Workers' Guard.

Reuven's Russian, like Samuil's, had remained close to fluent, accented only faintly with Yiddish and Latvian.

—Where from? the guard asked.

—Riga.

—How did you come here?

—A truck to Gulbene. On foot from there.

—You walked with these people?

—Yes, Reuven said.

—They say they were attacked by German aircraft. You see any German aircraft?

—We saw.

—Show me your rifles, the guard said.

They handed over their rifles and the guard peered into the barrels and sniffed the muzzles. He opened the actions and inspected the chambers.

—You have ammunition? he asked.

—What we were issued in Riga, Reuven said, and he extended the box of shells they'd been given to protect the bridge.

—You too, the guard said, and Samuil did the same.

He opened the boxes and counted the rounds.

—All there, he said disdainfully.

—Yes, Reuven admitted.

—You call yourselves Communists, the guard sneered, but you let the German motherfuckers strafe defenseless people without firing a single shot. Who behaves like this? Not Communists, I assure you.

He leveled his revolver at them and pointed in the direction of the border station, to join the others under armed guard.

—Soon enough, we will find out who you really are, he said.

They took their places with the other suspects and waited for several hours. Intermittently, an NKVD officer would select a half dozen men and lead them into a little copse behind the border station. Short moments later there would come a volley of rifle fire.

Samuil understood that the jaws of death had opened to consume them, and would have consumed them if not for Eduards's intervention. They were at the front of the line, with one foot in the other world, when he came running to the NKVD officer, waving his Party card, his Gorkom identification, and a personal letter he'd once received from Litvinov.

They evaded death again the next morning, or so Eduards contended, when they leaped from the back of an open troop truck. They had boarded the truck in Pskov with Eduards, his family, and some fifteen others. Several kilometers from the border, Eduards saw the driver wave his hat at an NKVD colonel parked by the side of the road in an Emka staff car.

—Jump now! Eduards had commanded.

They'd jumped and the truck had rattled on without them.

Later that same evening he and Reuven evaded death together for the last time. Stukas and Messers dropped from the setting sun and tore up the road. They took cover in a cherry orchard, and watched through the ripening fruit as the planes skimmed so low overhead that they could see the faces of the German pilots. When the attack ended, a convoy of trucks appeared and there was a frenzied call for men to board. Red Army soldiers rushed about, forcing men into the trucks, and in the twilight and the commotion Samuil was pressed into one vehicle and Reuven into another. It happened in an instant. Samuil supposed that they were all destined for the same place, but at some point during the night his truck went one way and Reuven's went another.

18

One afternoon in late August, on his way home from picketing the Israeli embassy, Lyova witnessed the election of the new pope. After five hours of circular and monotonous marching, he'd stopped and set his sign down at the edge of St. Peter's square.

—Looked like a nice fellow, Lyova said. You could almost imagine that Jesus Christ himself had had a hand in his election.

They decided that they would go to see his inauguration, scheduled for the following week.

—You still expect to be here? Alec asked.

—Unfortunately, I've no reason to expect otherwise, Lyova said.

—No action at the embassy?

—Some Italian Communists showed up with anti-Zionist placards and offered to march in solidarity. We nearly came to blows. Despite what some people say, I still have my limits. I'm not so far gone yet that I'll join up with a bunch of idiots who get a sexual thrill from shouting, *Zionism is racism!*

—What happened to your enemy's enemy?

—Sometimes your enemy's enemy is still your enemy. Incidentally, this is how my late grandmother used to refer to me and my sister. It was how she explained her boundless love. *Do you know how come Grandmother loves you so much? How come, Grandmother? Because you're the enemy of Grandmother's enemy.*

—And the enemy?

—My mother.

—Her daughter-in-law?

—No, daughter. They were very close, but always arguing. You've never heard it phrased this way? I always thought it was commonplace. It's how my mother now refers to my son.

At the mention of his son, Lyova grew morose. He was so often hustling, clowning, and crusading that Alec had assumed he was unaffected by the kind of loneliness and melancholy one would expect in a man who hadn't seen his wife and son in more than a year. After all, as Polina hadn't failed to point out, nothing tangible was stopping him from boarding a plane to Tel Aviv. That he chose not to do this suggested that he preferred the life he was leading in Rome. It occurred to Alec, not for the first time, that he had completely misread someone. At that moment, Lyova seemed to be defined precisely by the feelings to which Alec had believed him to be impervious.

As Lyova brooded, Alec's mind turned to Masha. He wondered what Masha would have made of Lyova in his state. Just as he'd wondered moments earlier if she'd have been amused by their conversation. Ever since he'd first seen her at the orientation he pictured her presiding in some upper gallery of his mind. He performed for her delectation. He noticed things he would have otherwise ignored, and saw with fresh eyes what was familiar to him.

Though who she was and what she really thought about anything, Alec had no idea. He'd seen her only twice. Once during the orientation and once more in the lobby of the pensione. Both times he had been under the scrutiny of Masha's mother and brother. A powerful neurotic force seemed to bind the three of them together.

He'd confided this to Karl, with the hope that Karl might have a lead on an apartment or some job for the brother.

Through some unspecified connection, Karl said that he knew of a good place coming available in Ostia.

—How good is good?

—You want a private tour?

—A description would help. I have to tell them something.

—Tell them. A separate bathroom. A separate kitchen. Clean, no bugs. In short, a palace.

—You don't know of anything in Ladispoli? Ladispoli would be more convenient, Alec said.

—This is what I can do, Karl said. I'll need an answer tomorrow.

—I'll ask.

—Ask, Karl said. As a favor to you, I'll reduce my commission. They'll get a nice discount and you'll get yourself another little chickadee.

—She might be more than that.

—It doesn't matter to me, Karl said. Do as you like. Nobody ever accused you of good sense. The lunacy with Polina proved that. Although, there, I could almost see why. Anyway, if I didn't know better, I'd recommend some self-restraint. Leave well enough alone. Particularly at a time like this.

—When isn't it a time like this?

—Spoken like a proper imbecile.

—You don't think it's true?

—You talk a lot of shit, Karl said. Careful you don't step in it.

Alec saw no point in reminding Karl that he recalled a time, not all that long ago, when Karl was not too far removed from this sort of shit. In this respect, they were both their father's sons. When they'd reached a certain age, they'd learned why their mother had spent so many nights sobbing behind the bedroom door. And if their parents had managed to conceal Samuil's infidelities from them while they were young, the infidelities were common knowledge to almost everyone else. This was something Alec realized on the occasion of Samuil's fifty-fifth birthday, when Yuli, their mother's cousin, got drunk and, in a failed attempt at humor, made some inappropriate comments during his toast.

At the factory, nobody ever mentioned it. People feared Samuil, and knew that he had a network of informants. But though Alec never heard anything said, he knew that strains of the gossip persisted. He inferred as much from the contemptuous smirks and glances directed at him when he chatted with some girl at work. There was more to those glances than simple resentment over his privileged status as the son of Samuil Leyzerovich. Implicit was that he'd inherited his libidinous appetite from his father, and the suggestion of something more odious, the libel of the rapacious, satyric Jew—which cast him and his father shoulder to shoulder, leering toothily, their trousers agape, members aloft, ready to defile the virginal daughters of the motherland.

In reality, of course, such a thing would have been impossible, not least because Alec couldn't remember the last time he and his father had exhibited anything resembling coordination of purpose. And beyond that, there was also the matter of the virginal daughters, who had few representatives among the female collective of the VEF radio-technical factory.

Before he took up with Polina, he'd had a few desultory affairs. Without these, the boredom would have been unendurable. Other coworkers dealt with the same problem differently. For lunch three men would each throw in a ruble for the price of a bottle, but Alec didn't have the right constitution for this. He resorted to persuading some Mila, Luba, or Luda to accompany him into a small utility room that smelled heavily of phenol.

When he met Polina, however, an alternative to the phenol-smelling room had miraculously presented itself. After living under the strict regime of his in-laws for six years, Karl had succeeded in obtaining a separate apartment in a cooperative that was being built in Teika, within walking distance of VEF. For two years, as it was slowly being constructed, he had passed the building every day on his way to work. When it was finally completed, people received letters telling them that they could take possession. Vans and movers arrived. Curtains and lamps appeared in the windows of his future neighbors. Karl was impatient to join them, but Rosa refused to move until the apartment had been prepared to her taste. She and her mother hired an interior decorator and spent weeks deliberating over the wallpaper, carpets, furniture, and appliances. The decorator had come recommended in the typical way, as a resourceful person, capable of getting her hands on merchandise of incomparable scarcity. However, months elapsed between the deliberations and the arrival of the wallpaper, carpets, and furnishings. Rosa, her mother, and the interior decorator made intermittent visits to the apartment, which otherwise remained unoccupied. The glaring fact of this incensed Karl every time he passed the building to and from work. In retaliation, he began to use the apartment on his own. He invited friends to drink and play cards. He let Alec use it for his liaisons. On occasion, he brought women there himself.

For Alec, it was in this apartment that much of his courtship with Polina transpired. Sometimes they would sneak away during the lunch break; other times Polina would invent an excuse delaying her after work.

The apartment, which lacked a stove, chairs, carpets, and wallpaper, had almost everything else. There were two little beds in the children's room, and there was a larger bed, albeit without linen, in what was to be Karl and Rosa's bedroom. A velour couch and coffee table occupied the main room. Karl made some token effort to tidy the place up, but there was usually an array of dirty ashtrays and empty wine bottles on the kitchen counter. To Rosa's and his mother-in-law's objections, Karl responded that he would resume living a normal family life when they moved into the apartment.

Rosa refused to make what she considered a premature move. For months there was, between her and Karl, a rancorous impasse. It was finally breached when, one afternoon, Rosa, her mother, and the interior decorator arrived unexpectedly at the apartment. When Rosa opened the door she was confronted by a distressing tableau. The tableau featured Karl in the foreground, on the sofa with a uniformed policewoman in his lap; and in the background, Alec, with his shirt unbuttoned, framed in the doorway to the boys' bedroom. Alec recalled the terrifically stunned expression on Rosa's mother's face, a look of total incomprehension, as if she were witnessing something altogether alien, which her mind simply couldn't process.

—Oh my God, Alec heard her say, he's gotten himself involved with the police.

Alec also recalled the scandalized expression on the face of the interior decorator, a tall middle-aged woman, prim and self-possessed, wearing a beige polyester pantsuit, the height of fashion. She looked at Karl and then Alec as if at moral garbage—coarse, low people.

Rosa, meanwhile, turned white.

Karl regarded her with the sublime equanimity of a Chinese.

—You have only yourself to blame, he said.

The policewoman extricated herself from Karl's lap and smoothed her uniform. Also, Polina emerged quietly from the boys' bedroom, and thus earned herself Rosa's unwavering enmity.

—Taking up with common sluts, Rosa said, the tears starting to flow. I'd expect this of your sex maniac brother, but never of you.

—Now, now, Karl replied. No need for insults. Besides, Tatyana has recently been promoted to the rank of investigator, and Polina is a graduate of the polytechnic and a valued employee of the VEF mechanical engineering department. Hardly common.

Alec couldn't remember where or how Karl had met Tatyana, and that day in the apartment represented the first and last time he ever saw her. Still, because of her uniform, and the capricious, vindictive authority it represented, her role in the episode acquired a special prominence. Mostly, Alec felt, this was because of the way Rosa had behaved. An ordinary person would have been intimidated by the uniform but, to Rosa's credit, she had been entirely unmoved. And despite the insults she directed at him, Alec admired her subversive integrity.

—I'll never forgive you for this, Rosa whispered. I wanted to make a beautiful home for us and instead of thanking me you've humiliated me in front of my mother, our children, and Alla Petrovna.

—Look, don't overdo it, Karl said. I told you a thousand times, I've had it living with your parents. We finally got an apartment and all I asked was that we move in. And what did I get instead? Alla

Petrovna. By the way, Alla Petrovna, since you're here, perhaps you could update me on the progress? Any word on our chairs? Our carpets? Our stove?

Flustered, Alla Petrovna was slow to respond.

Rosa's mother spoke for her and alluded to the item Alla Petrovna was holding in her hands. Everyone turned to look and saw that, yes, in her hands was a thin sample roll of wallpaper. Alec noted a constellation of brown spheres on a pale yellow background.

Considering it, Karl screwed up his face in disgust.

—You're telling me we waited three months for this revolting pattern? Looks like shit floating in piss.

—What a despicable bastard you are, Rosa sobbed.

Nobody spoke for some time. Karl shook his head ruefully and emptied the contents of a bottle of plum brandy. Everyone seemed to contemplate the next step. It was then that Alec decided to walk Polina out of the apartment. He started to button his shirt. As he did so, the policewoman broke the silence.

Speaking in the declarative, forthright manner of her profession, she said, Karl, you are mistaken. It is a very attractive pattern.

Three days later, Karl, Rosa, and the boys moved into the apartment. The fecal-motif wallpaper went up. A stove was procured. Someone donated a carpet; someone else, chairs. Karl stopped drinking, playing cards, and chasing after women. Finally the master of his own house, he devoted himself to home improvement, a preoccupation more arduous and demanding than fist-fighting or bodybuilding. Just to wangle ceramic tile for the bathroom, a man pitted himself against the mighty arsenal of the Soviet state. In effect, it was as if Leonid Ilyich was himself personally opposed to the tiling of a bathroom. It was the supreme challenge, eclipsing every other human endeavor—sport, sex, philosophy, art, and science. Karl, a pragmatist by nature, had always been inclined this way. And had he remained in Riga, his future would likely have been as a shady, jittery operator in the mold of Alter Schlamm. But instead Karl caught the break Schlamm never had. For the bargain price of five hundred rubles, the state allowed him to forfeit his citizenship and book passage to the fabled, capitalist West, where speculation was neither a dirty word nor an indictable offense. Where—had he not been confounded by history—a man of Schlamm's considerable talents would have owned city blocks and factories, not to mention a limousine, a mansion, and a yacht.

Alec didn't doubt that Karl would attain all this. Though, at present, he was engaged in a lot of petty hustling. Boris the Bodybuilder had departed for San Francisco and bestowed his cart upon Karl as a parting gift. Thus Karl had succeeded Boris in the relocation industry. In the afternoons, Rosa could be seen taking a shift at Piazza Marescotti, holding Boris's old sign: MOVING SERVICES. MAN WITH CART. Karl also acted as broker for some landlords in Ladispoli and Ostia. He made his mandatory appearance at the Americana on Sundays. And then there were additional involvements of a more abstruse nature, about which Alec knew no more than what he heard via rumor—of moneychanging, of used automobile sales, of an illicit traffic in icons.

His brother was tireless and liable to appear anywhere, selling anything. On the day of the pope's inauguration, Alec had expected to see him among the scores of peddlers dotting the streets leading to St. Peter's Square. He saw other Russians, some familiar, who were taking advantage of the unique fiscal opportunity. As in the case of the papal funeral, there were many religious knickknacks on offer, as well as postcards depicting the outgoing and incoming popes. Their presence was drowsily tolerated by a cordon of green-clad policemen who ensured that the peddlers kept a prescribed distance from the square.

Alec, Polina, and Lyova pressed forward as far as the crowd would allow. Lyova took the lead, banking on Christian goodwill, and tried to plow his way through the Catholics. When someone objected, Lyova pointed to Polina and delivered a short speech in Italian that caused everyone within earshot to gaze at her with a mixture of curiosity and sympathy.

—What did you say to them? Polina asked, when they'd advanced moderately forward.

—That you are pregnant and Russian and that you want to get near the pope so that he might bless your unborn child, whom you have liberated from a godless land.

To his mischievous smile, Polina responded with a grim look that cast a pall over everything. Lyova stopped trying to press ahead. They hit the final marks reserved for them as minor players in the pageant, beside a skinny African priest, four Capuchin friars in their brown robes and knotted sashes, and two Irish girls with plump freckled shoulders against whose earthly allure the Church could never enlist enough priests.

In the end, however, Alec didn't remember the inauguration for the freckled Irish girls, or Polina's injured mood, or his pinwheeling thoughts about Masha. He didn't remember it for the opulence of the ceremony—the censers, and scepters, and the ranks of shuffling clergy. He remembered it for his father's friend, Josef Roidman, whom he spied in the crowd sometime near the conclusion of the ceremony. Roidman had caught his eye accidentally, only because Alec happened to turn his head at a particular moment. Before he recognized Roidman's face, he saw the gleam of the Soviet medals pinned to his blazer. From the medals, Alec raised his eyes to see the face. After the slightest pause, they both smiled in recognition. Roidman even waved genially with the top of his crutch.

But by the time Alec gained Polina's attention, Roidman was no longer there.

—Who? Polina asked.

Alec looked again but didn't see him. Then he heard a sound, like a collective intake of breath. A second later, he spotted Roidman through the crowd, remarkably on the opposite side of the security barrier, hobbling onto the red-carpeted path that formed a straight line to the pope. Throughout the crowd, various cries rang out. Roidman didn't slacken his pace. Swinging forward, he reached inside his jacket with his free hand and produced a small Canadian flag on a stick, the kind handed out by the Canadian embassy. He managed to wave it energetically a few times, and to shout something unintelligible, before he was scooped up by the police. He didn't put up any resistance, and they carried him off like a little parcel. Just as quickly as he'd appeared, he'd disappeared. The entire incident hadn't lasted more than a few seconds, and Alec wasn't even sure how many, of the thousands present, had observed it. Or if it had caught the attention of the pope or of the dignitaries to his left, including the man for whom the display had been intended.

Grinning proudly, Alec turned to Lyova and Polina, and said: Ours.

SEPTEMBER

1

My dearest Lola,

It's always sad to see the summer end, but this year more than ever. That's because it occurred to me that we will have now been parted for an entire season. Compared with a week or a month, an entire season sounds like a lot. Here the very first leaves are starting to turn and so I notice more that you are not around.

I know you want to hear our news, but there isn't very much to tell. Mama and Papa are about the same. The main difference is that Papa has been given a promotion. Well, I call it a promotion. He isn't sailing anymore, but he is working at an administrative position within the ministry. So he is home all the time now and we get to see more of him. He's still getting used to the change, but I think it's for the best. He wasn't going to sail forever.

For me, it is back to school, of course. Before classes I was invited to attend a meeting of the Komsomol. You will probably not be surprised to hear that the Komsomol leader was very curious to know how you were faring in Rome. He and some of the other comrades enlightened me about the true state of affairs in the West. They turned out to be remarkably well informed about the conditions in Italy as well as in America. They read me accounts in Pravda *and from our own local Komsomol newspaper. Naturally, I told them that I was familiar with much of this information, since these were precisely the sorts of articles that Papa has been considerately leaving around the apartment. The meeting concluded on the warmest possible terms. I agreed with them that you had made a dreadful error, and that I, in my capacity as your sister, had failed to dissuade you from making this destructive and counterrevolutionary decision.*

As I wrote you before, I have become quite friendly with your mailman. He has introduced me to others like him. I've found them all to be very intriguing and energetic. They've been kind to me and have treated me almost as if I were one of them. Twice already I've spent an evening with them at one of their apartments. Did you know that your mailman sings and plays the guitar remarkably well? I don't think I've ever met anyone quite like him. He knows by heart literally dozens of songs in Russian and Latvian, but also many others in his native language. Just like our songs, theirs are beautiful and sad—and, if anything, sadder. He's made an effort to teach me, but as you know, memory has never been my strong suit. He claims that my forgetfulness is no match for his perseverance. I think he may be in for quite a shock.

2

As the saying went, Wonders will never cease, Alec thought.

He'd gone before the dour Riva Davidovna and offered the Karl-sanctioned apartment but she had declined it. The previous day, her son had found them a place in Ladispoli. She thanked Alec for his offer, and mentioned a family from Dnepropetrovsk that was experiencing tremendous difficulties in this regard.

The family from Dnepropetrovsk could burn, Alec thought, and cursed himself for not having acted more swiftly. By the next morning the Horvitzes' underthings would be part of the Soviet undergarment exhibit, dripping on some balcony in Ladispoli.

Alec had his exchange with Riva Davidovna in the pensione corridor, outside the door to their room. Other émigrés scavenged about the corridor, en route to continue their scavenging elsewhere. As Riva Davidovna prepared to return to her room, her son appeared at the far end of the corridor and skulked balefully over to them. With him was another man, all but recognizable at a distance, and then altogether unmistakable.

—This is the friend of Dmitri's who helped us find the apartment,

Riva Davidovna said, referring to Minka the thief, who extended his hand for a meaty shake.

—As you can see, Minka said, I am still here.

—You have my sympathies, Alec said.

—I'm sure, Minka replied.

—You know each other? Riva Davidovna inquired.

—We have a mutual friend, Alec said.

—Something like that.

Alec wasn't sure whose friendship Minka was calling into doubt. Or why exactly Minka had bothered with the clarification at all?

—It's a small world, Minka philosophized. Take me and Dmitri. It's been more than three years. When we last saw each other it was on another planet. On that planet, there was no Rome. No Rome and, you could say, not much of Minsk either, eh, Dimka?

—No Rome, that's for certain, Dmitri said churlishly.

—Yes, Minka affirmed. And now look. Here we are. Two wandering Jews. Searching for a home.

Strictly speaking, this was true, Alec thought. Though with their scarred brows and tattooed arms, their pictures would never grace the fund-raising brochures.

Putting her hand on the doorknob, Riva Davidovna informed her son about Alec's offer.

—Is that so? Dmitri said. You find apartments for everybody or just us?

—You're the first, Alec said.

—Yeah, and why's that?

—Something turned up, and I remembered you.

—Me personally? Dmitri derided.

—All of you, Alec said.

—"All of us," Dmitri mimicked. I know who you remembered.

As Riva Davidovna opened the door, Minka asked Alec about the apartment. Where it was; how he'd found it.

—Ah yes, your brother, Minka said meaningfully. He's very adept.

Minka pointed two fingers at Dmitri and continued, in a tone more menacing than admiring, He and his brother, Dimka, these guys know how to get ahead.

These last words Alec barely heard, because the door had been opened and he was looking at Masha. She seemed slightly disoriented, as she smoothed her dark hair and her peach-colored cotton dress. They had woken her. She had been sleeping in the afternoon heat. Her eyes drifted from her mother to her brother to him and finally to Minka the thief. Alec worked to tease out some meaning from the moment her eyes had come to rest upon him. But if he was to be honest with himself, she'd paid him no special regard. If anything, her eyes had brushed quickly over him, and lingered, if anywhere, on Minka.

Tonelessly, Riva Davidovna thanked him again and shut the door behind her. Dmitri and Minka turned for the stairwell with barely a parting glance. Left alone, Alec waited thirty seconds, long enough for Dmitri and Minka to reach the street, before taking the stairs down into the worn-out little room that served as the lobby. He was about to leave and make his way back to Viale Regina Margherita and the briefing department, when he heard the sound of footsteps on the stairs. Wishful thinking, reinforced by the pace and lightness of the steps, caused him to turn back. Nearing the bottom of the steps, he saw dark hair and a peach-colored dress. Whether she was there by accident or by design, he couldn't yet tell, but whatever the case, he felt instantly vivified.

Masha reached the bottom of the steps and made it clear that her appearance was not accidental. Looking at him directly, she said, I'm glad you're still here.

Two émigrés shoved past them coming up the stairs. Above their heads was a squalling of infants to rival a nursery.

—I'm sorry, Alec said, better over here.

He took Masha by the arm and led her to a spot at the base of the banister. She allowed herself to be touched and led.

—My mother said you found us an apartment, Masha said.

—I did, but it seems your brother found you a better one.

—Where is the one you found?

—In Ostia.

—And the one my brother found?

—Ladispoli.

—And why is Ladispoli better?

A strange question, Alec thought, if only because it seemed that all émigrés, including little children, seemed to apprehend the difference almost preternaturally.

—Some people prefer one, some the other, he said.

—What about you?

—What do I prefer?

—Yes.

—Neither.

—So where do you live?

—In Rome.

—Near to here?

—Not really.

—How far?

—Do you know the city?

—You think I would know the city if I don't know the difference between Ostia and Ladispoli?

—I don't know what you know.

—Not much. But don't worry, I'll learn. I'm a quick study.

—I don't doubt it.

—So where do you live?

—Across the river from the Jewish ghetto. The neighborhood is called Trastevere. Do you want the name of the street?

—Is there anything special about the street?

—Other than that I live there?

—Yes.

—No.

—Who do you live with?

—A guy named Lyova who rents the apartment, and a woman.

—A woman or your wife?

—Both.

The admission didn't appear to faze her.

—Is your place far from Ladispoli?

—About an hour, depending on how the trains are running.

—And from Ostia?

—About the same.

—If Ostia is so far from you, why did you find us an apartment there?

—It's the only apartment I knew of.

—And how did you expect we would see each other?

There was no flirtation in the way she'd put the question. It was of a piece with everything else—assertive, declarative, and either extraordinarily candid or extraordinarily cunning. In any case, she'd made the leap and all that remained was for him to follow.

—I imagined I'd take the train, Alec said, precisely as he'd imagined it.

—How often?

—As often as I could.

—The train costs money.

—My work issues me a pass.

—And the time?

—I'd figure a way.

—The same for Ladispoli?

—Ladispoli is a little easier. My parents live there with my brother.

—Easier because of what you would tell your wife?

—Yes.

—How long have you been married?

—A year.

—That's not very long.

—No.

Alec couldn't tell if her implication was that a marriage of such short duration warranted a higher or lower standard of fidelity.

Masha didn't inquire further about his wife. She wanted to know when they would meet again, and then went back upstairs to her mother.

3

ompared with what he saw around him, Alec believed that he might have had the most honorable of marriages. It had been founded on an act of kindness, whereas boredom, impulsiveness, and desperation seemed to be the foundations of too many others. Too many wives and husbands acted as if they wanted to annihilate each other. Incidents began as early as Vienna, with tales of wives running wild, abandoning their husbands. And in Ostia and Ladispoli, there were the common occurrences of one man leaving his wife for that of a friend. This was then typically followed by threats and imprecations and the obligatory loopy fistfight—the whole sorry spectacle played out before somebody's distraught five-year-old.

Some couples would have divorced years earlier if not for the complications inherent in divorcing and then leaving the Soviet Union. They'd remained together just long enough to get to the free world—whose freedom they'd defined in no small measure as freedom from each other. Their stories, at least in spirit, were the negative impressions of his own.

When he started seeing Polina, he had no thought of leaving Riga. It was the summer of 1976, and most of the people leaving Riga were Zionists. These were the sorts of people who organized surreptitious Hebrew classes. They were the ones who took jobs baking matzoh in Riga's last remaining synagogue, and who demonstrated at Rumbuli and Bikerniki forests—gathering on the anniversaries of the massacres to collect and bury loose bones, recite prayers, and sing the Israeli national anthem. Alec had joined them once, out of curiosity—his grandmother was among the dead, her bones jumbled anonymously somewhere under the stiff November grass. This was a fact that Samuil had never tried to conceal from him and Karl. He laid flowers twice a year. He never spoke about it except to say that he was going—once to mark the anniversary of his mother's death, and again on the anniversary of the death of his brother, whose actual grave, deep in Russia, was too far away to visit. Besides the fact that they were dead, Alec knew almost nothing about them.

It wasn't much of a surprise to Alec that the one time he had attended the memorial service, organized by the putative Zionist agitators, the information had gotten back to his father. When the KGB didn't send uniformed officers equipped with megaphones to disperse the participants, they sent plainclothes officers to take photographs and record names. Or just their informants.

If he'd expected sympathy—and in truth, he had—Samuil granted him none. In one motion, Samuil had opened and shut his case. Alec was a fool for gambling with his future.

—Tell me, how is it that you still haven't learned that there is a right way and a wrong way to do things?

To listen to his father, someone might have thought that Alec was an ideologue or an activist, whereas such things didn't interest him at all. In 1972, he was twenty, the same age as some of the conspirators who'd participated in the failed hijacking plot: a Soviet plane from Leningrad to Sweden—and from there, somehow, to Israel. He'd even known one of them, Zalmanson, an ordinary Jewish kid from Riga. When he'd read about the incident and listened to the accounts of the cartoonish show trial, he'd had a difficult time understanding the hijackers' motivations. To him it sounded like histrionics. Was life for a Jew in Riga so intolerable? He was a Jew; he lived in Riga; granted, it was far from perfect, but he managed all right. He certainly didn't feel the need to hijack a plane.

Other than the one time at the memorial in Rumbuli—and three years at the synagogue for Simchas Torah—Alec didn't involve himself with so-called dissident activities. Then again, going to the synagogue for Simchas Torah didn't, to his mind, entirely qualify as a dissident activity. It was more like a riotous party that incidentally happened to take place at a synagogue and involved some prancing around with a torah. Jews pranced, but so did Russians and Latvians. Those who feared the KGB took the precautionary measure of doing their dancing across the street—even if, on so narrow a street, the concept of "across" was merely semantic. Those who were more daring, or more seriously committed to getting a drink, danced in the synagogue's courtyard. And the boldest of all invited statutory perdition by taking the scrolls for a spin.

In September of '76, not long after the fiasco in Karl's apartment and several months into his and Polina's affair, Polina let Alec sweep her into the hora in the synagogue's courtyard. Two bearded Jewish youths and a tall, burly Latvian had whirled in the middle of the circle—with the Latvian, full of drink, raising the velvet-covered torah in exuberant protest against the Soviet occupiers. At the synagogue that day had been many of the familiar faces, the fixtures of his life in Riga. Both brothers Bender had been there—Syomka still recovering from the devastation of Lilya Gordin's betrayal. Rosa's parents and brother, who had already applied for an exit visa, were there too.

Each time he and Polina were together, Alec suspected that it might be the last. Whenever he neared her, he saw something guarded in her eyes, like a failure of recognition.

Through the summer and fall they carried on the affair. At times they saw each other quite regularly, other times weeks might pass between their meetings. Polina had her marriage to Maxim, and when she wasn't available, Alec took what life cast his way.

All this time, unbeknown to them, the train of their departure was approaching. At first distant and barely audible, but gaining momentum with every passing week.

Until, on a blustery afternoon in March of '77, after Karl had expressed his desire to emigrate, and shortly after Alec had moved into a small bachelor apartment, Polina had come to see him. Cold, and drenched from the rain, she sat down at the kitchen table and let the water drip from her hair and the hem of her coat. They exchanged all the questions and answers. *Was she sure? Yes. How could she be sure? She was sure.* And then the more delicate, unpleasant questions which he couldn't restrain himself from asking. *And she was sure? Almost certain. But not certain? As certain as she could be. Did he want her to go into details? To provide a tally? She could do it. It wouldn't take long. No, he didn't want that. They could wait until it was born, then they could run the tests. Was that what he wanted? No, he didn't want that either. So what did he want?*

As gently as he could phrase it, he'd told her what he wanted.

—I did that once, she'd said. I swore I'd never do it again. Not that I believed I'd ever be faced with the choice.

He'd been unable to think clearly. His mind had raced erratically, seeking a way out. It hadn't helped that in her condition, soaked and chilled, her lips nearly drained of color, Polina had cast an image of injured, poignant beauty.

Afterward, he'd consulted with Karl and there had been the agonizing enumeration of options.

Did he want to marry her and raise the child?

Did he not want to marry her but let her raise the child?

Alone or with her husband?

Did he want to leave Riga? And what then? Marry her? Bring a pregnant woman along? Or an infant? Emigrating was hard enough without that added burden. Karl knew of happily married women who'd aborted their pregnancies when they received their exit visas.

And what were her designs? What did she want? What could be done about her?

Even if men did it all the time, Alec had said, he didn't want to leave his child behind. He didn't think he could simply forget. It would always trouble him.

But what alternative did he have if she wouldn't agree to an abortion?

Three days after she'd delivered the news, Polina came back. The day was cold but clear, and Polina arrived this time in a very different state. Instead of martyred, clinical. Under her coat, she wore a heavy, gray wool turtleneck, whose collar rose to the line of her chin. She matched this with a long navy skirt and high black boots. Except for her face and hands, she was darkly, thickly covered. The clothes seemed chosen to negate her body, to discourage any sensual thoughts, in him or in anyone else. What other reason could there have been for such an overtly shapeless outfit? Not to conceal the pregnancy. The tiny being that had latched on inside her was less than three months old. Alec imagined it having the size and vascular translucence of a gooseberry. He pictured it in the red convection of the womb, growing, thriving, and encroaching upon his life. He'd tried to think of it in other, more positive terms, to envision it as a source of happiness. Why not? Many people were glad to have children. He also wasn't categorically opposed to someday having a child. At some future time, he could see himself surrounded by children, horsing around with them, walking them to school, putting them to bed. Only not like this. Like this he foresaw only a tangle of complications.

And of all the tangled complications, Alec's mind seized upon the most perplexing. By the third day, he'd seized upon it to the exclusion of everything else. It was much the same as when he'd been a very young boy and his parents had failed to come home on time. Then, too, his mind fastened on the disastrous. No amount of his grandmother's soothing or Karl's reasoning had any effect. He could nod and say yes, but his phantasms burned above reason. He recalled his parents' walnut-veneer clock, and his terror at the barely perceptible creeping of its white, plastic minute hand. Again and again came the fatal automobile collision, with the sudden jolt, flailing necks, and spray of glass. The terror eased only when he heard the clatter of heels in the corridor, the key in the lock, and inhaled the waft of his mother's perfume as she enveloped him.

Now as he thought about the worst possible scenario—emigrating and leaving a child behind—the emigration began to feel like an imperative. He pictured himself conscience-stricken somewhere in the abstract West or, conversely, stranded by his conscience in Riga, unwilling to deny his paternity.

—Screw conscience, Karl had scoffed. Conscience is the least of your problems. You could get stuck here regardless of your conscience.

By this he meant that if Polina had the child and he was proven to be the father, he'd need her written permission to leave the country. She'd have to sign an affidavit stating that she had no claims on him. That she absolved him of material responsibilities.

—It goes without saying, Alec declared, that if I left a child behind, I'd send money. Polina would know that.

—She might or she might not, Karl countered.

—She's not vindictive. She'd never cause problems.

—Have you ever stiffed her with a kid before?

—She's not the type. Of this I'm sure.

—You don't know, and you can't know. Even if you'd stiffed her before, there's no telling how a person will react from one day to the next. There's only one way to avoid a problem and that's not to create it in the first place.

—Well, the problem exists.

—It does and it doesn't, Karl said. But wait much longer and it will be *finita la comedia*.

—She won't agree to it.

—Is this the first time you've gotten a woman pregnant?

—What does that have to do with anything?

—You charmed your way in; charm your way out.

—Charming in is a lot easier.

—Yeah, well, write that on your forehead so you'll remember for next time.

—Anything else?

—What else? You have to take care of it. I can't do it for you. But if you haven't got one yourself, I know of a good doctor. Quiet, expert, and clean.

—Rosner?

—You've used him?

—Never needed to. Have you?

—I know him strictly by reputation.

Apart from recommending a doctor, Karl was of little help. On the subject of what Alec could possibly offer Polina in exchange for her compliance, Karl proposed, as an option of last resort, Alec's new bachelor apartment. Karl contended that, if necessity demanded, he would have no trouble proposing such a barter. As for whether it was morally reprehensible or not, he wanted to know what could be bartered against a human life that *wasn't* morally reprehensible.

Nothing, Alec thought. That was the trouble. Though a distant runner-up to nothing was another human life.

As they sat in his tiny kitchen, it felt like Polina had trailed in the chill of the outdoors. It adhered to her like a personal climate and caused Alec to feel as if the temperature in the tiny kitchen were a few degrees colder than the temperature two meters away in what passed for the adjoining room. To warm himself, her, and the space between them, he filled a kettle and set it to boil. He asked Polina if she wanted coffee, tea, or something stronger. In a cabinet he had the greater portion of a bottle of brandy and a brown clay bottle of Balzams, less beverage than unit of exchange. He wanted to forestall, for as long as he could, the unavoidable conversation because—though he couldn't have articulated it at the time—the conversation promised to be the first serious one of his life. Life, which he'd treated as a pastime, and which he'd thought he could yet outdistance, had caught up with him. And he'd discovered, much as he'd suspected, that once life caught up with you, you could never quite shake it again. It endeavored to hobble you with greater and greater frequency. How you managed to remain upright became your style, who you were.

Style was the difference between him and Polina. On that March afternoon he wanted to approach the problem from the side, circle it a few times, until, sidling over with such roundabout movements, the two of them would discover themselves at the destination as though by happenstance.

Polina, meanwhile, wanted to get there directly.

—It was an accident, Alec began, you wouldn't have planned it this way.

—How could I plan something I thought impossible?

—But if you could, would you have planned it like this?

—No. But what does that matter? It happened. I'm not sorry that it happened. Even if you want me to be, Polina said with controlled defiance.

—I don't want you to be sorry, Alec said. I want you to be happy. Will having the baby make you happy?

She didn't answer immediately but seemed to carefully consider.

—It might.

Gently, Alec tried to enumerate the options he'd hashed out with Karl.

—Would you be happy having the child with Maxim?

—If this is where you begin, Polina said, you don't need to say anything else. I have my answer.

—I think you're wrong.

—Do you want me to have the child?

—No, Alec said.

—So I'm not wrong.

—If that's the only question, then, no, you're not wrong.

—It's the only question that matters, Polina said.

—And about what happens to the child and to you?

—We'll find our way somehow. We won't be the first.

—Here in Riga?

—I imagine. Where else?

—Living with Maxim or on your own?

—Or, in time, with someone else.

—Yes, there's that, too. Raising my child.

—Biologically.

—That isn't insignificant.

—To whom?

—To me.

—I'm afraid you can't have it both ways.

—It may also not be insignificant to the child.

—Alec, that is also having it both ways. You can't claim to care for the feelings of the child you want to abort.

There was logic in what she'd said, but it didn't change the fact that Alec felt quite certain that he *could* care for the feelings of the child he wanted to abort. That is, once the child was born.

—If I could agree to having the child, I would. If I could be a father to it, I would.

—I never asked you to be a father to it.

—So what did you hope I would say?

—I don't know. Or rather I do, Polina said, and laughed dryly. It wasn't what I'd hoped you'd say, but what I'd hoped you wouldn't say. That's all.

A stillness of denouement settled upon her, or she summoned it from within. Somehow the conversation he'd planned had escaped his control. It wasn't even that he'd misled himself by thinking it would be easy. He'd imagined a thorny path that led, in the end, to a favorable resolution. He pictured Polina's happiness, gratitude even, at his proposal. But now, in actuality, he feared that he'd misspoken and miscalculated. He feared that she would leave before he could even make his big redemptive offer. The offer that would recast him radically and heroically not only in her eyes but in his own.

Sensing that his time was short, he rushed ahead and told her that he was leaving Riga.

He then unfurled his grand plan, like a carpet to a bountiful future. Polina would divorce Maxim. The two of them would marry. An expert doctor would perform the operation with incomparable care in an atmosphere of total privacy. It would be nothing at all like the savagery of the public abortion clinic. No harm would come to her. She would still be able to conceive. Once they settled somewhere, they could try again properly. This was their once-in-a-lifetime opportunity to slip the shackles of the Soviet Union.

—It's all very rosy, Polina said.

—It could be. I think we could make a good life together over there. I truly believe it.

—Don't try so hard, Alec, Polina said. Next you'll tell me you love me.

With the warning she bracketed a great length of silence, long enough to accommodate everything that had happened or would happen: the abortion clinic, Maxim, Alec's parents, the private doctor, her parents, their spiteful coworkers, the snarling officials, and the dreadful, sunny day when she would sit on a park bench waiting to say goodbye to her sister.

One afternoon at the military hospital in Simferopol a number of patient-musicians had put on a small concert. Their singer was a squarely built young Tatar woman, a surgical nurse. The musicians took up their places under a banner that predicted "Victory over the Fascist Invader." The ensemble played and the nurse sang traditional Russian songs and the popular songs of the day, ballads of heroism, homesickness, love and loss. In the aisles between the beds, comrades paired up and danced together. Samuil had made captain by then, and as there were no able-bodied officers for partners, he had watched the enlisted men dance.

He was reminded of it when he heard "Where Are You, My Garden?" played by a very different ensemble at Club Kadima. The man who sang it, Samuil had to admit, was as appealing in his own way as that Tatar surgical nurse of long ago. He was a small, bald man of Samuil's age, a veteran, who sang and played the accordion. A girl, young enough to be his granddaughter, but a graduate of the Leningrad conservatory, accompanied him on the piano. The third member of the group was a cornetist from Riga, a fellow his sons' age, who had played in the restaurants. They were an unlikely combination, but quite capable. The main credit had to be given to the singer, who had a sure, soulful voice. His repertoire included Russian and Yiddish songs, and, in either language, he tasted each syllable and didn't go in for any melodramatic tricks.

Samuil had attended the concert reluctantly, at the persistent urging of his wife and of Josef Roidman. They had assured him it would be an evening of musical entertainment to suit his taste. Skeptical, he had arrived with low expectations, but the musicians had exceeded them. They had started with the old standard "Uner Erster Waltz," and treated it not like some confection but like a task of honest work, each note precise as a rivet. This they followed with "Shpiel, Fidl, Shpiel," performing that, too, as if they were closely aligned with the old feelings.

The evening had been advertised to appeal to people of their generation, and some two dozen had come. Couples like him and Emma, single men like Roidman, and widows who arrived in the company of other widows. Scattered among them were younger people, though not very many. The friends and families of the musicians, Samuil supposed. Of the older people, few remained seated for long, but reported purposefully to the dance floor. Samuil did his obligatory turn with Emma, taking some pleasure in executing the steps. Around them other couples danced as they did, cohesively, in marked contrast to the modern trend where all thrashed about like epileptics and it was uncertain who was dancing with whom. Was it any wonder, with such culture, that his sons had taken the wrong path?

But what did it matter in the end? he thought as he danced with Emma, surrounded by their dwindling cohort, who danced the steps from memory and nursed the infirmities of old age. They were all obsolete, a traveling museum exhibit of a lost kind: Stalin's Jews, unlikely survivors of repeat appointments with death. And if he allowed himself to feel any kinship with these people, what was the good of it? It was a kinship with the past. And a kinship with the past was no kinship for a revolutionary. A revolutionary allied himself only with the future. But as it sickened him to even think about the future, his revolutionary days were over.

Samuil sat down when the band began "Where Are You, My Garden?" Roidman had requested the honor, and was now hobbling with Emma on the dance floor—one arm around Emma, the other on his crutch.

When they returned from the dance floor Emma and Roidman were joined by the rabbi. Samuil had noticed the man circulating around the room, approaching guests or being approached. People more than twice his age—people who should have known better—took his hand reverentially, and drew him near to mouth a joke or a confidence, which the rabbi received with the lofty humility of a sage. A Soviet education, the war, and decades of Soviet life, and still the kernel of religious servility hadn't been eradicated. It had lain dormant, like a suppressed vice—a prejudice or superstition—waiting for an opportune moment to resurface. Now the moment had come, personified by this man with the pale, thin wrists and patchy beard—purveyor of discount chicken.

Emma led the rabbi to the table. Here was the generous rabbi who had shown such kindness to their grandchildren. He was a gem of a man and a holy person.

—Every Jew is holy before God, the rabbi said to Emma's approbation.

—Rabbi, I am not a believer, Samuil said. This sort of talk doesn't interest me.

—I understand, the rabbi said. Your wife has told me. You are not a believer, but you are still a Jew. You carry within you the holy spark.

—These terms are meaningless to me. I would never speak like this about my origins.

—But are these not your origins?

—You're interested in an account of my origins?

—If you wish to tell me.

—I was born in 1913 in the town of Rogozna in the Kiev region. My father managed a woods and owned a general store. I am Jewish by nationality. I did not complete my higher education. When I was six years old, my father was murdered by the Whites. After his death, my mother became a seamstress, and remained a member of the proletariat until her death at the hands of the German fascists. At the age of fourteen I was trained by my uncle as a bookbinder. I worked at this trade until the war. At age sixteen I was a member of a Communist cell. In 1940, when the Latvian SSR was established, I joined the Party. During the war, I volunteered for the front and rose to the rank of captain in the Red Army. After demobilization I was finance director of the VEF radio-technical factory. Until six months ago, I was a member in good standing of the Communist Party of the Soviet Union. I was never expelled from the Party and never had any Party penalties assessed. I have the following awards: Order of the Red Star, Order of the Red Banner, medal for bravery, and medal for Victory over Germany in the Great Patriotic War, 1941 to 1945. You will notice that I make no mention of any spark, soul, or God.

—Syoma, don't get upset, Emma said. The rabbi means well.

—He means what he means, Samuil replied, and I mean what I mean.

—Your husband is right, the rabbi said. It is a shame that we mean different things. But I respect your husband as a man of his convictions. Samuil Leyzerovich, if you had applied the strength of your convictions to the torah, I don't doubt that you could have been a great rabbi today.

—Nonsense. Had I applied myself to your torah, I would not be here today. The NKVD would have put me on a train, or the Germans in a pit.

—All the more reason to return now to the torah. Wouldn't you say? Out of respect for our martyrs.

—There were many kinds of martyrs. You honor yours; I'll honor mine.

Samuil excused himself and went outside. The rabbi had switched topics and begun to speak about Israel and the peace negotiations with Egypt. He spouted drivel about the age of redemption. For the first time since the destruction of the Second Temple, the Jews were once again masters over Greater Israel, the portion that the Almighty had promised to Abraham. All of this portended the imminent arrival of the messiah. Thus it was absolutely forbidden for

Begin to surrender any of the sacred land to the Arabs. God's covenant inhered in every stone and every shrub.

Outside Club Kadima, Samuil walked away from the building and leaned against the low wrought-iron fence. The security guard, a beefy middle-aged émigré, tossed a casual remark about the humidity inside the club. Samuil didn't bother to reply. He rested his hip against the fence and waited for the coolness and quiet to act upon his thoughts. The rabbi's remarks had agitated him too much and caused his blood pressure to spike. He'd become flushed and light-headed and he'd noticed Emma appraising him. He'd felt a tremendous urgency to get free of both of them.

Alone in the street, he calmed down. The talk of religion, martyrs, and Begin led him to think of his cousin. Begin was in America meeting with Carter and the Egyptian Sadat. The entire civilized world attended his every move. But who was Begin? A simple Jew from Brest, a Betar activist and disciple of Jabotinsky. Like Yankl, he'd been deported to Siberia in the summer of '41. A year later, he was pardoned and allowed to join the Polish army. It was possible that Yankl had met with a similar fate. And so it was possible that he'd survived the war and found his way to Palestine. His biography, up to a point, was sufficiently similar to Begin's or to those of many of the other Israeli leaders of the same generation. Ordinary Jewish activists like him had founded their country and were now international statesmen.

Samuil recalled his cousin's words from the final night. He had bet on one horse, while Samuil and Reuven had bet on another. That night it had seemed that Yankl's horse had lost. Nearly forty years later, this was no longer so. Now it seemed instead that Yankl had prematurely conceded the race. But the race had continued. The horses went around and around the track indefinitely, switching places. The race was never lost or won. All that happened was that, in the interim, men died. The trick was to die at the right moment, consoled by the perception of victory. More likely than not, Yankl had died too soon. As for himself, Samuil thought, he would die too late.

5

With the music still streaming from Club Kadima, Samuil pushed open the gate and walked in the direction of home. He felt no inclination to account for himself or his whereabouts. When Emma came looking for him, the security guard would tell her all she needed to know. Or not.

Samuil minded his steps on the sidewalk that led from Via Mexico to Via Napoli. In places, tree roots had buckled the concrete, making the footing treacherous. Few people were out in the streets, though the night was pleasant. Now that it was September, many vacationers had returned to Rome. During the afternoons, when he took his walks along the beach, he saw how the crowds had thinned. Soon enough, when the weather cooled some more, the Russians would have the beach to themselves.

It will be us and our stray dogs, Samuil thought grimly.

The dogs, mostly large breeds, the mastiffs and wolfhounds favored by Russians, roamed in hungry, scraggly packs around Ladispoli, often congregating along the shore. They had been abandoned by owners who'd flown off to Canada or America—who, after going to considerable lengths to process and transport the animals from the Soviet Union to Italy, had finally been dissuaded from taking them any farther. During the day, the dogs sprawled listlessly in the shade of the palm trees, and in the evenings they skulked about in search of food. As with people in similar straits, the largest ones fared the worst. Great, once proud beasts dragged themselves about with downcast eyes, begging for scraps. To feed them was only to prolong their misery. Samuil had seen Italians shooing the animals away using the Russian words for "no" and "scram."

Where Via Napoli crossed Via Italia, Samuil turned left and took the main road toward the beach. There was still life in the cafés along Via Italia, but it, too, had diminished with the waning of the summer season. Samuil noticed a proliferation of signs on the doors and windows of cafés advertising, in Russian, ice cream, pastries, and beer. A number of these signs were the product of Rosa's handiwork, done with paints and brushes at their kitchen table. Karl—who no longer lifted a finger unless there was a potential for profit—landed Rosa the job. Similarly, he'd gotten her a position making up signs to promote upcoming events at Club Kadima.

When Samuil had looked askance, Karl had said, If we're going to be here a long time, we will need the money.

His son's implication was that Samuil—singlehandedly responsible for the length of their Italian purgatory—was not entitled to issue critiques.

He and Emma had made two trips to the Canadian embassy to plead their case. At the first appointment, they had been cursorily dismissed on account of his medical results. But so long as they made a good impression, anything was possible. This was the homily Emma and Rosa repeated in their attempts to gain Samuil's cooperation the second time around.

He told them that he would go to the appointment and express to the Canadians that he would not become a strain on their health and welfare system. He would vow that if he became ill, he would jump from a window and spare everyone the trouble and the expense.

—Since this is what concerns them, Samuil said.

242

—Back home, when you wanted to accomplish something, Samuil Leyzerovich, you knew very well how to conduct yourself, Rosa said. Why not here?

—Please, don't speak to me of back home, Samuil cautioned.

—Syoma, you said you would try, Emma remonstrated.

—I said I would, and I will.

—To try means to try, Rosa said.

And he had. He'd allowed himself to be demeaned, even. Emma had done more of her secret plotting. He'd lived thirty-two years as her husband and wasn't so credulous as to be taken in by her tricks. The morning they were to depart for the consulate, Roidman had arrived and offered to lend Samuil his medals. He and Emma both vigorously denied that she had put him up to it. However, seeing as how his friend made the suggestion, Emma encouraged that Samuil accept it.

—Where is the deceit? Emma asked. You earned the same decorations.

He knew his decorations down to the serial numbers and the nicks in their enamel. How could he explain to Emma the disgrace of using the medals of a Red Army soldier to curry the favor of some petty capitalist official?

In the living room, Samuil watched Roidman fumble to remove the medals from his blazer. Emma hovered above him, itching to intervene. Unsteady progress obliged Roidman to sit. A sheen rose on his bald head. In time, he managed to unscrew the medals from their backings. Then, with more ease, he unpinned the ribbons. Emma didn't lose a second before she started to apply the decorations to Samuil's blazer, which she'd laid out on the coffee table. Samuil pretended to ignore her as she arranged and rearranged the medals.

—How did you used to have yours? she asked.

He didn't bother to answer.

With Roidman waving farewell at their doorstep, they left for the Ladispoli train station. Once inside the train, Samuil took the window seat and glared out at the passing countryside. Emma sat on the aisle and, in an attempt to quell her own anxiety, scrutinized and remarked upon the other occupants of their train car.

What an interesting woman. How old do you think, Syoma? My coeval? Back home a woman this age would never think to wear such a provocative dress. Even if she could get one.

Look at what a well-behaved little girl. There is an example of the difference between boys and girls. Could you imagine Zhenya sitting like that even for a minute?

If there is one thing I have noticed between here and back home, it's that I haven't seen any drunks. In Riga, I can't remember a time when I rode a train for so long and not a single drunk came into the car. Have you observed this, Syoma? Although from what I've heard, the Italians have a serious epidemic of pickpockets and purse snatchers. This is why women are advised to wear their purses with the strap crosswise, like so.

At Termini they filed out into the gargantuan space. Trains, in their rectilinear ranks, towered above them. They had been to this station once before, but that had been with Karl, and it hadn't made the same daunting impression. At the other major train stations, in Bratislava and Vienna, they had been part of the swirling émigré vortex. Now, for the first time, they were facing the vastness by themselves. Samuil felt Emma clutching his arm and pressing up against him, hobbling his thoughts and his stride.

—What is it with you? he asked.

Emma looked at him with sorrow.

—I'm afraid. I'm afraid to get lost.

With Emma pulling at his arm, Samuil pressed ahead. He set a harsh face not only against the people in his path, but also against the physical bulk of the imposing machines. He felt as though even the machines wished him ill. The feeling was new. A Soviet train, forged in a Soviet factory and meant to travel the length and breadth of the Soviet land, had never seemed to him malevolent.

Samuil steered them toward the huge board that displayed arrivals and departures, where destinations and times came and went with the synchronized clacking of hundreds of black plastic tiles. People with fixed objectives sped one way and another. Samuil saw stores, cafés, newspaper stands, and bookshops. By the entrance to one of these, a Gypsy woman squatted on the ground in her long skirt. Beside her, a boy no older than ten played a small accordion. Farther ahead, there were steps and an escalator leading to an upper level. Beyond this, the concourse continued, and he could see the possibility of a turn to the left and to the right. Samuil couldn't recall which way they had gone the last time they'd been at the station. He felt sorely conspicuous because of the medals. People glanced at him as if at some oddity.

For these indignities, Samuil blamed his wife and his son. Emma had insisted on the medals, and Alec, predictably inattentive, had specified a bus number, but not where the bus might be found. In a station like Termini, the size of a small town, such an omission was unforgivable.

Once they found the depot, boarding the bus brought no relief, only the fear of missing their stop. Emma supplicated the bus driver—a young, impassive dullard—babbling and holding the sheet of paper with their directions. She then sat apprehensively at the window, trying to read street names and recognize landmarks, not trusting the driver to call their stop. Though when the time came, the driver barked a word and one of their fellow passengers pointed conscientiously to the door.

The second meeting was worse than the first. They had been assigned to a total incompetent: a young man who did not wear a jacket or tie, but a yellow sweater over his shirt collar. On his table he'd had an open can of soda, from which he drank periodically and unapologetically during their interview. He also smiled, for no evident reason, from hello to goodbye. And when he spoke, it was only to utter some nonsense. Though Emma had admitted to no knowledge of English, the caseworker insisted that she nevertheless try to read several pages from an illustrated children's book about a polar bear. When she stumbled, which was at every word, he corrected her. To his invitation that Samuil also make an attempt, Samuil declined through the interpreter.

—If it's to demonstrate my ability, there's nothing to demonstrate.

—If it's to demonstrate your willingness to learn . . . Emma whispered.

—To learn or to be ridiculed? Samuil said.

On the subject of his fitness, Samuil delivered his standard response. He was fit enough for any work.

He believed that he had turned in a blameless effort, in spite of everything.

He'd even suffered in silence while Emma launched into the epic of his wartime service. The caseworker had nodded approvingly at Samuil's medals and contributed that his own father had seen action in the Canadian military. Here again, Samuil felt that he had responded prudently, and that his behavior had been beyond reproach. He had held his tongue. Instead of inquiring why it had taken the Western powers three years to open up a second front, he had said something complimentary about the Canadian army.

Nevertheless, he could tell that Emma hadn't been satisfied with how he'd comported himself. She would not admit to it, but her displeasure was immanent.

Returning home, Samuil and Emma occupied two of the last available seats, one behind the other. As they rode, they didn't have to look at each other or speak. But when the bus came to its inexplicable halt Emma tapped him on the shoulder. The doors had opened and the bus driver had climbed out and lit a cigarette. Passengers grumbled and cursed. Some left and started walking. Samuil heard a word repeated that sounded much like the Russian word for bus driver: "schoffer." A woman cradling an infant called out to the driver. Samuil saw him shrug his shoulders, not unsympathetically. The woman slid back into her seat, dug an orange out of her purse, and began to peel it. A man standing beside Samuil checked his watch and then turned the page of his newspaper.

They remained on the immobile bus for upward of two hours. The driver went away down the street, evidently abandoning his vehicle and his passengers entirely. When he returned, he climbed back into his seat as if nothing had happened, turned the ignition, and re-sumed the route.

At eight in the evening, many hours late, they descended from their train at Ladispoli Station. Before Samuil could take five steps, he saw his daughter-in-law and his grandchildren. Rosa was already in motion, issuing exclamations, rushing toward them, pulling the boys along by their hands. At the sight of Rosa and the boys, Emma nearly fell into a swoon of martyrdom and fatigue. It was a reunion for the ages, Samuil thought. Yet another one.

At home, Karl was waiting, the reverse image of his wife. As much as Samuil deplored Rosa's hysterics, he found that he also deplored his son's indifference.

—They waited over two hours on a stationary bus, Rosa ex-claimed.

—But what did I tell you? Karl said.

—So what? Anything could have happened, Rosa said.

—But what happened? Karl asked.

—Never mind, Rosa said. Look at your mother, she's half dead.

All that trouble for nothing, Samuil thought. They had dressed him up and dragged him to Rome for this. A farcical interview at the consulate and then a wildcat transit strike: sitting on a bus, going nowhere.

6

The second time Alec went to Ladispoli to meet Masha, he'd encountered his father walking the paved path along the edge of the beach. Alec was with Masha, going in the opposite direction. Before they drew close enough to speak, Alec had recognized his father's shape, even in the low light of dusk. His father peered directly and stolidly ahead. Alec thought for an instant to duck into a shuttered beachside café, and hide behind the stacked chairs and umbrellas, but he knew this was idiotic. Though when they approached each other, Alec saw in his father's eyes a grudging, regretful look—as if he was disappointed that Alec hadn't had the good sense to duck into the shuttered café, behind the umbrellas and chairs, and spare them both the inconvenience of this meeting.

With no recourse, they stopped and acknowledged each other. Alec saw his father give Masha the briefest glance, no more than a shift of the eyes, after which he didn't look at her again.

—You're still here? Samuil asked.

—I'm still here, Alec said.

Hours earlier, when he'd arrived in Ladispoli, he had seen his father, mother, and the rest of his family in the rental cottage. For the duration of Alec's visit, his father had remained in the living room, poring over a manuscript.

With a stricken expression his mother had said: He writes; he reads; he goes for walks.

Alec had seen the writing and the reading; now he'd seen the whole troika.

—When is the last train to Rome? Samuil asked.

—Ten fifteen, Alec said.

—See you don't miss it, Samuil said evenly, nodded his head, and resumed his walk.

Alec had deliberately chosen to walk with Masha along a part of the beach that he believed would be the least trafficked by Russians, among whom, first and foremost, he counted his family. They hadn't seen anyone until they met his father. That he was there, so far from where he should have been, seemed like an act of spite. At the same time, Alec couldn't help but feel sorry for him, in the austerity of his solitude. He turned and watched his father grow indistinct in the distance and the darkness. His father was becoming a recluse, rejecting everyone and everything, denying himself every pleasure except the pleasure of denial, whereas for Alec, the pleasure of denial—that high, weatherbeaten pleasure—was the one pleasure he didn't want.

The pleasure he did want was Masha. A pleasure much closer to the ground. In pursuit of this he'd gone to the apartment she shared with her mother and her hoodlum brother. He spent more than an hour eating dinner with them. Masha had told him to be on time, so that they could all eat together before her brother left for work. When Alec arrived, Riva Davidovna acted as if he were a favored and long-standing suitor. Even Dmitri, whose attitude couldn't be mistaken for anything other than hostility, wasn't hostile in the same way. Previously, his hostility had seemed a type of suspicion, now it seemed more seasoned—as if he'd known Alec for many years and had long held a negative opinion of him.

A place was set for him next to Masha. Riva Davidovna served, ladling out vegetable soup, inquiring if he wanted one or two spoonfuls of sour cream. She asked after his parents and after Karl and Rosa. A casual web of acquaintance connected them. Riva had seen Rosa at Club Kadima painting and posting her signs; she'd seen his mother at Piazza Marescotti tending to the boys; and evidently Karl had a stake in the auto body shop where Dmitri had found work. The impression created was of a respectable, industrious family, with Alec as the bachelor son. Facts inconsistent with this impression Riva willfully ignored—for instance, where exactly Alec went when he went home.

After the meal, Riva allowed him to take Masha for the unchaperoned walk. Just walking with her, he felt an almost ungovernable desire. He hadn't experienced anything like it in years. Not since he'd been a teenager and spent entire evenings with an erection straining against the fly of his pants. That was when he'd gone to dances to seek out girls who would chat breezily or look blankly over his shoulder while they returned his pressure with their hips and thighs. Alec had almost forgotten how exciting that had been, testing the limitations. A few years later, nobody took the limitations seriously anymore and everything changed. He certainly hadn't missed the limitations. But now that he'd encountered them again, he believed that they added to Masha's appeal. She was eighteen years old, of less than average height, with dark hair and eyes, and a figure that seemed to strain the laws of physics, like a glass filled past the brim. Had she been a deranged nymphomaniac, Alec imagined he'd be similarly hooked, but he preferred her this way: coy rather than wanton.

When he was alone with her, he felt the need to always be touching her. On their unchaperoned walk, Masha rested her head against his arm and he held her around the waist. Whenever his hand slipped down, she let it linger before she guided it back to its original place. And when he stopped to kiss her, she behaved like the dance partners from his teenage past and let him press his groin against her abdomen. The pleasure of it traveled the length of his body and resolved like a high note in his jaw.

Things didn't go too much further: she trapped his hand between her thighs; he stroked her breasts; she traced a line with her fingertips.

She was toying with him; her excuse, that she was a virgin and inexperienced.

—I see it's hard for you to believe, Masha said. Other women you've known are different, right? All you have to do is ask.

—Not always.

—No?

—Sometimes there's no need to ask.

To Alec, it didn't matter what they said to each other or even if they meant it. The thrill was in saying the words and having someone say them back. The conversation was always the same anyway. You repeated at twenty-six what you'd said at sixteen. And, if you were lucky, you got to repeat it again at fifty-six and ninety-six. To see yourself through admiring eyes, to tell a woman what you wanted—what could be better? How could you tire of that? Emigration had already spoiled too many pleasures and hadn't granted many new ones in return.

This was why he was so happy to have found Masha. With her, he was back on familiar ground. It was like Riga before the whole convoluted saga of the emigration. He'd seen a girl, become smitten, and pursued her. For the first time in a long time, the demands of emigration were peripheral. And as for Polina, he believed that one thing had nothing to do with the other. Masha was a complement, not a competitor, and so he felt altogether good, to the point of satiety, like a man who had everything.

On the ride back to Trastevere, as Alec was rocked into a near dream state by the iron drone of the rails, the dark fields in the window leaping up to become dark towns, an apparition of Masha's father filtered into his thoughts. He'd never so much as seen a photograph of him, but he'd assigned him a face: and this face was looking at him. A bald head, a strong brow, intense black eyes, lean cheeks, and a growth of stubble. It was the face of a man in late middle age, though Alec knew that Masha's father hadn't been forty when he'd

died. Alec examined the face to see if Masha's father approved or dis-
approved of him. He wanted him to approve, but the father's features
were grim, foreboding. Alec sensed that he neither approved nor dis-
approved—he didn't care. In his eyes, Alec was insignificant, not
worth a moment's consideration. Masha's father was consumed with
weightier matters. He stood accused of a commercial crime, a capital
offense. He was an astute man. He knew what awaited. His wife, a
widow, would be put out in the street. His children would grow up
without a father, stigmatized and humiliated. His boy was three, the
little girl, one. They wouldn't remember him. His son would become a
violent criminal.

Alec saw the face of a man condemned to hard labor in a uranium
mine. He saw him pry a gold tooth out of his mouth and bribe a
guard. He saw him swinging by his belt in his jail cell.

7

The bells at the Vatican were ringing the evening Polina and Alec
took the train to Ladispoli to attend the Rosh Hashanah pageant. Pope John Paul had died completely unexpectedly, having
served for barely one month; but at Club Kadima the principal
topic of conversation was that the Israeli parliament had approved
Begin's peace agreement.

Chairs had been arranged to accommodate the absolute maxi-
mum number of spectators. Alec's parents arrived in advance and
occupied seats two rows away from the stage. Emma held three
seats, two for them and one for Karl. As Polina and Alec squeezed
into their seats a woman raised her voice, challenging Emma's right
to save so many seats. The woman, in her fifties, her face red with
heat and indignation, charged Emma with effrontery. The woman's
husband glared in stern, wordless support of his wife. He was
scrawny, cerebral, with inordinately bushy eyebrows under a sky
blue cap. The woman was also saving a seat. Emma drew her attention to the hypocrisy. They sniped back and forth, taking umbrage,
invoking their credentials. The woman was an economist; her husband was a physicist. Emma retaliated with her medical degree,
Samuil's managerial position, his war record. The woman eyed

Polina and Alec as accomplices to the crime. As she became more emphatic, the woman took to leaning over Polina, as if she were of no consequence.

—To save more than two seats is vulgar.

—Where is this written?

—Written? Where is it written not to spit, not to root around inside one's nose in public? It is common knowledge for any cultivated person.

—My grandchildren are in the pageant. Their mother, my daughter-in-law, is in the choir.

—Mazel tov! So you think this gives you special privileges?

—If I want to save seats for my two sons and my other daughter-in-law—who don't live around the corner but had to take the train in from Rome—I don't need your permission.

Mercifully, a woman from Sachnut appeared on the stage and demanded the people's attention. Slowly, the talking and bickering subsided and the auditorium grew quiet.

The woman began with introductory remarks about the pageant. She explained everything at a rudimentary level, presuming that her audience was unfamiliar with the basic tenets of the religion. Everyone listened obediently. Polina noticed that the woman beside her, livid only moments earlier, had miraculously relaxed. She nodded her head and smiled receptively at the mention of the words "torah," "Rosh Hashanah," and "the Jewish people."

The pageant began with the adult choir performing three songs. They then exited to make way for the children, who marched in, sweetly self-possessed. From the audience came cries of instruction and encouragement. Also commands. *Larachka, be a big girl: don't cry!* The choirmistress scurried out and helped the little ones into their ranks. The older children tried to shepherd the younger ones. Watching the children stumble into their places, mount the risers, and straighten their costumes, Polina felt the familiar pang. She wondered if, for the rest of her life, she would continue to react this way. It wouldn't do.

The children sang five or six Hebrew songs to the accompaniment of violin and piano. Samuil's friend, the one-legged Josef Roidman, was the violinist. He smiled ebulliently now at the children, now at the spectators. The pianist was a boy in his teens—gangling and serious—the very opposite of Roidman. *A prodigy*, Emma whispered deferentially. *Sixteen years old. A big career ahead of him. His teacher was Horowitz's student. Practices here three hours every day. One time they didn't let him; he wept. A great talent. Hands of gold.*

The ebullient Josef Roidman, the solemn piano prodigy, the sweet disharmony of the children's choir: Polina felt an upswell of emotion, a tenderness that moved her nearly to tears.

Near the conclusion of the program, as the children's choir was complemented by the adult, Karl arrived and claimed the place Emma had so valiantly guarded for him. The choir had launched into the first verse of the Israeli national anthem, and the choirmistress had bid the audience to rise. Groans and the scraping of chairs greeted Karl as he edged into the row. As he brushed past the woman and her husband they both looked at him briefly, contumeliously, before they dared not look at him any more. Polina saw them turn toward the stage, pretending at patriotism. Polina, who hadn't seen Karl for a month, perceived the change in him. He'd always had a formidable character, but now he seemed somehow more intimidating, like a man grown contemptuous of talk, who could afford to say less and less to more and more people.

At the conclusion of the concert the woman from Sachnut held the stage for her closing remarks.

5738 promised to be a remarkable year. It would be a historical year for the state of Israel. After many wars and many sacrifices, 5738 would bring peace to the land. Those people who feared Israel because of war no longer had anything to fear. There is no longer any reason for a Jew to say "Next year in Jerusalem"—"This year in Jerusalem!"

With this exhortation, the woman from Sachnut signaled to Josef Roidman and to the pianist, who then led the choir in a final spirited Hebrew song—the youngest children joining together to dance in a circle around the woman from Sachnut, who clapped her hands, waved her fist, and encouraged the audience to lend their voices. The song was familiar to Polina from the drunken celebration that Alec had taken her to, now nearly two years ago, at the Riga synagogue.

That day at the synagogue she gave herself over, if not precisely to Alec, then to the affair, which she felt existed somehow independent of the two of them. She recalled even the moment of letting go, when Alec had pulled her into the frenzied circle inside the synagogue courtyard. In public, in view of coworkers, in the center of the city, under the watchful eyes of the police, she'd allowed herself to be claimed by a man who was not her husband. Even a child who had glimpsed them that afternoon would not have been deceived.

It was a wonder to her that word didn't reach Maxim that same day. A wonder that he gave no sign of suspicion, and that months later, when she'd made her decision to leave him, that he met her announcement with a blank and uncomprehending look. She might even have thought it a wonder that, after she'd submitted to the second abortion, he hadn't noticed anything awry about her emotionally or physically even though she bled and suffered from cramps for days afterward. Maxim never posed any questions, as if, being a man, he was unwilling to delve too deeply into that obscure gynecological precinct. And he'd also not protested or even remarked that Polina was physically remote in the weeks that led up to the abortion and also in the weeks that followed. All told, they hadn't had sex for months. But Maxim behaved as if he was unaffected by this. As if it didn't bear mentioning. What in courtship would have been grounds for separation, in marriage was accepted as a matter of course.

After the abortion, she'd felt as if there was nobody to whom she could turn for comfort. Naturally, she'd kept it from her parents. She'd also kept it from Nadja—whom she didn't want to saddle with the shambles of her personal life. She felt completely adrift. Her marriage was finished. It was only a matter of time before she informed Maxim and made it official. She no longer knew why she'd agreed to the abortion. Alec's proposal seemed absurd in the wake of what she'd done. How could she marry Alec or emigrate with him when she didn't even want to see him? She didn't want to see anybody. She felt as if she never again wanted to be spoken to, looked at, or known.

When, in the days immediately after the abortion, Alec had come to see her, she'd released him from all promises and responsibilities. He didn't owe her anything and should consider himself free to go when and where he pleased. She imagined that this would come as a relief to him, but even if it did not, and even if he was sincere in wanting to honor his promise, she was no longer willing to go along. When Alec returned a second time—to persuade her, or confirm that she was serious, or assuage his conscience—she'd told him the same thing again. He didn't need to feel bad or guilty or upset. She had no ill feelings toward him. She asked of him only that he let her alone.

Then, one afternoon, at the conclusion of the workday, she was visited by an older woman whom she'd never met before. The woman approached Polina at her desk. Polina had noted her when she entered the office, as had the others. Her entrance had been so tentative that she'd succeeded in arousing everyone's attention. As she crossed the room, seemingly in Polina's direction, Marina Kirilovna had leaned over to Polina and said archly, *Well, here comes Mamasha.*

Polina didn't know what Marina Kirilovna meant, but watched the woman come near, her face nervous, sympathetic, and polite.

The woman introduced herself by saying, *Forgive me, but if I am not mistaken, you know my younger son, Alec,* and she asked Polina if she wouldn't mind joining her for a short stroll.

For half an hour they walked the streets around the factory in the pale late-afternoon light. It was nearly April and spring was making its first cracks in winter's shell, but here and there, on the pavement, there remained patches of ice. Emma asked if she might hold on to Polina's arm for balance.

Emma began by saying that she had come to Polina of her own accord. Alec hadn't asked her and he didn't know that she was doing it. Though, in another sense, she believed that he had asked her and that he wanted her to help him—he had just not said it in so many words.

—Not long ago, Emma said, Alec told me and my husband that he was going to marry and apply for emigration. It was the first we'd heard about either of these things—neither of them being something a parent would take lightly. We were both quite shocked, though, I daresay, not for the same reasons. Now Alec changes his plans: he still intends to emigrate, but no longer to marry. When I ask about his bride, who she is, what happened, he doesn't say. But I'm his mother. Men believe they have secrets only because women pretend that they don't know.

Emma delivered this last line with a wry resignation, and Polina felt yet more warmly disposed toward her.

And then, without any further preamble, Emma related a story from her past.

Emma tried to conjure for Polina the image of herself as she was at the age of twenty-one, a young bride, innocent in a way twenty-one-year-old girls no longer were, wedded to a handsome man she barely knew, a man twelve years her senior, a Red Army officer and a veteran of the front, experienced in life in ways she couldn't imagine and didn't dare ask about. They were living in Baltinava, the small town where Emma had been born, and from which she and her parents had fled when the Nazis invaded in 1941. In the woods surrounding the town were bandits of various stripes. Most days, there was shooting. It was dangerous to go into the streets at night, and even more dangerous to be on the roads outside of town. Her father and her husband were both military men. Time and again, they led raids into the woods.

This was in January, the winter of 1946. She was six months pregnant. For most of the Soviet Union the war was over, but for her it persisted.

—I was frightened every minute of every day, Emma said. I feared for the lives of my father and my husband, out in the woods, and I feared for the life of my unborn child.

There were townspeople who sympathized with the bandits. When her father and husband were away, only she, her mother, and her invalid grandfather remained in the house. Her father and husband left them a submachine gun, but the weapon terrified her and her mother both. If, God forbid, the need arose, neither of them trusted herself to use it.

The strain on her nerves led to complications with her pregnancy. From the very beginning, she had been unwell. What she desperately wanted was to quit the terrifying town and wait out the duration of her term in Riga, or at the very least with relatives in Karsava. But her father and her husband dismissed the idea. Her husband said that the conditions in town were nowhere near as dangerous as she made them out to be.

But she couldn't cast the worries from her mind, and she couldn't simply ignore the shooting that came from the woods. Finally, late one evening, under the weight of her nervous strain, something in her snapped. There were terrible pains and a great deal of blood. She was put into bed, and the white sheets were quickly drenched. Outside, a thick coat of snow lay on the streets.

—The town had no proper doctor, Emma said, only a medic in the Red Army garrison and two midwives. I had already started my medical training and I knew that there was nobody in town equipped to handle what was happening to me. I thought that my baby was going to die inside me, and that I would die too.

Through this anguish, she saw her husband standing at her bedside. She thought he was angry with her, but then, with great force, he said: *You will not die.*

He went out into the night and returned with his hat and the shoulders of his greatcoat covered in snow. With the help of her parents she was lifted from the bed, wrapped in wool blankets, and taken outside on a feather duvet. Her mother had used a rag to stanch the bleeding, but it didn't help. In front of the house was a horse-drawn sledge that her husband had hired from a neighbor. There were no trucks or automobiles to be had. Even the garrison had none—but even if it had, a truck or an automobile would have been crippled in such snow.

She was put on the sledge, and her husband took the reins.

From where she lay, she saw the back of his greatcoat. He had a submachine gun across his shoulder and a whip in one hand. He snapped the whip and they lurched off into the dark, frozen night.

They were headed for Karsava, fifteen kilometers away. At night, in such weather, the trip would take hours and hours.

—I lay in the sledge and felt the life draining out of me. Not just my own life, but also the life of the child. In my delirium, I felt the child's spirit float out of me and waft into the sky. I felt beyond all consolation. Only a woman who has experienced such a tragedy can comprehend it. I no longer cared about my own life. I was ready to let my spirit drift off after my child's.

Only her husband's will kept her from dying. It was as if Death had her by one hand and her husband had her by the other. And all night long she felt herself being pulled in opposite directions, until, finally, Death released its hold. For the sake of her life, her husband had been more unyielding than Death.

—I saw a part of him I had not seen before, Emma said. He was not only stern, but he was also gentle; he spoke sweetly to me; over the howling wind, he called my name. I could not put into words everything I saw of him that night. But it was what kept me alive. And not only that night, but also in the weeks that followed.

They were standing again near the front gates of the factory. Even as they stood quietly, Emma kept her arm linked with Polina's.

—I am grateful to you for your kindness, Polina said. It's very sad what happened to your child. But our experiences are not the same.

—I know you don't know me. You have every right to think: Who is this woman? What does she want from me? It's true that I'm Alec's mother and that I saw his unhappiness and I wanted to help him. But I am also a woman, and I came to speak to you as a woman. My dear, you are still young. Your life is ahead of you. Even if you don't make a life with my son, you mustn't punish yourself. Sooner or later, we all say, What's done is done. It is better to say it sooner.

Emma turned her head and glanced down the street. Polina watched her eyes settle on a black Volga, which responded by edging from the curb. The car rolled slowly toward them. Through the windshield, Polina saw the face of the driver, a lean, muted, sagacious,

Latvian face. The car stopped beside them, its rear passenger door level with Emma. The driver got out and came around to their side. He opened the door for Emma and remained in place, looking obediently, implacably into the distance. The heavy, polished car idled luxuriantly. Polina became aware of VEF workers, entering and exiting through the main gate, who paused to look at her. Emma paid them no mind.

—We are leaving this country, Emma said. Whatever you decide, my dear, decide so that you do not regret it later.

She released Polina's arm and lowered herself into the backseat of the car. She said, Thank you, Arturs, and Arturs expertly shut the door.

Never looking directly at her, his tone sedate, the man spoke to her in Latvian.

—If you were my daughter, I would tell you to use your ticket. Nothing is going to change here.

Arturs rounded the hood and resumed his seat. Polina watched the formal black car, with its two apostates, pull away and disappear down the road.

NOVEMBER

1

My dearest Lola,

Belated Rosh Hashanah greetings to you and Igor! May you both
have a good and sweet year! (See how I'm expanding my cultural
horizons!) How did you celebrate the holiday in Rome?

Here, I was invited by my new friends to a special dinner.
Thanks to you, I've been made an honorary member of their
circle. They've even given me a new name: Naomi. They're all very
amused by the idea of me as Naomi. The name is from the Bible,
which some of them claim to have read. As a work of literature,
it's gotten mixed reviews. Our mailman says that God was no
Tolstoy. But everyone agrees that it's the best source to consult
when you need to name a Gentile.

So now I have three names. The plain one, Brigitte, and
Naomi. Can you believe that an ordinary girl like me should
have so many identities? You'd think I was Mata Hari.

I've come to feel more and more at home with these new
friends, and with our mailman in particular. It certainly wasn't
what either of us intended to happen. In almost every way, it's
inconvenient, if not completely absurd. But I think he's witty and
sympathetic and resilient. And he says I'm the only free spirit in

Riga. So, for the time being, we're proceeding as if everything were normal.

This past month we've spent a lot of time together. I've kept this from Mama and Papa because I know that they would strongly disapprove. Our apartment is still gloomy, like the bottom of a lake, and we drift through the rooms silently, like eels. I am trying not to contribute to the gloom.

I know that I won't be able to keep this up indefinitely. You probably find this hard to believe, but I've been very careful. I've avoided going places where we might be seen. Only yesterday, people went to the Riga synagogue to dance and drink in honor of Simchas Torah. I thought better of it. Our mailman went. (I should give him a name. I'll call him Alain. After Alain Delon.) He said that he'd seen you there two years ago with Igor. You never told me. I didn't know you'd been so daring. What other secrets have you kept from me?

Do you recall how many people were at the synagogue two years ago? Alain says that most of them are gone. Alain and I have talked a little about what we might do if he were to get his permission to go. What do you think about it?

(Funny how it's Jewish women who are called "vehicles," when, with us, it's the men who provide the passage.)

2

Over the course of her brief stay in Rome, Masha had strayed from the pensione only a handful of times: twice to appear at the offices of HIAS; once for a disheartening interview at the U.S. embassy; and once to make some purchases at the round market in Piazza Vittorio. All of those times, she'd been under the supervision of her mother and brother. Consequently, she never got to see anything.

It was only because of her mother's trust in Alec that she had allowed Masha to take the train by herself from Ladispoli. Alec met her on the platform at Termini and led her down into the metro. They rode four stops to Flaminio and emerged at the gates of Piazza del Popolo. Traffic on the avenue that circumscribed the ancient walls had ground nearly to a halt. It was a Sunday, and a great number of people were gathered in the square. Alec saw nuns in full habit scampering down from the plinth of the Egyptian obelisk.

The warm November sun was directly overhead, and the obelisk cast only a thin rim of shadow. A crowd streamed down Via del Corso, where it formed something of a procession.

—What's all this? Masha asked.

From the little he overheard, Alec gathered that they had just missed seeing the new Polish pope. Only a few weeks into his papacy, he'd caused a sensation by going out among his parishioners on Sundays. The newspapers reported an epidemic of swooning nuns.

With the city before them, Alec asked Masha what she'd like to see.

—Show me what you think I'd like to see.

—It's a big city, Alec said.

—If you know me at all, you'll know where to take me.

Alec steered Masha away from the Catholic faithful and onto Via del Babuino, which ran like a spur directly to Piazza di Spagna and its famed steps—where one could see the city's birds in all their plumage: wily immigrants peddling their souvenirs and tchotchkes; American tourists, with the movements and features of overgrown babies; long-haired bohemian kids, their limbs casually intertwined, treating the steps like a huge communal bed; pious middle-European pilgrims, resting between epiphanies; and snooty Roman socialites returning from the elegant shops on Via Condotti. Alec proceeded past the window displays of the famous fashion houses, the Versaces and the Guccis. From Via Condotti through a series of tributary streets, they emerged in front of that great wedding cake ornament, the Trevi Fountain. After four-plus months in Rome, Alec's knowledge of the city inhered in him physically, like sense memory. He knew his way around just as he knew how to ride a bicycle or dribble a soccer ball. He looked to Masha to see if she was impressed.

With a note of petulance, Masha said, Is this all you wanted to show me?

—There's more, of course, Alec said, his tone upbeat. Not two minutes away is the Pantheon, with its perfect round blowhole; and not five minutes from that is Campo dei Fiori, where there is a statue of a monk whom the Church burned at the stake.

Masha's expression didn't brighten.

Alec went on: On the Corso, there's a large shopping center, unlike anything we had in the Soviet Union. And set off, practically on its own, is the Colosseum, where the gladiators fought and the emperors sent Christians to be devoured by lions. The stands remain. You can sit right where Caesar sat two thousand years ago.

Alec couldn't tell if Masha was genuinely peeved, or if this was just part of a game. But, glumly, she said, If that's all, then I guess you don't really know me.

They made one or two more circuits like this before Masha finally unburdened herself.

What she really wanted to see was where Alec went when he left her in Ladispoli. She wanted to see the square, the building, the very window that faced the street. She wanted to see more still—the apartment itself, and the bedroom, and the bed. But that exceeded even what Alec was willing to do.

It seemed reckless to show her where he lived and Alec knew that he would only be indulging a childish need in her. But then, his address wasn't classified. If she wanted to find him badly enough, she could. So better show her himself—and get the surge of tempting fate.

Through the ghetto and over the bridge they went. Past the pharmacy and the hospital on Isola Tiberina and across the second bridge to Trastevere. Alec steered Masha to the intersection of Via Anicia and Via dei Salumi, from where it was possible to see the building, its front door, and Lyova's window. Alec regarded Masha as she gazed up at the window and the apartment. No movement could be seen through the window. Lyova had, that morning, gone again to plead his case at the American embassy. Just to keep in practice, he'd said. Polina was at her job.

They stood there for some time, with Masha looking fixedly at the apartment house. At last, she relaxed and leaned against Alec.

—Well, now you've seen the palace, Alec said.

—Don't mock me, Masha replied in an injured tone.

—I'm not mocking, Alec said. It's a building like any other.

—No it isn't, Masha said. But I don't expect you to understand.

—What should I understand? Alec said.

—That I can't feel close to you if I don't even know where you live.

—All right, Alec said. So you know.

—Yes, Masha said.

—Are you happy now? Alec asked.

—Yes, Masha said, and slid her hand into the back pocket of his jeans.

3

Just south of Verona, on his most recent tour of northern Italy, Lyova had been involved in a car accident. Two women inside his van had started quarreling and Lyova had momentarily taken his eyes off the road. When he looked back, the rear of a bus loomed massively before him. To avoid the bus, he swerved to his right and collided with a Fiat. He sheared off the Fiat's side mirror and dented the driver's door. It had cost him a week's wages—one hundred thirty *mila* lire—to settle with the Fiat's owner and thus avoid police involvement. His own van had fared little better than the Fiat.

Ordinarily, Lyova would have fumed over the accident and the lost wages, but upon his return he'd heard some news that had lifted his spirits. Through a diplomat at the American embassy he'd been made aware of some new legislation before the U.S. Congress. The loosening of strictures that related to his case.

It didn't exactly mean he could start packing his bags, but it provided a reason for optimism. In the near term he would still have to keep earning money. The more the better. And for this, he needed to repair his Volkswagen, which had sustained superficial body damage, but also structural damage to the wheel well. Bent metal brushed against the driveshaft and caused a grinding sound.

At higher speeds, the grinding became more of a high-pitched squeal, and this is what Alec heard as he and Lyova drove the highway from Rome to Ladispoli. To help Lyova, Alec had proposed a visit to the body shop that Karl either owned, had a partial stake in, or managed—Alec didn't pretend to know the intricacies of the arrangement.

To find the body shop, they first stopped by his parents' house. Emma answered the door, a wooden spoon in her hand. A faint crackle of frying oil, and the associated smells of eggs, onions, and sausage, wafted over from the kitchen. It was eleven in the morning.

Alec said, Breakfast?

—For Papa, Emma replied. And added in a conspiratorial whisper, He's been sleeping late.

They followed Emma into the kitchen, where Samuil sat alone at the table. Rosa had taken the boys to the apartment of an acquaintance, where they could play with other children. Karl had left, customarily, at dawn. She'd stayed behind to attend to Samuil—he was alone so much of the time as it was. She didn't like the idea of him preparing his own meals and eating by himself.

Samuil eyed first Lyova, then Alec, and asked, Official HIAS business?

Emma said from behind the stove, where she transferred the omelet from the pan to a plate—We have plenty of food. Syoma, invite them to sit.

Alec watched his father raise an unenthusiastic eyebrow.

—If you're going to eat, you might as well sit, Samuil said.

—He doesn't mean to be impolite, Emma said, mostly to Lyova.

—Not at all, Lyova said. I'm grateful for the hospitality. And inhaling the aroma from the steaming plate, he asked, Are those veal sausages?

—They are, Emma said proudly.

With a butter knife, she divided the omelet into three sections.

She distributed the food and turned back to the stove. Alec watched his father poke absently at his eggs.

—I'll cook up some more, Emma said. It won't take five minutes.

—It's hard to find veal sausages here, Lyova said. Mostly, they sell pork.

—Rosa, our daughter-in-law, has become very close with the rabbi and with the rabbi's wife, Emma said. I go with her to classes on Jewish subjects. The rabbi's wife teaches us what is the right way. It's harder, of course, and you have to make an effort. But we do it. We have almost no pork in the house.

—I applaud your efforts, Lyova said, and dug into his omelet. I'm not religious, but I appreciate variety. In Jerusalem, for example, it is the other way around. There, it is nearly impossible to find a piece of pork. The religious Jews don't eat it, and neither do the Arabs. It's the one thing they can agree on. Unfortunately, they haven't been able to make it the basis for peaceful coexistence.

—You lived in Israel? Samuil inquired, exhibiting his first mild interest in his guest.

—Syoma, Emma said, he's the one who shares the apartment with Alec and Polina. I've spoken to you about him.

Samuil cast her a disparaging look that implied that he couldn't be expected to account for every piece of flotsam.

—I lived there for five years, Lyova said. Near Tel Aviv.

—And no longer? Samuil said.

—No longer, Lyova said. I'm a serial dissident. A rootless cosmopolitan, as they used to say. A "seeker of happiness," Lyova added, citing the title of the classic Birobidzhan propaganda film.

Samuil wasn't amused.

—I've heard of people like you, Samuil said. I've also heard of others who, having quaffed the Israeli waters, developed a thirst for home.

—There are those, too. Some unfortunates couldn't adapt, others were merely dopes, and a few were KGB plants, sent abroad to serve as object lessons for the benefit of the press.

—KGB plants? Samuil scoffed. According to whom?

—Lyova imagines KGB agents everywhere, Alec volunteered cheerfully.

—Naturally, Lyova said. I lived in the Soviet Union with my eyes open. I was an officer in the army, a tankist who rolled into Czechoslovakia in August of 1968. I have a healthy appreciation for Soviet power. What I'm saying is realpolitik, not criticism. In the history of the world, was there ever a nation that thrived without spies?

—They didn't need to plant you, though, did they? Samuil countered.

—I suppose I wouldn't admit it if they had, Lyova said and grinned.

—Now there's an idea that never occurred to me, Alec mused.

—Everything is a big comic revue for my son, you see, Samuil pronounced, but let me ask you a foolish question. If you had to return to one or the other place, which would it be?

Lyova surprised Alec by appearing to seriously contemplate the question.

—No, it's a good question, Lyova conceded. I think about it often, but nobody has ever asked me. When I go out with my placard to attend protests and I speak with journalists, they—depending on their politics—want to know either why I left Israel or why I will not return there. Even the Communists don't imagine that a person would trade life in the West for life in the Soviet Union. Other than Christina Onassis, who could afford to? This is why her story made headlines. It wasn't that the world's wealthiest woman had renounced her fortune and had thrown her lot in with the citizens of the workers' paradise. She renounced nothing. She kept her millions. That was the point: she proved what most people already suspected, that only a multimillionairess could afford the luxury of living in the workers' paradise. The average person knew that he could no more afford to move to the Soviet Union than he could afford a private jet. The only exception to this mind-set is that of the former Soviet citizen. Only the former Soviet citizen, dazed and pummeled by emigration, could yearn for home and imagine a better life in the Soviet

Union. Did I have these thoughts? I did and I do. Do I have similar thoughts about Israel? Yes. But don't we all have our pathological thoughts? Rapists and murderers also have pathological thoughts. So what separates a rapist from a normal person? The rapist submits to his pathological thoughts, and the normal person resists them. To return to Israel is, for me, pathological, and to return to Kishinev, also pathological. Which is worse? How to answer such a question? Which is worse: rape or murder? To a normal person, neither is acceptable. So that's all. *Zehu*, as they say in Hebrew.

Alec watched his father for a reaction. He'd heard Lyova expound like this before, many times, and had found it entertaining. Samuil said nothing, and instead looked at Lyova as if from the seat of an intellectual throne. When he finally deigned to speak, he said, with a mixture of pity and reproach, What you are looking for doesn't exist, and you're not going to find it.

Taking no offense, Lyova said, That may be so. Then again, I'm not looking for perfection. So far I've been a citizen of two utopias. Now I have modest expectations. Basically, I want the country with the fewest parades.

4

Karl's body shop was at the southern edge of town. From where Lyova stopped the van, they could gaze out at the autumn stubble of harvested fields. In the immediate vicinity there were a few small houses with crumbling stucco exteriors, spaced widely apart. The last of the houses on the street looked to be uninhabited. The second to last was the one that had been converted or commandeered to serve as the body shop. Three Fiats were parked bumper to bumper to bumper just shy of the house, their body panels sanded down and blotched with primer. Directly in front of the house two kids were kicking a white leather soccer ball around. Alec guessed that they were about fourteen or fifteen years old. One was fair, tall, and skinny, with knobby elbows jutting out of his plain white undershirt. He wore Adidas track pants from the Americana and Russian canvas sneakers. He had lank hair and a few blond whiskers emulating a mustache. His counterpart was shorter, darker, and stockier. He was clothed much like the first kid, but his features and body language identified him as Italian. Alec and Lyova watched them kick the ball around for a few moments before Lyova put the van in gear and rolled up to the house.

As the van crept closer, the boys looked up from their game. Both eyed the van with street-kid bravado. The Italian lifted his chin and called out first in his language.

—*Hey, dove stai andando?*

Lyova slowed the van to a stop.

—*Dal meccanico,* Lyova said.

—*Quale meccanico?*

—*Che cos'è quella dietro di te? Non è un'officina?*

—*Chi ti ha detto che è un'officina?*

Lyova grinned wickedly and said, *Tua madre*.

Naturally, this provoked the kid to fly at the van, spewing curses and their accompanying hand gestures. His Russian friend followed close behind.

When the Italian kid started banging on the hood of the van, Alec called out to the Russian kid to calm his friend. He received the inevitable response.

—Calm him down, if you know what's good for you, Alec repeated.

—Who the fuck are you?

—You don't want to know who I am, Alec said leisurely.

This got the kid's attention. He turned to his friend and motioned for him to desist.

—So who the fuck are you? the kid repeated.

—If that house behind you is a garage, and if the guy who runs it is named Karl, then I'm his brother. If not, then never mind.

At the mention of Karl's name, both kids' faces grew rigid. Their eyes flashed from Alec to each other.

—So I guess it is a garage, Alec said.

—Wait a minute, the Russian kid said, and hustled off to the back of the house.

The Italian kid remained as sentinel, his expression still hooded, suspicious and belligerent.

In short order, the Russian kid returned with Karl, who wore blue jeans and a denim work-shirt, its sleeves rolled up. Using a dirty rag, he wiped his grease-stained hands.

—You've become a mechanic? Alec asked.

—Not exactly, Karl said. But now and then I have to get my hands dirty.

Alec watched as Karl glanced ambivalently at Lyova's van. He then turned to his two lookouts, complimented them on their vigilance, and sent them back to their ball playing.

Karl stepped over to the passenger side and said, So what brings you?

—Have you met Lyova? He shares the apartment with us.

—Nice to meet you, Karl said, and raised his dirty right hand in lieu of a shake.

—As you can see, Alec said, gesturing toward the dented fender, Lyova banged up his van.

—Right, Karl said.

—And I thought, seeing as how you're now in the garage business, Alec said.

Karl listened stonily and made no motion to invite Lyova and his banged-up van into the garage.

—The accident cost him a lot of money. He gives tours of Italy, and he needs the van for work, Alec continued.

Karl's expression didn't mellow. He allowed his gaze to travel from Alec to the damaged van and then over to Lyova, who had been sitting patiently all the while, wearing a look of calm, worldly comprehension.

—All right, follow me, Karl said finally. He pointed at the pitted cement drive that led to the rear of the house. But next time you have a brilliant idea, do me a favor and ask me first.

Creeping along behind Karl, they went along the drive and, at Karl's signal, stopped the van at the entrance to a small workshop under a corrugated tin roof. Thin shafts of light streaked into the workshop through small holes in the tin. Inside the workshop, Alec saw four or five men—it was hard to be precise—two of whom wore handkerchiefs over their faces and were busy spraying white paint on a yellow Renault. A third man was engaged in removing a side panel from an Alfa Romeo. A fourth man was seated at a small card table beside the wall, drinking from an espresso cup. Alec didn't see a coffee pot, only a bottle of vodka. He believed that he saw a fifth man duck out of the workshop, but in the haze of dust and spray paint, he couldn't say for sure if he'd seen a man or a shadow.

Karl crossed to the man at the card table and motioned in the direction of the van. They exchanged a few words. Then Karl waved for Alec and Lyova to approach. As they did, the two guys in the handkerchiefs briefly paused to observe them, as did the guy working on the Alfa. At closer range, and despite the handkerchief, Alec recognized one of the painters as Dmitri. Alec nodded in passing, a gesture Dmitri didn't bother to reciprocate.

The man at the card table Karl introduced as Angelo. The house and the workshop were his. He looked to be in his fifties, powerfully built—heavy through the shoulders, chest, and gut. Karl spoke to Angelo in Italian, which, to Alec's surprise, he commanded admirably. He introduced Alec, the word "fratello" eliciting a smile from Angelo and an invitation to join him at the table.

—We taught him to drink vodka, Karl said. Lately we've been getting decent Polish stuff. It arrives in good quantities through Germany.

A chair was dragged over for Lyova, and Angelo poured shots of vodka into the espresso cups.

After they drank, Karl quickly sketched the situation.

—*Ma tuo fratello, che tipo di lavoro pensa che facciamo qui?* Angelo smirked.

—*Non ne capisce niente di queste cose,* Karl said. *Sa solo correre dietro alle ragazze.*

—*Anche quella è una dote.* Angelo grinned, and then turned to Lyova.

—*Parli italiano?*

—*Sì,* Lyova said.

—*È il tuo furgone?*

—*Sì, è mio.*

—*Niente male.*

—*Grazie.*

—*Funziona bene?*

—*Funzionava bene, prima dell'incidente.*

—*Qui non arrivano tanti furgoni come questo.*

—*Agli italiani piacciono le macchine piccole.*

—*Ma qualche volta fa comodo avere un furgone.*

—*Sì, qualche volta.*

—*Se ripariamo il furgone, forse saresti interessato a cambiarlo con una di queste auto?*

—*Una qualsiasi?*

—*Sì, eccetto l'Alfa.*

—*È molto generoso da parte tua ma per il mio lavoro mi serve un forgone.*

—*Peccato*, Angelo said, and turned the matter over to Karl.

Resuming in Russian, Karl told Lyova that there was only so much they could do for the van.

—If there's mechanical damage, our guys won't be able to fix it. We don't have the tools or the parts.

—And if it's just body work?

—That we can do, Karl said. Though it depends what you can afford.

—What Alec said is true. I can't afford much.

—Tell me what you think is fair.

Lyova named a figure and Karl accepted it without haggling.

—If you want to wait around, Karl said, I'll have Valera do it after he finishes with the Alfa. Or if you don't feel like waiting, you could leave it here overnight.

—If I leave it overnight, what are the chances it will be here tomorrow? Lyova grinned.

—I suppose anything could happen, Karl replied blankly.

—Anyway, it's our means back to Rome, Lyova said. I don't want to speak for Alec, but I'll wait.

—No problem, Karl said. I'd keep you company, but there are some things I need to do.

They spent the rest of the afternoon, several hours, in and around the garage. They had another drink with the idle Angelo. They rested their chairs along the rear wall of the house—as far from the dust and the fumes as possible—and watched the activity. Nobody paid them any mind. Dmitri and his partner finished painting the Renault, and Dmitri drove it out of the garage. A Ford Escort sedan pulled in, and its driver, another Russian, fetched several wooden packing crates out of the trunk. Karl greeted him at the back door of the house and helped him carry the crates inside. At the same time, two uniformed policemen dropped by to have a drink with Angelo. The afternoon ticked by.

Alec and Lyova made peace with the two kids out front, and periodically joined them to have a smoke and kick the ball around.

Eventually, Valera swapped the panel on the Alfa with another that he drew from a stack of body parts stored at the far end of the workshop. He then turned his attention to the van.

—It's some operation your brother's running here, Lyova observed.

—Is it? Alec asked, not because he didn't have a sense of its illicitness but because he found it hard to believe that the proceeds could compensate for spending so much time in such squalor.

—I'm sure I don't understand half of it, Lyova said, but the half I understand is no joke. To pull this off, he's got to be involved with serious people.

—Even so, Alec said, I haven't seen a sty like this since our fiasco at Chop.

Lyova had also crossed at Chop. His experience had been bad, but he'd freely admitted that Alec and his family had been subjected to a more diabolical order of humiliation.

The fact was that, one night, in July of 1978, in a small, dingy booth at the Chop railway station, a scrawny Russian customs inspector, who reeked of tobacco and looked like a prime candidate for cirrhosis, had said to him: *Bend over and hold your balls and your cock. I don't want them swinging in my face.* Clutching a flashlight in one hand, he had tried to force the rubber-gloved finger of his other hand into Alec's rectum. And when Alec's body had instinctively resisted, he had barked: *Don't play the virgin and open your ass! I didn't have this trouble with your father.*

They had all been subjected to this same violation. Samuil had gone first, followed by Alec and Karl. A matronly female customs inspector had taken charge of the women. First Emma, then Rosa and Polina. In a neighboring booth, equipped with a gynecological table, the customs inspector had done her work with the aid of a speculum. For long minutes after they emerged from the booth, they all averted their eyes and didn't speak. Even the boys, who were not spared, came out this way.

When the customs inspector had tried to take them, Rosa had shrieked with the ferocity of a jungle creature, *They are children! Seven and five! What kind of monster would do this to a child?* Karl had silenced her with a searing look. In a level tone, he had said to the customs inspector, *There is nothing on the boys.* The inspector remained unmoved. He took Yury by the wrist. Karl said, *What will it take to leave the boys?* The customs inspector leered and said, *We have our regulations.* As the inspector tried to pull Yury in the direction of the booth, Karl clapped a hand on his son's shoulder and shot the agent a withering look. *Their mother goes with them*, Karl said, *or, I swear to God, I will tear your throat out.* The inspector regarded Karl for an instant—long enough to gather that Karl wasn't the type to issue idle threats—and relented.

Resentful thoughts, like a flock of bats, wheeled around them. Alec tried hard not to blame Samuil. His father's stubbornness had incited the first customs agent to single them out for the cavity searches, because he had refused to part with his brother's letters from the front, or even to allow the customs agent to lay hands on them. The agent had already confiscated his father's medals. They had only a very short amount of time to clear customs before their train left for Bratislava. If they missed the train, they would be stranded overnight in Chop, a closed border city, without passports or permits, where they could easily be arrested. Alec felt the likelihood of this increasing as his father brandished one letter after another, taking pains to unfold them and display first one side and then its obverse. It was a ludicrous exercise. It seemed like every letter was written in Yiddish, in an alphabet the customs agent couldn't pretend to understand. Behind them, other families stirred impatiently.

In the end, after Zhenya, the last of the boys, had been searched, they already knew that they had missed their train. They were stranded in the station amid jumbled belongings. They now appeared very conspicuous. The customs agents who had impeded their departure eyed them darkly. And Alec felt other sinister characters in the station taking their measure.

We have to get out of here, Karl said. Rosa had looked despondently at their pile of baggage and asked, *How?*

At that moment one of the sinister characters, a Gypsy, detached himself from a pillar and sidled over to them. He was squarely built, unshaven, with a greasy forelock, shabby trousers, dingy canvas shoes, and an impressive red silk shirt. *Missed your train?* he asked, scanning them all, but gravitating intuitively to Karl. *What's it to you?* Karl said. *If you're in a bind, I can help*, the Gypsy said.

From the station they walked three kilometers to the outskirts of Chop, an area of partially constructed panel apartment houses. The Gypsy and his fourteen-year-old son had helped them load most of their belongings onto a cart harnessed to a lethargic donkey. The cart was large enough to accommodate all their belongings, but Karl and Alec elected to carry some things to allow the boys and Emma to ride instead of walk. Emma had confessed to feeling weak and lightheaded, symptoms she attributed to nervous exhaustion.

The Gypsies brought them to a clearing set back behind one of the apartment sites. The ground was rife with weeds and strewn with windblown trash. Lodged in the middle of the field, like a dinosaur egg, was the rusted drum of a concrete mixer. There was a large shanty at one end of the clearing, and a larger structure at the rear edge, abutting a little wood. The Gypsies deposited them and their belongings in the shanty, and retired to the other building. They'd arrived in early evening and had only a few hours to adapt themselves to their quarters. The shanty was derelict and dark. It had two windows, both thick with grime. The walls and floor were of plywood and infused with mold. Vodka and beer bottles were littered throughout the place, and along one wall were three stained mattresses, two of which were outfitted with crumpled, and equally stained, sheets. The place smelled heavily of rot, tobacco, urine, and debauch.

Where have you brought us? Rosa asked Karl. A question he disregarded. *How do I put the children down in this place? They are wearing their good suits,* she persisted. *We have all of our shit with us,* Karl said. *We have sheets, pillows, blankets, all kinds of crap. You're their mother. Improvise.*

They all regarded the place with disgust. Nobody wanted to touch anything. Emma gaped in horror and spoke one word: "Taman." Lermontov's epitome of squalor.

By nightfall they managed to clear a quadrant of the space for themselves. In a discarded barrel, previously used for a similar purpose, Alec lit a fire. Through the walls they heard the sounds of the Gypsies across the field. When Alec and Karl stepped out to smoke, they saw the lights aglow in the Gypsies' house.

At some point in the night, they fell asleep. Alec remembered drifting off beside Polina. He remembered saying, *A fitting way to spend our last night in the Soviet Union.* Then he'd been startled awake by Karl, in what felt like the middle of the night, but what was in fact not even midnight. Karl hissed, *Zhenya's gone. Get up.* Except for Rosa, who peered at them with blazing feral eyes, everyone else was still asleep.

They slipped from their shanty and out into the dark clearing. Across the way, the lights were still burning in the Gypsies' house. Karl hunched forward, his body coiled for violence, as he strode toward the Gypsies' house. Alec followed in step, and felt the same apprehension as when he'd feared that Karl's schoolyard enemies might come to their street for a brawl.

Alec remembered passing the black outcropping of the cement mixer, and then standing with Karl at the lit window of the Gypsies' house. The window granted a view of the living room. Inside, they saw mismatched furniture, a large ornate rug, and also the man who'd brought them there, his fourteen-year-old son, an old woman, two middle-aged women, and three small children. Two of the children were girls, the other was a boy roughly Zhenya's age. The boy, Alec was quick to note, was wearing Zhenya's little suit. Everyone was smiling, in high spirits. But there was no sign of Zhenya himself. Then Alec felt his brother tense beside him. He turned to see what had caused Karl to react. Opposite the Gypsy children, at the edge of the rug, stood Zhenya. He was naked except for his underpants. In the lamplight, his pale skin was translucent. Alec could see the delicate web of blue veins in his chest. He didn't look precisely frightened or upset. If anything, he looked confused. However, the scene was so bizarre that Alec didn't know what it implied. He had no time to consider it because Karl leaped past him and barged through the door.

Alec felt that he'd been only seconds behind Karl, but somehow, in that span, Karl had managed to seize the Gypsy by the ear and bend him over backwards. The women and children started shrieking, and Zhenya, who hadn't looked upset before, had burst into tears. Alec saw a trickle of blood at the Gypsy's earlobe and he feared that Karl might tear the man's ear off. He threatened to do as much if everyone didn't quiet down. Between gasps, the Gypsy protested that they'd done nothing wrong. Zhenya had wandered over to their house. They had let him in. The Gypsy's youngest son had admired Zhenya's suit. The Gypsy's wife had offered Zhenya a trade. For the suit, they would give something of theirs. His son was only trying the suit on to see how it would fit.

Karl said, *Enough.* He told the Gypsy's little boy that if he preferred his father with two ears, he should be quick about removing the suit. Alec helped the sobbing Zhenya get dressed. When Zhenya was clothed, Karl released the Gypsy. *Tomorrow*, Karl said, *I expect you to be there with the donkey at eight. No surprises. Everything like we agreed.* Alec didn't remember if the Gypsy said anything in compliance. The only sound in the room seemed to be Zhenya's sobbing.

On the way out the door, Karl slapped Zhenya sharply on the back of the head. *Keep quiet*, he said. *And not a word about this to anyone.* He looked over at Alec and said, *You, too.*

5

On the thirty-sixth anniversary of the loss of his leg, Roidman came to visit, armed with a bottle of cognac.

—I call it my second birthday, Roidman said.

Samuil invited him in and joined him at the kitchen table to raise a toast.

—So, a happy occasion, Roidman said and smiled. One has to remember to rejoice—especially when everything is not going quite according to plan.

By "not going quite according to plan," Roidman meant that, after nearly a year, and after all of his son's machinations, and all of the letters written on his behalf by Jewish ladies in Winnipeg, the Canadians still had no interest in him. Roidman confided that he would continue to wait until one of two things happened: either Canada accepted him or he finished his opera about Fanny Kaplan. He found Ladispoli to be conducive for musical composition. There was the seashore, the mild climate, stimulating company, and few practical obligations. This was how he had always imagined the way creative people worked in their exclusive rest homes and union retreats. How engaging and fulfilling it was. He had been working in one trade or another since boyhood: finishing boots with his father, a sapper's duties in the Red Army, later his occupation in Kiev, tooling leather. He'd never objected to the work, but it had never felt like anything other than what it was: work. His time in Ladispoli confirmed what he had always suspected—that artists were indeed the most fortunate people. What a charmed life they led! What they did could not even be considered work—it was such a pleasure. When he sat down to compose, the music simply poured out of him.

In his opera, he had now reached the most stirring and hopeful part of the story. Up to this point, much has happened. Fanny Kaplan is no longer a girl of sixteen. She has long since left her family and their traditions. Seduced away by the anarchist Mika, she has joined a terrorist cell. In a hotel in Odessa, she has helped to fashion a bomb for a tsarist governor. By accident, this bomb has exploded in the hotel room, wounding her in the eyes. Injured, she is abandoned by Mika and arrested by the police. A trial follows and a life sentence in a Siberian prison.

For more than a decade, she is exiled and imprisoned. Because of her injury she is nearly blind. She expects no reprieve from the tsar, and her future seems as bleak as the taiga. She waits and waits, and her youth and idealism drain away with the passing years. The only comfort she finds is with the other prisoners—radical revolutionists of various stripes.

In their captivity, she and her fellow prisoners plot the revolution and dream of a just world.

Will we forever be the childless mothers of the revolution? Up on the frozen brow of the earth, our hearts and wombs burn to give birth to the future. Our hearts and wombs burn to forge a new world.

Then, miraculously, spontaneously, comes the February revolution. The divine eternal tsar, monarch of the Holy Russian Empire, abdicates his throne. All that Marxist rhetoric and doctrine—previously just compressed heat and air—takes solid form. Amnesty is granted.

As a show of gratitude, Fanny is sent to a clinic in Kharkov. A doctor performs surgery. It is the spring of 1917 and she can see again. She is fit to take her place among the political workers. She is fit to instruct the masses.

—She is fit to shoot at Lenin, Samuil said.

—She is, Roidman said, but she has no mind to yet. This is still only the spring of 1917. The October Revolution needs to be waged. The Constituent Assembly dissolved. Armistice signed with the Germans at Brest. In the spring of 1917 Lenin has not yet become *Lenin*. There is no reason to shoot at him yet.

The spring of 1917 was as far as Roidman had progressed. He had arrived at the enchanted moment where, as in a fairy tale, the clouds part and the golden light streams in. In a fairy tale, this is where the story ends. Not so in life. But that doesn't detract from the enchanted moment. The moment remains the moment. And that which comes later, comes later.

For the enchanted moment, Roidman envisioned a scene in the hospital ward. All is white. The iron beds painted white, the bedsheets white, the doctors and nurses in their coats white, shafts of white light through the windows, and Fanny in a white nightgown with white bandages over her eyes.

Carefully, a doctor bends down and removes the bandages, placing them in a white enamel bowl. Fanny's dark eyelashes are revealed, her eyes still closed. Slowly, tentatively, like petals to the sun, her eyelids open.

With a contented grin, Roidman said: Our day will also come, Samuil Leyzerovich. I am certain of that. Our patience will be rewarded and we, too, will be released.

6

My dearest Lola,
Prepare yourself, because I have some big news . . .

Alec had collected the envelope from the mail slot and, as was their habit, he'd left it on the kitchen table for Polina to discover when she came home. He then went out to the corner store for groceries and cigarettes. When he returned, Polina was at the table with the letter spread out before her. At the sound of his entrance, Polina raised her head and gave him a tentative, perplexed look.

Alec asked, What is it? and joined her at the table.

—Arik Farberman got his visa, Polina said.

—Imagine that, Alec said. They're really cleaning house.

Polina paused.

—He's proposed to Nadja, she said.

—You don't say.

—She asks me what I think she should do.

—Arik is a real Zionist, down to the bone, Alec said. Or at least he was when we left.

—He still is, Polina said.

—And is there more going on between them than just the visa?

—There is.

—A lot? Alec asked.

—How much does there need to be? Polina asked dryly.

In response, Alec could only smile.

—If Arik is the same as when we left, he won't go to Canada or America. Only Israel. Is she ready for that?

—She says she is, but he's filled her head with ideas and you know how she can be.

—What are you going to say?

—She's my sister; I love her, and I want to see her.

—So then tell her.

—Is that reason enough, that I want to see her? It's not like I'll be next door.

—You think she'll be worse off in Israel than in Latvia?

Alec had asked the question almost without thinking, as if it could have only one plausible answer. But in the way Polina received it, in the flash of acrimony in her eyes, he saw himself reflected as a dullard and a fool.

—She is asking if she should leave her home and abandon our parents in their old age to follow a man she hardly knows to a strange country: What would you have me tell her?

—If you put it like that, then of course, Alec said, feeling a swell of anger. You must write to her immediately and keep her from making this terrible mistake.

Polina continued as if she hadn't heard him.

—And she'd be going to Israel, with its wars, its terrorist attacks. Where she would never be completely accepted.

—Into the lair of the Zionist aggressor, Alec said, now surprising himself with this upsurge of patriotic indignation.

—Don't twist my words, Polina said. I'm not saying anything I haven't heard you or Lyova say.

—Fine, so what are we debating? It seems we are all in agreement. You, me, Lyova.

Alec found that Polina's invocation of Lyova also irritated him. He thought: What is Lyova doing in our private conversation?

Polina looked at him coldly and said, I see that I was wrong to say anything to you.

It felt to Alec like a storm had blown in out of nowhere. He couldn't understand what had given rise to this strange disagreement. Why was he being attacked? He hadn't designed the Soviet Union. He hadn't founded the state of Israel.

They sat locked in this stalemate when the intercom buzzed and Alec got up to go to the device. Through the speaker, swirling with electric clicks and pops, a man's voice burbled out. The voice wasn't one Alec could place immediately. Who's asking? Alec said, and the response came back: It's me, Iza. Iza Judo.

—It's not a good time, Iza. Come back later.

—Would I bother you for no reason? Iza said.

—Later.

—Five minutes, Iza said. I'll come up.

Alec looked ruefully at Polina.

—Go, I'm not keeping you.

—Wonderful, Alec said, and trudged down the stairs.

When Alec opened the door, he came face-to-face with Iza, who wore an overeager expression, as if he'd been wound up like a child's toy. Or, more precisely, wound himself up.

Since the day Iza had propositioned him in front of the briefing department, Alec had seen him only in passing, now and again, usually at one of the pensiones, where Iza would be accosting a batch of new arrivals. But it had been weeks since he'd seen him last. If Syomka hadn't still been employed by the briefing department, Alec would have assumed that the brothers Bender were safely naturalized in Australia. Instead, here was Iza, emitting urgency and venality.

Over Iza's shoulder, the late afternoon sun had ripened and saturated the pastel colors of the buildings down to their grains. Iza's close-cropped head was rimmed in ocher. His tan vinyl jacket, the sleeves pushed up over his thick forearms, had a warm translucence.

Assessing the building and the street, Iza mused, I don't think I know anyone else who lives around here.

—It's not popular with Russians.

—How's the rent?

—Not too bad.

—A lot of drug addicts?

—They keep to themselves. And, besides, we don't have anything to steal.

—It's all right here. Very Italian. If you like that sort of thing.

Iza grinned and interrupted his patter long enough for Alec to take note of a white Fiat 500 parked half on the sidewalk just at the edge of the building. The driver's window was rolled down and Dmitri was leaning out, watching them. Beside him in the passenger seat, white as a bulb, was Minka the thief. Neither of them twitched a muscle in greeting.

Iza glanced at the Fiat and back at Alec.

—Something big is going down, Iza said conspiratorially.

—What's that?

—A serious deal. High stakes.

—Great, Iza, but what's it got to do with me?

—Your brother's involved.

—I'm sure it's not the first time. But I don't meddle in his affairs. Which is how he likes it. Me, too.

—Not this time.

—Not this time, what?

—This time he wants you along.

—Why's that?

—I couldn't say. Those were his words. I didn't think to ask why. You know him. He doesn't like to be questioned.

—It doesn't seem a little strange to you, Iza? This is how you prepare for a big deal? Karl wants me along but I don't know anything about it? Instead he sends you over without any warning? Let's say I wasn't here.

—But you are here.

—What if I wasn't?

—What if? What if? Look, if Grandpa had tits he'd be Grandma.

Alec considered Iza to be a dolt and he wasn't thrilled about the prospect of going anywhere with him, or with tight-lipped Dmitri or with Minka the thief, but at the same time he felt a masochistic urge to spite Polina—to punish her by going on this rash, dubious adventure.

—Where's this happening?

—Ostia.

—And how long will it take? Alec asked.

—No time, Iza said and grinned, tasting victory and enamored of his powers of persuasion.

He spun himself around and headed toward the car.

—And what about getting home? Alec called.

—Don't worry about it, Iza said, glancing backwards.

—I'm not interested in taking the train, Alec said.

At this, Iza turned dramatically, a pained expression on his face, as if Alec had just uttered something petty and outlandish.

—What train? Iza said. Who said anything about a train? We do this and you go home in a taxi.

On the way to Ostia, Dmitri drove without uttering a syllable, the back of his neck a truculent pillar. Minka the thief gazed out the window and smoked indolently. Iza was the only one to do any talking. The other men's silence did nothing to inhibit him. He was full of energy, twitchy and garrulous. As they jounced together in the back of the Fiat, Iza announced to Alec that his and Syomka's documents had finally been approved for Australia. In six days, they would be on the plane to Melbourne.

—Eleven months of chasing my tail in Rome, Iza said, but that's all over now. No more HIAS, no more Joint. No more groveling like a schlepper from one office to another begging for handouts. That's it. We finally go and live like free men in a free country. Over there, you have money in your pocket, you do as you please. No more of this bullshit where some bureaucrat with a pike up his ass goes: *Not for you; unavailable; off-limits; forbidden*. Twenty-nine years of that was enough. I think about my mother, who nearly died giving birth to me and Syomka. Did she go through all that so we could live our lives like neutered dogs? You can be sure, I'm kissing all that shit goodbye.

The glorious Soviet Union, the refugee caravan. Let me ask you, by the way, when you leave here, how many bags will you have?

—Leave Rome?

—That's right.

—I couldn't say.

—I've got none, Iza said. A round zero. You know why?

—Why? Alec obliged.

—Because there's not three things worth keeping from the entire Soviet Union. And everything I bought in Italy is also crap. The only thing worth bringing from here is capital. Dollars. For which you don't need a suitcase. So that's what I'll be leaving with. Capital and my Australian passport. And fuck everything else in the eye. You get what I mean? Iza asked.

—Sure, Alec said.

—That's why I'm doing this deal. My last deal in Italy. A serious deal with real money on the table. Not like the Americana and the pensiones. That was crumbs; this is the loaf. I do the deal, I take my profit, and *arrivederci Roma*.

They drove west toward Ostia. Ahead of them, beyond the horizon, the orange sun eased itself gently into the sea. Everything went orange in the expiring light. Orange-hued cars barreled along the orange-hued Ostiense until Dmitri pulled up and veered off onto a side road. The road led to a paved parking lot, with posted signs from the tourist bureau and a ticket booth. But for their car, the lot was empty and the ticket booth closed.

—I thought we were going to Ostia, Alec said.

—We're in Ostia, said Minka.

—Ostia Antica, Iza elaborated.

Dmitri turned off the ignition and got out of the car. Minka and Iza followed suit. Alec, observing the others, did the same. Dmitri went around to the rear of the Fiat and opened the trunk. He reached inside and retrieved two identical brown leather briefcases. He handed them to Minka and bent down to get two more. These he gave to Iza. He repeated the process once again and extended the next two briefcases to Alec. When Alec didn't immediately reach for them, Dmitri snapped, What are you waiting for? We don't have all night. Dmitri bent one last time into the trunk and collected the final two cases. He slammed the trunk closed and started in the direction of the ticket booth. Minka fell in step, and Iza followed only slightly behind. Alec picked up his pace and joined Iza.

They walked past the unattended ticket booth and along a dusty path that led to the entrance to the ruins of Ostia Antica. As they advanced, nobody spoke. They went with single-minded purpose past the jagged wrecks and orphaned columns. Dmitri led the way with practiced, confident strides. From the main road, he cut to the left and went through a complex of redbrick walls and stone foundations. Fragments of bricks and loose stones crunched underfoot. Lizards darted through the coarse grasses and scampered up the walls. Set into these walls were niches, meant for funerary urns.

Dmitri led them out of the necropolis, past a statue of a headless, armless man in a toga, and along a street of bleached stone ruins, with their exposed floors mutely resigned to the whims of sky. They passed an amphitheater, remarkably well preserved, with curved stone benches and, upon the stage, stone masks mounted atop marble columns—their petrified mouths laughing, leering, and grimacing.

Dmitri pressed ahead. The evening light began to fade. Alec thought for sure that in a matter of minutes they'd be stumbling around these ruins in the dark. So far as he knew, nobody had bothered to bring a flashlight. And he didn't expect to find any in the briefcases. What there was in the briefcases, he could only speculate. His appeared to be packed tightly, with nothing shifting about. Both cases were of equal weight. They had a heft, a solidity. Alec guessed at something between books and cigar boxes. Though for such a caper, Alec presumed something more substantial. Swiss watches in velvet cases or stacks of dollar bills. The one thing he couldn't understand, though, was his role. So far as he could see, he seemed to have been brought along because they needed another pair of arms.

Following after Dmitri, it seemed to Alec like they covered the entire length of Ostia Antica, passing through all manner of squares, temples, and interchangeable ruins. But Dmitri kept going, leading them beyond the heart of the settlement, through a field, and toward the lights and sounds of an adjacent road. He finally came to a stop not far from a fence that separated the ancient site from the intermittent traffic. Where he stopped, there was one last ruin, not unlike the others—collapsed walls, jutting columns—only it was essentially isolated, set apart.

The headlights of passing cars flashed between the pillars. Silhouetted in the headlights, Alec saw the form of a large fat man. The man came toward them and, in a booming, gregarious voice, greeted them in Italian. At his side was a second man. Backlit, their faces were obscure, but as they drew near Alec was able to identify them. The larger man was Angelo, owner of the garage, and the smaller one was the Italian kid who'd been playing ball outside the garage when he and Lyova had first pulled up.

As Angelo approached, Dmitri set his cases on the ground and shook hands with the Italian. Angelo, looking jovial, grinned broadly at everyone.

—*È un piacere vedere tutti i miei amici Russi*, he said.

Dmitri, not one to accommodate to social graces, kept his face blank, but Alec saw that Minka and Iza Judo bared their teeth and made obliging noises.

—Where's Karl? Alec asked.

—Looks like he's not here, Dmitri said.

—Looks like, Alec said. Is he coming?

—How should I know? Dmitri said.

—Iza said he'd be here. That's why I came.

—Looks like Iza was mistaken, Dmitri said. Karl's not here. And you are. Looks like that's the way things stand.

—*Cosa c'è?* Angelo inquired.

—*Cerca Karl. Ma Karl non c'è*, Dmitri replied.

—*Ho capito*, Angelo said, and smiled at Alec. *Certamente, è normale che vorresti tuo fratello. Tu gli vuoi bene. Anch'io gli voglio bene. Karl è bravo. Molto bravo. Ma Karl non può essere dappertutto.*

—What did he say? Alec asked.

—He said what I said. Karl's not here.

—That's all he said?

—What's with you? Dmitri snapped. Karl's not here. You see that. I see that. Everybody sees that. So why are we still talking about it? What are you so worried about?

Alec felt the eyes of the other men on him. Their eyes were full of impatience, smugness, and rebuke. Their eyes said that he was behaving badly, dishonorably.

—Who said I was worried? Alec said. What's there to worry about? Just because it's night, we're in the middle of nowhere, and I don't know what the hell's going on?

—This isn't the middle of nowhere, Minka said. It's a famous touristical destination.

—And what do you need to know, anyhow? said Dmitri. Are you some kind of child? You need to have everything explained to you? Wait one fucking minute and you'll see.

Alec concluded that there was nothing more to say. He had no grounds to complain. He'd been sober when he signed up.

Snatching the briefcases from Alec's hands, Dmitri said, Here, give me those fucking things so we can get down to work.

Minka said, Let's step inside and do this.

Carrying his two briefcases, Minka lifted a leg, stepped over a low stone ledge, and effectively "entered" the ruin. Since there were no walls to speak of, everyone could still see him just the same as before. Where they were, the terms "inside" and "outside" were arbitrary. Even so, everybody filed in. All eight briefcases were lined up. Angelo and the Italian kid switched on the flashlights Alec hadn't noticed they'd been carrying. They shone the beams on the briefcases and on the floor. The pale floor bounced the light back into their faces. It also roughed in the dimensions of the ruin and picked out details in the floor itself. Alec saw the vestiges of a crude mosaic. He discerned two objects composed of small black tiles—one looked like a lemon, the other like a candelabra.

—Let's get to it, Dmitri said.

Iza Judo, who'd been standing next to Alec, stepped forward and released the clasps on one of the briefcases. He lifted the lid and Angelo turned the beam of his flashlight onto the contents. Alec saw dozens of slim objects, each wrapped in green felt. Iza reached inside, withdrew one of the objects, and unwrapped it for Angelo. Angelo fixed his light on it and Alec saw a glint of gold. Held this way, Alec was now able to identify it as an icon. He was far from an expert in icons, but to his eye it looked impressive, authentic, probably valuable, and certainly contraband. These were the sorts of things that could never have left the Soviet Union through legitimate channels. Somebody somewhere had bribed a whole legion of customs agents.

—*Bene? Bellissimo?* Iza asked.

—*Benissimo*, Angelo said, taking the icon in hand for closer inspection.

Alec looked around at the other men. Minka and Dmitri were opening the clasps on the other briefcases and examining the icons. The Italian kid also reached inside and took one. As he fixed his light on it, Iza eyed him apprehensively.

—*Ei!* Iza said. *È Gesù Cristo. Molto caro*.

Iza turned to Dmitri and warned, Watch he doesn't damage that. That's a fragile thing and he's pawing it like a piece of ass.

Dmitri, unflappable, ignored Iza and made no move to caution the kid.

—Now this is more like it, Minka said, admiring the icons and clucking his tongue approvingly. You know who would have liked this?

He said this to everyone and no one in particular.

—Who's that? Iza asked.

—My grandfather. A shame he didn't live to see it. It would have warmed his heart. In Minsk, everyone knew of him. Isn't that so, Dmitri?

—Sure.

—You remember him, right?

—Could be.

—Sure you remember. He did business with your late father.

—A big fat guy?

—Like a steamer. Twice as big as Angelo. Lived to be eighty-five. He used to tell stories about what it was like before the Revolution. His father traded, smuggled, made a good living. My grandfather learned from him. Those were some clever Yids. He told me, *You know why the Bolsheviks closed the synagogues? Because they wanted to stop the trading.* It had nothing to do with religion; it was because Jews made deals in the synagogue. All those musty Jews sitting in the dark, mumbling in their strange tongue—the tsar's agents had no idea what was going on in there. But a lot of the Bolsheviks were Jews and they knew. So they turned the synagogues into theaters, stables, and warehouses. Oh, how my grandfather hated Soviet power. He missed the old days when a Jew could come to the synagogue and do some business.

Minka paused as though out of solemn respect for his departed grandfather.

—If he could look down and see us now. Just like our ancestors. Jews in a synagogue once again, doing business. That's why we left that Soviet shit heap. Isn't that so, Dimka?

Dmitri picked up another icon and didn't bother to answer.

—You know how old this synagogue is? Minka asked.

Sensing a limited audience, he'd put the question to Alec.

—Old, Alec said.

—Very old, Minka said. Older than these icons. Maybe older than Christ himself.

The beating started soon after. Dmitri, Minka, and the Italian kid rained blows down on Iza Judo. They beat him savagely, the Italian kid even using his flashlight to strike Iza on his hands, shoulders, and back, after Iza curled up in a ball to protect himself. Briefly, Iza had put up valiant resistance. He'd hurled himself at Minka and wrenched Minka's hand until he'd howled with pain. Beneath the howl, Alec had heard the crisp sound of a twig snapping. Minka fell back temporarily, but Iza hadn't been able to seize the advantage. Dmitri and the Italian kid descended on him with insatiable ferocity and quickly overwhelmed him. They kicked and punched him indiscriminately until he sank to the ground, and they kept beating him as he curled up, grunting and moaning pitiably.

Alec had been stunned by the display; he'd stood and watched, unable to budge or to speak out. The whole thing had flared up so quickly and the scene itself seemed so unreal. Much of it transpired in the dark. He intuited what was happening mostly from the sounds. But then a car would pass on the road and its headlights momentarily illuminate the grisly scene. Or the beam of the Italian kid's flashlight would slash across Dmitri's face or Iza's body as he beat him with the heavy metal barrel.

One minute, everything had been calm, even jovial, with Angelo approving the icons and Minka spouting his nonsense about his grandfather and the synagogues. If there had been any evidence of hostility, Alec had thought it was directed at him. But then Angelo had started to negotiate the terms with Iza. Angelo claimed that he'd expected a certain number of icons and that Iza had brought fewer than this number. Iza had objected, saying that he'd brought precisely the number they had agreed upon. Dmitri, speaking on Angelo's behalf, offered Iza less money since he'd fallen short in the quantity.

—The hell I'm going to take less, Iza had said. I did my part. Don't try to jerk me around.

—If Angelo says you're short, then you're short.

—Angelo can say whatever he likes. He can say the earth is flat. He can say day is night. That doesn't make it so. We had a deal, and now he's making up tales.

—Here's how it stands: you should take what he's offering, before you get nothing at all.

Alec had watched Iza swell with rage, his neck engorging, like a bullfrog's.

—You say how it stands, Iza fumed. I say differently. If I don't get the money I was promised, fuck this, the deal is off. This fat shit can go crawl back up his mother's cunt. I got others who'll pay what the icons are worth. Maybe more.

—Who's going to carry the cases back, Iza? To what car? That's not the way this works.

It was at this point that the situation crystallized. Everyone realized it. Including Iza, though evidently too late. Alec saw a hunted look enter his eyes. He lost the arrogance of the predator and took on the edginess of the prey.

—You think you can just do what you please? Iza demanded. You can't do business like this. People will find out. I've got a witness.

—Who's your witness? Dmitri asked, and motioned disparagingly to Alec. Him?

—That's right, Iza said.

—First you get him out here so we can smack him around, and now he's supposed to be your witness?

—Now don't *you* go making up tales, Iza said bitterly, and sought Alec's eyes in solidarity. We're friends from way back. He knows the truth. He knows nobody would dare touch him, because they'd have Karl to answer to. Everybody knows this.

—Is that right? Dmitri asked. Is that what everybody knows?

It was after this that the violence started.

When Iza fell silent, Dmitri, Minka, and the Italian kid stopped beating him. They stood panting from their exertions and the Italian kid trained his flashlight on Iza's huddled form. Dmitri kneeled down and placed his hand on Iza's neck to check for a pulse. He then frisked him, going into his pockets and pulling out loose change, his wallet and passport. The passport was the only thing that held his interest. Alec watched him open and study it.

—Stupid piece of trash, Dmitri said to Iza's inert body. I should piss on your fucking Australian passport. A piece of trash like you gets out while I'm stuck in this shit.

He flung the passport down on top of Iza.

He then wheeled around and slugged Alec in the face. Alec felt the impact like black shards inside his head. Before he knew what had happened, he found himself on the ground next to Iza.

—So that you understand who you're dealing with! Dmitri spat.

He peeled off a number of bills and threw them in Iza's general direction.

—That should be enough for a taxi to the hospital.

Alec didn't bother to get up as Dmitri, Minka, Angelo, and the Italian kid packed up the briefcases and took them away. Minka, with his broken hand, could carry only one case, so the Italian kid carried three. They stepped out of the ruin and into the field. Before too long, their flashlight beams were swallowed up by the dark streets of Ostia Antica.

7

A t four in the morning, from a hospital in Ostia, Alec was finally able to call home. Polina picked up after one ring, and answered in a voice completely alert.

—I thought I'd have to apologize for waking you, Alec said.

—Where are you? she asked, her tone balanced on a point between anger and fear.

—In Ostia. In the Villa del Lido hospital.

—What happened to you?

—Nothing too terrible. It's just my face. A few stitches over the eye. I think they'll still let me into Canada.

—What's the name of the hospital again?

Alec heard Polina turn from the phone and ask, Do you know where the Villa del Lido hospital is? She turned back and said, Lyova says he knows. We'll be there soon.

It took an hour, and Alec spent that hour sitting in the emergency waiting room, drifting off to sleep and then jolting awake when his hand made accidental contact with the plaster over his left eye. Dmitri's punch had cut him for six stitches, and he'd done a considerable amount of bleeding before the Italian doctor had treated the wound. On the dark road on the outskirts of Ostia Antica, his swollen, bloody face hadn't helped him to flag down a car. Several cars had slowed, only to speed away when they caught sight of his face. Add to that his poor command of Italian and then, worst of all, Iza—compared with whom Alec looked like the picture of health. Hours passed before an elderly couple picked them up, the old man even helping Alec to lift the unconscious Iza over the fence—no easy task—and put him in the car. Alec didn't have the words to craft an explanation for their predicament, he managed only *grazie* and *ospedale*. It didn't much matter since the man and his wife, though kind, were not naïve. They even declined the money Alec offered. As they drove, Alec's main concern was that if Iza croaked, he'd have the courtesy to wait until they were out of these people's car. As for himself, he tried his best not to bleed on their upholstery.

Polina and Lyova arrived just before dawn. Alec saw them from a distance and watched as Lyova detained a doctor who pointed them in two directions, neither of which was correct. Alec rose from his seat long enough for Polina to spot him. She walked briskly toward him, her expression becoming graver the closer she came. She stopped before him, regarded his injury, and then, almost as if she might cry, brought her hands up to cover her mouth.

—My God, who did this to you? she said.

—It doesn't matter, Alec replied.

—Did you call the police?

—It wouldn't do any good.

Lyova drew up and also appraised Alec's eye.

—What did they do that with, a belt buckle?

—I think just a fist.

Lyova leaned in closer to inspect the wound. He clucked his tongue appreciatively.

—In the end it will be an improvement. You were too handsome for your own good.

—It's not a joke, Polina said, reaching across to touch Alec's cheek below the wound. It's horrible.

—Have they discharged you? Lyova asked.

—I think so.

—In that case, you'd probably like to go home.

They left the hospital together and crossed the street to where Lyova had parked his van. Alec felt exhausted, but he made a point of walking under his own power. When they reached the vehicle, Lyova turned to Alec and said, I imagined telling you this under happier circumstances, but I've received some good news. I told Polina last night. The Americans gave me a visa.

Alec had been leaning on the van, but he straightened up and shook Lyova's hand.

—Congratulations, you're a free man.

—More or less, Lyova said.

—What's the less? Alec asked, and stumbled back. He felt a dark wave wash over him. Lyova still had hold of his hand and prevented him from falling.

In the van, Polina cradled Alec's head in her lap. They rode in silence. Alec's mind cleared and he thought gratefully that Polina hadn't brought up Iza Judo, and so spared him the trouble of getting into it. When they got back to Rome, he planned to contact Syomka. Syomka could assume responsibility for his idiot brother. One way or another, Alec was sure that Syomka would manage to get Iza on the plane to Melbourne. If his arms and legs were broken, he'd put him in a wheelchair and stick his passport in his mouth.

—What did you decide to tell Nadja? Alec asked.

—I decided to tell her what's in my heart.

—To come?

—I can't tell her not to come. She's the dearest person to me. I want to see her. Besides, she would be hurt if I wrote her not to come. But I'll tell her to choose for herself. I'm no longer there. I can't help her. Not with our parents, and not once she leaves. And I'll accept whatever she decides.

It was still very early when they returned to Trastevere. The neighborhood was only just beginning to stir. In the apartment, Polina asked Alec what he intended to do.

—Take a shower and sleep, Alec said. And you? You didn't sleep either.

They went into the shower together and Polina washed the dust of Ostia Antica from Alec's skin—also the blood: some of it his own, most of it Iza Judo's.

In the bedroom they drew the shutters and slipped into bed, Polina resting her head between Alec's shoulder blades.

—I'm to blame for last night, she said. I sent you out to him.

Her words reached him from the rim of sleep. His body felt like a bottomless cavity through which he plunged in glorious free-fall. The wound over his eye pulsed like a beacon, its round blue signal growing fainter the farther he descended. He tumbled into a dream in which he was pursued along the dark streets of Ostia Antica by large brown Roman dogs, a breed depicted in ancient mosaics. He heard them snarling and panting and felt their breath on the back of his neck. He sought vainly for a place to hide in the ruins, but the dogs kept coming. They would soon catch him and tear him to pieces. Up ahead, standing by the side of the road, Masha watched in impassive silence.

8

round midday, Alec opened his eyes. At first he felt immobile, as if he had been buried in sand. He turned his head and saw Polina's indented pillow. The left side of his face ached. The ache had dimension and shape and it extended beyond the familiar plane of his face.

He willed himself out of bed and headed to the bathroom. The cold floor under his feet sobered him. Each step brought him closer to lucidity, until he was standing in front of the bathroom mirror and looking at his reflection—which dispelled any lingering doubts. He saw the bulbous purple swelling and the white plaster from which two sutures peeked out like insect legs. His face looked so gruesome and garish that the only reasonable response was to laugh. Alec stood in the bathroom and laughed, and a lunatic laughed back at him.

He dressed and went into the common room, where he found Lyova at the dining table sifting through a stack of documents. There were coffee cups on the table along with juice, bread, vegetables, cheese, and salami. Alec saw no sign of Polina.

—Have a seat, Chapayev. Your wife left you breakfast, Lyova said.

—Where did she go?

—To send a telegram to her sister.

Alec made himself a sandwich, and chewed delicately.

—She waited for you to wake up, but the telegram office was closing.

—I couldn't go out like this anyway.

—Do you want to say what happened?

—I'd rather not.

—Whatever it is, is it finished?

—I think so.

They sat for a time without speaking. Alec nibbled his food and Lyova sorted his documents.

—Did I dream it, or did you say the Americans granted you a visa?

Lyova grinned and said, You didn't dream it. I have a visa. Now all I need is a passport.

Alec didn't pretend to understand.

—My Jewish luck. The Americans grant me a visa just as my Israeli passport expires. I didn't even know it was due to expire. I haven't looked at it in months.

—How hard is it to renew?

—Not hard if I go back to Israel. But if I go back to Israel, I'm cooked. The bureaucracy. And I don't expect they'd let me travel. My American visa is only good for thirty days. The alternative is a temporary travel document from the embassy here. But it's purely at their discretion, and the first question they ask is why you allowed your passport to expire abroad. And the second question is why you don't return to Israel to renew it through the proper channels.

—Still, you should go. What do you have to lose?

—You're right: nothing. I went yesterday.

—They turned you down.

—I had a very pleasant exchange. As a rule, the Israeli foreign service is stocked with the most rigid apparatchiks, but I drew a nice guy. He looked at my documents and we discovered that we had a lot in common. He was my age. Married with a kid. Served in the Sinai.

Lived near Netanya. And his wife had also been driving on the coastal highway when the PLO killed all those people on the bus last March. He was sincere in wanting to help, but he said he'd never get approval from above.

—So what does this mean?

—It means, I think, that I have one last card to play. In five days, I have an appointment with the Ufficio Stranieri. They could issue me a temporary travel document. Or, of course, once they discover that I'm in the country illegally, they could deport me. But, at this point, I've got nothing to lose. Worst case, either the Italians ship me back to Israel or the Israelis do.

In the five days that remained before his appointment, Lyova worked to put his affairs in order. He mailed some of his belongings to Netanya, and tried to sell off the rest. For his books, he went to a secondhand bookseller in Trastevere. For his van, he thought of returning to Angelo and the garage in Ladispoli.

This was two days after the incident in Ostia Antica, and Alec's face, if it was possible, looked even worse than it had before. Alec hadn't ventured out of the apartment—not to go to his job at the briefing department, not even to go to the corner store for cigarettes. But when Lyova mentioned his plans to go to Ladispoli, Alec volunteered to come along.

When they were on that same road, a few streets shy of the garage—but past the neighborhood where his parents lived, and also past Masha's building—Alec asked Lyova to let him out of the van. It seemed an arbitrary place to stop—there was nothing there apart from the highway and a street of nondescript residential houses. There was no restaurant, café, or even a bus stop. The only other features of the landscape were the occasional palm trees that lined the road. Alec pointed to the nearest one.

—I'll wait for you there, Alec said.

When Lyova did not immediately drive off, Alec added, If you see my brother, don't mention I'm here.

Hiding behind the palm tree, so that he could not be easily seen from the highway, Alec tried to formulate a plan. He tried to envision different scenarios and how he might best behave in each. But no matter how hard he tried to focus, his thoughts became diffuse and drifted apart. It was impossible to plan without a clear objective, and he didn't have one. He didn't know what outcome he wanted.

After a time, Alec saw Lyova returning. This time on foot. Alec didn't step out to meet him, but continued to wait behind the tree. When Lyova reached him, his face bore a sly smile.

—You look unharmed, Alec said.

—Sometimes it's easier to deal with thieves.

—Tell me, Alec said, who was in the garage?

—I think the same crew as before.

—Can you be more specific?

—Angelo, the fat Italian who bought the van. I caught a glimpse of your brother, though he didn't come out. Valera, who fixed the van last time. And one young Russian hood. Dark hair, tattoos on his arms—he was painting a car.

—All right, Alec said, and stepped out from behind the tree.

They walked back the way they had come, following the highway north. The road wasn't meant for pedestrians and so they had to skirt the edge to avoid passing cars. As they neared the more residential section of Ladispoli, a sidewalk appeared. They followed it until they came to the front of Masha's building, where Alec paused.

—Can I ask a favor?

—What's that?

—Could you wait here a few minutes while I go inside?

Lyova looked at him with faint amusement, as at an impetuous child.

—A girl? Lyova asked.

—I won't be long, Alec said.

Alec went into the building and rode the elevator, the same as he had when he'd visited in the past. He padded through the corridor and faced the door to Masha's apartment—straining his ears to detect movement inside. He knocked and waited, straining still for any sound, as if his entire being were concentrated in his ears. As he prepared to knock again, he heard footsteps come toward the door and stop. He felt the weight of another human presence on the other side.

—Who is there? Riva Davidovna asked.

—Alec.

He believed he heard the sound of another set of footsteps withdrawing.

After a short moment, Riva Davidovna opened the door. He saw her stern face study him, though not unkindly. Her eyes passed fleetingly over his brow.

—Somebody hit you.

—It will heal.

—I am the mother of a son, you don't need to tell me.

They remained for a few seconds without speaking. Riva continued to calmly study him, while Alec tried to glance subtly beyond her into the apartment.

—I feel like we haven't seen you in a long time, Riva said. I just recently remarked this to Masha.

—Masha isn't home?

—No, I'm afraid she's not, Riva said. I would invite you in, but I don't expect her until later.

—Of course, Alec said. Tell her I'm sorry to have missed her.

—I will, Riva said, and started to slowly shut the door.

As Alec took his first step toward the elevator, he heard the door swing open again. His pulse leaped and he turned back to find Riva Davidovna in the door frame, looking like she had reconsidered something she had said or failed to say. She hesitated, as if weighing her words, then said, The best thing for your eye is a vinegar compress.

9

When the time came for Lyova's appointment at the Ufficio Stranieri, they said their provisional farewells in the apartment. Alec offered to escort him to the ministry, but Lyova didn't see the point.

—If they detain me, you'll just end up waiting in the street.

Before Lyova departed, Polina surprised him by producing a small gift, a leather wallet from her store, which she had wrapped neatly in butcher paper.

—Something for your American documents and dollars, she said.

—And if they send me back to Israel?

—I hope you can use it there, too.

Alec and Polina watched him walk out the door and Alec was quite certain they would never see him again. The thought wasn't pessimistic, only empirical. In the emigration, when somebody left, he left for good.

With Lyova's departure, the sound of his footfalls receding to nothing on the stairs, Alec and Polina were left in a pristine silence. It felt as if they were being reintroduced after a lengthy separation—a jail term or a sea voyage. The place seemed suddenly too quiet and too big. Without Lyova's mediating presence, Alec felt as if they had each been made transparent and their hidden thoughts exposed.

—I don't think people were made to live like this, Polina said.

—Like what? Alec asked, fearing something devastating.

—To form attachments only to have them broken.

It was late morning, and they busied themselves tidying the apartment, as if it were a compulsory act, the period at the end of the sentence. Lyova had left his remaining possessions stacked up in one corner, the easier for them to ship to Netanya in case he didn't return. Alec watched Polina sweep carefully around the stack, as around a household shrine.

When they had finished, Polina considered the contents of the refrigerator and said, I should go to the market.

—Would you like me to come with you?

—You're no longer worried about frightening the neighborhood children?

—I'd thought it was getting better.

Polina crossed from the kitchen to the dining room table, where Alec was sitting, and lightly traced the perimeter of his bruise with her fingertips.

—Alec, if you'd like to come, come. But only if you want. I don't plan to pick up more than a few things.

—Well, maybe for the sake of the neighborhood children, I'll give it another day.

Once Polina had gone, Alec lit a cigarette and sat by the window that overlooked the street. He picked up a copy of the *Herald-Tribune* left behind by Lyova and he read about some kind of reverse pogrom where a mob of Orthodox Jews stormed a Brooklyn police station and injured sixty policemen. He read articles about the civil war in Beirut and the revolutions in Rhodesia and Iran. He read an article about Soviet workers being conscripted for the annual potato harvest. From his perch at the window, an Italian cigarette between his lips, Alec felt a momentary tranquillity—as though, like a lord, he was gazing down at the grubby idiocy of the world. For that moment, his own grubby idiocy seemed trivial.

Alec finished his cigarette and prepared to flick the butt out the window and into the street. As he did so, he saw a familiar figure walking briskly along Via Salumi. He leaned his head out the window for a better look, to make absolutely sure. But there was the loose-jointed, storklike gait and the wild conflagration of hair. Lyova spotted Alec in the window, broke into a wide grin, and raised a triumphant fist in the air.

Upstairs, Lyova showed Alec the dark green, clothbound little booklet: his temporary Italian passport. His picture had been affixed, his American visa stapled, and the pages bore the official stamps and signatures.

—So tell me, Alec said.

—There's almost nothing to tell. After all this time, I didn't have to plead or weep. I showed my papers, Carmela said she deplored the way the Israelis were treating the poor Palestinians, and I said I did too. What the hell? This way, at least one of us gets to go free.

—*Mazel tov*, Alec said, and fetched a bottle of grappa.

When Polina came through the door, grocery bags in hand, Alec and Lyova were still at the table. They looked up and watched her rein in her delight.

—Don't be afraid, Alec said. He's an American, not a ghost.

Polina smiled and came over to the table.

—Congratulations, she said. I'm happy to see you again.

—Thank you, Lyova replied.

Polina looked down at the grocery bags in her hands.

—I'm sorry, I didn't get nearly enough. I didn't think you'd be back.

—No need to apologize, Lyova said. I didn't think I'd be back either.

To celebrate, Lyova went down for a bottle of Chianti and a box of chocolates. Polina threw together a mongrel dinner of boiled potatoes, white Italian bread, cottage cheese with sour cream, green onions, cucumbers, prosciutto, figs, and a wedge of parmesan.

They sat at the table and drank in honor of friendship, Rome, health, wives, fortitude, prosperity, and the future. Polina nursed the same glass of wine, while Alec and Lyova polished off the grappa and most of the Chianti as well.

The sky darkened as Lyova talked about what he expected from America. He'd lived abroad for nearly a decade, and so he didn't think he'd suffer the shock of the new Soviet transplant. He had taken pains to learn English and to stay current on American affairs. His son had received some English instruction in school. The boy had a good ear for languages and Lyova thought he'd have little trouble adapting. His wife was a different story. Since she neither wanted to leave Israel nor believed that Lyova would succeed in getting them out, she had stubbornly refused to study English. Consequently, she would arrive in New York resentful and ill prepared—not a good combination. But Lyova hoped that once she inhaled American air it would trigger a chemical reaction and her outlook would change.

—What did she say when she found out? Polina asked.

—I haven't told her yet.

—You didn't call?

—No. Not her and not my parents.

—You do intend to tell them.

—I intend to tell them, but not over the phone. I don't need to pay to hear their disappointment. They can read it in a telegram.

—What will you say?

—I haven't decided.

—How about: "Pack your bags," Alec said.

—Yes, Lyova said. "The voice of America is calling."

—You might want to consider having a woman write it, Polina said.

—That's a marvelous idea, Lyova said. You'd be doing me a great favor. There are some things men aren't suited for.

—The favor is for your poor wife and son, Polina chided, and began to clear the table.

As she carried the cups and plates to the kitchen, the intercom buzzed. Polina looked over her shoulder at Lyova and Alec and, the hour being late, the three of them exchanged inquiring glances.

The buzzer sounded again—a longer, more insistent note.

—Maybe the Italians have reconsidered, Lyova said.

Alec rose from his chair and went to answer the intercom. He tried to give the impression of lightheartedness. An infinite number of people could be at the buzzer, including delinquents, junkies, and stray tourists—but nothing felt as plausible as the thing he feared. As he approached the intercom, he tried to read Polina's and Lyova's faces. If either of them harbored fears akin to his, their faces didn't show it.

Alec pressed the button and spoke. Masha's voice surged up in response. She said, It's me, Masha, her voice pouring into the apartment like a swarm of bees, peevish and severe.

Alec turned from the intercom and looked at Lyova and Polina. Neither of them had moved. They looked at him stiffly, Polina with a keen edge of disgust. From below, Masha pressed and pressed the buzzer relentlessly, sending jagged currents through the silent apartment.

Alec pressed the button again and said angrily, Have you lost your mind?

—Let me up, Masha replied.

Alec removed his finger from the button again and stared at the intercom as it shrieked at him. He didn't turn to face Lyova or Polina, but he felt their eyes upon him. Though he knew he had no right to, he resented them for bearing witness to his scandal and compounding it by the simple fact of their presence. Still, he had no intention of letting Masha up. Go home, Masha, he said, this is not the way.

—Let me up, you bastard, or I'll scream, came her reply.

From behind him, Alec heard Polina say, in a firm, steady voice, Let her up.

Alec pressed the button that released the downstairs lock and opened the door to their apartment, letting it swing wide. He stepped back and leaned against the wall in the vestibule. Polina set the dishes she'd been holding on the kitchen counter, wiped her hands on a towel, and took her stand at the mouth of the kitchen. Lyova remained at the dining room table. They listened as the echo of

Masha's steps spiraled up the stairway, and waited for the article in its spectacular detail.

Masha did not disappoint. She appeared in the doorway irradiant, her dark eyes burning and her color high from the climb up the stairs. She wore her peach cotton dress, short-sleeved and hemmed above the knee, exposing the soft tan flesh of her arms and her strong, smooth legs. Her black hair, its generous brushstrokes, framed her face to striking effect. But for all this, the focal point was at her mouth: her upper lip was split and swollen.

Masha took two steps beyond the threshold and let her eyes roam around the apartment, taking in the surroundings and the principals. Alec watched her glance at Lyova and then look defiantly at Polina. Him, she studied last, and Alec sensed something fleeting, like a silent gasp, as though the condition of his face had unnerved her. But just as quickly, she seemed to regroup.

—It looks like I interrupted a party, Masha said.

—What did you come for, Masha? Alec asked.

—You're not happy I came?

—Say what you came to say.

Masha gazed once more around the apartment and settled on Polina.

—Such a lovely apartment, and such a lovely wife. How nice to finally meet you.

—I can imagine, Polina said.

—And this here, Masha said, directing herself at Lyova, this is your housemate? The one you helped go to America?

—That's right, Carter came for tea and signed his visa in the kitchen.

Masha looked at him with hatred. A hatred mostly, Alec sensed, at being mocked. Like a self-serious child who has not been taken seriously. He watched her fumble for an instant, as from a loss of confidence, and what anger he felt toward her drained away.

—We'll see how you joke when I tell people what you did to me.

—What did I do to you, Masha?

—This, Masha spat, and motioned sharply to her swollen lip.

—I did no such thing, Masha, and you know it.

Masha turned the force of her fury on Polina.

—He took advantage of me. Got me into a state. And when I wouldn't agree to an abortion, he did this.

She pointed again to the violence that had been done to her, but Alec was no longer looking at her but at Polina, who stood as if holding her breath.

—Nothing she says is true, Alec vainly declared.

—Believe what you like, Masha said. But I'm here to tell you that if he thought he could get away without consequences, he's very mistaken. There will be consequences, I can promise you that!

Masha stared at Polina as if to evoke a reaction. Polina held her gaze for a moment before she turned to Alec and said with cold precision, *Get her out of my sight.*

Masha didn't protest, but with a small, satisfied smile, she left of her own accord. Alec stole a glance at Lyova, who sat solemnly at the table, before he pursued her down the stairs. Alec reached the bottom just in time to catch the front door as it was swinging shut. He sprang out into the street only a few steps behind Masha and called her name. She spun to face him and, in the darkness, they studied each other, each other's wounds.

—What did you do this for, Masha?

—You helped your friend go to America, but you did nothing for us, she said, now with flagging conviction.

—You know I never raised a hand to you. I've never raised a hand to any woman.

—So what? You did worse. You caused all of this to happen.

She said nothing more, and turned back to the street, where Alec now noticed the white Fiat 500, with Dmitri at the wheel. He watched Masha climb into the passenger seat and the two of them drive off.

Alec stood on the dark street and contemplated what he might do. He thought to walk around the neighborhood for a while, to allow them all some time to recover, but he couldn't even do that. In his haste to catch Masha, he had left the apartment without any shoes. He felt the rough, cold pavement through his stocking feet.

The front door to the building had locked behind him, and so he had no choice but to ring the buzzer. Nobody answered, but Alec heard, just as when he and Polina had first come to inspect the apartment, the sound of a door opening inside the vault of the building and the descending pattern of Lyova's footsteps. Presently, the lock clicked and Lyova opened the door—though he remained in the door frame, a forlorn smile on his face.

—I have no shoes, Lyova, Alec said. I'd like to get my shoes.

—I'll get you your shoes.

—Is that so?

—Alec, don't be dim. You think I like any of this?

—You'll forgive me if I say that I'm not particularly concerned right now with what you like or don't like.

—I'll bring you your shoes, Alec. What else do you need?

—My wallet. My jacket. My keys.

Lyova balked at "keys."

—I need my HIAS keys, Lyova, or I'm sleeping in the street tonight.

—You're going to sleep in the briefing department?

—Unless you have a better idea, Alec said. By the way, where are you going to sleep tonight?

Lyova drew the door shut behind him and returned a few minutes later with Alec's shoes, jacket, wallet, keys—and toothbrush for good measure.

—Things will be brighter in the morning, Lyova said.

Alec gathered himself and walked the nighttime streets to Viale Regina Margherita and the briefing department. He had never been inside the building at that hour. There was a light switch on the wall in the entryway but he elected not to press it for fear of attracting attention. He rode the elevator and walked the darkened corridor feeling like an intruder, apt to be arrested. Quietly, he inserted his key into the lock and slipped inside the office. Light from the streetlamps spilled through the windows, casting shadows. He picked his way between desks and chairs to where the large photocopier stood against a wall. Beside the machine were stacks of folders, fat with émigré case files. Alec slid these out of the way to clear a bare patch of floor. He lowered himself onto this patch and lay staring up at the ceiling. He'd kept his jacket on for warmth, so he had nothing to cushion his skull from the hard marble. With his left hand, he reached out and took hold of several file folders and placed them under his head. Like this he tried to sleep, shivering a little from the cold, the Persecution Stories of a half dozen émigrés for his pillow.

10

fter Lyova gathered Alec's belongings, Polina closed the door to the bedroom and turned off the lights. Unwilling to lie down, she sat on the edge of the bed and saw the woeful scene replay itself. It had the grotesque character of a bad dream: the knot of shrillness, violence, and perversity, too strange and horrible to be true. She hadn't believed everything the girl had said but the simple fact that she was in their apartment proved that there was some underlying substance to it. If nothing else, Alec had allowed himself to become involved with this mixed-up, angry, voluptuous child, and he had brought this ugly scandal into their lives. She recalled Marina Kirilovna's warning—Alec, a boy with a butterfly net. She had disbelieved her words and disregarded her warning. She'd instead nursed the belief that she saw in Alec what other people failed to see, did not try to see. On the strength of this belief, she had staked her future and her family bonds. Now she was flooded with shame and self-reproach.

Like a swooping bird, the most despicable memory assailed her: when her parents had refused to sign the consent form, she had, in her own hand, written that they were dead. What authority could pardon her for that?

Polina sat stiffly in what felt again like a strange room in a strange city. She saw no way forward with Alec. What options remained for her? If Nadja went, to follow her to Israel? To return to Riga? To venture somewhere else, entirely on her own? The choices made her feel at once captive and terribly adrift. She was dismayed to find herself in this predicament. How can it be, she wondered, to have lived a life that she would have never described as reclusive. To have been loved and nurtured as a child. To have been, at every passage, surrounded by classmates and friends. To have never felt shunned or excluded. To have worked for years amid colleagues—a participant in every party and celebration. To have been twice married. To have been a guest in countless homes, and to have hosted countless guests in return. And after all this, to make a tabulation—sitting in the dark, in tears, in this unfamiliar room—and to discover that you have passed through life like a knife through smoke. That almost nothing has adhered to you. From a lifetime of society, only Nadja, one single wisp.

The prospect of sleeping in the bed, of staying in the room, sickened her. She rose and opened the door. The rest of the apartment was also dark. She had half expected to find Lyova up, reading at the table or in his bed, but she was glad for the darkened apartment. Lyova had drawn the brocade curtain, but Polina brushed it aside and entered his half of the room. She saw the outline of Lyova's body in his bed. He was facing the wall but, at her approach, he turned toward her. Polina felt that she understood what had brought her to Lyova—the simple wish not to be alone. But she was also aware of another manifestation of this idea: the need to see if she could still act to gratify her desires.

Lyova seemed to wait for her to speak.

—I can't sleep in that room, Polina said.

He sat up and, after a moment's hesitation, said, You can have my bed.

Polina easily imagined a scenario in which Lyova gallantly relinquished his bed, and in which nothing more happened between them.

Without saying a word, Polina knelt on the edge of the bed. If she were mistaken, Lyova could still protest, but he didn't. Instead, he edged toward the wall, making a space for her beside him. For a few moments, they lay silently facing each other before Polina put out her hand and placed it on Lyova's ribs. She felt Lyova's hand slide through the bedsheets and onto her ribs in return. She then felt the press of his mouth on hers, and the contortions to undress—the tangle of clothes with the bedsheets and the blanket. The act itself felt like they were assembling a complicated machine for the first time, with pieces strewn about and then forced into place. In the midst of things, Polina thought of Alec, and how this very disorder must have appealed to him.

Afterward, they lay side by side in the narrow bed.

—What will you do? Lyova asked.

—I'm not sure, Polina said.

—I wish I could offer you some help.

—Don't concern yourself, Polina said. There's nothing you could do. I'm just waiting for my sister's letter. When I get it, I'll know what to do with the rest of my life.

11

ot long after the girl departed, Samuil left the house and set off for the Ladispoli train station, the late autumn sun bright and bolted high overhead. Emma's exhortations trailed after him as he pressed forward, disregarding her completely and wishing that she might finally sprout the good sense to quiet down.

Syoma, don't go alone, she called. *Rome is a zoo. What if you get lost? Let someone come with you!*

As he reached the foot of Via Italia, he heard Emma's voice fade to the point of irrelevance. Pocketing this small satisfaction, he headed toward the station. As he went, he attempted to quell his emotions. He did not want to undertake the trip in a state of excitement. As a soldier and as a manager—if not always as a husband and a father—his greatest strength had been his ability to maintain his composure. He credited it for his successes, and he tried to invoke it here once again.

The morning's spectacle had deeply unnerved him. The frantic banging on their door. The girl raving in their kitchen. Spewing her wild accusations. Causing a shameful, disgusting scene in front of his grandsons, his daughter-in-law, and his wife.

When Samuil had heard enough, he had said to her, *My son is capable of many things, but not this. Get out of our house.*

By the time the train touched off, his anger had subsided. He looked about the train at his fellow passengers—Italians—and, for once, he did not feel estranged from them. He saw people like himself—with a destination, attending to the practical affairs of their lives.

Out his window, he watched the brown countryside unfurl, the fields harvested and tilled. The sky was a flawless blue. Small black birds glided effortlessly across it.

The farms gave way to larger settlements. Samuil saw more pavement and with it more people, more vehicles. Then, curiously, the train slowed, and presently stopped. There was no station, so far as he could see. There was not even a town to speak of. Looking out, Samuil saw a narrow road that ran beside the tracks, he saw scattered houses, low buildings, with many vacant patches between. He turned to regard the other passengers, and saw many of them also peering out the windows. Then a man's muffled voice sounded over the public address. Even before the man concluded his statement, passengers began to grumble and shake their heads. Some gathered their belongings and made for the doors. Others he saw settling into their seats—some in frustration, some in resignation. Samuil was casting about for another Russian émigré when he caught the attention of a man of his generation, dressed neatly, wearing steel-framed glasses, his eyes gentle, considerate.

The man walked up the aisle to Samuil.

—*Non parle Italiano?* he inquired.

Samuil shook his head.

—*Français?* the man asked.

Samuil shook his head again.

—*Español?*

Samuil shook his head once more and, though his knowledge of the language was spotty, proposed, *Deutsche?*

It was the man's turn to shake his head.

—*Ruskii? Iddish? Latviesu?* Samuil asked for the sake of formality.

The man smiled regretfully and then paused, as if considering one final, doubtful possibility.

—*Ĉu vi parolas Esperanton?* he said.

Gingerly, Samuil nodded his head.

He saw the man smile, delighted.

—Many years ago, Samuil said.

—Well, let us try.

—Very well.

—You would like to know why the train is not going?

—Yes.

—The engineers have called a strike. All the trains have stopped.

—For long?

—They did not say. It could be for long.

Samuil digested this.

—How far is it to Rome?

—Fifteen kilometers. Perhaps more.

His feet crunching the gravel of the rail bed, Samuil walked the length of the train, feeling the warmth emanating from its sides, like a great horse at rest. He passed the locomotive and saw in its window the engineer, sitting at his console, reading a newspaper. He could feel no resentment toward a worker asserting his rights in a capitalist system. In the Soviet Union, where socialism had been achieved, workers worked. The country hadn't seen a strike in seventy years. There, if a train had stopped, he would have gone directly to the engineer and demanded: *Comrade engineer, what is the meaning of this?*

After he passed the locomotive, a broad panorama opened up on all sides, the railroad tracks running down its middle, like a zipper on the mantle of the earth. Ahead of him, he saw a string of figures picking their way along the tracks. He looked behind him and saw dozens more, some empty-handed, some with bundles, and others with young children—women carrying the littlest ones in their arms.

As a soldier, he had marched with his division along roads and rail lines, at times covering as many as seventy kilometers in a single day. He had walked in every kind of weather: in the mire of the *rasputitsa*, with the mud pulling at his boots with its ghoulish hands; in the coldest frosts of winter, where comrades made macabre statues out of the frozen German dead; and in the heat of summer, the army crossing the land as a towering pillar of dust.

Compared to all of that, Samuil thought, was he to be deterred by a walk of a mere fifteen kilometers in mild weather? Not to mention that, as a soldier, he had also carried as much as twenty kilos in equipment, ammunition, and kit. Now he was encumbered by nothing other than his blazer. The blazer he removed after fifteen minutes and draped first over one arm and then the other.

From the opposite direction, also along the rail line, he saw other commuters trekking west. He looked, but could not see their train, and, checking behind him, he could no longer see his own. The rail line had snaked and curved, and he had walked a considerable distance. He regretted that he did not have any water with him. There were a few buildings and houses about, but he did not want to stray from his course to appeal to strangers who did not speak Russian. In the time he would lose searching for water, he could gain several kilometers and bring himself closer to the city or the next station.

He walked another half hour. He saw the train that had stopped on the westbound tracks. And he saw, on the horizon, the geometry of some larger settlement, perhaps an outer suburb of Rome. His thirst made his legs feel heavy, his chest tight. The tightness forced him to labor slightly to draw a full breath, and so he decided to rest.

He scrambled down from the rail bed to the dry, weedy embankment. He spread out his blazer and lowered himself onto it. He sat with his knees bent, his hands resting upon them, and his head up and chin raised so as to better draw breath. He gazed ahead, his field of vision incorporating the long stretch of track. The view was bare. Not a soul passed in either direction. Samuil did not know what had happened to the people who had walked before him. He had passed some of them as they rested beside the tracks. Nor did he know what had happened to the people who had followed behind. The people with bundles, the men and women with children. It seemed as if they had abandoned the course. Few had persevered so long and come so far as he had. Samuil thought of his family, of Emma and Rosa, all of them, and how they had misjudged him. How surprised they would be, and how none of them had ever fully appreciated.

Samuil surveyed the scene around him. He saw mindless gravel, railroad, and sky. He thought to rise and continue on his way, but to his consternation he felt as if, rather than diminishing, the pressure in his chest had increased. He tried to rise nonetheless, but felt as if the sky had dropped to prevent him. He inhaled and felt something zealously squeezing his lungs, as if his heart, after biding its time, had finally chosen this moment to revolt. He felt a fleeting panic that quickly turned to rage. His own heart was betraying him, like an enemy inside the walls of his body. He was determined to attack it and bend it to his will. He would wage a battle against it. His treacherous heart would have to wrest the breath from his lips.

12

A t the end of the workday, a man who identified himself as an employee of the Joint appeared at the briefing department looking for Alec. He was in his middle thirties, balding, slightly flabby, and with the typical Russian look of fatigue—acquired in the womb, marinated in that broth of disappointments. He said he had an important message to convey and suggested that they retire to the corridor for privacy. Alec felt his colleagues' eyes upon him as he followed the man out.

He had been the object of curiosity all day. He'd crept out of the office at dawn and lurked about the neighborhood, reporting for work only when he saw others start arriving. His colleagues reacted with shock at the sight of his face—more shock than he'd anticipated. He'd thought that, after a week, it was no longer quite so ghastly, but based on their reactions it occurred to him that he had simply grown accustomed to it.

In the corridor, the man from the Joint looked at him dourly before speaking. Alec felt a mounting apprehension and imagined what else Masha might have done.

—Is your father Samuil Leyzerovich? the man asked.

—Yes, said Alec.

—I'm afraid I have some sad news for you.

They went by foot from the office to a mortuary where the Jewish Burial Society had brought Samuil's body. The man opened the door to an antechamber where Alec saw a shrunken old Jew in a yarmulke sitting on a chair and mumbling something from a small black hymnal. At his shoulder was a long table that supported the weight of a body enfolded completely in a white sheet. The little Jew barely looked up from his mumbling as Alec and the man from the Joint entered the room.

—You'll forgive me, the man said, but we need you to confirm it's your father.

Alec approached the figure, drew aside the folds, and uncovered a wax replica of his father's face. He saw the full head of gray hair, the stern brow, the distinguished masculine nose, and the shiny white granules stippling the cheeks. Someone had shut his father's eyes and removed his dentures. The latter detail had distorted his face, collapsing his mouth and making him seem ancient. Alec's impulse was to look away, but he resisted out of a duty to see all. He tried to reconcile this pale waxwork with the father who had been such a vital, dominant presence in his life. He felt crushed by the mortal paradox: how it was that his father lay by his side and that his father was no more. He studied his father's face and understood that there was such a thing as a soul and that it had departed and left behind a corpse.

—Is it him? the man asked.

—Yes, it's him, Alec answered.

He covered his father's face and looked to the man from the Joint for further instruction.

—What happens now?

—The funeral. They like to do it as fast as possible. Tomorrow afternoon.

—I suppose, Alec said. I still have to tell my family.

As they left the room, Alec glanced at the little Jew mumbling his stream of gibberish.

—What's he doing?

—He stays with the body all night. So it's never alone.

—Is that necessary?

—Does it bother you?

—I don't know.

—It's a Jewish custom. You want him to go away?

—It doesn't matter.

—It's his job. He's paid for it.

—Then leave him, Alec said.

Alec caught a nine o'clock train out of Rome. He arrived in Ladispoli after ten and walked the dark, empty streets to his family's house. He saw the world with the clarity conferred by the knowledge of death. He saw everything as it truly was. Every mundane thing existed in terms of death. Everything was tinged by this tragic impermanence.

The lights were on when Alec came to the house. He knocked on the door and heard exclamations and frantic scrambling. He felt the imminence of what was to come. The door would soon open and he would have to look into his mother's eyes and speak the words so that they entered irrevocably into the world. He felt his intransitive physical bulk on the doorstep. Somehow the fate of his life had designated him for this.

The door was thrown open and he saw his mother—her anxious, haggard expression. Pressed up behind her were Rosa and the boys, followed by Karl, who took Alec's meaning from across the room. For an instant, his mother was confused, distracted by Alec's mutilated face.

—My God, what did you do to your eye?

—An accident. It's nothing.

Then his mother seemed to remember what was uppermost in her mind. She asked nervously, as if fending off the knowledge, Alec, you're alone? Where is Papa?

Alec managed only to slowly say *Mama* before she interrupted him, her eyes gaping with terror, and pleaded, What happened, Alec? Where is your father?

On the train and walking the dark streets of Ladispoli he had silently practiced the words. Now he opened his mouth and they tumbled out: Papa is gone.

His mother wailed, *Oi, Syomachka!* as if something had cracked inside her. Rosa drew her close and the two of them wept into each other's neck. The boys, bewildered, also started to cry. Karl said, Come, let's go inside, and they all trailed into the house, Alec shutting the door behind them.

They settled in the living room, where Samuil had spent so much of his time writing his secret memoirs.

—It's my fault, his mother bemoaned, looking up from her anguish. I should have never let him go by himself.

—It isn't your fault, Emma Borisovna, Rosa responded. She looked bitterly at Alec and added, It was because of your slut that your father went off to Rome. If not for that, he would still be alive!

—Don't say that! his mother snapped. Don't say that to him! He's not to blame. Syoma went to help him. He was a father concerned for his son.

That night Alec slept on the floor of the living room. Karl stayed in the bedroom with the boys, and Rosa slept in his mother's bed so that she would not have to be by herself. Before she joined his mother, Alec heard Rosa soothing the boys with a lullaby. The lullaby she sang was familiar, though not because he recalled anyone ever singing it to him.

The half moon shines above our roof
Evening stands at our yard
For little birds and for little children
The time has come now to sleep
In the morning you'll wake
and the bright sun will rise above you again
Sleep little sparrow
Sleep little son
Sleep my dear little chime.

Alec lay on the floor and listened to her sing. He could not have said precisely why he was so moved. The words and the melody pierced his heart and he lay on the floor and quietly wept.

In the morning they scurried to make arrangements for the funeral. Karl went to coordinate with the rabbi and Rosa deposited the boys at a friend's apartment. Alec was left alone with his mother. He watched her comb fastidiously through the house collecting the stray items his father had left behind: his reading glasses, his slippers, a newspaper he had been reading. When she finished, she looked at Alec dolefully and he waited for her to say something more about what had sent his father to Rome.

—Will you call Polina? Emma asked.

—I don't think I can, Alec said.

She studied him for a moment, with a wisdom for which he seldom credited her, and didn't insist further. Instead she sent him to Club Kadima to find Josef Roidman. He was his father's friend, and she believed that he would want to attend the funeral.

Alec found Roidman at Club Kadima, sitting alone with a newspaper. He apologized for disturbing him and asked if he remembered who he was.

—What's to remember? Roidman said merrily. But for the eye, you're the spitting image of your father.

Alec told him that his father had died.

—It can't be, Roidman said.

—The funeral is today. I am here to see if you wish to come.

—*Vey, vey*, the old man said and shook his head despondently.

Roidman gathered himself up and hobbled for the exit.

—I am not properly dressed to pay my respects. Is there time enough for me to go home?

Alec accompanied the old man to his apartment, where he put on a cap and the same blazer with the medals Alec had seen him wearing the day of the pope's coronation.

Karl secured transport to ferry them all to the cemetery. Despite it having been repainted, Alec nevertheless recognized it as Lyova's old Volkswagen van. Piled inside were all the members of his family—minus the boys—along with Josef Roidman, the rabbi, and six other Jewish men: three of the rabbi's bearded adjutants, as well as two idle Russian pensioners and one teenage boy, whom the rabbi had recruited with the promise of a break from their routine and a complimentary meal.

The rabbi directed them to the cemetery and Karl turned off Via Tiburina at Piazzale delle Crociate, where an iron gate stood ajar. They followed a paved road into the grounds. The road, lined with cypress trees, stretched deep into the cemetery and curved away at a high mausoleum wall. Not far from the entrance, at the edge of the road, was a black hearse with a uniformed driver. The rabbi directed Karl to park the van in front of the hearse. The rabbi exchanged a few words with the hearse's driver and then gestured for everyone to follow him to the graveside. Even without the rabbi's instruction, everyone had already noticed the mound of freshly turned earth with a simple pine coffin beside it. At the sight of the coffin, Alec heard his mother and Rosa begin to whimper and to call his father's name. He and Karl lagged some distance behind, at the tail of the procession. Alec looked at his brother to see how he was taking all of this. Karl's face was grim and brooding.

—You're a fool, you know that? Karl said.

Alec didn't think he had anything to say in his own defense.

—You can't tell when you're climbing into a nest of vipers?

—I thought it would all come out differently.

—Fool, Karl said with disgust.

He halted and peered up at the sky, as if he could no longer bring himself to look at Alec.

—They'll go to Germany. They can be smuggled in. I'm sure they'll prosper. There's plenty of opportunity. Let them be the Germans' problem.

His brother went ahead to join the others and Alec followed.

At the graveside, added to their number were two young Italian groundskeepers who indicated how the coffin needed to be lifted and positioned onto the straps. Karl and Alec both stepped forward to take up the coffin, but the rabbi stopped them.

—Immediate kin do not lift the body.

Alec and Karl then watched the rabbi and his assistants perform the task. The neighboring plots, Alec saw, were already occupied by other Russian émigrés who had failed to complete their journies. The white stones were thin and bore no decoration, save for an etched Star of David, the name of the deceased, and the dates each came into and departed the world.

In an aching, reedy voice, the rabbi sang some verses from a prayer book. At certain predetermined moments his assistants responded, *Omayn*. They were the only ones. Nobody else knew what he was doing.

When the rabbi finished his portion, he flipped through the book and extracted a laminated card that he'd filed away between the pages. He presented the card to Karl.

—It is the kaddish. For you and your brother to read together.

Alec stood at Karl's side to read. The card was typed with Hebrew words transliterated into Russian.

—What does it mean? Alec asked.

—It sanctifies God's name, for your father's sake.

—Our father wasn't a believer. If it's for his sake, he'd want nothing about God at his grave.

—Alec, the rabbi is showing us how to do it according to the rules, his mother admonished.

On the rabbi's cue, he and Karl read the unfamiliar words, mispronouncing some. But after they'd read everything on the card, Alec still felt troubled by misgivings. He asked the rabbi what more there was to the ceremony.

—Only to fill the grave. Though if there's anything you wish to add, there's no law against it.

—I feel we should do something he would have wanted.

—And what is that? the rabbi asked.

—What is done at the burial of a Communist?

—What is done? You want us to sing the "Internationale"? Rosa asked.

—Not a bad idea. At least everyone knows it.

—You'd ask the rabbi to sing the "Internationale"?

—Why not? I'm sure he also knows the words. The rabbi was probably a Pioneer and maybe even a Young Communist. Am I wrong, rabbi?

—We all make mistakes in our youth.

—But do you have any objections against singing this song in our father's memory?

The rabbi smiled faintly and shrugged his shoulders.

Alec expected that Karl would disparage the idea and so put an end to it, but his brother didn't say a word.

The first to sing was Josef Roidman. He raised his voice martially and proudly. Alec turned to see the little man standing at attention, his eyes wet, gripping his crutch, his chest with its medals thrust forward.

Arise you branded and accursed,
The whole world's starving and enslaved!

Roidman began and the others gradually joined in. The old men and the teenage boy who had come along for the car ride and the free meal. His mother, her arms linked with Rosa's. Karl with his heavy bass. And singing softly, the rabbi and the other bearded men.

13

After the funeral, instead of returning with the others to Ladispoli to begin the week of mourning and eat the kosher dinner furnished by the rabbi, Alec boarded the train to Rome. His family's grief, and the expectation to grieve with them, was too oppressive. That house, with its rigors, felt like the one place where he wouldn't be able to mourn.

Riding the train, Alec tried to think about his father and about himself as his son. If he were honest with himself, he would admit that it had been many years since he and his father had shown any affection toward each other. To no small extent, as soon as he had been able, he had structured his life so that it intersected only glancingly with his father's. Now, guilt and sentiment bade him to repudiate this fact and to imagine that things could have been different between them. Could he have made more of an effort? Had he been guilty of making a conveniently low assessment of his filial debt? How great was his portion of the blame? But he knew that these questions were irrelevant and had nothing to do with what he actually wanted, which seemed like a very small and humble thing. And what was it? Merely to sit in the same room with his father once more. Exchanging not a word. Only to gaze at him, at his face and at his hands, to perceive him again in the realm of the living, and to inhabit that feeling for as long as he could.

The sun was beginning to set as Alec walked from Trastevere Station back to the apartment. In his mind he felt a sense of mission, as though he were about to make of himself an offering, to abase himself before a righteous judgment. The last time he had felt this way had also involved Polina. Then, too, he had taken a long walk through an industrial suburb. He had carried forms that needed to be signed by Maxim, Polina's ex-husband. Alec had never seen the man before, but Maxim had asked for him specifically. *Send your pimp*, he'd told Polina.

Alec met him in the communal apartment where he and Polina had lived together. Alec had gone, uncertain of what awaited him. Did Maxim have any intention of signing the document or was it just a ruse? What indignities might he have in store? But the exchange had been nothing like he'd anticipated. The man he'd met had been like a bad actor playing a role for which he was sorely ill cast. He seemed to be clumsily following someone else's script. His role demanded that he project indignation and anger but his true emotions seemed closer to confusion and hurt. It looked like he still did not understand why all this misery had befallen him. Alec suspected that a woman's hand guided him. The word "prostitute" recurred too often in the script for it to have been written by a man. Alec pictured some squint-eyed crow perched on Maxim's shoulder, playing on his bewilderment, dripping poison in his ear.

—Nobody gets a prostitute for free, Maxim had stammered.

So Alec had signed his apartment over to Maxim, and Maxim had signed the form, absolving Polina of her "material obligations" to him.

At the time he had come away from Maxim's feeling as if he were coated in grime. But now the recollection evoked a different feeling. He felt ashamed of everything to which he had subjected Polina.

Alec reached the building on Via Salumi and stood before it under the weight of his grief and shame. In his pocket he had a key, but it didn't occur to him to use it. He had lived in the apartment with

Polina for nearly five months, but after two nights away, he felt utterly banished.

Lyova answered the buzzer.

Though he did not want to desecrate his grief, Alec nonetheless said, *I just buried my father. I'd like to come up.*

The lock released and Alec entered the lobby, which was cool and quiet. He mounted the steps, counting the flights, regretting that only three separated the lobby from the apartment. He still didn't know what he might say to Polina, and three flights didn't offer enough time to compose his thoughts. He imagined a climb of thirty flights, arduous and purifying, like one of the pilgrims crawling on his knees along Via Conciliazione.

From the landing he saw that the door to the apartment was open. As he neared, he found Lyova waiting for him in the vestibule, where he himself had stood and waited for Masha.

—My condolences, Lyova said, and put out his hand.

Alec accepted the hand and allowed Lyova to usher him into the apartment. Polina sat at the dining room table and regarded him silently. Alec looked at her, and then, instinctively, past her, around the apartment, alert to any changes that might have cropped up in his absence. The curtain separating Lyova's half of the apartment was partially drawn, and the kempt bed visible. The door to their bedroom was open, but there, too, Alec detected nothing incriminating.

—I'm sorry about your father, Polina said. What happened?

—He died walking to Rome to straighten me out.

Alec looked meaningfully at Lyova, laying claim to what negligible rights remained to him.

—I'll go, Lyova said, then took his coat and tactfully withdrew.

Alec and Polina were left together in the apartment, as if under a vast ponderous cloud. Alec thought to speak, though without any confidence in what he might say, but Polina preempted him.

—Alec, there is nothing to say.

As she spoke the words, Alec noticed that on the tabletop, framed between her hands, was a Soviet airmail envelope.

—It's from Nadja?

—Yes.

—What does she say?

Polina smiled grimly and slid the envelope across the table.

—Read it for yourself.

Alec eased himself into a chair at the table and examined the front of the envelope. He saw Nadja's familiar script, addressed, for the first time, to Polina and to him using their real names. He removed the pages and unfolded them.

The letter began:

My dearest Sister,

It is so hard for me to write this because I imagine that it will cause you disappointment and pain. Even as I write the words, my tears are falling. I have made the most difficult decision I have ever had to make and I am still not sure that I have decided correctly. But after thinking about everything a thousand times over, I have decided not to marry Arik and not to go with him to Israel. I have decided to stay here, in Riga, with Mama and Papa. Does this sound crazy to you? It still sounds crazy to me. But every time I thought of leaving them it broke my heart . . .

Alec turned the pages facedown on the table. He raised his eyes to meet Polina's and perceived the change in her—as if a tenacious light had finally been extinguished.

—I'm sorry, Alec said.

—What are you apologizing for?

—I have enough to apologize for.

—It doesn't matter to me, Alec.

—I understand that, Alec said. But it matters to me.

Polina looked at him blankly.

—I'm serious, Alec said.

—Alec, it's too late.

—I don't agree. It doesn't have to be.

Polina rolled her eyes with exasperation.

—Alec, I knew who you were when I chose to go with you. Nobody forced me. If I've made a mess of my life, and am now left alone, it's my own fault.

—You don't have to be alone.

—Alec, please don't be dense.

—I'm not being dense. I have lost your trust—I recognize that. You don't want to go to Canada with me—I understand. You regret leaving your family—so return to them. The same borders you crossed to get here, you can cross in reverse. It needn't be hard. For all we know, it might even be easier in reverse. If that's what you want, you should do it. And if it's what you do, I will go back with you.

—Alec, now you're being more than dense.

Alec prepared to object. He didn't see it that way at all. Instead, he had begun to feel illuminated by the idea of returning. It had dawned on him purely spontaneously, but it possessed a seductive logic. If he was looking to commit an act of sacrifice, there was no better altar. If he wanted to prove his devotion to Polina, here was the perfect symmetry. She had forsaken her family for him, now he would do the same for her. He envisioned their return, and his mortification. He saw himself making public statements and disavowals— maybe even on television and radio. He saw himself prostrating himself before one official body after another. He saw himself entering into moral compromises. Becoming a tool of the KGB. Joining the Party. Giving formal speeches against internationalism and in support of the Revolution. Fervently espousing beliefs he did not hold.

14

The following morning, they bade farewell to Lyova for the third and final time. They descended with him to the street to await the taxi that would take him to the airport. Their farewell was muted, colored by everything that had just passed. When the taxi arrived, Lyova embraced each of them in turn—first Alec, then Polina. With a vagabond smile, Lyova uttered the old Red Army creed: *Nothing and nobody is forgotten!* He then ducked his head inside the taxi and was gone.

The night Lyova left, Alec slept on an eiderdown on the floor in Lyova's half of the apartment. Once Lyova was gone, he assumed his bed.

Before the week of mourning was over, they received word about their papers. Without Samuil, there were no longer any constraints to their application. After such a long period of waiting, they were once again obliged to rush. They packed up their things quickly. The majority of what they'd brought to Rome they had sold, and they'd purchased very little in exchange. Polina did most of the packing, maintaining a barrier of activity between them.

Days before their departure, Alec and Polina traveled to Ladispoli

to allow Polina to finally pay her respects and to help with the preparations. The house, when they arrived, was in a state of upheaval.
Objects and clothes were piled up in the corners. In the kitchen, Alec
saw his mother displaying one of his father's shirts for Josef Roidman, who stood before her and examined the garment. On the table
before her, neatly folded, were other of his father's clothes—his
shirts, his trousers, his blazer. Also on the table were a pair of tailor's
shears and a knitting kit with needles, thimbles, and multicolored
spools of thread. When his mother saw them enter, she beckoned
them into the kitchen. Seeing Polina, her face flushed and she wiped
her eyes with the backs of her wrists, overcome again as if for the
first time.

—He is gone, Polinachka, Emma said.

Polina went to embrace her, and everyone observed a solemn
moment, until Emma collected herself and remembered what she'd
been doing.

—I don't want them to go to strangers or to waste, Emma said.
Josef was his friend. Your father would have been happy for him to
have them. Unless, of course, you want anything.

—It's probably better that Josef take them, Alec said.

—I consider it an honor, Roidman replied.

—They just require some alterations, Emma said.

Polina offered to help, and joined her at the table.

—There are more of your father's things in the other room,
Emma said. It breaks my heart to touch them. But if you feel you can
do it, you should do it. And look to see if there is anything you want
for yourself.

As he started away for the living room, Alec heard Roidman say,
God willing, I will come to Canada soon and visit you wearing this
shirt.

In the living room were several cardboard boxes of his father's
things. Alec sat down to sort through them. From the bedroom, he
could hear Yury and Zhenya chirping some song in what may have
been English. Rosa opened the door and the boys' voices spilled out
louder. Seeing Alec amid Samuil's effects, she came over.

—Karl took your father's wedding ring and left you his watch, Rosa said. He's the firstborn son, so I hope you don't have any objections.

—No objections, Alec said.

Alec saw Rosa glance at the kitchen, where Josef Roidman was wearing his father's blazer, with Polina folding and pinning one of the sleeves.

—So she took you back after all.

—She says she will leave me once we get to Canada.

Rosa kept her eyes on Polina as she went about her task.

—She would be right to, Rosa said. But I suspect she won't. That's the way we women are.

She looked away and returned to the bedroom, leaving Alec alone with the boxes. They consisted almost exclusively of papers, notebooks, and documents. There were very few personal items. He saw his father's razor, an unopened bottle of cologne, two pairs of pewter cuff links, and the inexpensive watch, of Soviet manufacture, that Rosa had bequeathed to him. He found that he was able to handle these objects without feeling too much distress. His father's papers and notebooks he felt far less equipped to handle. To look at his handwriting felt exceedingly personal and painful. He glanced quickly through the documents and packed them away for some future day.

Among the papers, at the bottom of a box, he came upon the stack of letters that his uncle had sent from the front. They were yellowed, brittle with age, and carried the scent of loss and the past. For that reason they seemed hallowed, but also because Alec knew that these were his father's dearest possessions. Alec leafed through them carefully, unfolded them, and regretted that he would never understand what they said. The only thing he could decipher were the dates, which his uncle had written in Roman numerals at the top of each letter. His father had filed them chronologically, beginning with the first correspondence from the summer of 1941. Alec counted more than sixty letters in total, ending in late December of 1942. This final letter was composed in Russian and in another hand.

29 December 1942

Dear Comrade Krasnansky,

I am still entirely under the influence of the great tragedy which today befell you and your loved ones. I am here undertaking the sad task to tell you that your brother Reuven was killed by a German bomb near the zemlyanka *where we live. Just by chance he went out and at that very instant a Messerschmitt flew past. It dropped two bombs and one bomb exploded near your brother. In the time we tried to help him and carry him away from there, he died. We buried him in the same place where the bomb hit.*

It is a terrible task to tell you this, but I see it as my duty to him and to you. I know what it is like when one sits and waits for a letter from the front. Together with this letter I am also sending 336 rubles and some photographs we found in your brother's pocket. You will be surprised that I am writing to you since we do not know each other well. My name is Chaim Obadya and I was a student in Riga at the 2nd Grunt School.

This is all I can tell you about this sad end. Take hope, my friend. You, too, are a soldier and understand that this is war and many of our friends, brothers, and loved ones have already fallen. We don't know what any moment will bring us. It is possible that many more will meet the same fate as your beloved brother. But we will go forward and find our compensation in the struggle against dark reactionary fascism.

Acknowledgments

I would like to thank my agent, Ira Silverberg, and my editors at Farrar, Straus and Giroux, Lorin Stein and Eric Chinski.

Excerpts from the novel appeared in *The New Yorker* and *The Walrus*, and I am grateful to Deborah Treisman and Jared Bland, respectively, for their editorial contributions.

Lucia Piccinni, John Montesano, and Giorgio Bandiera helped with the Italian translation, Esther Frank with Yiddish, and Detlef Karthaus with Esperanto.

Rosalba Galata and Susan Davis provided information about HIAS and JDC, and Enid Wurtman offered her expertise on the Soviet emigration process. Any errors of fact remaining in the novel are mine.

Nell Freudenberger, Wyatt Mason, and Anna Shternshis read early drafts of the manuscript, and I am indebted to them for their insights.

I am grateful to the many people who shared their recollections of the period, particularly Sara Bezmozgis, Alexander and Musia Mozeson, Lev Milner, Michael Vilinsky, Seva and Irina Yelenbaugen, Hirsh and Stella Vivat, Lev and Elena Aleinikov, and David and Emma Tsimerman.

ACKNOWLEDGMENTS

I offer my enduring gratitude to Simon Friedman (1935–2003) and to Zebulon Sharf (1915–2008), whose story is intimately connected with that of his brother, Mordecai Sharf (1913–1942).

The John Simon Guggenheim Memorial Foundation, the Canada Council for the Arts, the Ontario Arts Council, and the Toronto Arts Council provided financial assistance, and the MacDowell Colony offered its hospitality: this book would have been much harder to complete without their help.

A Note About the Author

David Bezmozgis was born in Riga, Latvia, in 1973. His first book, *Natasha and Other Stories*, won a regional Commonwealth Writers' Prize and was a 2004 *New York Times* Notable Book. He has been a Guggenheim Fellow and a Dorothy and Lewis B. Cullman Fellow at the New York Public Library. In 2010, he was named one of *The New Yorker*'s "20 Under 40." For more information, visit his website at www.bezmozgis.com.